ABSENT LIGHT

Eve Isherwood

D1613254

Published by Accent Press Ltd – 2007
ISBN 1905170823 / 9781905170821

Printed and bound in the UK

Cover Design by Joëlle Brindley

The publisher acknowledges the financial support
of the Welsh Books Council

In loving memory of my mum

May Reeves Isherwood

ACKNOWLEDGEMENTS

This book would not have been written and published without the help, support and enthusiasm of certain people. Firstly, I'd like to thank my publisher, Hazel Cushion at Accent Press, and Broo Doherty, my agent, editor and friend at Wade and Doherty.

For background information on police procedure, my thanks go to Matt Hunt and certain friends in the police force who prefer not to be named. Thanks also to the lovely staff at the Worcester office of St John Ambulance who cheered me up one morning while also giving advice on Helen's treatment after her dip in the drink. Thanks, too, to David Boucher, Service Administrator at Okehampton Training Camp for giving me some sense of the visual impact of live firing on Dartmoor. It should also be mentioned that anyone trying to find the cottage described in the book would be disappointed – far too dangerous for people to actually live there!

While acknowledging people's generous assistance, any mistakes are entirely my own. Last but by no means least, thank you to my husband Ian Seymour for keeping the home fire burning, the gang fed and watered, and spurring me on.

PROLOGUE

DEATH WAS IN THE air. Unmistakable. After seven years as a Scenes of Crime Officer for West Midlands Police, Helen Powers recognised it the minute she set foot in the building.

The only light came from a bare bulb hanging in the stairwell. Walls, once a shade of red, now tobacco brown, were aged by years of dirt and neglect. A metal handrail, kicked and beaten into submission, offered minimal support and the tread on the stone steps was so badly chipped and worn that Helen had to take care not to miss her footing and drop the camera equipment. She'd lost count of the number of times she'd been to places like this: seedy, deprived, without hope.

There was noise. Always was. Deep in the bowels of the block of flats came the sound of a screaming child. From somewhere else, a heated exchange between male and female. Repetitive gangster rap hammered out over her head, boxing her ears.

"All right?" she smiled, half-turning to Elaine Peterson, another SOCO.

"Never better," Elaine grinned, protective clothing rustling as she moved. Small but sturdy, she'd been charged with carrying the forensic and fingerprint kit.

As they reached the top they were met by two police constables. One, who looked impossibly young, was trying to keep a small group of onlookers at bay. The other, face pale and drawn, had a handkerchief clamped over his nose and mouth.

"Peterson and Powers," Helen announced, by way of introduction.

Reluctantly removing the handkerchief, the pale-faced officer made a note in his scene attendance log and jabbed a thumb in the direction of an open doorway partitioned off by crime-scene tape.

"Grim Reaper here yet?" Helen asked, towering over him. She wondered whether bobbies on the beat came smaller these days.

The policeman's eyebrows drew together in a questioning frown.

"Barnaby?" Helen persisted. Barnaby Finch was Head of Scenes of Crime and her supervisor.

The police officer nodded, unwilling, it seemed, to share the joke.

A wicked smile crept over Helen's face. "Got any gum, or a packet of mints?"

This was met with an anguished shake of the head.

Helen let out a laugh. "Better make a note to remember for next time, the stronger the better." Personally, she'd never had a problem with the smell from a dead body. Either you could spend time with a corpse or you couldn't.

Elaine drew alongside. "Jesus, next time you can carry the kit. In here, is it?"

"What the man says," Helen said, winking at him as she plunged past.

The flat was freezing cold and filthy, one of the most squalid she'd ever visited. It looked as if a fight between two rival gangs had taken place among the cheap furniture. Everything was smashed: television, chairs, china, glasses, tables. And anything that couldn't be smashed was ripped or destroyed. Blood spattered the floor. The droplets were quite small,

2

Helen observed, rounded one side, irregular in shape the other, suggesting that the victim had moved at speed, probably in a desperate attempt to escape.

There was a fair bit of human activity. Two plain-clothes police officers hung round the perimeter talking in muted voices. They shouldn't be here, Helen thought, wondering why Barnaby hadn't kicked them out. Tougher-looking than her, both appeared visibly shaken. No welcoming smile. No exchange other than a brief nod of the head. None of the usual banter. And there was something else. Something she couldn't quite place. A certain edginess, hostility even. Despicable crimes engendered that type of response.

Further inside, Barnaby was conferring with Detective Chief Inspector David Dukes. Short, fat and balding, Dukes was old school with a distinguished service record. He had a reputation for an anarchic and often black sense of humour, a cover for the rampant cynicism associated with almost thirty years in the Force. But there was little comedy in his eyes today, Helen thought. His skin seemed almost sweaty in the bleak January light.

Barnaby broke off and turned to Helen, his heir apparent. As thin as Dukes was overweight, Barnaby had dark eyes and cadaverous features. "I've already asked the constables outside to maintain a perimeter. They'll be logging names, excluding anyone other than those who have a right to be here," he paused, fixing both SOCOs with one of his most piercing expressions. "Victim's a young teenage girl. According to neighbours, her name's Rose Buchanan."

"Appears there was a boyfriend on the scene," Dukes interjected, "a bit of a violent type."

"Sign of forced entry?" Helen asked.

3

"No," Dukes said, clipped.

Making the boyfriend a prime suspect, Helen thought. "Forensic examiner arrived?"

"He's with the victim."

"Pathologist?" Helen pressed.

"Still waiting." Dukes looked and sounded impatient.

Barnaby took up the conversation. "Usual ropes, girls, diagram of the scene, note and record of possible items of interest. There's a particularly suspicious sequence of footprints near the victim. In fact, on the surface, there appears to be a treasure-trove of evidence." He gave Helen a hawkish look. What Barnaby really meant, Helen thought, was make an informed choice about what to collect. Processing evidence cost money, and there was little point in collecting it unless you were fairly certain it had come into contact with the murderer. Selection was key. Otherwise it just overloaded the forensics team and wasted funds.

A sound behind them signalled the appearance of Dr Stephen Forbes, the middle-aged medical examiner. "Judging by the rigidity in her jaw," he told Dukes, "I'd estimate she's been dead for roughly eight hours – Bill should be able to give you a more precise time – and with regard to the manner of her death, there's some evidence of physical and sexual abuse. Cause of death most likely stab wounds."

"Doesn't take much expertise to work that out," Barnaby said drily, inviting Helen and Elaine to take a look.

Apart from the dull grey light bleeding through the netted windows, it was dark in the room. Helen blinked, accustoming her vision to the absent light.

4

She'd seen many crime scenes, some appalling, some less memorable, all unique. But this…

Blood. Blood everywhere. On the ceiling, spattered across the walls, staining the bare-boarded floor, more blood than it's possible to imagine. The room was slicked with it.

A small divan was pushed up against one wall. Helen observed it with dispassionate interest. Beds were likely sources for semen samples, but this indicated something else. Something that was both sick and disturbing. Whoever had slashed the sheets and clothing was sending a warning: worse to come.

At first she didn't make out the body, the beating heart of any crime scene. It didn't seem real. Looked too small, too insignificant, and far too vulnerable to be the focus of such rage. It was the blood that drew her line of vision. Dark as tar, it pooled underneath the girl's broken body, soaking into the only rug in the room.

Helen crossed the floor to where the victim was curled in a foetal position, palms facing upwards in a pose of supplication. She had chestnut-coloured hair that once might have looked lustrous but now was a tangled mess of dried sweat and blood. Her blue-grey eyes were open, searching, as was her bloodstained mouth. Helen let out a sigh that was partially muffled by her mask. She briefly imagined the girl imploring her assailant to take pity.

Roughly pushing the image out of her mind, Helen crouched down and made a visual survey of the girl's injuries. Just below one eye, she noticed a mark. Elaine noticed it, too.

"Looks like a bullet wound."

Helen shook her head and looked more closely. "Cigarette burn," she said, her voice low and detached. "Same here," she pointed, with a gloved hand, to several marks on the girl's legs. There were numerous wounds to the torso, but the really sickening part was the vicious injuries to the girl's stomach, clearly visible because of the way her skirt had been wrenched up above the waist, cruelly exposing her naked buttocks.

"One for the pathologist," Elaine said. "Bound to find semen either around her mouth or genito-anal regions. What do you make of the wounds, Helen?"

"Penetrating. Sharp-edged, inflicted with a single blade, judging by the appearance, most likely a kitchen knife." Helen could only conclude the injuries were committed by someone whose rage was as personal as it was violent.

"She's been beaten," Elaine said, pointing to the bruising on the girl's thighs.

Maybe not for the first time, Helen thought, deciding to photograph some of the shots of the body using ultraviolet. UV had the advantage of revealing scars, bruises and burns long after all visible signs had faded.

Bill Durrant, the pathologist, strode into the room. Built like a small ox, he quickly took charge of proceedings. Within minutes he was simultaneously taking intimate swabs from the victim and giving instructions.

"Make sure you get some carpet fibres from the rug."

Helen bent over the body. "What you clocked?"

"These," he pointed to fibres on the victim's legs.

Elaine dealt with the body first, fibre-taping it and sealing the evidence in a clear plastic bag labelled with Health Hazard tape marked for the lab, while Helen, after collaboration with Barnaby, was charged with getting on with the photography, the most powerful tool in the armoury for recording an image, however vile.

She began by videoing the entire flat, from the point of entry to where the corpse lay, then she photographed the perimeter of the scene, including the entrance and approaches, taking wide-angled shots, continuing with close-ups. She used colour film, three rolls of 36 exposures each, shot with a Nikon Single Lens Reflex. By tracing the pattern of blood spatter, she was able to work out and record the direction in which Rose was travelling to escape her assailant. The drip patterns indicated that Rose had been wounded in the living area and fled to the bedroom, her attacker pursuing her at close-quarters. Blood on the ceiling pointed to the weapon being drawn upwards, blood from the blade flicking off. She mentioned this to Bill Durrant who, after examining it, concurred with the theory. Then she moved on to the body itself. With clinical detachment, she took shots from every angle, the conscious part of her focusing on the job. Only later would she struggle with what she'd seen: the snuffed-out remains of a young life before which hadn't even begun.

Fibre evidence, trace evidence, any impression that could be identified, was photographed and treated.

"Shit," Elaine said, "we really ought to have permission from the owner before we start ripping up this floor."

"Problem?" D.C.I. Dukes said, stalking up behind them. He'd been snapping at their heels for a fast result from the moment they started. Given the circumstances, Helen found it easy to make allowances.

"We need to recover an impression," Helen pointed out. "I've already photographed it but we ought to lift the floorboard."

"The place is a shit-hole, for Chrissakes," Dukes burst out with uncharacteristic anger. "Just get on and do it, and fuckin' get a move on."

Elaine exchanged a *what the hell's got into him* look with Helen who shrugged and turned away. Yes, it was bad, she thought. Nauseating and senseless, it ranked as one of the nastier crimes. Police officers were only human and they had a right to feel, but she also sensed an emotion more compelling than anger. There was a definite undercurrent. Fear. It had been there from the moment she stepped through the door. Something was going down, she thought. Something serious.

Once they'd completed the job, Rose Buchanan was lifted into a zip-up body bag, and taken to the mortuary to be formally identified. Meanwhile, extreme care was taken to ensure the correct packaging was selected for each piece of forensic evidence. Then there was the filling in of forms, the signing and dating, the distribution of copies, totalling four in all.

After finishing at the crime scene, Helen returned to Thornhill Road to write up and file her report. Then she pushed off home and cracked open a bottle of wine, selected a spine-tingling track, *The River,* from an Eric Clapton album, and mulled over the savagery of the day's events. So lost in thought, she didn't hear

Adam put the spare key in the lock and creep up behind her.

"Jesus, I wasn't expecting you," she blurted, as he put his arms around her, buried his face in her neck, making her skin tingle.

He pulled away, gave her one of his lop-sided smiles and kissed her. "Looks like a rough day," he said, eyeing the half-empty bottle.

"I've had better," she sighed in agreement.

"Want to talk?"

"Not especially. Want a drink?"

"Not especially," he grinned, drawing her close.

They ended up in the bedroom. Always did.

"How long have we got?" she said at last, rubbing a finger across his chest. Her life seemed to be made up of questions like this.

"Long enough for you to tell me what happened today," he said, plumping up the pillows beside her.

"Ghoul," she laughed.

"Think of it as professional interest. Remember, I'm the detective."

So she did. That's when she realised she was more shaken than she thought. She wasn't going to break down or anything, but you'd have to be as cold as winter not to be affected.

"Poor kid," Adam said at last, his eyes dark and solemn.

"Yeah," Helen sighed. "And you should have seen the place, Adam, it was a real hovel. A young girl should be living at home with her mum and dad, not somewhere like that." She snuggled up next to him. "Odd, but I thought what a nice name she had. It had a sort of ring about it, as though she came from a good family. Pure conjecture, of course."

Laughter trickled out of Adam. "You're daft," he said, stroking her hair away from her face. "What was her name then?"

She looked up into his eyes. "Rose Buchanan."

The eyes hardened. The smile froze. "What did you say?" His voice sounded strange, strangled.

She repeated it more slowly.

He let go of her, sat bolt upright. He looked as though he'd been punched in the head.

"What's the matter?" she said, aghast.

That's when the questions started and the compassion abated.

"Where was the flat?"

"Lozells Road, number…"

"Who was the Senior Investigating Officer?"

She told him. He quizzed her about the medical examiner, the pathologist, what *exactly* had been said, what evidence found. His tone became more and more urgent.

"For God's sake, Adam," she cut across him. "What's this all about?"

He didn't answer, just tore out of bed, grabbed his clothes.

"Adam, would you please tell me what's going on?" She was cross. She couldn't help it.

He looked back at her with the same kind of hostility she'd encountered at the flat. "I know who did it."

"You know who the killer is?" Now she was worried.

He carried on getting dressed.

"I don't see how," she said slowly.

"So do you." His eyes were boring into her.

10

"You're not making much sense," she gave a shaky laugh.

"You have to promise me something."

"Promise what?" She didn't like the sound of this.

"To say nothing." There was anger and frustration in his voice and, although she'd glimpsed it before, she saw full-on the ruthlessness of his ambition.

"About what?" she said, confused.

"Everything." It sounded like a warning. "Fuck, where are my shoes?" he snarled, rummaging under the bed.

"Over by the door," she said dully, getting up, reaching for a robe, following him. She rested a hand on his arm.

He looked straight into her eyes. "It was Warren Jacks, Helen."

Her hand flew to her mouth. She couldn't speak. She felt as if someone had sucked all the air out of her.

"Got to go," Adam said. "Try and sort this Godawful mess out before I'm completely fucked."

She stared at him in frozen disbelief, knowing that her world had suddenly changed. Then he was gone.

She didn't foresee that the images captured on film that day would be committed to memory forever. She neither expected the event to become imprisoned in her brain, nor the outcome to finish her prospering career.

That would come later.

CHAPTER ONE

PART ONE
FOUR YEARS LATER

THERE WAS NO WARNING. No indication of what was about to happen. One minute she was looking across water that gleamed and glistened like snakeskin, the next she was falling. No time even to scream.

The icy cold took her breath away as expertly as any punch to the stomach. Foul, slimy, diesel-infused water rushed up her nose, stinging her eyes, filling her ears, pouring into every part of her.

She thought herself a good swimmer, but warm water and a calm swimming pool environment had clearly deluded her. This was different. This was deadly. As she spluttered and choked, her limbs flailing blindly, each movement drew a fresh surge of filth into her mouth. She felt as if her lungs were exploding, and the more she tried to push to the surface, the more her sturdy winter clothes and boots dragged her down.

Try to shout, she thought, but the connection to her brain felt uncoupled. Instinct kicked in. Her body curled up. Her muscles went into spasm. In short, the cold was killing her. Even if she could force her limbs to unbend and move, the steep sides of the canal guaranteed no exit.

Kicking frantically, she surfaced to grab some precious air before the canal came back to claim her. As she sank for a second time, she had a strange vision of afterwards, the swarm of police activity, the grim task of retrieving her swollen corpse, *bloated floater,* as known in the trade. The tell-tale froth discharging from her nose and mouth would be noted and observed, as would her skin, which would peel easily if she were left too long in the water, especially from her hands and feet. Then there'd be photographs of her cadaver and the surrounding area. Because she was fully clothed, suicide would be ruled out, murderous intent ruled in. But was it, she wondered weakly?

The strength was fast draining from her as surely as if she were bleeding to death. She could literally feel the fight going out of her. Gulping for more air, she inhaled water, further disturbing the natural osmotic balance of her body. This time she had no energy to struggle. Was it really as quick as this, she thought feebly? Did it really take only a few minutes to die? Water to water, not ashes to ashes, dust to dust?

Life is supposed to flash before your eyes when you're drowning, she thought muzzily, freeze-frames of family and loved ones, of happy and memorable times. She ought to make out her mum and dad, close friends and past lovers, but all she could see, as her body finally capsized, were bright lights and people laughing. The sadness was that, while she was dying, they were only yards away.

"Can you hear me?"

She was lying on her side. Faces stared at her. From far away she heard the insistent wail of police sirens. Someone had taken off her coat and wrapped her in a blanket. She was wet and stinking and chattering with cold. Her mouth felt parched and tasted of sewers. Her stomach ached from retching. She felt hollowed out, like a fish gasping its last floundering

13

breath. A small light was shone into her face, dazzling her eyes, making her see double.

"What's your name, love?"

"Helen," she rasped, retching again, "Helen Powers."

"Good girl, you're going to be all right, Helen. I'm Paddy, by the way. I'm your paramedic. We're just going to wrap you in a special blanket, warm you up a bit."

They could do anything they liked, she thought drowsily. She couldn't care less.

"Give us some room," she heard a woman's shrill voice pierce the darkness. Then there was the sound of people scattering, muttering among themselves as they receded into the night.

She let herself be rolled over and tucked up into a blanket that had a shiny, metallic surface. Her carers were gently efficient. She felt pathetically grateful. After they loaded her onto a stretcher, she was carried briskly up some steps, the paramedics' feet clattering as they crossed over the bridge and along the other side of the canal, up another flight of steps and into a waiting ambulance. As the doors slammed shut, she feebly asked Paddy how she'd been saved.

"A passer-by, my love, a young man."

"But he must have been half-drowned."

"Grabbed hold of your collar and fished you out from the side. Obviously a strong fella."

Yes, she thought, trying and failing to strain her head to make out her hero and thank him.

"Don't you fret now," Paddy said. "Once he knew you were all right, he didn't hang around."

*   *   *

They took her to Accident and Emergency at Selly Oak. She didn't remember much of the journey, and only had vague impressions of the hospital, mostly the surgical smell and clamour. She felt confused and wanted to sleep, something that seemed to bother the doctors. It was some hours later before she was able to piece events together. By that time she'd been peeled out of her wet clothes and every piece of her anatomy studied and checked. She dimly overheard a spirited discussion about whether she would need a cocktail of drugs to guard against hepatitis, tetanus, and Weil's disease, an infection picked up from swimming in stagnant water polluted by rats. In the end, it was decided that, as she was young and in generally good health, and had miraculously suffered no abrasions or injuries to her body, tetanus would be sufficient.

"You're lucky not to have died from shock. Bodies aren't good at tolerating sudden and drastic changes in temperature," a female house doctor soberly informed her as Helen lay in a hospital bed, warm at last, cosily curtained off from the rest of the ward.

I know, Helen thought. She had no energy to speak. She felt heavy with exhaustion as if her body were still waterlogged.

"Do you know how it happened?" the house doctor asked.

"I was mugged," she managed to reply.

It was three days after Christmas. She'd gone to meet Freya Stephens for a drink at the Pitcher and Piano, a fashionable bar and restaurant in Brindleyplace, an area of redevelopment based around the city's network of canals, but Freya, who was new to Birmingham, hadn't shown up. Helen was particularly annoyed because she didn't normally do drinks with clients. She'd taken a bit of a flyer. Season of goodwill and all that. To be perfectly honest, she was never comfortable with Christmas. It was the ultimate intrusion. Having spent weeks leading up to it in a froth of activity and optimism, she found the great day never measured up. It couldn't. Worse, it encapsulated all life's disappointments. When she'd been little, it boiled down to not getting the particular toy she'd lusted for. As a grown-up, she was painfully reminded of her single state, of an overwhelming sense of loneliness, of always looking back and wanting things to be different. The forced jollity, the material excess, the way all normal life ground to a halt seriously unnerved her. It was as if the whole world seemed to take leave of its senses during the month of December.

The bar was a lot busier than she expected and, as she ordered a glass of red wine, her eyes methodically scanned the sea of bucolic-looking faces, but there was no sign of Freya Stephens. Instead, the light wood interior was mainly populated by groups of young men and women in their late twenties, early thirties, only half a dozen tables were taken by older people.

A couple of solitary men were hanging out at the bar. One glanced over in her direction. He was blonde, not particularly good-looking. He smiled at her. She returned the smile and turned away, gazing out of the window.

Outside, lights from the nearby restaurants lit up the darkness. A vast Christmas tree swayed and tinkled in the gathering wind. Jazzed-up versions of Christmas carols were belting out of public speakers. There were hardly any people outside. It was too cold.

Twenty minutes later she asked one of the staff collecting glasses if he'd seen a woman with long dark hair, in her twenties, on her own. He shrugged, shook his head. "Maybe, maybe not. It's a busy night."

Helen gave it another ten minutes, sipped her drink, and studied her surroundings. There were plenty of people on the pull. Men with seductive eyes. Women with *have me* smiles. Two interesting-looking guys came into the bar and struck up an animated conversation. She thought they might be brothers. Similar in appearance, they also had a naturally easy way of joshing with each other. The taller of the two was waving his arms about. He caught her eye but didn't smile. Pity.

Freya wasn't going to show, she thought with tired irritation. Pulling on her coat, she went outside into the night. That's when it happened.

The punch came from behind. One movement. Expertly carried out. Smash and grab. This is what she told the two CID officers: a black female detective, Detective Sergeant Christine Harmon and a Detective Constable with slicked-back hair and the kind of tight expression that made Helen consider whether word about her identity had mysteriously leaked out. Apparently, they'd been waiting to speak to her since her admission. In contrast to *Slick*, Harmon was small, with a stocky build, and sympathetic.

"So just to recap," *Slick* said, "this friend of yours didn't turn up."

"No, not friend exactly, client."

Slick frowned and made an alteration in his notebook.

17

"You say you went outside," Harmon said, "walked along by the canal, intending to go home."

"Yes."

"You stop at all?"

Helen screwed up her eyes, trying to remember. She hated canals but she'd paused for a moment and looked up at the bridge to see if Freya was coming. She told Harmon this.

"And that's when your attacker struck?"

"I think so."

Slick gave Helen a penetrating look. He had beady blue eyes that lacked warmth. "Do portrait photographers normally meet clients socially?"

Portrait photographer, Helen thought. It still sounded strange even after four years. She didn't think she'd ever really get used to it. "Depends whether they like them," she smiled.

"Would you agree to meet a man?"

"Wouldn't rule it out."

He cast her a look that was entirely unreadable. "So what happened to your client?"

"Not a clue," Helen replied. "I've had rather more pressing things to think about. Like staying alive," she said, with a stab of humour that was lost on the policeman.

Harmon gave her an encouraging smile that seemed to imply she didn't like *Slick* any more than Helen did. *Slick* looked away and scribbled some more.

"You say you've no idea about your assailant," Harmon spoke softly.

"I presume he was male."

Slick scratched behind his ear with his pen. "You had absolutely no knowledge of someone creeping up on you? You didn't hear anything?" There was a disbelieving note in his voice.

"I was taken by surprise." Giving him a distinct advantage, Helen thought.

"Did he grab your bag or give you a shove first?" Harmon said, a thoughtful light in her eyes.

"Like I said, it was more of a push and grab." Which meant, Helen mused, that he was taking a risk. She could easily have gone into the water, taking the bag with her. And then another more chilling idea took root.

"What I'm trying to establish," Harmon said, as if reading Helen's mind, "was whether you fell as a result of him grabbing your bag, or whether he intended you to go into the water."

"You mean whether he meant to kill me?"

"That what *you* think?"

I don't know, Helen thought. "Whether it was accidental or not, the fact is I could easily have drowned. It wasn't as if he asked whether I could swim," she added gamely, eliciting another smile from Harmon.

"Attempted murder?" The D.C. muttered to Harmon.

"Difficult to prove," Harmon said cautiously. She turned back to Helen. "Were there any witnesses?"

"Potentially dozens, though I wasn't aware of anyone in particular. What about the guy who pulled me out?"

"He didn't hang about but we'll put out an appeal," Harmon assured her.

Don't leave it too long, Helen thought. Time is the enemy of the witness. "Are there cameras in the area?"

"Yeah, we'll be checking CCTV," Harmon confirmed.

"It's pretty well-lit," Helen continued. "The bar was packed. There must be a chance someone saw him."

"Not exactly ideal for a mugging," the D.C. said.

"On the contrary," Helen interjected, "it was a perfect foil."

The policeman's brow furrowed. "How do you work that out?"

"There were lots of people. Everyone was having a good time. They felt secure. It's the last place you'd expect something like that to happen."

"She's right, Wylie," Harmon said, a hint of admiration in her voice. "Dead easy for someone to appear and then fade away. Naturally, we'll be following up enquiries," she told Helen.

"Are Scenes of Crime checking the area?" Helen said, "Only you might strike lucky, a foot impression, maybe, or some other evidence."

Harmon opened her mouth to speak but Wylie beat her to it. "You a copper or something?" His eyes were hard with suspicion.

Helen flashed a nervous smile. "No, erm…read a lot of books."

Harmon nodded thoughtfully. Wylie looked relieved.

"Any news on my handbag?" Helen asked.

"We found *a* bag near the scene of crime," Wylie replied, cagey.

"Brown leather, fairly large, tear-drop shape?"

"Yes," Harmon said, her voice ringing clear.

"Let me guess," Helen sighed, "empty?"

"'Fraid so."

"No wallet or credit cards?"

Harmon shook her head.

"Keys, mobile phone?"

"Sorry," Wylie said, flicking his notebook shut. "He took the lot."

CHAPTER TWO

HER MUM AND DAD came to pick her up the following morning. Both looked pale and worried.

"You sure you should be coming home?" her mum asked anxiously. She was quietly spoken, quiet in every respect. A large-boned woman, she carried little weight because of a fondness for gin in preference to food. Her face, though lined, was softened by expertly applied make-up, giving her a gentle appearance. She had small hooded eyes that nestled like a couple of dark blue sequins. Her tinted ash-blonde hair was thick and curly. Helen looked nothing like her. In appearance, she was her father's daughter.

"I'd rather not stay here," Helen said, taking the clothes her mother brought with her. It beat her how anyone ever managed to rest in a hospital ward. It was never dark or quiet. There was always a single light shining somewhere, always some drama.

"We could get you upgraded," her father said authoritatively, fixing his dark brown eyes on her. Well into his sixties, and over a decade older than her mother, he still had a handsome charm. He was tall with an abundance of steel-grey hair that once was raven-coloured. When Helen was growing up, her friends pointed out, much to her embarrassment, that she had a dishy-looking dad.

"I just want to come home," Helen said, appealing to him.

"But surely, after what's happened to you, darling…" Her mother's voice trailed off, the familiar features contorting with distress, an unusual sight and one that Helen found faintly alarming. She was more used to her mother's smooth self-composure, the maintenance of which stemmed from a rigid system of self-medication. Not one to show depths of emotion, she largely floated through life, more a spectator than a participant. It was strange to see her this connected, Helen thought, watching her mother glance at her father for guidance.

"It was a very nasty attack, Helen. You could easily have drowned." His voice was steady but his eyes expressed concern.

"But there's nothing more the doctors can do."

"They can keep you in for observation," her mother said, darting another anxious look at her husband.

"I've been thoroughly checked over," Helen smiled reasonably. "No injuries. No lasting trauma. Anyway, they probably need the beds."

"If you're sure," her father said, with some reluctance. "It's your decision, Helen."

She beamed at him. "Won't be a moment," she said, scurrying off to the nearest lavatory to change.

Her father drove them back in the Jaguar. Helen settled into the pale cream leather, closed her eyes, and listened to her father talking. "You'll need to contact the bank and put a stop on your cards. Lose much cash?"

"About thirty pounds."

"And you'll need to get the locks changed at the flat. Did you have the keys to the studio with you?"

"No, thank goodness."

"Tell you what, I'll get Vic to organise a locksmith today then you can have a new set to go back with."

"Have the police talked to you yet?" her mother half-turned. There was strain in her voice.

"Yes."

"You've made a statement?" her father interjected.

"Uh-huh."

"What did they have to say?" her mother pressed.

"Not a lot."

"Any ideas on the culprit?"

"There's not much to go on," Helen said. "He'll probably get away with it."

"He?"

"Most muggers are blokes, Mum."

Her mother let out a laugh. It sounded like air seeping out of a rubber ring. "Silly me, of course."

"Probably an addict wanting to feed a habit," Helen continued, looking out of the window at houses gaudy with Christmas decorations. Children were riding along pavements on newly acquired bikes and skateboards. Adults, eager to shake off the excesses of the recent festivities while preparing for the next, walked briskly in the winter sunshine. She felt strangely detached. She guessed it was a hangover from her previous line of work in Scenes of Crime. Christmas and New Year was awkward territory. Both festivities signalled a rise in the death rate. With so much excess booze and soaring emotions, it wasn't surprising. The obligatory merry-making not only provided the right atmosphere for strangers to talk to each other, but families, too, sometimes at considerable cost.

"You sound remarkably relaxed about what's happened," her father said, glancing at her in his rear-view mirror.

Helen smiled. She'd always been good at masking her true feelings.

*   *   *

Keepers was a large six-bedroomed country house in rural Staffordshire, some seventeen miles from Birmingham, and had been the family home for the past twenty years. It was her father's reward for building up a massively successful print business in the centre of Birmingham. A forward-thinker, Jack Powers had taken full advantage of the leaps forward in computer technology, and set up a dedicated design studio over a print works housing the latest state-of-the art equipment. Although not a graphic designer himself – his background was in engineering – he'd cherry-picked a select team of computer nerds so that all print material could be designed and reproduced in-house. With a regular source of business from like-minded captains of Midlands industry, the company went from strength to strength. Within ten years, Jack Powers's talent for assembling the right people, his basic business acumen and entrepreneurial spirit turned what was a good idea into an extremely lucrative enterprise. At the age of sixty, he sold up, making a fat profit.

Helen felt a familiar flood of memories as her father drove up the long and winding drive. After such a frightening experience, roots and family mattered more than ever.

As soon as she got home, she phoned the bank and made the necessary arrangements. Afterwards, she went straight to bed. She felt unspeakably tired and was happy for her mother to assume a caring role. It was what her mother did best. Operating as if on auto-helm, she glided through the house, dealing with things calmly, giving quiet orders, noiselessly tidying,

25

wordlessly organising, all her actions efficient and designed to anaesthetise from life's pains and tribulations.

The house was spotless. Even the furnishings were guaranteed to soothe. Nothing too vibrant. Her mother was the queen of pastel. Peach and apricot in the downstairs rooms. Upstairs, soft lilacs and greens. But, underneath her mother's smooth exterior, Helen sensed there lurked a nervy personality, a woman with seriously screwed-up emotional wiring. As her mother enquired whether she wanted more pillows, more newspapers to read, more this and more that, Helen knew that her mother was stealthily helping herself to more drink.

"I'll be fine, and Mum," Helen said.

"Yes, dear?"

"Try not to worry."

Her mother flashed a fragile smile and closed the door. Although she was glad to be in safe and familiar surroundings, Helen also felt a measure of relief to be alone. She wasn't quite sure when she'd realised that her mother had a drink problem because it had gone on for so long and was concealed under the guise of conviviality. She'd grown up to the sound of ice chinking at midday, to her mother's occasional bouts of forgetfulness, of her slurred speech in the evening, and her need for absolute quiet in the morning. She'd also grown used to making excuses for her, for pretending that her mother's capacity for booze was not outside the norm. Her mother didn't conform to the stereotypical drunk; she was careful with her appearance, always fragrant, never foul-mouthed or aggressive, rarely maudlin. When she hit the bottle, it was as if she became out of synch with life, inhabiting a shadowy, lonely world where she couldn't be reached. The funny thing was her mother intermittently enjoyed good patches where she hardly seemed to drink at all. Then there were times when she drank a lot but appeared to tolerate it well. On other occasions, she drank and became confused very quickly. It all seemed quite random. And, in the rare moments, when her mother was completely sober, Helen came to realise that, at heart, her mother was fundamentally a decent person, not warm and easy to be around exactly, but fair-minded and predictable. With these poignant periods of remission, there came a sense of dread because Helen knew that it was only a matter of time before the dark side took over.

She slept fitfully most of the day. Shock, she guessed. Her mother brought her soup, tucked her up in extra blankets, gave her a hot-water bottle, ensured she had tissues, newspapers and a radio. Apart from the time she'd suffered from glandular fever, she'd never felt so cosseted. She neither read nor listened. Sometimes she stared at a round penny of light on the ceiling. Sometimes she lay, flexing her legs, examining all her working parts, checking that she was really alive. She thought about phoning Ed and Jen but didn't have the energy. Around three in the afternoon, she got up and took a hot bath, soaping and scrubbing herself with vigour to rid herself of the lurking smell of canal on her skin. Her dark, close-cropped hair meant she could wash and dry it in record-time.

Having plastered herself in her mother's Chanel body lotion, she dragged on a robe and went to a wardrobe in one of the guest bedrooms. She still kept some clothes and make-up at home. She didn't know why she did it. It wasn't exactly a safety net because, wary of being tagged an only child of wealthy parents, she was fiercely self-reliant. To prove the point, she'd moved out when she was seventeen in a dramatic bid to find both personal and financial independence. It proved harder than she thought.

Just for a moment, she allowed herself to remember the thrill of landing her first proper job with the police as a trainee Scenes of Crime officer. The job title varied from force to force – sometimes they were called crime scene examiners, and the Metropolitan Police tended to have their own cutting-edge labels and jargon – but the work was basically the same. She was primarily an evidence-gatherer. Again, while some forces still employed dedicated Scenes of Crime photographers, she trained and worked with constabularies where it was expected for her to cover any and every aspect of the job.

With a smile, she reminisced over her initial month based at Brierley Hill, working with experienced officers. It had been a baptism of fire but she knew from the outset that this was what she wanted to do, something real and important at last. Then there had been the nine weeks training at Harperley Hall, County Durham, followed by a posting of two years as part of a development programme. After that, she transferred to Birmingham where she stayed for seven years. The smile faded as she remembered Adam Roscoe, detective inspector, her married lover, the man who for six years had dominated her life, had been her dark obsession. One of those charismatic, deeply ambitious men you come across maybe once in a lifetime, their very first meeting took place soon after her appointment to Thornhill Road. She'd been called out

28

to a drive-by shooting resulting in a fatal road accident.

Jesus, she thought, surveying the scene. It was dark, belting down with rain, and there were swarms of vehicles: police, ambulance and fire services. Two dead black men, the passenger with a caved in head from a gunshot wound, lay slumped in the wreckage of their top-of-the-range Mercedes, the bonnet of which was buried deep in the entrails of a Ford Escort. While firemen were using cutting gear to free the unfortunate female driver of the Escort, Helen was charged with securing the scene and taking photographs.

"Can you hurry it up?" a young detective constable snapped at her from the sidelines.

"Doing my best," she called back. "Not easy competing with the flashing lights from all these vehicles."

"I'm not interested in excuses. Either you can do the job, or you can't."

She said nothing. Biting her lip, she tried to work out how she could time her shot so that it wasn't over-exposed.

"I hate these fucking black on black killings," the D.C. continued to carp. She wondered how he could be so sure that's what it was.

"Come on, for Chrissakes," he cursed, "how long you going to stand there before you take the shot?" He took several steps towards her.

"Stay right there," she barked, straightening up.

"What?"

"You come any further and you're going to contaminate a crime scene."

"Who the hell…"

"You heard what she said, Davies. Shift your size tens. And, while you're about it, make sure everyone else keeps a respectful distance."

Helen turned, saw the man who'd spoken, saw his remarkable face, the sleek clean-shaven features, dangerous-looking eyes, the blackness of his hair. There was something else about him, something off-centre, she thought. He wasn't conventionally good-looking, but he was immensely attractive. Slim and tall, he wore a dark leather jacket. He winked at her.

"D.I. Roscoe," he said to Helen. "I don't care for people getting in the way of progress – not when it's my investigation."

She smiled awkwardly. "Thank you."

"No, thank *you*," he said. "I've a lot of respect for SOCOS."

Then he was gone. No great fanfares. No celestial choirs. But, from that moment, she was hooked.

She shook her head in an effort to obliterate the memory. The image of Rose Buchanan's lifeless body, however, was not so easily erased. Neither was Warren Jacks, Rose's killer. Helen remembered him, all right. Good-looking and charming, he was also a pathological liar, rapist, and police informer, *Adam's* informer.

Helen stood for a moment, willing herself to be calm. In the end, she'd done the best she could. She'd turned against her lover, exposed an injustice, cut herself loose, and joined Raymond Seatt's Photographic Agency as a portrait photographer. Had she been turned down on that initial interview with the police, her life would be quite different, she thought, cowering inside, picking out a pair of smart pale denim hipsters with a slight flare, a thick white sweater and a pair of pointy tan leather boots.

She put on her clothes, put one hand on her hips and surveyed her tall, slim reflection. Even with her colouring, she looked pale. Her eyes were ringed with shadows. Reaching for her make-up, she blended foundation into her olive-coloured skin, brushed highlighter onto her brow-bones to accentuate her dark eyebrows, swished eyeliner over her heavy lids, and applied black mascara onto her upper eyelashes to open up her eyes, not forgetting a smudge of deep cherry-coloured lipstick on her small but full mouth. Instantly feeling better, she decided to get some fresh air before it got too dark. Wrapping herself in one of her father's old jacket, she slipped down the stairs and outside.

It was bitterly cold, the icy air punching tears from her eyes and, just for a moment, she had a horrible recollection of the night before. She'd never been afraid of the dark but she wasn't keen on open water, canals in particular. She found them deeply threatening. Unlike rivers and seas, which were moving, organic expanses, canals were static, weed-infested places, with steep sides, impossible to escape from. She'd literally only given it a cursory glance and then she'd been pushed. At least, she *thought* she'd been pushed. In the beginning, she'd been certain. With hindsight, she couldn't be sure. It seemed as if time had robbed her of judgement. When she thought what might have happened to her, the slow asphyxia as her air passages, lungs and stomach filled with water, she felt shards of panic. And what had happened to Freya, she thought? Why hadn't she phoned?

She wasn't sure of Freya's age but reckoned she was around the twenty-five mark, roughly eight years younger than herself. They'd hit it off from the moment she'd walked into the studio. Helen guessed a part of the attraction was that Freya reminded her of how she used to be a long time ago, before she'd had her confidence stamped on. Sparky and fun, Freya had an unstoppable quality, something Helen admired, yet there was also loneliness in her eyes. She seemed vulnerable. And the city preyed on people like that. Especially at Christmas.

Keepers had several acres of landscaped gardens, including a tennis court and a wild, spirited area of natural woodland. As Helen walked across gently sloping lawns, childhood memories flooded her mind. She thought of warm, sunny days sprawled out in the grass, listening to the drone of bees and steady clunk of ball on racquet. She remembered hiding in the greenhouse, with its aroma of vines and geraniums, the magic of hearing rain against the glass. It was quite an isolated upbringing. Her dad always seemed to be at work, her mother in a world of her own. Helen wasn't ignored but the focus was always on her mother, or rather her mother's drinking. For this reason, and for as long as she could remember, she was wary of taking friends home. She couldn't bear them to notice that her mother, and by reflection herself, were different. She couldn't endure the embarrassment. She supposed deep-down she felt ashamed of her mum, which, in turn, made her feel ashamed of herself.

In spite of it all, she pretended that life was fine, that her mother was more often happy than sad, that it didn't matter if they weren't particularly close, didn't get on. She tried not to think of the time her mother shut her out in the rain, or got drunk at a summer party and fell over while dancing, breaking her ankle. She tried to forget four years before, when she'd hidden herself away from prying cameras and baying newspaper reporters.

She returned to the house as the light was fading. A police car was outside. She removed her boots in the porch and walked into the drawing room where Harmon and Wylie were drinking tea with her parents in front of a blazing log fire. Her mother had that instantly recognisable slightly pissed look on her face. Both C.I.D. officers stood up as Helen entered. Her father took charge.

"D.S. Harmon and D.C. Wylie were wondering whether you can remember anything else about the attack last night."

Helen lowered herself into a plumply furnished chair. "Not really."

"Pity," Wylie said, eyeballing her in a way that made Helen feel uncomfortable. If she wasn't certain before, she was now; he knew about her past.

Helen looked at Harmon. "No leads?"

"Nothing. Witnesses have been hard to come by. It seems most people were keeping warm indoors."

"What about the bloke who hauled me out?"

"Hasn't come forward yet."

Helen guessed it wasn't that unusual and it was still early days. "You were going to check the CCTV."

"We did," Harmon said, looking awkward.

"And?"

"Wasn't productive," Wylie intervened snappily.

Harmon flashed him an exasperated look. "It was useless, I'm afraid," she told Helen.

"Don't tell me," Helen groaned, "they forgot to put a tape in."

"The tape was in, all right," Harmon said, "but it had been used that many times, the quality was awful. We just got a load of grainy images."

Helen wasn't that surprised. In spite of the searing clarity in high profile locations, the general quality of CCTV was so poor you'd have a hard time recognising your own parents on most footage.

"A bloody outrage," her father growled.

"I can see where you're coming from," Wylie said stiffly. Actually, he had no idea, Helen thought, mildly amused, as her father blistered on about incompetence, accountability and the need to *catch the bastard.* "He ought to be done for attempted murder," her father ranted, "never mind mugging."

Harmon smoothly reasserted her authority. "In the absence of witnesses, that might be difficult to prove, sir."

"We're doing all we can," Wylie chipped in, though Helen suspected that, in his own mind, he'd probably already wrapped up the case and moved onto another. It was to do with priorities. This wasn't a courtesy call: it was a kiss-off. And, actually, she didn't really care. She just wanted to forget all about it and get on with her life. She looked across the room. Her mother's eyes were rheumy with booze and emotion. Her hands were shaking, and she was twisting a small lace handkerchief round and round her fingers. Helen could see the knuckles gleaming shiny and white.

"That's it then," her father said, in a clipped voice. He got to his feet, indicating that the interview was over. Harmon turned to Helen, reiterating that she'd be in touch.

"We've given your bag to Mrs Powers," Wylie told Helen, his lip curling as he glanced over in her mother's direction. Helen read the contempt in his face and instantly felt on the defensive. How many times had she registered the disapproval of others? People could be remarkably prissy about women who drink. Blokes were just being blokes.

"It's upstairs," her mother said, rising unsteadily to her feet, "on the landing."

"It's all right, Mum. I'll get it."

While her father saw the police out, Helen went upstairs, picked up her bag and returned with it to the drawing room. She vaguely noticed that something was different, though she couldn't quite put her finger on it. It wasn't the Christmas decorations. Wasn't the cards suspended from the beams, the wreath hanging over the fireplace, or the tastefully dressed Christmas tree.

"You've had a change-around."

"What?" her mother said muzzily.

"Things look different, somehow." The furniture and furnishings were the same. Everything in the usual places, but…

Helen stared at a tall vase of large purple-headed tulips that spilled over the rim like a clutch of hissing snakes. The only departure from the soothing surroundings, Helen didn't know why she hadn't spotted it immediately. And it flagged up something else.

"That's it," she said brightly, "it's the Royal Worcester."

Her mother gave her a befuddled look.

"You know, the porcelain arrangement of birds. It's not where it usually is."

"Oh," her mother broke into a smile. "I've sent it off to be cleaned."

"Well, that's that," Helen's father said, stalking back into the room.

"Let's hope so," Helen's mother smiled tightly. "Sun's over the yardarm. Anyone fancy a drink?"

Dinner was a tense affair. Bit by bit, Helen watched her mother slide into an alcoholic stupor. The irritation in her father's eyes was clear. Although he adored her mum, he'd never been able to completely cope with her drinking. Most of the time, he pretended not to notice, glossed over it, made excuses. Not this evening.

"Popped in to see Gran on Boxing Day," Helen said, trying to make conversation.

"Don' know why you bother," her mother said thickly, pushing food around her plate with no interest. Her bottom lip and teeth were black, stained from wine.

"Makes her happy," Helen said simply.

Her mother rolled her eyes. "Doesn' know you from Adam, dear. Jus' a shell."

Helen looked down at her plate. She wasn't Gran any more, she wanted to say, but she was still a person. "She appreciates visitors."

"Never used to," her mother said in a detached fashion, taking a pull of her drink. "She was too obsessed with herself to have time for others."

Helen glanced up. Her mother's face was devoid of expression. Only her voice betrayed resentment. Helen turned to her father. His jaw was grinding. His eyes

36

were cold. In every other respect, he viewed her mother as the model wife. It was required. Expected. And although, most of the time, her addiction was in check, it was a source of huge frustration to him that he remained powerless to keep her sober. It was as if he regarded it as a personal failure. It explained why he loathed seeing her so drunk, hated seeing the crack in the apparently serene exterior.

"Gran gets quite soppy about presents," Helen smiled, trying to smooth things over. Her grandmother had developed a sweet tooth since her illness and Helen was in the habit of taking chocolates or sweets with her when she visited. It was worth it just to see the old woman's eyes light up. Gran might be going senile, she thought, but she knew what it was to be fussed over and loved, which seemed more than her mother was capable of.

Helen's father twitched a sympathetic smile at her. "That's good, isn't it, Joan?" he said, curtly addressing his wife. "At least we made sure the old girl's comfortable."

Helen supposed that was something. As private residential homes went, Roselea was in the higher echelons. And at least it didn't smell of pee.

Her mum eventually flaked out shortly before nine o'clock. Once Helen's father helped her upstairs, he rejoined Helen in the drawing room.

"She's getting worse," Helen said.

Her father offered no comment. He was sick of it, she thought. They'd done this one countless times before. They'd even developed this peculiarly veiled way of talking about her mother's drinking so that neither of them had to mention the dreaded word *booze*. She guessed it was a form of denial, the result

37

of years of putting on a perfect and united front. Her dad, if pressed on the subject, put it down to biology. Her mum's father had been a heavy drinker, driven to it, some said, by his wife. Whatever the truth of it, Helen's dad didn't want to talk about it tonight.

"You look tired, Helen."

A classic decoy, she thought. "Not surprising."

He agreed and chucked another log on the fire. "I've been thinking. You don't reckon there's more to this mugging than meets the eye?"

"How?"

Her father hesitated. "Could it be connected to your previous work with Scenes of Crime?"

She didn't say anything. She didn't want to think about it.

"You worked with the police, remember." He was speaking softly, his Midlands accent more pronounced, but there was relentlessness in his eyes.

"*For* them," she said quietly. "I wasn't a police officer. I wasn't at the sharp-end."

"Not at the sharp end?" A quizzical smile played on his lips.

"Well, all right," she conceded sheepishly, scuffing the pile on the carpet with her foot. I really don't want to revisit this, she thought.

Her father was speaking again. "Criminals have long memories. You were a part of the process of bringing them to justice."

"Dad," she laughed uneasily, "I was a faceless part of a team. An evidence-gatherer. And it was a long time ago."

"Four years."

She knew. Sometimes it seemed like yesterday, other times a lifetime ago. She wondered whether Adam felt the same.

"And you made enemies," her father continued.

"Other policemen," she pointed out with more levity than she felt. "And they're not generally in the habit of assaulting or attempting to bump off their foes."

"Not even Roscoe?" His voice was hard.

She could hardly bear to hear his name. It seemed strange now. She adored him from the moment she clapped eyes on him in that dirty little street with the blood running into the gutter. She would have done anything for him and, in many ways, she did – until her final and very public betrayal. "Not even him," she said softly.

He said nothing for a moment, took a pull on his drink. "Did you mention your past to Harmon and Wylie?"

My past, Helen thought, that far-away place where I betrayed my lover, confessed to my superiors, went to the press. I didn't need to, she thought, feeling vulnerable. "You make it sound as though I did something wrong, Dad."

Her father took another pull of his whisky. Too much time elapsed before he gave the answer she needed to hear. "You did what you felt was right."

Eventually, she thought. "I had no choice."

"No," he agreed.

They'd debated the subject endlessly. He'd wanted her to be pragmatic. She'd wanted to come clean. In the end, she'd done it her way. Mostly.

Neither of them spoke for a moment, each lost in their own thoughts, staring at the fire. The truth was her dad didn't understand. It wasn't his fault. She never told him the full story. Never told anyone. And, however many times she tried to explain the nature of her then employment, it was a dark mystery to anyone outside the police force.

Scenes of Crime, at its best, swung into action with the smooth running of a well-oiled machine, and she had been but a small cog in it. It required the ability to work both as part of a disciplined team and as an individual. She didn't remember exactly how many cases she'd covered, how many people in theory she'd contributed to put away but she couldn't imagine any crook, even less a police officer, wanting to single her out for special treatment. She considered herself to be a backroom girl, a civilian. In her father's eyes, not only had she'd been working for the police, but with the dead. That always generated an element of fear. Helen broke the silence. "I don't think last night's incident has any connection to the past."

"Simply a case of wrong place, wrong time?"

"Unfortunately, it happens a lot."

Her father gave a weary smile, drained his drink and stood up. Briefly touching her shoulder, he wished her goodnight.

CHAPTER THREE

THE CHILL AIR FELT as if it were penetrating her jacket, seeping through her skin, freezing all her bones, but, the next day, she was glad to be back in her own surroundings.

The studio was situated on the Hagley Road, one of the main arterial roads into Birmingham. Helen's flat or, to put it more accurately, coach-house, was in the garden of the studio, tacked onto the main body of the building. A former stables, the coach-house had separate access via a private drive at the back, providing a tiny, almost rural haven of peace while still being in the centre of the city. Thirty or so years before, the entire site housed a public relations consultancy. Now it was home to Raymond Seatt's Photographic Studio, except that Ray was taking it easy, somewhere in the West Indies, she believed.

She felt more settled among her own belongings: the poster-red leather sofa bought in a fit of indulgence, the mounted photographs on the walls, the Moroccan rugs, the clutter of books and brochures on the floor because she'd run out of shelf-space, the cobwebs. Nothing was neat and tidy. Ethnically messy best described it.

There were two messages on the ansaphone. The first was from Jen reminding her of preparations for the New Year's Eve party, the second from Ed informing her of *a drama,* as he put it, concerning a woman found *in the drink* at Brindleyplace, near his flat. Some drama, she thought wryly, hanging up her new set of keys and deciding to make a cup of heart-starting coffee.

Standing there, waiting for the kettle to boil, she stretched and looked out of the window. Even though it was past noon, the grass was edged with a thick layer of sparkling frost. A robin perched on the naked branches of a tree through which a low winter sun sent shafts of reddish-gold light. Then she remembered Freya Stephens, and flicked off the kettle.

Helen recalled that Jewel had taken the initial phone-call from Freya, talked through the requirements – two sets of 8 x 6 shots, black and white, soft focus – discussed prices, suggested make-up and clothes, and arranged the appointment. Within hours of making the call, Freya phoned back and spoke to Helen in person, introducing herself and changing the date. She mentioned that she was optimistically looking for publicity work though she didn't really specify what form it might take. Helen explained that she didn't do glamour photography but Freya insisted she only wanted head and shoulder shots and it had to be a female photographer, "not some pervy guy who wants to sleep with me in the pursuit of artistic excellence."

Her first impression of Freya Stephens was that she was striking to look at. Roughly the same height as herself, but thinner, she wore a long black leather coat with a red roll-neck sweater and black leather trousers. She had chocolate brown eyes. Freya's hair was long, much as her own had been before she'd taken the decision to chop it all off. She had an engaging smile and, although she seemed a little nervous to start with, not unusual for someone inexperienced in having their photograph taken in a professional setting, she was eager to co-operate, a huge plus, in Helen's experience.

"So you say these are for publicity purposes," she said to Freya.

"Uh-huh."

"I'm trying to understand the image you want to project."

Freya gave an earthy laugh. "Does it matter?"

"Do you want to look friendly, mysterious, sexy…?"

"Sexy," Freya grinned, "definitely sexy."

Helen took out what she called her bag of tricks, an odd assortment of hats, scarves and glasses with the lenses punched out. "Even though I'm shooting in black and white, your sweater will show up as a greyish tone. Thinking of keeping it on?"

Freya raised an eyebrow and, without uttering a word, peeled off her coat and sweater, revealing impressively full breasts on a tiny frame. Helen briefly wondered whether she'd had a boob-job.

"Now put your coat on," Helen said, "but leave a couple of the top buttons undone."

Freya did as she was told. As she reached for her coat, Helen thought she noticed some suspicious-looking marks on the inside of Freya's arms. It was such a fleeting impression, however, she thought she was mistaken.

"What do you think?" Freya said.

"The coat's gorgeous," Helen grinned.

Freya beamed. For a second, Helen had the strange impression that the coat had been chosen to impress her. "Tonally speaking," Helen continued quickly, "the arrangement's perfect. I just wonder whether to introduce a little more light to your face," she said, holding up a gold-coloured scarf. "How about draping this around your neck?" She handed it to Freya, catching the scent of cheap perfume.

"Like this?" Freya said, arranging the scarf so that it trailed like a sleeping snake over the leather.

"Lovely. I'll take some shots with, some without."

"Oooh, is this the moment I'm supposed to say *cheese*?"

"God, no," Helen laughed. "This isn't school. Just relax. Try not to think consciously about smiling. It's more of a smile from the inside."

"Sounds dirty," Freya laughed.

"Behave," Helen joked. "I'll ask you to perform certain actions, maybe turn away and look at the door as though a friend's just walked in, that kind of thing. We're going to tell a story."

"A story?" Freya looked intrigued.

"Your story," Helen said, taking a light reading.

"Wow," Freya said, her face gleaming with excitement. "Can you make it into a thriller then?"

"I can but try," Helen laughed.

She didn't know why but somewhere, crouching in the back of her mind, she had the vague suspicion that Freya might be connected to the mugging. Ridiculous, she thought. It was too outlandish, too far-fetched. She blotted it out.

The studio wasn't officially open. Jewel, the receptionist, had been given the Christmas and New Year holiday off en bloc. Prior to her stint in hospital, Helen popped across the garden each day to open and sort the post, check emails, catch up on any paperwork, and log any phone messages. She enjoyed the time to work alone without either the hassle of the phone ringing, or clients making demands. When it came to work, she was extremely methodical, another hangover from her previous occupation, she guessed.

Among the rest of the mail and belated Christmas cards, an envelope had arrived from the lab marked *photographic prints – fragile*. She opened it and slid out the contact sheets. At a glance, she could see that Freya Stephens took a good photograph. Personally, Helen always found blondes easier to shoot, especially in black and white, but the soft-focus lens had worked particularly well in this instance, and the brief flash pre-exposure had increased the film speed by about a stop. Slipping the sheet back into the envelope, she opened up the computer and retrieved Freya's details, including her mobile phone number. Next, she gave her a call. It didn't even ring. The phone switched straight to a messaging service. Vaguely unsettled, she locked up, and spirited the contacts back with her to the coach-house.

Flicking on the kettle again for strong coffee, she took out the sheets for a second time and laid them on the kitchen table. There's a saying that the camera never lies. Richard Avedon, the great celebrity portrait photographer, maintained that while all photographs were accurate, none of them told the truth. Helen held a slightly different opinion: while the camera might tell the truth, it never told the whole story. Smiles and happiness can be phoney, but you can never fake the expression in the eyes.

Or the terror.

Her nerves sharpened. A needling pain jabbed at the back of her head. She could feel the fear lapping at her. She blinked, shook herself, pulled herself back from the brink.

45

Stirring two sugars into her coffee in a lame bid to jump-start her system, Helen took a sip and went across the hall to her own personal makeshift darkroom which, in a previous life, was an old bathroom. Now it also doubled as a home for assorted pieces of photographic gear. The darkroom was pretty much redundant in the modern professional setting. Nearly all studios, including Ray's, used specialist photographic labs for the development of prints. Helen found it rather sad. There was something deeply satisfying about messing about in the dark, developing your own work, even if it was laborious.

Stretching up to a shelf, she retrieved a polychrome eyepiece and took it back to the kitchen. Placing the eyepiece over the first of the proofs, she bent over and put her left eye to the lens, squinting her right eye shut. The dramatic choice of lighting had added a sensuous quality to her subject's skin, something that was generally less apparent in colour work. The first shots were usually of a poorer quality in the non-professional subject, nerves being the main stumbling block. The smiles tended to look forced, the poses wooden. Freya Stephens was no exception. The first takes made her look years older than she appeared in the flesh. Once she'd got used to the camera, however, the results were sensational. The look was alternately raunchy and sensual, but the very last shot was most telling. Enigmatic smile, mysterious light in the eyes, an expression of secrecy. So what makes you tick, Helen wondered, widening her eye to have a better look? Are you a games player? Do you like leading people on? Were you in on the mugging, she thought, thinking again the unthinkable and shaken by the prospect?

She got up, put some washing in the machine, tidied up the sitting room, thought about what to take out of the freezer for dinner, going through the motions, then she phoned Freya's number for a second time with the same result. This time she left a message asking Freya to call her as soon as possible. Unable to settle, and not wishing to be alone, she returned Ed's call. He seemed to spend more time out than in, so she was surprised and pleased when he answered after a couple of rings.

"Thought you'd be at the sales," she said.

"Lack of funds."

"Christmas over-expenditure?"

"I'd rather not say." There was a playful note in his voice.

"Fair enough." Ed's hedonistic tendencies often confounded her.

"You got my message," Ed continued.

"Yeah, I…"

"The place was swarming with police. They actually shut off the entire area for hours. You can imagine what that did for trade. The guys in the International Convention Centre are all moaning like hell…"

"Ed," Helen interrupted his flow.

"Yes?"

"It was me."

"What?"

"It was me in the drink," she said. "I damn nearly drowned."

Ed's flat was the sort of place she dreamt of. As befitted a graphic designer, it was stylish and luxurious, with views over the water and city. Well, all right, forget the bit about the water, Helen thought, pressing the entry buzzer. Much as she loved her quaint little coach-house, part of her aspired to a more grown-up style of living. She reckoned a change in habitat might also effect a change in her personal circumstances. Swimming in the right sea, she'd meet the right fish. If she met the right fish, she'd feel better about herself. Oh, if only it were that simple, she sighed, as Ed pressed the buzzer and let her in.

Helen passed through a wide and brightly lit glass-fronted reception area manned by a female concierge. Rather than taking the stairs, she took the lift.

The door to Ed's apartment was already open. Helen walked inside, took off her coat and slipped off her shoes, letting her toes sink into the plush woven carpet. The smell of cologne wafted from down the hall. Ed was standing in the German-applianced kitchen armed with a bottle of red wine and a corkscrew. He looked sleek and gorgeous as usual, she thought. Blond with green-eyed good looks, he was also tall. His well-built frame was clothed in a black cashmere sweater and a pair of soft black Italian trousers.

Ed put down the bottle of wine and rushed towards her. "Christ, you look exhausted," he said, kissing her on both cheeks.

She gave a weak smile.

"But you're all right?" he said, holding her shoulders, looking at her with serious eyes.

Of course I'm bloody not, she thought. "So what about this wine," she laughed lightly.

Ed opened the bottle and poured out two glasses, handing her one. "Good health," he said with a twinkly smile.

"Long life," she said in return, meaning it.

They chinked glasses, took a drink. Ed gave her one of his appraising looks. "Maybe you should take up yoga. It's excellent for stress."

"Not my kind of thing," she cringed.

"Good for your sex-life, too."

"What sex life?"

"Touche Eclat?"

"What?"

Ed's face split into a grin. "A wonderful little cosmetic by Yves St Laurent that hides the circles under your eyes."

She broke into a sunny smile. Ed was the only man she knew who regularly wore moisturiser. She'd even borrowed some once.

"Great after a heavy night out," Ed enthused. "It's in the bathroom if you want to try some."

"Later." This was better, she thought. She was beginning to feel more sane.

Ed smiled and took a sip of his drink. He was leaning against the granite-topped work-surface. "You going to tell me all about it then?"

"S'pose I'd better," she said, wondering how and where to begin.

They went through to the sitting room, a den of dark colours with Gallic overtones. The lighting was tastefully subdued, carpet so thick you could sleep on it. An entire wall housed an armoury of books, from large, glossily illustrated design tomes to the latest contemporary fiction. A vast antique Venetian mirror hung over the facing wall, making the room look twice the size, and a full-length painting of a woman by Mark Spain hung on the other. Helen lowered herself into a dark brown leather sofa. Ed sat at the other end and swung her feet up into his lap.

"So?" Ed pressed her, running his fingers along the tips of her toes.

She snuggled in, making herself comfortable, and told Ed about the aborted meet and the mugging. She told him she thought she was going to die.

"You poor baby," Ed said, kneading her toes. "Shouldn't you have some counselling or something?"

She almost choked. It hadn't even crossed her mind. She didn't believe in that kind of scary stuff. Ed cast her an indulgent smile. "So this woman you were going to meet, you haven't spoken to her since?"

"Nope."

"And she hasn't phoned?"

"Not yet."

"Mmmm," Ed said.

She took a deep drink. So did Ed. "Don't you think you were a bit reckless?" Ed said pointedly.

"A crowded bar, a single woman, where's the threat?"

"She might have been the lure."

"You've been reading too much fiction," she laughed.

"Quite probably, but you can't trust anyone these days, male or female. Didn't the cops teach you anything?"

"I wasn't a cop." She hadn't meant to sound chippy but, from the dismayed expression on Ed's face, she knew she hadn't quite pulled it off. She took a deep breath and smiled. "Sorry," Helen said, squeezing his arm.

"You're forgiven," Ed said, giving her the sort of look that was reproving and mischievous at the same time. "Didn't mean to sound flippant."

"Yes, you did," Helen teased him affectionately. And maybe, just maybe, Ed had a point.

As soon as she left Ed's, she screwed up her courage and walked the short distance from his flat to The Pitcher and Piano. She told herself that she was simply taking a look, nothing heavy-duty, no camera shots, no fingertip search, no checking for missed evidence, none of the paraphernalia: lifting tape, powders, Zephyr brushes, vinyl sheets, magnifying glass, search lights. The chance of something happening again in broad daylight was remote so there was absolutely nothing to worry about. Nothing at all. She couldn't quite admit that she was about to review her own scene of crime.

Wanting to retrace her route, she entered the bar from the top entrance, walked into the modern interior through a crowded eating area, then down the stairs to the ground-floor, scanning faces in the same way she'd done two nights before. She spotted a certain sort of tiredness in the expressions, a result of too much boozing, too much eating, too much time spent inside confined with people one should care about but couldn't. She also registered the dogged determination to keep the momentum going – by ordering another drink. Someone was sitting at her table but it didn't really matter. That wasn't what she was there for.

Deliberately sauntering through the busy bar, glancing at her mirrored reflection, she passed through double opening-doors and out onto a paved area from where she could see the water winking menacingly at her. A blade of sun penetrated through a break in the clouds. This was it, she thought nervously. This was where it happened. Her professional expertise deserted her. She felt no adrenaline rush, no crucial sense of cool detachment, vital to carry out the job. Rather her fists were clenched and her palms were sweating. A sharp pain inserted itself behind her left eye, signalling the start of a blistering headache.

There were a couple of white plastic tables and chairs for those brave enough to sit outside, the rest of the outdoor furniture stacked against a brick-built wall. Beyond this, a tarmac path ran alongside the canal. To her right was one of the many tunnels, the footpath hived off from the water by a single metal, slightly kicked out of shape, handrail. She thought it might have been a good spot for someone with malign intent to hide, but the presence of a light at the opening of the tunnel meant the individual was exposed to some risk of being seen.

She looked to her left where a solitary painted barge, selling teas and coffees, lay anchored. Her gaze transferred to the pedestrian footbridge leading to the International Convention Centre. That wouldn't work, she thought. She would have heard the clatter of footsteps, and met her assailant head-on. The attack had come from behind, she reminded herself. So, she thought, pivoting slowly on one foot so that she was facing the Pitcher and Piano, there was only one other possibility. Whoever mugged her had waited inside and followed her out.

CHAPTER FOUR

ADAM WAS STANDING THERE, a kitchen knife in his hand, fresh blood on the blade.

"What have you done?" she screamed.

He said nothing. Just stood there with his lop-sided smile.

"Please, Adam, please…"

"It's all right," he said soothingly. "She's in here. She's not really dead. Look."

Heart in her throat, Helen followed him down a dark corridor into a small, windowless room. A pile of clothes lay in a corner. She knew the body was underneath.

"Go on," he said encouragingly. "See for yourself."

She nodded, as if in a dream, crossed the room, drew back the clothing, saw the face. *Her* face.

"Christ Almighty," Helen sat up and switched on the light. She was bathed in sweat and her limbs were trembling. The spectre of Adam Roscoe seemed to inhabit every corner of the room, even though he'd never even set foot in the place. She saw Adam standing by the window. Adam taking her clothes off. Adam joyous. Adam angry. Tossing back the bedclothes, she leapt out of bed and headed for the bathroom. Putting the thermostat on its hottest setting, she closed her eyes, trying to wash him out of her head. But the image of that filthy flat, the wrenched-up clothes, Rose Buchanan's broken body, the baby already dead inside her, just wouldn't go away. She let out a bitter laugh. All the time she'd been there in the flat, taking photographs, combing through every piece

53

of detritus for evidence, she hadn't known that Adam Roscoe, the love of her life, had unwittingly contributed to the young girl's murder. She was blissfully unaware that Adam knew for months that Rose Buchanan was at risk from Jacks. She'd no idea then that Adam's blind desire to protect his informer, at all costs, meant Rose's life, or any girl Jacks took up with, was deemed a necessary sacrifice. Worse, she didn't yet understand the significance of an earlier case of indecent assault, in which both she and Adam were professionally involved, and in which the charges were later dropped. *About which she'd stayed silent.*

Fuck it, she thought, stepping out of the shower, reaching for a towel, willing herself to be rational. The mugging had understandably upset her equilibrium, resurrecting a series of unpleasant events that were history. Simple as that. Nothing more to it. No links. No connections. What was needed was focus. Thank God she'd arranged to go round to Jen's first thing to help prepare for the New Year's Eve party that evening. Anything to blank out the mugging.

Anything to eradicate the past.

She dressed in black jeans and a thick polo-neck sweater, and decided to give breakfast and make-up a miss. Grabbing a thickly padded jacket, she bowled down the stairs, swiping her car keys, and let herself out onto a sharply gravelled path, her ears keening at the steady drone of city traffic.

In spite of the sun, the chill air made her teeth ache. Digging her hands deep into her pockets, she tramped up the path that led out onto the back of the property to where her car, a chilli red MR2 Roadster, was parked. She climbed into the black leather interior, and once she'd defrosted the windscreen, slipped Robert

Palmer's *At His Very Best* into the CD player, and started the engine, revelling in the throaty roar. When she'd worked as a SOCO, she'd received driving instruction as part of extra training. She was commended, she remembered with some pride. She was always up for things then: charity events, marathons, even a self-defence course for female officers. She did it for a laugh, or so she said, but really it was to prove herself to Adam Roscoe, to give her an edge, to impress him, to make her worthy of his love. She expelled a heavy sigh. In spite of all her good intentions, she couldn't help but remember.

"Goodness, you scrub up well," Adam said admiringly.

She was sitting having a drink with some colleagues at the Gate Hangs Well, a popular haunt for police officers and associated staff.

"Not that difficult. Protective suits must be the most unflattering outfits on the planet."

"I reckon you'd look good in a bin-liner," he said. "Can I buy you a drink?"

"Thanks," she said, flattered. "Gin and tonic, please."

He ordered the drinks, picked both of them up, and walked to a corner of the room away from the others.

"Oh, shouldn't we…" she began, half-looking over her shoulder at her friends.

"I'm sure they won't miss you for five minutes. Anyway, I wanted to thank you."

"For what?"

"You did a good job on the shooting."

She bridled a bit. She thought he sounded patronising. "It's my job. It's what I do."

"A pity people like Davies don't appreciate it."

"No harm done," she said, sipping her drink. It wasn't wise to slag off officers, whatever their rank, whatever she thought.

He nodded and let his dark eyes rest on hers. "Didn't have you down for a complainer."

"What did you have me down for?" she smiled flirtatiously.

"Someone who cares."

Oh, she thought, the last thing she dreamt he'd say.

After stopping off to collect some wine for the party, she called in at the car jet wash in the expectation it wouldn't be busy. There was only one car ahead. She took her place and switched from CD Player to radio, hoping to catch some news. Slade's Merry Christmas was blasting out from the speakers. She'd never particularly liked it but found herself singing along until riveted by the driver of the car in front, a dark blue Audi A4. Dressed in galoshes, yellow waterproofs and wearing Marigolds, the Audi's driver attacked his car with the hose as if it were a dog that had rolled in fresh cow-shit. Every time she thought he'd finished, he pushed the button for an extra wash. There was a lot of fumbling underneath, the hose poised just so to get the full effect. It looked highly suspicious, forcing her to seriously consider what he was eradicating. She switched off the radio, and found herself watching with a professional eye. Water was the enemy of forensics. Critical trace evidence could easily be washed away. Fibres might remain – if you were lucky. Then she pinched herself, jolting back to the present. You're not in the business any more, she told herself, you walked away, left it all behind.

Twenty-five minutes later, he waved her in and drove off. Probably a wannabe BMW driver, she concluded with a smile, as she got out and fed the meter.

Jen lived in Bristol Road, in an annexe of her parent's Regency townhouse. She represented the new breed of stay-at-home older children who ate into their parents' pensions. While Helen fled from her home environment at the first opportunity, Jen chose a rent-free roof over her head the size of a football pitch, her washing done, meals when she wanted them, and all the freedom because Jen's parents were fond of travelling. At the present time, they were whooping it up in Cuba.

Helen parked on the gravelled drive. Loud music was belting out from Jen's side of the house. Helen walked in and was greeted by George, the family's bearded collie-cross. As she squatted down to pat him, he stuck both muddy paws on her chest and licked her face. Not much of a guard-dog, she thought fondly, stroking his hairy head.

"Tell George to bugger off," Jen called from a small galleried area that had been converted into a kitchen. The rest of the annexe was open-plan, which meant that guests could as easily sit on the large double bed as on the sofa. The idea was that certain spaces had their own distinct functions but Jen was so pathologically untidy, everything seemed to meld into one big mess. The bathroom was the only sane bit, tucked at the other end of the gallery with proper doors that locked.

Helen gave George an affectionate shove, crossed the obstacle course that covered several hundred square feet of floor, and went up the two steps to the kitchen.

"What do you reckon to this?" Jen said, holding out a soup ladle. Pink-faced, she was wearing denims and an old sweater that failed to conceal her voluptuous build. Her long blonde hair was unceremoniously pinned up on top of her head.

Helen sniffed it. "What is it?"

"Chicken Gloop."

"Sounds dodgy."

"Oh ye of little faith. Go on, give it a try."

Helen tasted it. "Funnily enough, it's quite nice. What else are we cooking?"

"Industrial-sized quantities of Beef in Beer, George's favourite," Jen regarded him affectionately as he trotted into the kitchen and slumped down near her feet. "What is it with dogs? They always park themselves in the most inconvenient places." She gave him a gentle nudge with her foot.

Helen knelt down and stroked his soft, fluffy coat. George gave a contented grunt and closed his eyes.

"No, you don't," Jen said, clapping her hands, "Come on, up Georgie boy, you'll have to go in the parent-pad." George twitched his hairy eyebrows, got up with great reluctance and threw Helen a reproachful look.

"What do you want me to do?" Helen said as Jen carted George away.

"Saved you a special job." Jen had a wicked light in her eyes.

"What's that?"

"Make a start on the onions."

"Wow," Jen said, goggle-eyed.

Helen flinched at Jen's too obvious enthusiasm.

They were taking a well-earned break. Helen was beginning to wonder whether she'd ever recover. God knows how many onions she'd peeled, but the rims of her eyes were bright red and her eyeballs felt on fire.

"Any idea who rescued you?"

In a random moment, she wondered if it was the taller of the two guys she'd spied in the Pitcher and Piano, the better-looking one. Wishful thinking. She shook her head.

"Hot chocolate?" Jen said, as if Helen's near drowning were cause for celebration.

"Thought you were on a diet," Helen teased.

"After New Year, silly. Anyway, chocolate's good for you."

Unlike Jen, Helen didn't have to watch what she ate. She'd always kept reasonably physically fit by twice-weekly swimming – not that it seemed to have done her much good. She shrugged a *fine by me* and scrabbled in her handbag for a tissue.

"And you say you were pushed," Jen continued ghoulishly, pouring a pint of milk into a saucepan.

"Well, I…"

"God, he could have killed you."

Helen was beginning to regret her confession. Jen's strange fascination with the misfortunes of others was something that had, up until that moment, been mildly amusing. If something terrible was reported in the newspapers, or on the radio or television, it was guaranteed that Jen would call and let her know. Jen's collection of true-crime stories was awesome, her memory for ghoulish events irrefutable. She should have been a copper, Helen thought. Instead she worked in the alien, blokeish world of the motor dealer, selling Jaguars.

"So you're helping the police with their enquiries," Jen said, whisking chocolate powder into the boiling milk. That was the other thing about Jen, Helen thought, she loved the jargon.

"Don't say it like that," Helen let out a laugh. "Makes me sound like a potential suspect. How many are you expecting tonight?" she asked, rapidly changing the subject.

"I've invited sixty but I don't know if they'll all come."

"Be a crush if they do."

"S'pose if the worst comes to it, we could always spill over into the parent-pad."

"They'll love that," Helen grinned, with heavy irony. Jen looked unconcerned. She put two mugs down on the table. "Got enough booze?" Helen asked.

"Hope so," Jen replied. "Ed's collecting two barrels of beer and four cases of wine." She lowered her gaze. "Did I tell you Martin's coming?"

Oh shit, Helen thought. "No, you didn't."

Jen blew on her drink and took a sip. "It's OK. He's bringing some woman with him."

"Good," Helen said.

"Really?"

"Really," Helen insisted.

"Told you he'd get over it," Jen said with a shrewd smile.

Dear sweet Martin, Helen thought, as she drove slowly back to the coach-house. He'd genuinely loved her. Of that, she was certain. It should have been enough. *He* should have been enough. Wasn't as if she hadn't

60

cared or had strong feelings for him. But these had come at the wrong time, if that didn't sound too perverse. The truth was that she'd been on the rebound. Adam was under her skin. Still was.

With Martin she'd felt such a rush of unfamiliar happiness, such a strange, uncomplicated and unaccustomed emotion that it was no surprise she'd wanted to run for it. Perhaps it was her upbringing. There were always boundaries not to be crossed. Getting too close wasn't welcomed and it wasn't advisable to try. She was schooled to be solitary. If ill, carry on. If unhappy, say nothing. There was a certain family philosophy in which she'd been steeped: work hard and trust nobody.

One day, she and Martin were walking together along New Street. It was a bitterly cold January afternoon and the light was fading. They passed a young lad who was sitting huddled in a vacant shop doorway. He asked for some change. With his pinched face and sunken eyes, he couldn't have been much older than fourteen years of age. Something in his despairing expression tugged at her. She sensed his loneliness, his bleak isolation. She knew of old that he was a potential victim of crime statistic. As she slowed down, Martin pulled at her sleeve.

"I'll be back," she called over her shoulder to the boy as Martin bundled her away.

"What do you mean?" Martin said, confounded.

"Won't take a second," she said, absently scanning the shop-fronts. "Here, this will do," she said, darting into a bakery.

"You can't be serious," he said, half of him appalled, the other fascinated.

She ordered a meat pie, one cheese and onion pasty, and asked for both of them to be heated. She asked for a carton of hot vegetable soup and two rounds of sandwiches, one cheese and tomato, the other ham and salad.

"And I'll have two of those iced buns and a doughnut," she said. "You can stay here, if you want," she said to Martin mildly, as she offered a crisp ten pound note to the shop assistant.

"You must be joking. I'm coming with you. He might turn funny and demand money with menaces."

But he didn't. He looked astonished and grateful.

As they walked hurriedly away, Martin said in bewildered tones, "I've never been with anyone who's done that before."

"No big deal," she said dismissively. "Had I given him cash, he might have spent it on drugs."

"That's not really what I meant," Martin said, slowing down. "You really feel, don't you?"

"Feel what?"

"Other people's pain."

She gave a puzzled shrug. "Just being a decent human being, that's all."

Martin stopped and turned towards her. He put both hands on her shoulders. "Are you afraid to be happy, Helen?"

She smiled awkwardly.

"Are you?" His eyes were so darkly penetrating they wiped the smile from her face.

"No," she whispered, feeling the denial catch in her throat.

"Is this about Adam?"

"No," she said, fiercely this time. It's about me, she thought.

"And *are* you happy?"

She sighed, touched his face with her fingers, her heart clenching with sadness because she knew she couldn't tell him the truth. She knew it wasn't his fault, but hers.

Even though she decided she'd nothing to wear, Helen eventually settled for a claret-coloured dress with long, slinky sleeves, and a flattering neckline. She dug out a pair of black stilettos – the heels could fell a male at thirty paces – and strapped them on with the same precision as if she were carrying an undercover weapon. With a swish of muted grey eye shadow over the lids, red on her lips, the vampish look was complete. Then it was on with her coat and off into the freezing night air. She'd arranged for a taxi. It took less than ten minutes door to door.

Jen's annexe echoed with music, loud but not deafening, a constant burble of voices, odd guffaws of laughter, the chinking of glass. The open-plan living room, enveloped in a non-politically correct nicotine haze, was awash with people, bright-eyed, their faces sheened with warmth, alcohol and lust. Helen knew most of them by sight if not by name.

The car-dealer fraternity gathered in two tightly delineated groups: Jaguar versus BMW. Then there were the petrol-heads and the type of thrusting young-bloods who regularly appeared, along with the great and the good, on the back page of the Birmingham Post for the grip and grin shots, as Helen termed them.

Helen slipped off her coat and chucked it on the pile on Jen's bed. As she helped herself to some white wine, she heard her name being shouted. She turned and recognised one of Jen's work colleagues, a guy called Mark Horton. Holding court on the other side of the room, he had the typical car salesman's stance: feet wide apart, chest sticking out, blokeish grin. He was signalling frantically for her to come and join him. She nodded and waved, weaving her way slowly through various groups of people, stopping every so often to say hello, dipping in and out of conversations.

"Smashing dress," Jen commented, a little tipsily, Helen thought.

"You look pretty good yourself," Helen said. Jen's enviably curvaceous form was squeezed into an electric-blue creation with a plunging neckline, her blonde curls, newly unleashed, cascaded over her shoulders. She was standing next to a man Helen didn't recognise.

"James Saunders," Jen said, doing the introductions. Although he wasn't particularly short, in her heels Helen towered over him. With his small eyes and heavy-framed spectacles, he looked all head and no body. She guessed he was an academic.

"Hi," he said.

Helen murmured the usual pleasantries.

"Helen's a photographer," Jen explained. "Portraits."

James cracked a smile.

"She works for Ray Seatt," Jen laboured the point.

The smile widened. "Oh, right," he said in a knowledgeable fashion.

"You know him?" Helen asked.

The smile faded. Ridges appeared across his brow. "Don't think so."

There was a stilted silence. Jen flashed a weak smile in Helen's direction and took the opportunity to disappear to *see to the food*.

"Nice party," James said, smiling again.

Helen muttered a meaningless reply, secretly cursing Jen for dumping him on her. "So what do you do, James?" It was a pretty lacklustre opening but she couldn't think of anything else to say.

"I'm a court welfare officer," he said firmly, proud of it.

"Here?" Helen said.

"In Corporation Street. My work's mainly with children."

"So you're a sort of social worker," Helen said.

"A mediator. Often between warring spouses," he laughed lightly. "I work for CAFCASS."

She felt the blood leach from her cheeks. She could have gone on the attack about the cases that slipped through their bureaucratic fingers, about focusing on the detail and missing the obvious. She could have asked if he remembered a girl called Rose Buchanan. Instead she forced a smile. "Must be challenging," she mumbled, trying to conceal her dismay. She took a quick snatch at her drink.

"Extremely rewarding. The work's varied, and you get to meet some interesting people," James said, warming to his theme.

"I can imagine." She heard her own voice sounding artificially bright as she glanced over his shoulder.

"I like to think we enjoy a fair degree of success," he twitched a smile.

"Mmmm." Nausea wended a speedy path to her throat. "Well, it's nice talking to you, James, but I think Jen could do with some help."

She shut herself in the bathroom, washed her hands, went to the loo, washed her hands again. Perhaps she shouldn't have come, she thought, looking in the mirror at her strained reflection. It was too soon after her stay in hospital. She was still fragile. Somehow she couldn't shake off the feeling that the Fates, not content with being thwarted, were conspiring against her. By the time she'd recovered and joined Mark, he was in full spate.

"I mean, can you believe it?" Mark said, his voice rasping from a pack-a-day habit, "this bloke actually wanted to name his son after his motor."

"And what was that?" a guy with a pockmarked complexion chipped in.

"Maverick," Mark grinned.

"Good job he didn't drive a Hyundai," Helen said.

The assembled gang roared with laughter, fuelled more by booze, she suspected, than her sparkling wit.

"How you doing?" Mark said, slipping his arm around her waist and giving her a playful squeeze. He was already showing signs of a distinct beer-gut, which she took pleasure in pointing out to him.

"Give a man a break," he grinned. He lowered his voice. "Jen muttered something about you being in some bother."

Bit of an understatement, Helen thought. She smiled sweetly.

"So it's true then. Someone tried to drown you."

"I was mugged."

Mark raised an enquiring eyebrow.

"During the attack, I fell into the canal," she explained.

"Fell? Jen said you were pushed."

Jen would, Helen thought. "You know Jen," she laughed softly, "she's a sucker for death and destruction."

"So what do you reckon happened?"

Helen gave a wide-eyed *no idea* shrug. "Wrong place, wrong time," she said, stealing her father's phrase.

"You're all right then?"

"No harm done," she smiled, disentangling herself from further conversation. She fluttered from group to group, wandering in and out of discussions on movies, the state of the economy, the vague and unconfirmed rumours of closures at yet another of the local factories, horse racing, the terrorist threat. Around ten o'clock, she balanced a plate of Chicken Gloop and rice in one hand, and a glass and fork in the other. She ate standing up while talking to a couple, whose names escaped her, about the perils of starting up your own business. Someone let George out. Exploiting every cute expression in his repertoire, he was fed a vast array of leftovers, the evidence clear for all to see as he promptly threw up on Jen's Chinese rug. While several women squealed and headed off, Helen alerted Jen and went in search of a mop and bucket.

Clearing up dog's vomit didn't phase her, though she could have done without the small gathering of onlookers as she scrubbed the carpet, especially the men who made helpful suggestions from fifty paces. Humans were endlessly fascinated by the grim and gruesome, she thought. It was that same fascination that drove motorists to slow down near fatal road accidents, to collect around a crime scene, to read with relish every sordid detail of a sexual killing over their breakfast toast and marmalade.

She'd just finished clearing up, and helped herself to another drink, when a familiar voice spoke behind her.

"You look stunning."

She turned. It was Martin. She'd spotted him earlier in the evening and done her best to avoid him. He was wearing a tailored jacket that clung to his lean physique. He looked darkly handsome, sleek, like a well-groomed cat.

"Thanks," she said, anxiously looking around for the attractive-looking redhead who'd accompanied him.

"Sarah's in the bathroom," Martin said with an amused smile. Helen smiled back and tried to conceal her relief. "How's things?" he asked.

"Great," she nodded, wincing at the heartiness in her voice. "And you?"

"Good. Very good," he added with emphasis.

"I'm pleased," she said, genuinely happy for him.

"Thought I wouldn't be," he said steadily, mouth close to hers, "but I am."

"Look, Martin, I wanted to say…"

He put a finger to her lips. "Don't say anything, Helen. Not now."

Not now? Had he heard about the mugging, too? What did he mean, she thought, nerves jangling?

"This looks pally," a piercing voice came from nowhere, the kind of voice, Helen thought, that could strip paint. "Aren't you going to introduce us?" The woman, who she took to be Sarah, was tugging at Martin's hand like a child trying to get its mother's attention. Small and pretty and pale, she wore a black strapless taffeta dress exposing creamy-white arms. Helen wondered if Martin had chosen her because she was the physical opposite of herself. Funny, she thought, she'd found Martin attractive precisely because he was so similar in looks to Adam. Same dancing eyes. Same enslaving smile.

The introductions were made. Helen smiled and murmured that it was nice to meet her. Sarah clung on to him like a limpet, Helen noticed. She wondered whether Martin found it attractive or whether, eventually, it would drive him away.

"Heard so much about you." Sarah's blue eyes were pure ice.

"All good, of course," Martin hurriedly spoke up. Helen offered another smile and felt her cheeks flush. Oh God, this was really difficult.

"I hear you're a photographer." The haze of blue didn't waver. Helen grunted a yes. "Maybe you could take my picture some time."

You have to be kidding, Helen thought, the fixed smile hurting her face. "How much do you charge?"

"Seventy-five pounds for a sitting, prints are extra."

Sarah gave Martin an appealing look. "I don't know whether that's expensive or not."

"Well, I..." he mumbled.

"I think you'll find it competitive," Helen said evenly. "So how did you two meet?" she said, deciding to be proactive.

"Sarah joined our P.R. wing," Martin explained.

"Handy," Helen said, inwardly cursing for not thinking of something smarter to say.

"It means we understand each other's work," Sarah said. "We often discuss campaigns at home. Some of our best ideas have originated over a bottle of wine," she said with a silvery laugh.

"Right," Helen said, draining her glass. Sarah followed suit. Helen considered whether she was copying her.

"Could you get me a refill, darling?" Sarah held out her glass to Martin.

Martin glanced from Sarah to Helen, his expression one of wincing apology. "And you, Helen?" he added, looking uncertain.

"Thanks," she smiled, handing him her empty glass.

"Won't be a moment," he said, pushing his way through the scrum of people.

Sarah possessively watched his retreating form and turned back to Helen. It was evident from the look in her eye that she wanted to make plain the ground-rules. "You're quite a tough act to follow."

Helen gave an embarrassed shrug.

"I think poor Martin thought you were *the* one."

Don't make me feel any worse than I already do, Helen thought.

"He was quite cut up until I came along," Sarah continued.

"I never meant…"

"I'd hate to see him made a fool of again." Sarah was smiling sweetly but her eyes gleamed with malice. This was the stay-away speech, Helen thought. What a silly girl. More than anything Helen wanted Martin to be happy.

"Look, Sarah, you really have nothing to worry…"

"You think I'm interested in your opinion?" Sarah cut in haughtily.

"Drinks, girls," Martin said, clearly pleased to find that neither woman had yet attacked the other.

"Thanks, sweetie," Sarah said, tipping up on her toes to give him a kiss and reassert ownership. Crisis over, Helen thought. At heart, Sarah was just a jealous cow. A bit of her worried about what Martin had let himself in for.

"Martin said you used to work as a crime scene photographer for the police."

Helen glanced from Sarah to Martin. He looked as startled as she felt.

"Not as simple as that. I…"

"Weren't you involved in that case that hit the papers?"

Martin paled. In a space of seconds, Helen felt herself turn from a reasonable person into an *I want to get my hands around your throat person*.

"Which case was that?" Helen replied dead calm.

"There's Chloe and Chris," Martin cut in, ludicrously animated, "remember you wanted to ask them round for supper, Sarah. Sorry, Helen, catch you later," he said, pulling Sarah with him.

Helen stood rooted. In just a couple of days, it felt as if her life were unravelling, her own near-death experience opening up her past. Could there be any connection, she thought anxiously? Maybe Jacks harboured a grudge. Maybe Adam wanted payback for her betrayal. No, silly. It was too long ago. While Adam was a lot of things, he wasn't a vengeful man. But, perhaps, he'd turned bitter. Perhaps life had treated him badly. She'd heard his marriage had collapsed but that was no great surprise; it had been on the verge of disintegration for years. She looked across the room, saw Martin and Sarah together, listened to their bright, to her ears false, laughter.

Eventually she drifted away to find another drink. Christmas was for couples, she thought, for close families, for old friends. It didn't have room for people like her, for the lost and the lonely. Wafting in and out of other people's conversations, she felt more like Banquo's ghost with every passing minute.

About eleven-thirty, the music changed tempo. As Steve Tyler and Aerosmith belted out a catchy version of Road Runner, several couples started to dance. Ed, who'd arrived late with an imposing-looking black man, grabbed hold of Helen, making her squeal. "Come on," he said.

They danced until midnight. The New Year was seen in with a drunken rendition of Auld Lang Syne. After that, Helen kissed people she knew and those she didn't, including Ed's new friend, Charles. Champagne was popped, and people stole away with whole bottles of the stuff. The party began to fold around four in the morning when she eventually caught up with Jen.

"Want a hand clearing up?" Helen said, slipping off her shoes and tweaking her strangled toes.

"Let's leave it," Jen said, also removing her shoes. "Had a good night?"

"Lovely," Helen lied. "What did you make of Martin's new girl?"

"Never had the pleasure of talking to her," Jen replied.

"You're lucky."

"Jealous?"

"No," Helen said vehemently.

"In fact I never got a chance to talk to anyone properly," Jen complained.

"The penalty of playing host," Helen smiled.

Jen yawned and rubbed her eyes, sending smuts of mascara down her cheeks. "Want to stay over?"

Helen looked in the direction of Jen's bed. "Looks like you already have company," she laughed.

George was conked out on the covers, hairy head on the pillow, eyes tightly shut, legs extended in a pose of sheer luxury.

"Terrific," Jen moaned. "How come I only get dogs to sleep with?"

Charles and Ed insisted on walking her home. Drunkenly linking their arms through hers, they joked they were bodyguards. She wasn't complaining.

A fierce and bitter wind had picked up, and there was a lethal-looking layer of ice upon the ground. She set her chin down into her coat and, zigzagging up the road, exchanged greetings with inebriated passers-by. It was all good-natured, which was lucky, she thought. The season of goodwill was often a flashpoint for violence.

Somewhere in the distance, the night sky was lit up with fireworks. They all stopped and watched for a few moments before the brutal cold drove them on. As they drew close to the studio, she explained that she could manage on her own.

"It will only take a couple of minutes to walk down the road and round the back."

"You didn't bring the studio keys?" Ed said, with concern.

"Ray would go bonkers if I lost them," Helen laughed. "Seriously, it's fine."

"You sure?" Charles said, the whites of his eyes gleaming in the darkness.

"Go on, boys," she said, kissing both of them.

"We'll watch your back," Ed said, standing on the corner with his arms crossed.

"Have it your way," she laughed, setting off down the road with a determined step.

The wind buffeted against her face, lifting her hair, numbing her ears. She called to them and they called back but their voices were carried away, sucked into

73

the sound of New Year breaking over the city. She stood for a second, feeling nervous, wanting to run back and join them, to say she'd had an attack of nerves and changed her mind. Instead, she did what she always did. She summoned up her courage. She took a risk. Giving a last wave, she turned down the private road that led to the back entrance, taking out the bunch of keys to the coach-house from her bag. Together with the thinning slice of moon, there was enough of a duff glow from the street lamps to light her way. She listened to her own footsteps, which seemed loud in the darkness. She saw plumes of hot breath escape from her mouth and cut through the cold. She felt her heart hammer in her chest. Get a grip, for God's sake, she told herself sternly. It would be fine. A few more paces, that was all. At any moment, a security light was timed to come on.

Only it didn't.

Perplexed, she waited. Still nothing happened. She glanced behind her, checking for someone in the shadows, but there was nobody. With a faltering step, she moved forward, one arm stretched ahead of her like an elephant's trunk, feeling her way. She could just make out the outline of her MR2 Roadster parked in its usual slot, and the white painted door that led to the rear garden and her home. Emboldened, she walked on, touched the car, her fingers connecting with and briefly sticking to the frosted metal, hoping to God that nobody was lurking behind it. Then she heard the noise: the heavy-duty sound of an engine starting up. And it was coming from in front of her.

It came out of the darkness with vicious speed. A flash of white. Swerving towards her. Clipping her smartly. Sending her and the keys sprawling. Even though her hands and knees took most of the impact, the intense pain in her hip rivered through her as she fell. Gasping with distress, she twisted her body round, her eyes searching the night. White van. Blocked-out windows. No plates. Stationary. Oh Christ, she thought, watching the brake-lights glow a simmering red, he's coming back to finish the job off.

Crying out with pain and fear, she grabbed hold of the side of her car and levered herself to her feet. She'd lost a shoe. Her tights were ripped to shreds and her hands were bleeding. Dragging her left leg, she tried to melt into the darkness, hugging the bushes near the side of the road. Still the van waited, taunting her. Got to get out of here, she thought, desperately trying not to panic. Got to find the keys. She dropped back down to her hands and knees, her desire to stay alive greater than the agony in the left side of her body, and raked the ground with her fingers.

That's when the van slowly started to reverse.

CHAPTER FIVE

THE PRIVATE DRIVE WAS a cul-de-sac. The van was hemming her in with deadly intent. In too much pain to make a run for it, her only ally was the moon. A chink of light shone on the frozen ground and, guided by its gleam, she searched furiously to locate the keys, but the van was still crawling at a menacing pace towards her. By now, it was no more than two yards away. In desperation, she raked the ground again with bleeding hands. Still the van backed. She felt as if it were already on top of her. Then she caught sight of her key ring glittering in the moonlight. Crawling towards it, she recognised the metallic disc with her initials engraved upon it. She calculated that she had seconds to strike and get clear. No more. At any moment, he could put his foot down and reverse over her, crushing her bones, leaving pools of blood and bits of her on the tarmac. She lunged forward. At the same time, she heard the wrench of the handbrake, heard the tyres locking. Crackling with fear, she lay there, waiting for her assailant to get out of the car to do God knows what. Had she been uninjured, she would have faced him and taken her chances. In her current state, it was unthinkable.

Heart thumping, blood drumming in her ears, she held her breath until she felt dizzy. Then the engine gave an unexpected roar, the brake lights vanished, and the van took off at speed, *forwards*, disappearing down the drive, jerking left towards the main road, and out of sight.

Scrabbling for the keys, she moved back onto her haunches, and forced herself to her feet. Her only focus was the door. She fumbled for the lock, jabbed in the key, turning it, pushing her way through, taking care to bolt the door shut behind her. Then she lurched along the path to home, tears streaming down her face.

Once inside, she headed straight for the bathroom, locking the door, something she never did, and collapsed onto the floor. Deathly cold, she was shaking all over. Her teeth chattered. Everything hurt. She felt sick and her mind was rambling. Another shock like this in so few days couldn't be good for her, she thought wildly. Tea, sweetened tea, that's what you're supposed to have. But first she needed to get up, and she couldn't. She just couldn't. She stared at her hands. The nails were broken and there was grit in her palms. Same with her knees. Her dress was wrecked and the left side of her body felt all stiff and swollen. She didn't know how long she stayed there on the bathroom floor but, very slowly, she managed to pull herself up. In between moans, she gingerly peeled off her tattered clothes and threw them into the corner. She was cut and grazed all over. Her hip and left thigh had started to swell and change colour but, as far as she could tell, it was all soft tissue; there was no major damage. After making a half-hearted effort to bathe her wounds, she decided to run a shallow lukewarm bath and get it over with in one go. While it was running, she slipped on a robe and went downstairs to make herself a drink.

The kitchen clock said five fifty-five in the morning. Apart from the moon clinging tenaciously to the sky, she could see very little outside, which made her feel safer. Ought to be checked over by a medic, she thought vaguely, sipping her tea. Ought to phone the police and speak to Harmon. She thought of D.C. Wylie showing up, imagined his swagger, his disapproving expression. She wouldn't be believed, she thought numbly. Half of her didn't believe what had happened either.

Returning to the bathroom, she immersed herself in water, grinding her teeth as it flowed over her wounds and made them sting. At least she was alive, she consoled herself.

For the second time in less than a week.

Two hours later she awoke in bed. Every part of her body had stiffened. Her muscles ached from where she'd instinctively braced. Her skin felt sore as if sunburnt. Gently touching the back of her head, she found her hair was matted with blood and that there was a noticeable bump. But more than all these physical injuries, she was consumed by one question: why?

He could have killed her. She was unarmed, vulnerable and totally at his mercy. There were no witnesses. The van was plain, no markings, rather like a scenes of crime van but this one had no plates on it, indicating it was stolen. Afterwards, all he had to do was get far enough away, torch it and go to ground.

But he didn't run her over.

So killing her wasn't part of the agenda. Then what did he want, she thought anxiously? Was he simply intent on roughing her up, on frightening the life out of her? But that neither explained his motivation nor indicated what he wanted. And she couldn't rule out the connection between last night's incident and the mugging a few days before. Oh God, she thought, was it just possible that Jacks had a hand in it?

She remembered what her dad told her, but the idea that present events could be linked to her past simply didn't ring true. Convicted criminals often had policemen and judges in their sights. The threat to witnesses and jurors was real enough, but former scenes of crime officers didn't come in for that kind of attention. Not even people with her history, she thought, feeling a sudden weight of guilt so strong it hurt.

She struggled to sit up. In the chaos, she'd forgotten to draw the curtains. Although her clock told her it was morning, she could see that the moon was reluctant to make an exit. So what if her past was also refusing to go away, she thought with a shiver? What if it had come back to smack her round the face? What if it was all connected to the case that was branded on her mind? The one that made her leave, the one that destroyed her lover's career, her own career, the one that threatened her sanity? She swallowed hard. For four years she'd done her best to bury it. She'd tried to build a different life, to recreate a new persona, to immerse her entire being in work, to switch off, to escape. She'd also taken a personal vow of honesty. Exhibiting the same zeal as a reformed smoker, she'd become obsessed with truth, the need to know it and, where it counted, to tell it, even if that meant leaving her vulnerable and putting her at a disadvantage. But, in spite of all her efforts to twist and turn away from her past, to lay it to rest, it kept seeping through to the surface. It kept coming back to haunt her. That's why she got the headaches, she reckoned.

Her mind flipped back to the party. First there'd been goofy James, the CAFCASS bloke, then Sarah. She believed that women were finer observers than men, better at picking up non-verbal clues, expert at dishing out covert insults, not that Sarah was particularly clandestine in her attack, she remembered with annoyance. While she only felt peeved that Jen had gossiped to Mark Horton, it worried her that Martin had discussed her history with someone who'd used it as a weapon against her – even if it was to be expected. Lovers invariably talk about their pasts. It was a kind of currency, a chance to reveal, share, sometimes show off the most attractive facets of one's personality, but she'd believed, naively perhaps, that when she'd confided in Martin it was in strictest confidence. She imagined him telling Sarah. Perhaps it had been dropped into the conversation after one too many glasses of wine, or shared with her after sex. A chill crept up her spine. Pillow talk was a dangerous thing.

After another hour of trying to doze, she gave up. Pulling on a loose-fitting pair of sweatpants and a navy fleece-lined top, she shuffled to the bathroom, rooting through the medicine chest for painkillers. Her clothes lay in a bloodied heap upon the floor and there was grit in the bath from where she'd picked out bits of road from her skin. At least she didn't have a hangover, she consoled herself, swallowing a couple of paracetamol with some water. She knew that, if she were anyone else, she ought to report the incident, but, as it was her, a discredited and corrupt individual by many police officers' standards, it was out of the question.

Putting on a jacket, she hobbled downstairs, grabbed the camera she kept for personal use, a Leica with a zoom lens, and let herself out.

After a rough and windy night, the garden was an oasis of calm. A watery sun bled light onto the grass. She walked down the path to the rear door, unlocked it and, checking both ways to make sure she was entirely alone, carefully studied the area of disturbance. One of her stiletto shoes lay near the fence. Patches of fabric and fibre from her dress and tights were clearly visible to her trained eye. She crouched down painfully, her good knee resting on the ground, right elbow resting on her right leg. She hurt so much she found it difficult to keep the camera steady, crucial for a pin-sharp shot, and took the precaution of ensuring that the shutter speed was fast enough to hide any camera shake. She took several shots of both shoe and fabric, and one of the security light that had failed to come on. Where the van revved and sped off down the road, there were distinct rubber-marks, which she also snapped. Walking back down the drive to the entry to the next-door building, she noticed a narrow weed-infested patch that had been clearly flattened by a vehicle. She limped over and, gingerly resting on her haunches, examined the verge for tyre tracks or foot impressions, but the frozen, unyielding ground made it impossible to make anything out. Painfully straightening up, she noticed a number of spent matches aimlessly thrown towards the middle of the drive. Applying Locard's Principle – every contact leaves a trace – she took a closer look. There was no sign of cigarette-stubs, but she estimated this was roughly the spot where he'd holed up. This was the place he'd lain in wait for her. All quite deliberate. No chance of coincidence. Again she took more shots, this time using the macro facility on the zoom lens to a get a close-up. The simple act of recording what happened seemed to concentrate her mind. Returning to the coach-house, she knew exactly what to do next.

An hour later, she was sitting in her colourfully painted kitchen with Detective Inspector Joe Stratton.

"I wasn't sure if you'd be at work. Pulled the short straw?" she said with a warm smile.

"Volunteered for it." His deep, well-spoken voice sounded clipped. He'd lost weight, she thought, making him look taller than his six foot build. His dark hair was cut short, and his skin was pale, lending his eyes an unusual intensity. She briefly wondered if she'd made a mistake asking for his help.

"Thanks for coming," she smiled again, nervously.

"Didn't think you'd want to come to Steelhouse Lane."

"Too much like going into the bear pit," she joked.

Stratton agreed, eyes smiling. "Looks as though you landed on your feet," he said, looking around. "Ray's a good guy."

"And I'm a good photographer," she batted back.

"Must be quite a change from photographing corpses."

"My present clients smell a lot better," she grinned.

"But talk back," Stratton let out a laugh. That was more like it, she thought, more like the Stratton I know. It felt like the old days; black humour to cover the dreadful nature of some of the work.

"Want a drink?" she asked him.

Stratton requested coffee, no milk, no sugar. They sat down at the kitchen table. Now that he was here, she didn't know where to begin. Neither did he, by the look of him.

"So run through what you told me on the phone again," Stratton said.

She did.

"And you reckon this is connected to the mugging four days ago?"

"You already heard about it?"

"Hard not to. After your call this morning, I checked out the paperwork. It's not absolutely crystal-clear that you were pushed."

"No."

Stratton inclined his head in question.

"Truth is I'm not sure," she said, shuffling on her chair. No matter how she tried to sit, she couldn't get comfortable.

"Why didn't you report last night's incident to Harmon and Wylie?"

It was the obvious question. She'd been waiting for it. "I did *think* about it."

"And?"

She looked straight into his dark brown eyes. "I won't be taken seriously."

He glanced away.

"You want me to spell it out?" she said softly.

Stratton pulled a face.

"Corruption's a dirty word, Joe. It's like the big C."

His look inferred *so that's why you got me here*. "You weren't corrupt."

Helen arched an eyebrow. "Remember Lou Crosbie?"

Stratton let out a sigh and nodded. Detective Constable Crosbie's superior officer was found to be on the take, a crime for which he was arrested and eventually sent to prison. Even though Crosbie was innocent, he was shunned and eventually forced to resign, the assumption being that Crosbie must have been in the know. Helen didn't believe for a second that Adam Roscoe had been corrupt but there were plenty who did, and that meant her card was marked.

"I know the score, Joe. If I report what happened, my complaint will be written down, all the right noises made, and the details filed in the bottom of a very large filing cabinet." She couldn't say that she suspected Harmon and Wylie were the types who'd follow orders without question, would always close ranks. She couldn't say that Wylie appeared to have a view. "That's why I thought you were better placed."

"Bloody hell, Helen."

"Look, Joe, someone's out to get me."

"I'm getting deja vu. Next you'll start banging on about conspiracy theories and cover-ups."

She flinched, glanced away for a second. "I was right."

"Only to a point," he said a warning look in his eyes. "And I don't need reminding of it."

No, he didn't. One of the few who'd been good to her, he'd defended her when others had wanted to tear her limb from limb. The police were no different to the rest of society. They had no love of whistle-blowers. They turned against those who betrayed their own.

"Sorry," she said humbly.

"OK," Stratton said, his features relaxing a little. He took a sip of coffee and studied her. "Suppose someone *is* out to get you, as you say, the question you have to ask is what do they want?"

"Revenge."

His eyes locked with hers.

"You're the only one I can trust, Joe."

Stratton put his mug down on the table and gave her a straight look. "The fall-out from the Warren Jacks case is in the past. It's highly unlikely it has any bearing on what happened either last night or four days ago."

"But possible."

"Anything's possible," he carped. "It's whether it's probable."

"But surely it's the first place to start looking."

He broke into a wide smile. "Exactly."

She frowned. "I don't understand."

"You've just answered your own question."

"Because it's obvious, it's unlikely?"

"Helen, Jacks has no axe to grind with you."

"I nailed him."

"He nailed himself. All you did was collect the evidence."

"And shout about it."

He waved his hand in a dismissive gesture. "If he'd really wanted to have you taken care of, he'd have done it a long time ago, believe me."

"From inside prison?"

Stratton nodded gravely.

"That's encouraging," she said with a dry smile, "but I wasn't only thinking about Jacks."

Stratton looked uncomfortable. "You mean Roscoe?"

She nodded.

"After he left the force," Stratton said, "I gather he set up as some kind of security adviser."

"Right," she said, thinking what a waste.

"You knew of the likely consequences." There was no accusation in Stratton's tone. It was more a simple statement of fact.

Yes she did, that's why she'd agonised over it, she wanted to say.

"However you dress it up, Helen, he was bent."

Bent, such an ugly word, she thought. "He wasn't on the take," she pointed out fairly. "He didn't fit anyone up. He didn't profit from drugs busts or robberies. He didn't leak information to criminals. The operation had been cleared at the highest level…"

"But not the way he handled it," Stratton countered uncompromisingly. "He got too close to Jacks. He overstepped the mark to protect his informant, for God's sake."

She spread her hands. "He believed it to be in a noble cause."

"His own," Stratton said with a steely glare. "And everyone knows that noble-cause corruption is only the first step to financial or worse. If he was that bloody innocent, why did he resign instead of fighting his corner?"

"At least he didn't go on the grounds of ill-health," she said: the classic get-out clause for dodgy officers.

"He went before he was pushed."

She sighed. How could she defend the indefensible? And why the hell was she defending Adam Roscoe, in any case? He hadn't done her any favours.

Stratton glanced away. She was quick to pick up on it. "Is there something else?"

"Last I heard, he went out to Iraq."

"Iraq?" she gasped.

"There's good money to be had – if you can stay alive."

Maybe he doesn't care any more, she thought. Adam always was a risk-taker. He liked the buzz, the power it conferred. Contrary to what some had hinted at, he'd never displayed much interest in money. That wasn't what motivated him. "What about the others?"

"Apart from a couple of officers who left of their own accord, everyone directly connected to the case has kept their jobs. In some cases they've moved higher up the food-chain."

"Glad to see putting my neck on the block made such a stunning difference."

His eyes connected with hers. "It made the difference, all right."

"Another enquiry, another report and, in the meantime, everyone's got smarter at covering their arses." She said it smilingly in an attempt to disguise the spike in her voice.

"I mean you caused a cultural shift," he parried.

She gave a deep sigh. "The police will never dispense with informers, registered or otherwise."

"With good reason, Helen," Stratton said with more than a hint of irritation. "Most police work is human intelligence gathering. Sure, technology and systems have a valid role, but nothing beats solid information. It's why informers play a routine part in lots of criminal investigations. They're a necessary evil. Without them, information dries up and crime increases, and they're a damn sight more useful on the street than banged up in prison but, believe me," he added, "no one wants a repeat of the Jacks case."

"In case the lawyers come down on you?"

"Unlike you to be so cynical."

87

"Sorry," she muttered, catching too late the humour in his eyes. Oh God, she thought, would there ever be a time when she could talk rationally about it without getting this exercised?

"We're better trained now," Stratton said, "more informed about the inherent risks. Less experienced officers are more likely to listen to advice from superiors and less likely to make deals they can't possibly keep. There's been a real clampdown on backhanders and soft jail terms."

I've heard it all before, she thought, sipping her coffee thoughtfully. She didn't say anything. Sometimes it was better to let an argument go, especially one with such high emotional stakes. "You ever hear from Elaine?"

"She works for West Mercia now. Seems happy enough. Not so much blood and guts," he said, cracking a warm smile. She smiled back. "I'm not attempting to play this down, Helen," he said, reaching over and touching her hand. "I'm just trying to help you see what's behind it." His eyes were softer now. As she looked into them, she knew he was batting for her. She glanced down at his hand over hers. The skin felt warm and supple. But it shouldn't be there, she thought warily, abruptly pulling away. He seemed not to notice.

"I'm going to play Devil's Advocate with you," he said brightly.

"Now *I'm* getting deja vu."

"How do you know last night wasn't some prank by a lunatic drunk?"

"That's the sort of thing Harmon's sidekick, Wylie, would come out with," she protested.

Stratton continued, undeterred. "People get pissed on New Year's Eve. They do all sorts of mad things."

"Like this," she said, standing up, rolling up her left trouser leg. "This is just the edited highlight. Believe me, it's a lot worse further up."

Stratton's jaw slackened. "Christ, have you seen a doctor?"

"If you think I'm queuing up in casualty to see some quack who's been working round the clock for the past twenty-four hours, you have to be kidding," she let out a laugh. Still less do I want to see a scenes of crime officer, she thought more sombrely, and have my photograph taken.

"All right," Stratton said slowly, "show me where it happened."

They went outside into the garden and walked up the path together to the back gate. Any sun had given way to a grey and grudging sky. It felt cold enough for snow. "It was rumoured you'd had some sort of breakdown," Stratton said as he opened the gate.

She'd heard the same. In reality, she'd teetered on the brink. She'd felt as if she were suspended in time. How she thought she felt was not how she really was. And she'd been particularly affected, she remembered, by noise. Anything and everything made her jump. The world was a monstrous clamour, but nothing sounded as loud as the noises in her head. She would have liked to put Joe straight, but decided it was best left unsaid. "Whatever I felt then, I'm fine now," she said with a brisk smile.

She let Stratton study the scene for himself. He walked up and down, crouching briefly by the rubber marks, examining the security light, which, according to him, had been tampered with.

"It was thought-out, perfectly timed. He could have killed me."

"But he didn't," Stratton said, as if thinking aloud. "He had the opportunity but he didn't take it. Why would he do that?"

She shrugged her shoulders. "To create fear?"

"Maybe he wants to punish you."

"Which brings us neatly back to grudges," she said, hoping to be spared the psychoanalysis.

They went back to the coach-house and she made more coffee.

"Can you think of anybody you might have offended, intentionally or otherwise?" Stratton asked.

"No one."

"No rejected males, no broken hearts?" he said, flashing the type of admiring glance that made her feel vulnerable. Stratton was married, after all. She wasn't falling for that one again.

"Why has it got to be a man? It could be a woman."

Stratton rejected the idea out of hand.

"Why not?" she said, with interest.

"Driving vans at people is a man thing."

"Sounds sexist."

Stratton laughed. "You always come out with stuff like that when you're losing an argument."

"No I don't," she said, playfully slapping his arm. "Actually, now you come to mention it, there *is* another woman in the picture." She told him about Freya Stephens and showed him the contact sheets. Stratton examined them. There was no flex in his jaw, no quickening of his eyes. He put them down and studied her for a moment.

"You tried to contact her?"

"Her mobile was switched to a messaging service."

"And she hasn't been in touch since?"

"No."

"Sounds flaky."

"I know." It was one thing to suspect, another to have it confirmed.

"So what's your take on this woman?" His brown eyes fixed on hers in a way she found vaguely unsettling.

"That's a difficult one." What could she say? She hardly knew the woman. "On the surface she seemed very charming. We got on well."

"You liked her?"

"Yes. She was direct, irreverent, different, I guess."

"Like you," Stratton said with a spry smile.

You don't know me any more, she thought sadly. "There was nothing about her that triggered my alarm signals."

"Until the mugging," Stratton chipped in.

"Uh-huh."

He looked at her with meditative eyes. "You think the meeting was a ruse?"

"Could have been," she admitted.

Stratton looked thoughtful. "Got anywhere else to stay?"

"What's wrong with here?"

"You're on your own."

She gave him a level look. "You think I'm in danger?"

"In anyone's book, last night was a serious incident, which is why I don't feel comfortable about you not reporting it." He leant towards her. "I hear what you're saying, and, sadly, knowing how sensitive cops are about corruption, I agree with your general conclusion, but isn't it worth giving Harmon…"

91

"No," she burst out. "I've just told you…"

"Okay, okay," he said putting up a hand defensively. He watched her for a moment. "All right," he said slowly. "I'll do some discreet digging."

"Thanks, Joe," she said, trying to contain the relief in her voice. "Is this going to cause a problem between you and Harmon?"

"Not at the moment," Stratton said. "Depends what I unearth."

"But you might need to share it with her?"

"I might," he said neutrally. Except, Helen thought, the very rigid nature of police hierarchy meant that Stratton could always pull rank. Breakdowns in communication were not uncommon. He could play it however he chose. "Got an address for this Freya woman?"

"Her details are in the studio," she said, getting stiffly to her feet.

"And I'd like her number," he said. "Can I borrow these?" he asked, holding up the contact sheets.

"Sure."

When she returned, he was still studying the proofs. "I've written down my mobile number for you," he said, "easier than going through the switchboard."

And easier to keep it quiet, she thought.

"You always shoot in black and white?"

She shook her head. "Most of my work's colour. Black and white is generally for the purists. They reckon you get more of an artistic effect. It allows the photographer to let his subject impress his or her personality on the picture, give it more of a visual impact. From a practical perspective, it's also cheaper to produce."

"Why do you think Freya Stephens chose this particular medium?"

Good question, she thought. "With hindsight, I'd say she had a taste for drama. She wanted to create an impact."

And she certainly did, Helen thought.

CHAPTER SIX

SHE WAS DUE AT her parents for lunch. A New Year's Day ritual, enshrined in family history, it was designed so that her mother could recover from one hangover before embarking on the next. Several of her parents' close friends joined them and Helen attended with whichever boyfriend she was dating at the time. For the past two years Martin had accompanied her. It felt strange, this time, to be alone.

With her left hip and leg so badly bruised, she wasn't entirely certain how she was going to drive. Changing the clutch would be painful but what bothered her most was her cover story. She really wanted to come clean but she couldn't afford to, because, aside from her mother, who was spooked out enough already, she feared her father's reaction. Her dad was a doer. He expected results. He was not good at delegation, especially when it came to his daughter's safety. If she told them the full story, he'd be on the phone to the Home Secretary. The situation called for verisimilitude. She could say that she was drunk – who wasn't on New Year's Eve – and had stumbled into the road where she'd been accidentally knocked off her feet by a passing motorist. However, the idea of being economical with the truth made her feel so sick she decided to say nothing at all.

It took her ages to get changed. A skirt or dress was definitely out. She decided upon a navy loose-fitting trouser suit, smart-casual, as her mother would say. Just before she left, she called the lab. Although closed until after the weekend, she intended to leave a message.

After two rings, the phone was answered.

"Carl?' Helen said in amazement. "What the hell are you doing there?"

"That's a fine greeting," he gave a raucous laugh.

"Sorry, I'm just amazed you're open."

"We're not. I happened to be in."

"On New Year's Day?"

"You know how it is, can't keep away from the place."

"Christmas that bad?" she laughed.

"You haven't met my wife's side of the family," he joked, but in a way she suspected there was a grain of truth in it. "So what can I do for you?"

"You sent proof sheet references J6878/9."

"Yeah, I remember."

"Could I have another set, and can you print numbers eleven and twelve, fifteen and seventeen."

"Size?"

"Eight by six should do it."

"Any particular time frame?"

"Soon as you can."

"Will do. And Happy New Year, Helen."

"Same to you, Carl," she said, cutting the call.

Fortunately, she found some Co-Codamol lurking in the back of the medicine chest, the only painkiller that seemed to ease her frequent headaches. The pills didn't knock you out, thank God, but they subdued the pain to a manageable level. She just hoped the tablets would hold out for the necessary length of time.

The drive was uneventful. Roads were quiet. People were few. While Christmas decorations were already being dismantled in some homes, the majority were still intact, just.

As she drove, she listened to Norah Jones singing *Come Away With Me*. With bitter poignancy, she was reminded of Martin. They were at his flat. He'd cooked a lovely supper. Norah Jones's dusky soulful voice was seeping out of the speakers. They were at that mellow stage in the evening when she knew they'd soon fall into bed.

"Marry me," Martin said softly.

It was so unexpected she stupidly asked him to repeat what he said. He smiled, took her hand, kissed the inside of her wrist. "Marry me, Helen."

She felt like a rabbit caught in headlights. Here was this lovely man offering to make her his wife. She really did care for him, loved him, maybe. Not like Adam, but still lots. So easy to say yes. So easy. "Martin, I…"

"It's all right," he smiled. "I'm not rushing you. Take your time."

"It's not that," she swallowed. "I just don't think I'm the right…"

"Helen," he spoke gently. "You're everything I've ever wanted. Let me love you."

What he really meant, she thought, tracing his face with her fingers, was *let me save you*.

And, sadly, she knew he couldn't.

Judging from the glossy selection of vehicles outside Keepers, most guests had already arrived. She got out and crossed the drive, steeling herself to be social. The heavy oak door was already open and she stepped through a forcefield of dry heat and into the wide, open hall where Hilary and Vernon Rudge were divesting themselves of their coats. They greeted her with the smug warmth of the well-heeled.

"Lovely to see you," Hilary said, crushing her in a hug that near enough made her cry out. Always tactile, Hilary Rudge was one of those women, Helen thought, who'd lose the power to communicate if they lost their hands.

"We hear you've been having a bit of a rough time of it," Vernon said, a corpulent man with a deep laugh.

"I'm on the mend," Helen assured him, taking their coats, escaping to the downstairs cloakroom, a perfect design of coat-hooks and potpourri, hand-wash and tissues, scent and soft towels. She caught sight of herself in the gilt-framed mirror. She looked tired – to be expected – but there was something else. Faint marionette lines had appeared at the corners of her mouth. Her skin seemed lifeless. She looked haunted. Fear slithered over her body. A fear of being found out.

As she made her entrance into the drawing room, people turned and looked at her, the steady burble of conversation briefly dipping before it cranked up again. A log fire was blazing in the fireplace, windows staunchly closed. With the under-floor heating at full belt, she found it difficult to breathe. Bowls of crisps and sweating peanuts were dotted around the room though nobody seemed that interested. Apart from the Rudges, there were roughly twenty others. All were smartly dressed, the men in ties and jackets, the women in Christmas reds and greens. The air smelt of perfume, after-shave and money. Heaps of it.

Her father was playing host, topping up his guests' glasses from a bottle of Krug. He immediately pushed a glass into Helen's hand and kissed her.

97

"All right?" he said, his brown eyes searching hers.

She nodded. It probably wasn't a good idea to drink on top of the strong painkillers but she took a sip. What the hell, she thought. "Where's Mum?"

"In the kitchen."

"I'll go and see if she wants a hand."

Her mother was putting the finishing touches to a whole poached salmon.

"Hi, there," Helen said.

Her mother gave a start. "Oh, it's you." She put a hand over her heart. "Sorry, these kind of gatherings make me nervy." Always thin, she looked much thinner. Her skin was ashen. She looked, Helen thought, as if the lights were on but nobody was in. She couldn't tell if it was hangover or worry.

Her mother wiped her hands on her apron and forced a smile. "How's things?"

"All right," Helen said, resting her rear against the Aga. "Partied at Jen's last night. The usual crowd."

Her mother turned her attention to the fish again. Her fingers were trembling, Helen noticed. "Everything else all right?" her mother said. "No more problems?"

"Nothing for you to worry about."

"Really?" her mother flashed an anxious look.

"Honest," Helen said, skin creeping at the blatant lie.

Her mother's features melted into relief. She picked up her glass, a heavy-based tumbler of gin and tonic, and took a deep drink from it. As she went to put the glass down, it seemed to slip from her fingers, tumbling onto the tiled floor where it smashed into dozens of glittering pieces. She put both hands to her head, pressing the fingers hard to her temples, and let out a long, heartfelt wail.

Astonished by her mother's response, Helen moved swiftly towards her, cradling an arm around her shoulders. Her mother began to sob.

Christ, how many had she had, Helen wondered, the strong scent of juniper catching her nose? "Shush, shush," Helen soothed, as if comforting a child. "It's only a drop of gin, and the glass won't break the bank."

But her mother was gone. "I'm so sorry, Hels," she gulped, "so very sorry. I didn't mean..." she broke off, crying again. Her shoulders heaved as if she had all the sorrows of the world on them.

"I know," Helen said, gently rubbing her back. Her mother hadn't called her Hels since she was little. Must be the booze, she thought.

"You don't understand," her mother said, with desperate eyes.

"I do," Helen said simply. You're drunk, you're worried, you're unravelling. "Now go upstairs, splash your face with water. I'll clear up."

Her mother stood mute for a moment as if trying to process a decision. "Yes," she agreed at last, her voice little more than a whisper. "But the food."

"No one's going to starve. Most of them look as if they could do with missing a few meals," Helen laughed, forcing a weak smile from her mother.

"That's better," Helen said, kissing her mother's wet cheek. "If you're not down in five, I'll come and get you."

It took an age to find all the shards, even with the aid of the Hoover. Fortunately, everyone was too busy jawing and drinking to notice the blip in the

99

proceedings. By the time Helen emerged, her mother had recovered her composure and joined the party. Helen watched her. She was laughing politely at a joke cracked by Vernon Rudge, but there was no sparkle in her eyes, no warmth.

Eventually, the room thinned out as people drifted through to the dining room where they queued in typically British fashion. Helen found herself bringing up the rear with the Mainwearings, her parents' nearest neighbours. They were extolling the virtues of gardening. Even though she had little interest, she tried to make the right noises.

"Our big project this year is a water feature," Celia Mainwearing was saying. Small and dumpy, with weather-beaten features, she talked at speed.

"I've never been quite certain of the difference between a water feature and a pond," Helen said, wondering too late if she'd put her foot in it.

"Oh, a feature's *much* more complex," Dennis Mainwearing opined.

"More architectural," Celia backed him up.

The table looked as though ravaged by locusts by the time she got there. The cold roast beef was decimated. There was one tiny piece of salmon. The salads were stripped of all the choicest ingredients, and the garlic bread was reduced to half a dozen dried-up end pieces. Only the puddings looked unsullied. Worst of all, there was nowhere to sit because everyone had bagged places and disappeared into their own little cliques. Amid so many people, she suddenly felt displaced. This was her home and she didn't really belong. Never had.

She stood on the periphery of a heated conversation about asylum seekers, and ate standing up, wondering when she could slope off without causing a stir. Already the tablets were beginning to wear off and she was dreading the drive home. She was just considering how to make her escape when her cell phone rang. She deposited her plate on the nearest side-table, walked out of the room and into the empty hall, and picked up the call. It was Stratton.

"We have a problem," Stratton said. "Freya Stephens doesn't exist."

She felt as if someone had thumped her in the throat.

"You were given a false name and address," Stratton continued.

"I see." She didn't really, but she couldn't think of anything else to say.

"Any idea why she'd conceal her identity?" Stratton asked.

"Not that I can think of."

"You're absolutely certain she didn't give out anything about herself," he pressed, "any clues to her personal circumstances?"

"Not really."

She heard Stratton expel a sigh. "So what now?" she asked.

There was a lengthy pause. Poor Joe, she thought, it would be so much easier if he could share the information but, even if it were possible, how could she explain that she didn't want the torrent of questions, didn't want the drama, hated the idea of being in the spotlight again? She'd had enough of it last time.

"I'll try shaking a few trees for info."

Sounds like we're back to informers again, she thought, her stomach giving a sickening lurch. Then

101

she had another idea. "It's a bit of a long shot, but wouldn't Jacks have had contact sheets?" These were forms filled out by an informant's police handler.

"Yes, of course," Stratton said apprehensively.

"Could you get hold of them?"

"Helen, I'm not sure…"

"They might contain something, a name or a clue, something we're missing." It would also tell her about how Adam recorded the information, she thought but didn't say.

Stratton almost groaned. "Why do you still think Jacks is connected to the attack?"

"Just keeping my options open," she said brightly.

There was a baffled silence.

"Please," she said.

"I'll see what I can do," he said, his tone long-suffering. "But I'm not making any promises," he added in a reproving fashion, then softened a bit. "What are you up to?"

"I'm at my parents. New Year buffet."

"Sounds fun."

"It isn't, actually."

"Least it keeps you out of trouble," he laughed.

Helen drove back home in the late afternoon. The countryside looked exposed and bleak, houses and buildings, normally hidden by trees and undergrowth, laid bare: secret places revealed. The sky was a dark band of grey smudged with white, as if some unseen artist had taken a palette knife to it.

Freya, or whatever she was called, had lied to her. People who gave false identities were usually criminals trying to conceal a greater crime. It looked as if Freya had set her up, but was she in on the mugging?

Was she in on last night? Helen wondered with a shiver.

She took the precaution of parking at the front of the studio. If anyone wanted to attack her again, they'd have to do it in front of a busy main road and passing pedestrians. She double-checked to see if she had company and, seeing none, stiffly got out of her car, recoiling from a bitter wind. By now the light had completely faded, making her hurry across the small car park to the front door. On the floor, just inside, was a thick padded envelope. She crouched down and picked it up. It was marked for her attention. She opened it. Carl had turned the prints around with impressive speed, she thought. Was it some kind of omen?

Her footsteps sounded loud in the surrounding silence, but everything was as she last left it. No messages flashing on the ansaphone. Nothing out of place in reception, or the small room used by clients for getting changed and retouching make-up, nothing disturbed in Ray's room or hers. The distance from the studio to the coach-house was minimal and, though she had to travel outside again into the garden, there was enough illumination from the undamaged security light attached to the wall of the studio to prove that she was alone. The only scary bit was hearing her own footsteps on the wooden veranda, the sound of her own ragged breathing, the chill of the thin night air whipping against her face. Once safely inside her home, she changed back into her sweatpants and top and, leaving the prints upstairs, went to the darkroom. She wasn't that keen on dealing with chemicals, but developing your own film was much easier than most people imagined, as long as you didn't mind working in the dark. Taking the film from her Leica, she shut herself in, snapped on a pair of disposable gloves, and ran through a ten-point programme of loading and pouring, agitating and timing, pouring and more pouring, then the final wash, to eliminate all chemical traces, before removing the excess with a squeegee, and clipping the finished film up to dry.

After helping herself to a glass of wine, she went back upstairs to the sitting room, sat down on the sofa and pulled out the photos from the lab. Who are you, she thought, staring into the woman's dark and mysterious eyes? What did you want with me? The finished versions made her seem more flesh and blood, Helen thought. She could see the lines around the eyes, the pores on the skin, moles on the cheeks. The woman's hair shone in the carefully distributed light. The smile that played across her full lips could almost be her own. As she gazed at the strong jaw-line, she couldn't help but consider the difference between the perfectly posed studio portrait and crime scene photograph. These pictures she held in her hand portrayed a rewritten past, a confident present, optimism for the future. A crime scene shot, by definition, was a negation of all faith and hope.

She got up, paced the room. If only she had the confidence to report it. It wasn't fair to load it on Stratton. In effect, she'd asked him to help her but had first gagged his mouth and tied his feet together. Maybe if…

No, Lou Crosbie had been a decent police officer, she reminded herself, but his occupational association with a corrupt D.I. meant that no self-respecting officer wanted to work with him. He was soiled goods. Nobody trusted him. Like the albatross, he was considered to be bad news, bad luck. If Lou could be run out of the force, Helen thought, she stood no chance.

In an effort to distract her thinking, she selected a favourite book on photography from her collection. Taking it back to the sofa, like a dog retreating to its favourite lair with a bone, she flicked through the pages, her eyes lingering on a luscious section on fashion photography depicting the work of Helmut Newton. She was immediately transported to another world, a world of luxury where women were strong and powerful and earthy. As she flicked through the pages and gazed into Newton's dark and sexy depictions of his privileged subjects, she felt a spectral chill. She glanced up, put a hand to the back of her neck as if to smooth the hairs back down, catching the eye of the woman in the photographs. She was essentially a stranger, Helen mused. Their paths had never touched or crossed before. Some link to the past, therefore, seemed unlikely. Stratton confirmed it. But...

She couldn't shake it off. Whether it was guilt, paranoia, or some deep longing to feel connected in a way she'd once felt before, she believed that Adam was in the mix somewhere.

Perhaps Freya was the bait with which to reel her in.

If she was right, it had worked. If it were true, she knew a way to find out.

CHAPTER SEVEN

THE NEXT MORNING SHE got up to a downcast day. Staring at herself in the bedroom mirror, she saw that the swelling in her thigh was undiminished, the cuts were scabbing over and her injured skin was turning a dramatic shade of amethyst. She felt stiffer than ever, as if her muscles and joints had shrunk overnight.

Determined to disprove her own reflection, she dressed in a long skirt and sweater, hid her battered legs with a thick pair of black tights, and slipped on a pair of loafers. After making and drinking two mugs of coffee, she retired to the darkroom where she spent an entire morning fiddling with the finished film from her camera, producing contact sheets, test sheets, experimenting with exposure, until she finally yelled *hallelujah* and hung up several enlargements to dry. She was on a mission, but it would be at least another twelve hours before she could examine the results of her handiwork. Even then, she wasn't sure what, if anything, might be revealed.

But, in the meantime, she had another idea. It was risky, maybe reckless, but it was worth a shot.

It took her twenty-five minutes to drive through lunch-time traffic and find a suitable parking slot in the Jewellery Quarter, a maze of streets and historic buildings, where every type of jeweller and goldsmith could be found.

For ten more minutes, she waited, drumming her fingers, thinking, reminding herself of what she already knew about the woman who'd been Adam Roscoe's wife.

"You're married," she said dully. She'd collared Adam in a corridor and dragged him into a side-room so she could confront him with it.

"Only in name," he assured her.

"Isn't that what all married men say? Next you'll be telling me your wife doesn't understand you." She wondered what his wife was like, dark and flashing, like him, mercurial?

"Helen," he said stroking her cheek.

"Don't," she said, brittle.

"We lead separate lives, honey."

She gave a hollow laugh. "You expect me to believe that?"

"It's the truth."

"Why live together at all?"

"Apathy."

"Not because of the children?"

"There are no children."

Thank God, for that, she thought. She crossed her arms in front of her. "What's her name?"

"Does it matter?"

"Yes." She was curious.

"Robyn."

"That's unusual."

"She's American."

"What does she do?"

"Helen," he sighed, trying to placate her.

She repeated the question. She wanted to know exactly what and whom she was dealing with.

"She buys and sells art, paintings, mostly. She has her own gallery."

"Sounds glamorous." And lucrative, Helen thought. Most corrupt officers were motivated by greed. In spite of the rumours, Adam definitely wasn't one of them.

"Only if you're interested."

She cast him a searching look. "So what went wrong between the two of you?" A stupid question. She'd only get his blinkered side of it. She guessed she was hoping for an explanation she could live with. Women did it the world over. Finding themselves drawn irresistibly to unsuitable men and falling in love with them, itself a kind of madness, they then tried to find reasons to justify their insanity.

He pushed a lock of her long dark hair behind her ear. "You know what the job's like, the pressures, the shit we have to deal with day in, day out. Not exactly the type of stuff you discuss over a candlelit dinner for two."

"Yes, but…"

His cell phone went. He offered an apologetic smile, stood up, walked away. She watched a vein pulse in his neck, listened to the charge in his voice, heard the chill.

"Yes…calm down. It's all right. Breathe, fuck you, and tell me what happened…Uh-huh. Don't worry, it can be sorted." He looked at his watch. "Be with you in ten. Don't move. Don't walk away. Don't disturb anything. You hear me?" He cut the call, opened his arms to her. "Sorry, my love. Duty calls."

Ugly rumours, Stratton said. She knew. She understood.

Adam wrapped his arms around her, whispered in her ear. "I need you and you need me. We're tuned-in to each other. We're soul-mates, you and I."

And as she looked into his eyes, she wanted so badly to believe him. "Then leave your wife," she said.

"I will."

But he never did.

They broke up for a bit after that, she remembered. That's the way their relationship played out: six months on, several months apart. She always promised herself she'd never slide back but something always happened to change her mind. It would be that look, that phone call, that touch of his hand, or that need in the night, which led to her downfall.

And to his, she thought, getting out of the car and slamming the door shut.

She walked round the corner from Ludgate Hill and into St Paul's Square, past The Jam House, a restaurant and renowned jazz club, crossing over near St Paul's Church, passing a letting agency on the corner, mentally cranking herself up. She reckoned she had two advantages: surprise and the fact that neither she nor Robyn had ever met.

The gallery, which was next to a pub called The Rope Walk, housed a collection of work by contemporary artists, some to her taste, most not. Carefully lit, with dark olive-green walls, it had the hushed air of a library. She went in, passing a smart-looking middle-aged couple on their way out, and felt her shoes sink into the carpet pile as she crossed the floor. Feigning interest, she walked straight over to a painting of a young woman wearing jeans and a leather jacket, smoking a cigarette. The artist was Spanish. She'd never heard of him.

"Glamorous, isn't it?" A sultry-looking black girl in her late twenties, poised and stately, glanced up from a smart iMac G5.

"And contemporary," Helen smiled, noting that the price of the painting was £15,000.

"That's the artist's wife," the black girl said, getting up. "She figures in quite a lot of his work. He's very keen on focusing on the sensual quality of the female form. We have some more paintings round the other side, if you're interested.

"Thank you."

"You're happy to browse?"

"Absolutely," Helen smiled.

"If you require any further information, let me know," the black girl said, smoothly returning to her desk to resume her duties.

Good, Helen thought, friendly but not pushy. She took her time, first studying a collection of bronzes, and then returning her attention to the paintings. She made two observations: the average price was a shade under £30,000, and most of the works of art were far too large to hang in an ordinary-sized house, indicating that they might be more suitable for a private collection.

The phone rang. Helen listened as the black girl raved to the caller about a particular piece of work that the gallery had managed to acquire.

"We thought it just the sort of piece you've been looking for," she said. "We'd be delighted to arrange a private viewing."

Helen waited until the black girl finished the call then casually sauntered towards her.

"Would it be possible to speak to Robyn Roscoe?" Helen said.

"I'm afraid not. She isn't here."

Helen smiled. "Could you tell me when she's available?"

"You wish to make an appointment?"

"Well, if you could tell me when she's free, I could arrange to pop in."

The black girl's eyes darkened.

"Or maybe I'll catch her at home, Kellerman Drive, isn't it?" Helen said, using the oldest trick in the book. She was waiting for the contradiction, the trading of information.

The black girl's brow creased with concern. She wasn't falling for it, Helen thought. "May I ask what this is in connection with?" There was a hint of suspicion in her voice.

"It's a personal matter," Helen continued to smile.

"I see." The eyes were unrelenting. "Well, I'm afraid Mrs Roscoe is in the States. She flies back tomorrow morning. We expect her back in on Monday."

"Right," Helen said, "thanks very much."

The girl's eyes fastened back on the iMac. She clicked the mouse several times. "So when did you wish to come in?"

"Monday would be good."

"She's tied up first thing but I could slot you in at three o' clock."

"Great."

"And your name?"

Helen felt her nerves prickle. This wasn't how she planned it. "Tell her I knew her husband," she said, making swiftly for the door.

Unsettled, she decided to light a fire in the sitting room. She took her time, lighting small pieces of wood to start with, adding a few more sticks, a little more paper then the coal. As the flames caught, causing the fire to sputter into life, it sounded like falling rain. She hoped it would make her feel safe and protected. It didn't.

She tried not to think about what was happening to her. She didn't want to try and slot the pieces together, to think about the mystery client, the Roscoes, Jacks. She'd actually been tempted to visit him. Jacks was locked up in Winson Green, an old, bleak Victorian prison that had undergone major expansion and renovation after coming in for severe criticism for its terrible conditions. However, it was unlikely she'd be granted a pass, and, in order to get one, she'd have to do a lot of explaining. Best left to Stratton, she judged.

After a while of sitting and staring, she made herself cheese on toast and ate it upstairs with a cup of tea, flicking through a book on Cartier-Bresson, not really looking at the text or pictures at all. Flames from the fire played shadows across the wall and, as she glanced up in the half-light, her mind suddenly clamoured with long-dead and forgotten ghosts: the suicides who, too late, had tried to change their minds, the women who fought for their lives and lost, the battered child, the drug-addicts, the road casualties, *Rose Buchanan*.

The knife and fork clattered against the plate.

As first in line, she'd seen the torn holes, the blood-spattered walls, the gunshot wounds, bruises and cigarette burns, the violated and defiled. She'd witnessed the cruelty and carnage of drug-fuelled murders, the violence of the fatal domestic, the senselessness of *honour* killings. She'd seen victims bumped off by a nobody who wanted to be a somebody. She'd examined the results of a flash-in-the-pan loss of temper and the final conclusion of systematic, daily warfare. There was a common misconception that Scenes of Crime was no job for a woman, but the truth was that mental stamina was more important than physical strength.

Sitting in the silence, the bald truth hit her like a blow between the eyes. Although she currently enjoyed being a portrait photographer, she missed the sense of doing something that counted. She always would.

She picked up her knife and fork again. The cheese had gone cold and chewy. She prodded it gingerly. It felt like dead flesh.

Helen studied each of the enlargements. The first few shots revealed an accurate record of the scene. No details to add. Nothing missed. Nothing of significance. When she examined the shot of the flattened grass, however, something caught her eye. At first, she wondered whether it was a scratch on the print, easily done when processing your own film, but, after taking a closer look, she could see that there was something definite near where the grass met the road. Whatever it was looked small, hoop-shaped, but she couldn't make it out and decided to take another look at the spot.

By now, the sky was the colour of ash, the usual drone of traffic muted by the cold. Helen walked down the garden, slipped through the gate and out onto the private drive, walking the short distance, the enlarged print in one hand, a pair of vinyl disposable gloves in the other. Crouching down for a second look, she pulled on the gloves and examined the area of road and grass again, touching it with her fingertips, inch by inch. That's when she saw it, or what was left of it. She picked it up with her fingers, rolled it in the palm of her hand. Flattened by a passing car, she might have mistaken it for a coin except it looked like real gold: a single hoop ear-ring.

She wondered whether it belonged to Freya Stephens.

He looked less gaunt, less austere in casual clothes, she thought. Stratton was wearing a navy shirt, tan leather jacket and jeans and he carried a slim-line box file. He smelt of something aromatic, musk, sandalwood, maybe. He hadn't shaved and there was shadow on his jaw. She offered him a glass of wine and he accepted. She briefly wondered whether to put on some music and changed her mind. She worried that the lighting was too low – didn't want him getting the wrong impression.

"Keeping all right?" Stratton said, laying the file down next to him. Simple enough in sound, she thought, but in truth, fully loaded.

"I haven't been mugged or run down lately," she said, twitching a smile. "Take a look at these," she said, handing him the prints. As he studied them she noticed his particularly dark colouring, as if he had Italian blood in the family. His nose was straight, lashes unusually long, eyes, in the half-light, almost black.

"What's that?" he said, picking out the shot where the flattened verge joined the drive.

"This," she said, holding up the remains of the ear-ring in a clean, clear plastic bag. The gesture reminded her of old times. She'd often held up evidence bags, sometimes containing the remnants of someone's life.

Stratton took it and glanced up at her. "Not exactly cast-iron evidence, is it?"

"Might belong to Miss Stephens."

"Could belong to anyone."

She conceded with a smile and sipped her drink. It had never been her job to investigate, just to collect and log the evidence. A certain amount of knowledge inevitably filtered through – especially when you're sleeping with a high-flying policeman. Like a kind of osmosis, you couldn't help but absorb some of the thinking that drove an investigation, namely: don't make it personal, don't get ahead of the evidence, and do not take any short cuts. Not that Adam ever seemed to take that much notice. Maybe, that's why, so far, she'd failed on every count.

"Are those the contact sheets for Jacks?" she said, eyeing the file.

He nodded. He had very expressive eyes, she thought.

"Thanks," she beamed. "Anything of interest?"

"Depends on your point of view," he said with an enigmatic smile. "Four hundred and twenty pages including some fairly quality information. Stuff on the Park Lane Boys mainly."

She gave an involuntary shiver. The Park Lane Boys had a formidable reputation. Based in Aston, they were principally a white gang who sometimes used black criminals to do their dirty work. Powerful, impressively armed, the Park Lane Boys not only ran large-scale protection rackets, but, through sheer terror, had made impressive inroads into the crack-cocaine business. Total loyalty to the gang was demanded. Any new member was forced to go through a form of initiation involving carjacking at gunpoint, any indiscipline punished by severe beating, any defector executed, usually by a shot in the face. When the police once tried to talk off the record to one of the few surviving victims of an attack, the former gang member asked for it to be recorded *on* the record that he knew absolutely nothing.

"Nothing that sends your alarm bells jangling?" she said.

"No," Stratton said firmly.

"Take a peek?"

He silently passed her the file. She opened it, scanning the list of meetings and phone conversations. As Stratton said, it was mainly a catalogue of information passed to Adam, with notes about the type of action taken. There were also numerous references to other criminals, mainly professional thieves, a couple of whom Jacks was asked to cosy up to. "Who's Damian Crawley?" Helen said, looking up.

Stratton smiled. "A light-fingered individual. Crawley's managed to successfully evade the law for a couple of decades. He steals to order and has been linked with any number of robberies, but we've never had enough evidence to charge him and bang him up."

"So that's why Adam was keen to exploit Jack's friendship with Crawley?"

"Yup, it was hoped that Jacks could find out when the next big job was in the offing."

"But nothing came of it."

Stratton shook his head.

"Probably wasn't enough time."

"Either that, or Jacks wasn't as well connected as he made out."

Helen read on. No dodgy dealing. No references to money unaccounted for. In fact, there was nothing to suggest that Roscoe was anything but above board. A bit of her felt vindicated. She handed the file back to Stratton. "Dead end," she remarked.

116

"A line of enquiry closed," Stratton corrected her.

She smiled at him. "I guess that's something."

"The problem is," Stratton said crisply, "what if something else happens to you?"

"I'll cross that bridge when and if."

His eyes levelled with hers. "You'd have to make it official, Helen."

She opened her mouth to protest but Stratton headed her off. "I've been giving it some thought. As long as we find the right people to talk to, I reckon you're in with a chance."

"What sort of a chance?" she said suspiciously.

"Fifty-fifty"

"Not good odds."

"Neither is doing nothing."

She couldn't think up a cogent argument so she said the first thing that flashed into her brain. "Are they really going to be that bothered?"

Stratton burst out laughing. "That's the kind of response I get from prostitutes and paedophiles. Everyone's entitled to be protected. What makes you so bloody special?"

She gave him a transparent look.

"For God's sake, Helen, you're old news. Sure, lots of people would have preferred it if you'd kept your mouth shut, or at least gone about exposing Jacks and his minders in a more subtle way…"

"I tried," she murmured. But not soon enough, she thought, miserable at the memory. When, eventually, she went to Barnaby Finch, who in turn went to Detective Chief Inspector Dukes, it was already too late. Somewhere after that the information looked as if it was going to get buried, and she lost patience.

"But there were plenty of us," Stratton continued, "who thought you did the right thing."

She gave a shaky laugh. "Could have fooled me."

"Corruption's a dirty word, Helen. You said so yourself. Everyone feels tainted by it. Makes people edgy."

Usually because truly corrupt officers rarely worked alone, she thought. "Which is precisely why no one's going to be interested in little old me. Anyway, Adam wasn't corrupt. That file exonerates him."

Stratton rolled his eyes. "Hardly. He just knows how to play the system. He was the classic *Lone Ranger*."

"Oh, for God's sake," she said, in spite of knowing that Stratton had strongly argued this to her superiors in an effort to distance her, and anybody else connected with the case, from Adam.

"He was bloody good at his job," Stratton admitted, "Popular and charming, I grant you."

"And trusted," she chipped in doggedly.

"But he'd been passed over for promotion and his marriage was struggling. Coupled with that, he got a buzz out of working alone, and, underneath that flash exterior…"

"Charismatic," she cut in, feeling the colour blossom in her cheeks.

"He was extremely manipulative," Stratton continued, unabashed.

"You've been reading too many reports," she said, barely keeping a lid on her composure. "He was a man, not a profile."

"And how do you explain his talent for covering his tracks?" Stratton countered, eager, it seemed, to have the last word.

She looked at him, took a breath, softened her voice. "There weren't any to cover." Oh, how she wished she could have said it with more conviction. The truth was she didn't know any more. The more she tried to remember, the more confused she felt. Deep down, she suspected, Stratton was right.

"How would you describe him, then?" he said, levelling with her.

She chewed her lip. "Misguided."

They stared at each other in stalemate. Stratton was the first to break the silence.

"As far as Harmon and Wylie are concerned, you're just another case. What you did or what you used to do has no relevance to them. You've got to dump the past where it belongs."

"What if it won't dump me?" She was painfully aware of sounding defensive. He sipped his wine, cradled the glass. He's embarrassed, she thought. Coppers don't like emotional women. That's what Adam told her, usually when she was banging on about his wife. "Do you know what day it is tomorrow?" she said quietly.

He looked blank for a second, then his eyes lightened with recognition. "The day Rose Buchanan was killed," he said, sombre.

"I can't forget," she murmured. "I don't think I ever will."

"Helen…"

"That call-out was bad," she said, cutting across him, needing to talk, "but it was no worse than some of the others. I'd seen dozens of dead bodies: mutilated,

119

raped, burnt, rotting. Any scenes of crime officer will tell you that it's always the kids who get to you most. Rose might have been old enough to have sex, but she was little more than a child really. Too young to be so brutally extinguished," she said, taking a morose pull at her drink.

"And then when Adam confirmed that it was Jacks, that he'd been running him for months, like it was a confession." She looked straight into Stratton's eyes. "You know, men say the strangest things when you're in bed with them. It's as if they think the bedroom confers some kind of confidentiality clause."

"Not just men," Stratton said with a smile, attempting to defuse her.

He was right. She'd done exactly the same with Martin. She looked away, shook her head at her own folly. "Sounds daft now, but I used to think of myself as a conduit for the victim. I felt as if I were responsible for telling their story, recording what happened, how it took place, the way they died. In my head, I was this great spokesperson for the dead. It sounded grand and noble, lifted a shitty day." She glanced at Stratton with defeated eyes. "Now it just seems poncey."

Stratton didn't say a word. Simply let her talk. Like the old days.

"It wasn't just because Rose Buchanan was pretty and vulnerable, but…"

"Because it could have been avoided," he cut in softly.

"If *only* one of the players had talked," she said, anguished. If only *I* had talked, she thought.

Stratton reached over, touched her chin with the crook of his finger. "You're not responsible for the failures of others. Like I said, Helen, you have to move on."

She nodded, pulled away, took a deep drink to relieve her aching throat and hide the guilt in her eyes. "I take it you didn't turn anything up," she said, coldly pulling herself together.

Stratton's face relaxed a little. This was easier territory for him. "As I thought, Jacks is doing his time, best behaviour and all that."

She clicked her tongue in disgust. "I suppose he'll be up before the parole board soon."

"You have to be joking," Stratton assured her. "As far as anyone else involved is concerned, there's no credible link to either of the attacks on you."

"You're certain?"

"As much as I can be."

"I should feel pleased."

Stratton scrutinised her with shrewd eyes. "But you're not?"

"It would have been simpler if there'd been a connection," she said. "Then it would make sense. At the moment I feel as if I'm on a train wearing a blindfold."

"Not sure of the destination?"

"Something like that," she smiled sadly. She wondered whether to tell him about her visit to Robyn Roscoe's gallery. Better not, she thought. Nothing to tell anyway. Not yet.

Neither of them spoke for a moment. She could still feel the spot where he'd touched her chin. "Anyway, enough of me," she said. "What about you?"

He looked startled. "I'm good," he said, a bit too brightly, she thought.

"And Annie and the kids?"

His face clouded. "We're not together any more."

She stared at him in astonishment. "I'm sorry, Joe. I'd no idea. When did you split?"

"About three years ago."

She felt her heart flip. "I hope it's nothing…"

"Occupational hazard," he cut in with a taut smile. Don't skewer me with kindness his look implied. "I see the kids. It's all quite amicable, as much as these things ever are," he added ruefully. "We've both tried to keep the legal side of things to a bare minimum. I've never had much time for solicitors, as you know. They always seem to make a bad situation worse." His eyes met hers. She tensed, not quite knowing what to say. The consequences of never being able to switch off during an active murder investigation, the long hours, heavy boozing, the tendency to respond to an important phone call first and let the family come second, often led to affairs, and frequently contributed to the disintegration of a marriage, but, in spite of Joe's insistence, the guilty part of her wondered whether she'd also been responsible for his predicament, whether his going out on a limb for her had precipitated its downfall. It was Joe who'd first warned her that Adam was married, that he was a manipulative individual, that there were ugly rumours about him, that any involvement with him could be dangerous to her. She thought it was borne out of envy. She hadn't listened. Not then.

"So where are you living?"

"I've got a place the size of a shoe-box in Stourbridge," he said with a wry smile, "not that I spend a lot of time in it."

She sensed his loneliness. They'd both lost their sparkle, she thought, or was it part of growing older, one of those horrible rites of passage when you suddenly realise that all your hopes are dreams, that you're never going to set the world alight, and that the things you chased weren't worth having in any case?

"More wine?" she said, picking up the bottle.

He glanced at his watch. "No, I'd better be going," he said, getting to his feet. "Thanks for the drink."

She felt a pang of disappointment but covered it with a smile. She followed him downstairs. He paused by the door and turned to her.

"Let me try to talk to someone, put it on the level."

So like Joe, she thought, remembering. The words were almost identical, only the last time he'd appealed directly to Detective Chief Inspector Dukes. She shook her head.

"What about Harmon?" he coaxed. "She's a woman and a good police officer."

"And Wylie?"

"He's a jumped up little prick."

She burst out laughing. "What's it worth for me not to tell him you said that?"

"You trying to blackmail me?" he said, his mouth slipping into a smile.

"Wouldn't dream of it."

He continued to look at her. She felt as if she had feathers in her stomach. "I mean it, Helen," he said, serious now.

She checked the impulse to protest loudly. "Or?"

He let out a sigh. "What if something more serious happens? You've put me in a difficult position."

Oh, I get it, she thought. If I don't say something, you will. Hadn't she said exactly the same to Adam four years before? "You giving me a choice?"

His reply was evasive. "I'll do everything possible to ensure your complaint's not buried."

How, she wondered? "With the greatest of respect, you can't."

Stratton's jaw tightened. He didn't argue. He knew she was right.

Guilt. It had to rate as the most corrosive of emotions, Helen thought, as she tried to sleep. Even misplaced, or survivor-guilt, as it was sometimes termed, attacks the soul in the most irrational fashion.

Sometimes she'd wake up and not remember. She'd spring out of bed with a lightness in her step, joy in her heart, then she'd look in the mirror, see the shortness of her hair, see her shame. It must be wonderful to be a psychopath, she thought crossly, plumping up her pillows for the third time. They never seemed troubled by wrongdoing of any kind. No conscience, no feeling, no pain.

She rolled over, pulled the duvet up around her head, trying to still the chatter of once-forgotten voices, failing. Nothing else for it, she thought, throwing back the duvet and switching on the lamp.

She kept the box on top of the wardrobe. Squirrelling it back to bed, she took off the lid and braced herself for the contents. The newspaper cuttings were already starting to weather with age. She hadn't filed them in any particular order so she simply took the first off the top.

THE BIRMINGHAM POST

WEST MIDLANDS POLICE UNDER ATTACK

Warren Jacks, a police informer for West Midlands Police, has been identified as the killer of fifteen-year-old Rose Buchanan by scenes of crime officer, Helen Powers.

Jacks, 30, who has links with the notorious Park Lane Boys, is thought to have turned undercover informer eighteen months ago. Although being documented as a danger to young girls – a previous charge of indecent assault against a minor was dropped – he was allowed to escape justice as a means to infiltrate the Park Lane Boys as part of an undercover operation.

Miss Powers, the daughter of Jack Powers, the wealthy print industrialist, took the unusual step of disclosing the information to the Press because she feared that there might be a form of cover-up. "While this is an obvious embarrassment for the police, it is an absolute tragedy for the Buchanan family," she said. When asked how she thought such an event had come about, Miss Powers stated that a demand for results coupled with a lack of leadership led officers to bend the law.

At the time of going to press, nobody was available for comment from West Midlands Police.

Helen gave a heavy sigh. After wading through a number of cuttings from local newspapers with titles like: **MOTHER WARNED POLICE THAT DAUGHTER WAS AT RISK**, she moved on to the nationals.

DAILY MAIL

SCENES OF CRIME OFFICER RESIGNS OVER INFORMER SCANDAL

Helen Powers, the controversial scenes of crime officer who exposed the recruitment of notorious gangland figure, Warren Jacks, by West Midlands Police, has resigned her post.

No police officers will be prosecuted over the case of the gangster who murdered his pregnant teenage girlfriend, Rose Buchanan, while he was an informant. The CPS has stated that there was insufficient evidence to support a prosecution of the officer handling Jacks. However, The Police Complaints Commission is still considering disciplinary proceedings.

A spokesperson for West Midlands stated that every informant was assessed for potential risk and reliability, and that Jacks was directly responsible for supplying high grade information prior to his arrest. Asked about Powers's role, the spokesperson maintained that Powers was right to raise concerns if she had them but, "while Miss Powers claims to have acted from the highest of motives, the manner in which she disclosed the

information was unprofessional and fell well below the standards expected of a scenes of crime officer."
No decision has been taken about whether or not to prosecute Miss Powers under the Official Secrets Act. Miss Powers was unavailable for comment.

Helen settled back on the pillows, wondering how or if she'd ever make her peace with the past. The cuttings only told part of the story, the bit she'd wanted to reveal. The truth was she'd messed up a long time before that. It wasn't a deliberate act. She didn't set out to do it. To her eternal shame, she didn't really consider it that carefully. It was something that happened because she wanted to trust the man she loved. She allowed herself to be persuaded because she was as ambitious for him as he was for himself, because she, too, was a rising star, hungry for success. When Adam Roscoe talked of the greater good, which he did often, she chose to believe him.

Adam sailed as close to the wind as anyone she'd ever known, but he got results. He was a maverick. She wasn't entirely certain how he managed to flourish – the police were more hidebound than ever by procedure. To stand up to the scrutiny of the court, let alone secure a conviction, everything had to be carried out to the letter. Speak to any police officer and they could all tell you tales of devious defence lawyers intent on disembowelling every piece of evidence, but somehow Adam seemed to circumvent it all. He'd taken a law degree while a serving officer, which he reckoned put him one step ahead. Either he was a genius or...

He used to talk a lot about the ends justifying the means. She thought it possessed the fine logic of a mathematical equation. Numbers were just that: figures. They were movable, expendable, but when you transposed the idea, put a face to the x or the y, when you flesh out that face with a family, a history, a person with hopes and dreams, then you have a problem. She knew that the previous indecent assault charge against Jacks should never have been dropped. She knew that she should have gone to her superior, spoken out. She knew that by saying nothing she was, in essence, guilty of withholding information. It didn't matter that the kid Jacks assaulted was on the wrong side of the tracks, had a history of care, and was destined for a sad life, she thought, remembering snatches of a previous conversation.

"I'm going to get Tracey on her own, talk to her nice and quiet," Adam said.

They were in bed. The sheets were tangled; they were always tangled.

Helen crooked herself up on one elbow, looked into his liquid brown eyes, smiled with disbelief. "What?"

"Get the kid to drop the allegations, forget pressing charges."

She snatched the sheets up to her chin in a hopelessly virginal gesture and sat up. "You can't do that. The girl's virtually been raped. We've got the evidence."

"*You've* got the evidence."

Christ, what was he asking her to do? The samples were sitting in the refrigerator at work, waiting to go off to the lab. She still had her statement to make, the report to write.

"Adam, you know as well as I that this bloke, Jacks, will do it again. Guys like him can't help themselves. It's in their blood. In their psyche. This was a really serious assault on a minor. The guy bears all the hallmarks of a rapist, for God's sake. The next time he offends, his victim might not be so lucky. He might even kill someone," she said desperately. "You've got to nail him."

"You're overreacting."

She could have hit him. She opened her mouth to protest loudly when another, more worrying, thought sped through her mind. "The girl was seen by a forensic examiner. You're not telling me you're going to get him to forget what he saw?"

"Don't be daft," Adam said in a way that was not entirely convincing.

According to the seriousness of the offence and volume of work, scenes of crime officers were either sent out singly on a job, or as part of a team. It was entirely normal for her to attend an indecent assault alone, but, the way Adam was talking, she began to worry that she'd been especially chosen, over and above anyone else. Did that mean that Barnaby Finch was in the know, she quaked inside? Adam was a relentless networker.

"Sweetheart," Adam said, turning towards her, sliding his body in between the sheet and her skin. "It would be doing her a favour."

"I don't understand," Helen said, feeling the warmth and weight of his body against her own.

"She's got a long sexual history," he said, sliding the sheet down to expose her breasts.

"How do you know?" Her voice was hot with indignation.

"I'm the detective, remember?"

"Adam, the girl's fifteen years of age."

"Which means the bastard lawyers would have a field day with her in court."

"Yes, but…"

He ran one finger along her lips, put it in her mouth. "She's not a credible witness. It's far kinder to protect her from the humiliation."

She bit his finger, making him withdraw. "But if this bloke gets away with it, he'll do it again."

"He'll be monitored," Adam said, sliding his hand between her legs.

"You can't monitor someone like that. He's not a little kid whose going to say sorry and behave himself."

"I'll make sure of it."

"How?" she snapped.

Adam gave a tense sigh. "When are you going to wake up and smell the coffee?"

She glared at him. Once before, admittedly in the privacy of her flat, he'd made out that she was young and inexperienced – at least when it came to policing.

"Jacks is an informant," Adam said. "Any court case would put him and others at risk."

"But that's completely immoral."

"So is this," he said, putting a finger inside her.

She braced. "Adam, I'm serious."

"So am I," he said, his voice hardening.

She stared at him. Was he acting alone, or were others involved? Is this what Stratton would term as corrupt? Was that why she'd had that uneasy feeling about Adam before? The truth was she didn't know. Like Adam said, she didn't have the experience. To her innocent ears, it all sounded like the kind of stuff that happened in films. No, this was crazy, she thought. Corruption had been seen off years before, care of a number of internal investigations. Adam wasn't bent. Couldn't be. He was just well-motivated, ambitious, and a bit frustrated by the difficulties of obtaining the kind of evidence needed nowadays to secure a conviction.

Adam was talking again. "Look, in an ideal world I'd agree with you, but sometimes you have to bend the rules a little. You know how much the system's weighted in favour of the criminal."

"I agree, but…"

"And I'm being honest with you about the girl. Do you want to see her shredded in court? She's already had a pretty crappy start in life. Think what it would do to her, Helen."

She gave him a wary look. He certainly had a point. "You really believe you can control him?"

"Absolutely."

"But I still don't see how you're going to get round it. What about the WPC who spoke to Tracey?" she said, feeling her body operate quite separately to her brain.

"I can square it," Adam murmured. Helen imagined his smooth talking. He'd talk about the *proper management of the issues* even though he didn't believe in them. At the back of her mind, she also wondered whether he'd tell the WPC that, if she wanted to progress, it was as well to keep in with him.

"But…"

"I can do anything," he whispered.

And she believed him because she needed to. She liked to think she knew him so much more completely than his wife. The thrill was that, while she battled

131

with her conscience, her body snaked with desire. So she stifled the voice in her head about justice, about the possible prevention of a far greater crime. Had she spoken out, Rose Buchanan would still be alive. Exposing the later act fell well short of redemption.

And that's why guilt was her bedfellow. It stole the smile from her face, took the edge from every simple pleasure. It followed her around like a star-struck lover, a constant living, breathing, slippery presence.

Someone once told her that certain personalities were more susceptible to feelings of blame: the perfectionists, the high-achievers, and the ones who expected too much from themselves and of others. She wasn't one of them. Her guilt was well deserved. There was nothing she could do to change what she'd done, or make things better.

Nothing at all.

Not ever.

CHAPTER EIGHT

SUNDAY FINISHED. MONDAY BEGAN.

As usual she drove down to the swimming baths at Moseley, an old-fashioned Edwardian structure with changing cubicles surrounding the pool. She swam the equivalent of a mile, half breast-stroke, half crawl. It wasn't simply a means of keeping fit but a way of coping. Afterwards she got out, showered, grabbed some breakfast and went to work.

She spent the first ten minutes reading through a job application from someone with a photographic degree from Bournville. In her experience, graduates were great at photographing saucepans but take them to a wedding and they didn't have a clue. She asked Jewel to send a polite letter of rejection. The next hour was spent organising advertising in a number of wedding magazines, and obtaining the necessary permits for some planned location shots. Then she decided to check camera equipment. At mid-day, she nipped down to Five Ways for a sandwich. An hour later and drinking her fourth cup of coffee, she had an informal chat with a young couple getting married later in the year. Weddings always presented something of a challenge. It wasn't easy trying to capture the day when half the guests were intent on getting to the bar. For this reason, she found it critical to get the brief as clear as possible in her own mind. Under her direction, the couple decided to ditch the classic static poses and opt for a more exciting, documentary approach.

"Are the contacts back for Miss Stephens?" Jewel asked as Helen sauntered back into reception.

"Er…yes."

"Shall I give her a call?"

"Er…no."

Jewel threw her a questioning look. Of mixed race, she was a pretty girl with coffee-coloured skin, dark eyes, and neat rosebud mouth.

Helen cleared her throat. "Miss Stephens has done a runner."

Jewel arched a perfectly plucked eyebrow.

"She wasn't who she said she was," Helen said, feeling a bit of a chump.

"Really?" Jewel said, eyes popping now.

"It's a little complicated," Helen said with massive understatement.

"How complicated?"

"Enough for the police to be involved."

"The police?" Jewel's mouth dropped open. "Just because she's not going to pay?"

"Like I said," Helen flustered, "it's not as simple as that. There's nothing for you to worry about," she added with a brisk smile. "I'm handling the situation."

"Right," Jewel said, eyes glinting with disbelief.

"So if you see any coppers hanging around, just point them in my direction. Any messages?" Helen asked, firmly changing the subject.

"No, it's pretty dead."

The next hour dragged by. She phoned her parents and had an incomprehensible conversation with her mother whose voice was thick with gin. Helen promised to call back later though she didn't bother to add *when you've sobered up*. She felt edgy and unsettled. And she knew why. Telling Jewel that she was popping out, she took her coat, and headed for her car. Even though nothing else had happened, she didn't feel inclined to park it anywhere other than round the front of the building.

All the way to the Jewellery Quarter, she wondered how Robyn Roscoe would react. It was hard to tell because Adam so seldom mentioned her. Either she'd be furious and have her thrown out of the building, Helen suspected, or she'd be one of those professional types who wouldn't care for a scene, and would, at least, be civil enough to give her an audience. The only thing she could bank on was Robyn Roscoe's status as an ex-wife. In Helen's experience, ex-wives were only too ready to dish the dirt. If Adam had some connection, direct or otherwise, to the recent attacks, it might be that Robyn would throw some light on it, even inadvertently. It was pretty tenuous, Helen realised. In essence, she'd been Adam's mistress; Robyn might as easily direct her bile at her. Still, it seemed worth a crack. Helen's real problem was that, however much she wanted to know the truth, with Adam she was always scared of finding it.

Without expression, the black girl opened the door and offered to take her coat. "Mrs Roscoe asked me to show you through to her office. She shouldn't be long. Had to pop out to collect her son from school because of a mix-up with the nanny. May I offer you tea or coffee?"

Helen thought she'd misheard. "Her son?"

"Michael," the black girl smiled.

Helen felt as though she'd been slapped across the face. But they don't have any children. Adam said so. Swiftly making mental calculations, she realised that the child was very young – it was only three o' clock and most schools didn't break up until later. That explained it, she heaved an inner sigh, the child was probably the result of a different relationship. "Coffee would be lovely," she smiled, collecting her wits.

"Milk, sugar?"

"Black's fine."

Helen was shown into a light, modern and airy office, in which there were a number of display cases housing a collection of ancient-looking books. They looked very old, very rare and incredibly valuable; intimidatingly so. Helen peered at them with the same fascination a bomb-disposal expert might view a highly sophisticated incendiary device. Overawed, she quickly turned her attention to the window and looked outside onto a fine view of St Paul's church. Minutes passed. She picked up and flicked through a trade magazine. It mostly provided information about stolen art and antiques, and carried a number of articles on aspects of art theft and the importance of documenting and photographing property to best protect it. Still no sign of Robyn Roscoe. Looking back out of the window, Helen wondered how long she'd have to wait, and whether it was deliberate.

Eventually the black girl entered and placed a cup of coffee on the desk. Helen gave a short smile of thanks and leant across to pick it up, her eyes skimming over the computer, the phone, the closed leather-bound diary, the collection of art books, the silver-framed photograph...

Her eyes widened. The coffee cup rattled in the saucer. Then the door swung open.

"Miss Powers, do take a seat."

It wasn't an invitation. It was an order.

Helen stepped aside and watched the cool-looking blonde cut a swathe from one side of the room to the other. Helen smelt the heavy scent of exotic and expensive perfume. She noted the tall and athletic build, the shoulder-length blonde hair, the lightly tanned complexion from which glinted a pair of ice-blue eyes. The woman's muscular physique was clothed in an expensive-looking charcoal-grey suit, which she wore over a fuchsia-coloured silk shirt. Her feet were shod in pale grey suede stilettos. She was full-breasted and had narrow hips. And yes, there was a distinct American accent. As Robyn Roscoe perched her rear on the edge of the desk, she appeared to be viewing Helen with the same intensity. The only difference was that she wore a victorious smile.

"You're not what I expected," Robyn Roscoe said. The smile remained.

Helen sat down, trying to think. "Expect you wonder why I'm here."

"It had occurred to me, but you wouldn't be the first."

Helen's gaze sharpened.

Soft laughter trickled from Robyn Roscoe's lips. "You don't really think you're the only one to fall in love with my husband."

"I…"

"Men can be so remiss," Robyn cut in, her voice assuming an all girls together tone. "Adam in particular. Didn't you used to find that?" she said, frowning slightly, looking at Helen as though she expected a detailed reply. "I mean I know it's not easy when you're a cop. The hours are a killer quite apart from the extra-marital activities. He could be *so* naughty," she said, eyes gleaming. "I expect he clean forgot to tell you about our special relationship."

Pinpricks of alarm began to spread through the upper part of Helen's body. The room seemed to telescope. She thought she was going to be sick.

"We had a modern marriage. Sorry, I'm being dreadfully British," Robyn Roscoe smirked, putting a manicured hand to her face. "You guys never say what you really mean, always have to go all round the houses. Used to puzzle the hell out of me. I'm from Texas, see, and we always tell it the way it is. Basically, he fucked other women. I fucked other men. Mostly," she added.

Helen clamped her teeth together to prevent her jaw from dropping open.

"You see it's about trust, sweetie," Robyn Roscoe continued, her voice taking on a menacing intonation. "Not that you'd know a great deal about that."

So that was the nub of it, Helen thought, rallying. Robyn hadn't cared for her husband's infidelity brought kicking and screaming out into the open. She forced a smile. "Oh very good," she said. "I've got to hand it to you. What better way to explain away a cheating husband than profess to be a willing party? It's the classic defence mechanism."

"That's crap, and you know it."

"Shame Adam isn't here," Helen countered, "then we could ask him for his expert opinion."

Robyn leant forward. The blue eyes narrowed. Her expression implied that the gloves were coming off. "You fucked things up for us."

Helen stared back at her. "There was no *us*, according to him."

Robyn gave a mocking smile. "Believe what you like."

Oh, I will, Helen thought, but this wasn't achieving anything. They could go on mud-slinging for the rest of the afternoon. "Why get me here?"

Another glittering smile. "I seem to remember you made the appointment."

"You didn't have to see me."

"I was curious."

"You thought you'd humiliate me," Helen said, hoping she'd agree.

"Maybe."

"You wanted pay-back."

"Some," Robyn said, the smile evaporating.

"A little intimidation."

Robyn Roscoe folded her arms. "Just what the hell are you talking about?"

Helen glared at her. Was she bluffing, or was she really in the dark? "In the space of a week, I've been attacked twice."

"Your point?"

"My point is that both you and Adam have a motive."

The blue eyes crinkled in amusement. "You clearly have a high opinion of yourself, lady. I've moved on. He's moved on. Something you obviously have a problem with."

"I only have a bloody problem when I'm threatened," Helen snarled.

"Then I suggest you convey that to the cops."

Helen opened her mouth and changed her mind. Robyn was quick to pick up on it. "Oh, of course, I see your difficulty, telling tales, and all."

"Grow up," Helen sniped. "Of course I reported it."

"Then why are you here?" Robyn laughed coldly.

Helen stood up.

"*Sorry* you thought it was the real deal," Robyn said, unable to resist having the last word, "but I'm more sorry you had to drop Adam in the shit." The blue eyes were steely.

"He did that all on his own," Helen said.

"It could have been smoothed over."

"By talking to the right people, buying them off?" Helen flared.

The iron look remained. "A bit of advice, lady. Move on. Get yourself a life."

"Try telling that to Rose Buchanan's mother, Mrs Roscoe."

She was still shaking by the time she got back to the car. Either Robyn Roscoe was telling the truth, or she was phenomenally clever. She wished now that she'd quizzed her more about Adam's decision to go to Iraq, how long he intended to be there, when he was coming back, where he was living in the U.K. Something that wasn't so easily squared was the evidence she'd seen with her own eyes. The photograph on the desk portrayed an older, smiling Adam. The boy, whose hand Adam held, looked to be about three years of age, the daughter seven or eight, and the image of her father. Every picture tells a story, Helen thought sadly. Maybe the Roscoes were, in spite of the rumours, still together. And, she concluded, if Adam was that happy, there was no need to come after her. Not now.

She drove away, not really thinking where she was going. She'd toughed it out in front of Robyn Roscoe, but Helen's sense of disappointment was as strong as a physical pain in her chest. Had it really been a game to him, she wondered, a bit of fun, something on the side to spice up a marriage? If so, she didn't even have the consolation of being able to look back on what she believed to be great times. They were all lies. His lies.

It was four miles before she realised where she was. St Laurence's Church lay in Northfield, a leafy enclave of well-kept houses, some of them Thirties-style, with cared for gardens. Coming to her senses, Helen was careful not to miss the narrow turning to the church and throw herself back into the one-way system. She parked the car near one of the gates and climbed out into a neat and ancient-looking street. The sun was lying like a bloodshot eye, seeping a watery light onto a row of small houses and trees. A car alarm blasted a raucous cry from a distance, but the village itself looked sleepy and kind and benevolent.

Letting herself into the graveyard, hearing the creak of iron and wood, she found herself watching for others. A young woman was tending a grave nearby. Lost in thought, a middle-aged couple walked towards Helen. They nodded absently, falling into single file as they passed, eyes dimmed with memory. She offered a brief smile of thanks and continued to walk along a formal pathway, peering at epitaphs, realising how much the graveyard was like a kaleidoscope, each death and each new tombstone subtly changing the landscape. There were a couple of steel bins piled high with dead flowers, milk cartons and empty bottles of pop. As she followed the circular path round the church, a chill and unexpected breeze blew underneath her coat, making it flap around her thighs. She could see the entrance and the pub opposite, aptly named The Great Stone. It seemed strange that, just a street away from this quiet, tended avenue, tatty apartments chucked up in the Seventies, by the looks of them, with their peeling paint and dirty net curtains, lurked among the dense roar of city traffic.

She left the path and climbed up onto the grass where there were a number of more recent graves, the heels of her shoes spiking the frozen ground, slowing her down. Gazing at fragments of other people's grief, reading the monuments of mothers and fathers, pausing over the dearly beloved and greatly missed, and those reunited at last, she found the plainly worded stone.

Precious Memories
of a Dearly Beloved Daughter
Rose Buchanan 1985-2000

A fresh Christmas wreath lay at the base of the cool dark marble. She reached out, touched the holly, the blood-red berries, pearlescent mistletoe. She thought of the Rose she'd seen in the family photo album: a slight, graceful girl, more child than woman, warm eyes, shy smile, the girl who had a future. Rose's mother spoke of a loving daughter who'd always been a good girl, always had the right friends, always worked hard at school. Until…

Helen remembered the bizarre period of time when she and Adam danced around each other, he fearing her betrayal; she not knowing what to do then realising, beyond a shadow of a doubt, that she had to do something. Already sensing her decision, Adam became contemptuous of her, distancing himself, rubbishing her. The whispering campaign started. If the spotlight fell on one officer, it fell on many. And, as the rumours intensified, she heard that she was, after all, nothing more than a poor little rich girl, a tart, a marriage-breaker, and grass.

She recalled sitting in the Buchanans' kitchen much later on. It was the only time she'd ever visited a relative of a victim. It had snowed. Sunshine smirked through the trees like a joke in bad taste. Warmly welcomed by Cherry Buchanan, Rose's mother, because of her contact with her daughter which had made her feel sick with herself.

The kitchen was vibrantly-coloured, like her own, and she wondered if it would change over the years, the colour fading as surely as the life had dwindled from Rose's body.

Whether it was because Helen was both a woman and not a police officer, Mrs Buchanan asked all sorts of tentative questions.

"The coroner said she died of a single stab-wound to the heart. I suppose that was good really."

Helen agreed, lying to protect her. Afterwards, she swore it was the last time she'd ever lie.

"The marriage hadn't been right for years," Cherry Buchanan confided, a softly spoken, articulate woman with luminous dark eyes, hair slightly too long for her age, but only just. The mug of tea in her hands seemed soldered to her fingers and she sat hunched, her shoulders stooped with grief. "You know how it is, you do your best, put on a front, make it work, but there comes a time when you can't do it any more. I was naive. Thought divorce would be more straightforward. Certainly didn't expect venom. Rose took her father's side and went to live with him."

"How old was she?"

"Fourteen," Cherry Buchanan replied with certainty, as if the number were inscribed on her heart.

143

"For twelve months she wouldn't see me and he did nothing to encourage it. Then she started truanting. She got into some minor trouble with the police. It was pretty clear that her father wasn't looking after her. I tried talking but he wouldn't listen, said I was over-protective. When I found out that Rose was often left to fend for herself, particularly at weekends, I went the legal route and got a load of vitriol thrown back at me from his solicitors. I talked to Social Services and had several miserable meetings with some bloke from CAFCASS, but nothing helped. They weren't interested in seeing fault. They seemed completely blind to what was really going on. If anything, they took my husband's side, even when my daughter's safety was in jeopardy. The common consensus seemed to be that I was the problem. Then I found out about Jacks." She broke off, looked straight at Helen with soulful eyes. "That's when I thought I'd made a breakthrough. They'll have to listen to me now, I thought. I believed I'd a real chance of getting my daughter back. I went to the police."

Helen could hardly bear to look at the woman. There was so much pain in her eyes, so much guilt in her own. "What were you told?"

The bereaved mother's voice was without expression. She spoke in a lifeless monotone. "That there was no evidence that a crime had been committed."

"But Rose was under the age of consent," Helen said in astonishment.

Cherry Buchanan shook her head sadly. "Even if Rose was having a sexual relationship with Jacks, as I suspected, there was little the police could do because she wasn't too far off her sixteenth birthday."

"You were actually told that?"

Cherry Buchanan smiled. "A good-looking young detective, Roscoe, I think. That's right, Adam Roscoe, a very caring sort of chap. Unusual nowadays," she said wistfully. "It wasn't his fault. Just telling me the way it was."

Helen felt her stomach clench. "Were you ever told about Jacks's criminal past?" Helen asked softly.

Cherry Buchanan looked straight into her eyes. "Never."

She let Stratton into the coach-house later that evening. She felt surprised, pleased, and nervous.

"Sure I'm not disturbing you? If you prefer, I could…"

"Come in," she smiled. "You hungry?"

"Not really," he said, "but don't let me stop you."

"It's all right. I've already eaten."

He looked around for a moment as if not quite sure why he was there. "Thought we might drink this," he said, holding up a bottle of wine. "The label says it's got lead pencil overtones, whatever that means, but the guy in the shop assured me it was good."

She handed him a corkscrew and, taking two glasses, led the way upstairs. She apologised for the mess. He eased the cork from the bottle and poured. "I thought it might be a difficult day," he said, passing her a glass of wine the colour of garnets. They were standing either side of the fireplace, feet away from each other. It might as well have been a chasm, she thought.

"That why you're here?"

He smiled enigmatically, took a snatch of his drink. No, she thought.

"Do you do this often?" she asked him.

He looked taken aback. "What?"

"Call on victims of crime?"

"That how you see this?" His dark eyes settled on hers.

"How should I see it?" Her mouth felt dry and her voice sounded slightly hoarse. And she was being unfair. It was she who contacted him. What was she trying to do, drive him away?

"As a friend visiting a friend."

Oh, she thought. She smiled uncertainly and invited him to sit down. He took the sofa. She took the chair.

"I went to St Laurence's today," she said.

"Thought you might."

"I'd hoped for guidance," she said bleakly.

"Did you find it?"

"Not sure. Maybe."

Stratton nodded thoughtfully. "Did you know Buchanan is still trying to sue us?"

She sat up. "*Mr* Buchanan?"

"For not properly monitoring Jacks."

"What about his failure to monitor his daughter?" she said, her voice full of outrage. God knows how Cherry Buchanan must feel, she thought.

Stratton shrugged and looked gloomily into the fire. She wondered whether he was considering his own fractured family situation.

"You ever get lonely, Joe?"

"Sometimes. You?"

"Not as lonely as when I'm in a relationship."

He looked at her and frowned. "Not sure I follow you."

She smiled unsteadily. "Not sure I follow it myself."

146

"Try." He leant forward. He looked genuinely interested. She felt suddenly embarrassed.

"I guess, in a relationship, I can never shake off the feeling that something terrible is on its way."

"What sort of terrible?"

"I don't know. Betrayal, I suppose. Good coming from me, isn't it?" She laughed without much mirth.

Stratton's eyes crinkled with humour. "Sounds like your choice in men is lousy."

This time her smile was genuine. He was still looking at her. He spoke so softly she almost missed it. "I wouldn't betray you."

She gazed into eyes that seemed to give nothing away. He put down his glass and stood up, taking her hand, pulling her to her feet. She felt awkward because she realised she didn't know him at all, at least, not like this.

Nothing seemed real. The room was all shifting shadows, the air electric. He kissed her once softly. Her head fizzed with wine even though she'd hardly touched her glass. Shouldn't be doing this, she thought, shouldn't get involved. He kissed her once again. His warm hands slid underneath her sweater. She pressed her body against his. This was crazy, she thought, dangerous to her, she was safer on her own.

"Are you sure?" she said. "Only I don't want you to think…"

"Shut up, Helen. I want to take you to bed."

Afterwards, he fell asleep, and she was glad. She didn't want him to be one of those guys who get up immediately afterwards, thank you for a good time and say they'll be in touch. She didn't want a post-mortem, a discussion of his ex-wife – a sure-fire passion-killer

147

– or displays of residual guilt. His head faced hers. The lids of his closed eyes were very dark. He looked quite beautiful, she thought, listening to the sound of his breathing against the fevered beat of her heart.

Later she fell asleep and woke shortly after three in the morning to find him awake, crooked upon one elbow, watching her dreamily. She turned towards him and smiled. He stroked her cheek tenderly. They kissed again, limbs reaching out, their bodies sliding over one another's, this time with more passion and less self-awareness. The next thing she knew the phone was ringing.

Her immediate thought was that phones ringing at that time generally heralded death and destruction. Messages like *taken a turn for the worse*, *come quickly*, or *there's been an accident,* acquire a chilling ambiguity in the middle of the night. But surely this didn't apply to her?

"Yeah," she said blearily, holding the receiver to her ear.

"Helen, it's Dad."

"Uh-huh." Must be dreaming, she thought, keeping her head on the pillows, eyes firmly shut.

"Mum's been taken into hospital."

Helen opened one eye, a surge of alarm shooting her into consciousness. She reached over and snapped on the lamp, Stratton stirring beside her. "What's happened?"

The tone was agitated. "She's suffered a heart attack. We're at Staffordshire General."

"How bad is it?"

"The doctors are with her now," he said evasively. "I think you should come."

Helen rubbed her face in dismay. "I'll be there quick as I can," she said, putting the phone down.

Stratton was already reaching for his clothes. "I'll drive you."

"No, I can manage."

"I know you can, but it will be quicker and safer if I take you."

"Yes, but…"

"Think of me as a cab-driver," he said, arching a challenging eyebrow.

Sweater, trousers, she was thinking, scrabbling for knickers and bra. Stratton was fully dressed, car-keys at the ready. She reached for her shoes and suddenly felt terribly lost. "Oh, Joe," she said, holding her arms out to him.

He held her tight, like he was trying to keep her strong.

Stratton was driving at speed. They went through Aston and briefly joined the M6 before turning off and heading along the Wolverhampton Road. It felt as if she were going out on a crime scene job. Same white-knuckle ride. Same sense of apprehension, not knowing what exactly might be at the other end, what was involved, but already sensing the chaos. Depending on the seriousness of the crime, the volume of work and priorities, she'd worked both alone and with others. Towards the end of her time, *departmental budgetary constraints* was the new buzz-phrase. God knows what it was like now, she thought. She'd attended private homes, industrial sites, remote fields, and motorways. She'd toiled in near impossible conditions: in water, at heights, confined spaces. She'd seen corpses of the very young and the very old, and those in their prime. The fact that she was a stranger to them was their one saving grace.

She went over and over what her father said, trying to extract meaning from the few words he'd spoken as if she were going through a terse letter of rejection and trying to find some hope. Deep inside, she always suspected her mother would be the first to succumb to serious illness but not now, not like this. She was only fifty-four, for God's sake. That still counted as young, didn't it?

Stratton dropped her off at the entrance and drove off to park the car. She rushed inside, not knowing which way to go. Spotting a tired-looking nurse, she stumbled forward, gabbled her story and was pointed in the direction of Intensive Care. She ran down corridors, feverishly reading the signs on the walls as she sped past as if following some macabre treasure trail, unable to shake off the coldness in her heart. Rounding a corner, she was brought up short by the sight of her father. He was seated, his face in his hands. She could tell from the set of his shoulders that he was crying. Swallowing hard, she put her arms around him.

"Dad," she said softly.

He pulled his hands away from his face. He was shaking all over. He looked grey and old, as if all his vitality was spent, his lust for life extinguished, and every value he'd come to rely on gone. "She died three minutes ago," he said hoarsely. Then his face crumpled and he started to cry again. "What am I going to do without her, Helen? What am I going to do?"

*   *   *

In the past, whenever she'd looked at a dead body, she'd compared it to her own, not in an intimate or voyeuristic way, but with detached awe. This time it was different. In looking at her mother, she felt as if she were catching a glimpse of her own future. And when my own time comes, will there be someone there to hold my hand, she wondered? Will a loved one be present to act as spiritual midwife, or will it just be an array of machinery and faceless people? The thought of dying alone filled her with fear. The thought of death among strangers terrified her.

Her mother looked more peaceful than she'd ever been in life. She was still warm to the touch. Her eyes were gently closed, as if she were asleep. There was no stiffness present in her limbs. Her hair looked soft and natural upon the pillow. Helen reached over, touched a strand that was out of place, gently repositioning it. Her mother had always cared so very much about a groomed appearance.

From her mother's serene expression, Helen sensed that she'd been unaware of her approaching demise. She felt grateful. Too often she'd witnessed the evidence of the alternative. There was nothing dignified about violent death.

Already it felt as if her mother wasn't there at all, as if the essence of her personality had disintegrated, and she was staring, dry-eyed, at its shell. Helen had no religious inclinations – she'd seen too much carnage to believe in a benevolent God. She neither imagined her mother going to some great gin-palace in the sky nor descending to Hell's version of Alcoholics Anonymous. She was just dead. Gone. Lost.

She held her mother's hand. Her throat felt tight. She couldn't cry. Not yet. She just sat there, shocked, trying to grasp the significance of what had happened to her, venturing to find some meaning. She attempted to summon up images of her childhood but couldn't find them. She'd never watched her mum putting on make-up, never talked to her while she did the ironing, never went shopping with her for clothes. It would have seemed like an intrusion. She'd once asked her mum if she could do some weeding in the garden. Her mother stared at her incredulously and asked why. They paid the gardener to do it, was the reply. It seemed as if all her childlike efforts to be independent seemed doomed to fail, like the time she'd tried to cook dinner for them and it had gone disastrously wrong, or the time she'd cleaned one of the cars and left greasy marks on the bonnet. The only things she could remember were symbols: coffee cake, doilies, cheese and neatly sliced apples for lunch, dried flower arrangements, clean linen, structure but no form. There were so many pieces missing, she was beginning to feel like her sick, senile grandmother.

She didn't know how long she sat there. She ought to be getting back to her father, she thought anxiously. He depended on her. As for Stratton…

Did the nurses come and chuck you out when they thought you'd had enough, she wondered crazily? Would they be anxious to lay her mother out, or whatever they did, and take her to the mortuary? It seemed strange to her that she didn't know the form, she of all people. Age and experience didn't come into it. Nothing prepared you for this, she thought.

She got up, took a few paces forward, feeling the strength draining from her legs. She stroked her mother's cooling cheek and kissed her once on the forehead, saying goodbye, turning away quickly before the tears slid down her face. Her dad needed her. That's all that mattered now.

CHAPTER NINE

THE NEXT WEEK WAS taken up with funeral arrangements. She moved back into Keepers. In between maintaining an eye on work and trying to comfort her grief-stricken father, she had no time to mourn. Her own problems slipped from the forefront of her mind. So did Stratton.

He was entirely understanding, appreciated her need for time, didn't put any pressure on her, offered his help in whatever way he could. She didn't admit to him that, after her mother's death, everything, including him, became a muddle.

A harassed-looking doctor assured her that her mother's heart attack, while unpredictable, could not have been prevented. Indeed it was not that uncommon in a woman of her age, he stated clinically. While Helen knew it all in her head, in her heart she felt uneasy. She couldn't help but think that the mugging had strained her mother's fragile constitution. She couldn't help but feel some responsibility.

Her father took to the sitting room in the evenings – the drawing room had been her mother's haunt. Helen disliked it because the lighting was drab but she guessed it suited their moods. She observed her father. He was staring at the wall. He'd lost weight with alarming speed. The collar on his shirt looked too big for him and his shoulders jutted out from his clothes. There was a sunken look about his sleep-deprived eyes. He seemed, to her, like a man who'd stumbled from a bomb blast while others had perished. Her mother had not simply been the epicentre of the family, she'd been the epicentre of his life. And Helen hadn't really taken it on board until now. Neither had he, she thought.

Helen was trying to tell him about the final arrangements but she could see from the vacant look in his eyes that he wasn't really listening. She hadn't realised how much work was involved. It wasn't simply a case of booking the undertaker and the church, as she'd fondly imagined. There were people to contact, flowers, hymns, readings to be chosen, catering to organise, order of service to be printed. There were phone-calls to field, cards to receive, announcements to be placed. She thought her dad would be more practical, that the activity might even take his mind off his loss, but he behaved like a man who was paralysed. In a sense, he was, she thought sadly. She was taken aback by his indecisiveness, his helplessness. This was the man who, for all her life, had been a powerhouse of energy, positive in every respect. Only a short time ago he'd wanted blood because she'd been mugged and now he didn't know what to do. She didn't know whether it would pass or whether he'd be stuck like that for ever. Maybe he'd feel better tomorrow, she hoped, when her Aunt Lily arrived.

She and her father discussed telling Gran. She dismissed the idea. Even if her grandmother understood that her daughter was dead, she would forget, and to keep repeating it would be a needless cruelty. Helen still thought it a good idea to phone Roselea and speak to the matron, Mrs Gillespie, to see if she agreed.

"She never had enough confidence," her father said, out of the blue.

"Gran?" she asked, confused.

He turned towards her with misted eyes. "Your mother. Came from quite a lowly background, you know. All that business when she was growing up left its mark."

"You mean when Gran fell ill?"

"You know the story," he said.

She did but, as in Chinese whispers, she wasn't sure how much of it had changed in the telling. As far as she'd ever been able to glean, her grandmother, in her forties at the time, mysteriously lost the use of her legs and took to a wheelchair. In spite of being taken to various doctors, and put through all manner of tests, no physical cause was ever established. By default, her only child, Helen's mum, became her carer. It was, by all accounts, a deeply unhappy childhood, and one from which her mother escaped as soon as she could.

"I think what hurt most," her father said, "was that when your mother went to make her peace shortly after your grandfather died, she discovered your gran in rude good health. She neither needed a wheelchair nor someone to look after her."

"But that wasn't Gran's fault," she said reasonably.

Her father gave a shrug. "Your mother felt as if she'd been hoodwinked, cheated of her youth. I believe it's why she found it difficult to form relationships, but I always knew she loved me, loved you, too," he said.

Helen wished she could believe it. She wasn't honestly certain whether her mother was capable of any great depth of emotion and, as she thought it, she wondered wildly if some of it had rubbed off onto her. She, too, found relationships a struggle. She, too, felt unworthy.

She turned back to her dad. At least he was talking, she thought, which was an improvement. She asked him if he wanted a drink. He said he'd have whisky. She offered to get it for him. She thought she'd have one herself. Maybe it would help her to feel less closed down inside.

The phone rang as she was crossing the hall. It was around seven. She couldn't think who it might be. The horrible thought that Aunt Lily couldn't make it darted across her mind. She picked up. "Keepers." Nobody spoke. "Hello," she said.

"Could I speak to Mrs Powers?" It was a man's voice. He had an accent but one she didn't recognise.

"That's not possible," she said cautiously. "I'm her daughter. Who's calling?"

"She phoned me a couple of weeks ago about some window-cleaning. Been a bit busy with one thing and another."

"Oh, right," she said, relaxing.

"So if you could pass on a message for me."

Helen cleared her throat. "I'm sorry but my mother passed away a few days ago." God, it sounded weird, she thought. She didn't think she'd ever get used to it.

There was a brief stunned silence.

"Maybe I could take your number in case my dad's interested," she suggested.

"It's all right," he said swiftly. "I'll call another time, erm…when it's convenient. Sorry," he dashed out before cutting the call.

She put down the phone thinking it was a pretty typical reaction. People got funny about unexpected death. They shied away from it as if any association meant that they were next.

She went into the drawing room and crossed over to the drinks cabinet. The air smelt of her mother's perfume. The chair in which she'd sat still seemed inhabited by her. Helen wondered how long it would take before the place was vacated by her mother's presence. She guessed as long as her mother's things were still here, her clothes, her jewellery, her ornaments, everything dear to her, then she would remain with them.

And that was good.

That night she phoned Stratton. She wanted to hear his voice, to find an anchor. She didn't know what to say.

"It's all quite strange, really."

"Bound to be. How's your dad?"

"Shell-shocked. I never realised how much he depended upon Mum. Always thought it was the other way round."

Stratton didn't say very much. He didn't know her well enough, she supposed.

"Helen?"

"Mmmm?"

"There's something I've been meaning to say."

"Sounds serious." Was he chickening out? she thought.

"It's about Adam."

There was a curdling sensation deep in the pit of her stomach.

"We're always going to disagree about him. You know that, don't you?"

"Yes," she said, rubbing her eyes.

"It's rather complicated, isn't it?"

"Yes, it is."

"I don't want him to come between us."

"It's all right, Joe," she said. "Don't worry."

Aunt Lily arrived like a tornado. She lived alone in Berwick-upon-Tweed and, although she visited rarely, Helen always looked forward to seeing her. She was shorter than her brother, and significantly more well-covered. She had salt-and-pepper-coloured hair, which she cut herself. Her clothes sense was non-existent and she had a penchant for cheap jewellery, bracelets in particular. It was all bluff. Underneath the sloppy exterior, Aunt Lily was a human dynamo.

"Poor love," Aunt Lily said, hugging her. Helen laid her chin on her aunt's shoulder. It was the closest she'd come to allowing herself to be comforted. "Can see your father's in a bad way."

"Not coping at all well," Helen confided.

"He idolised your mother, dear. Her death was bound to devastate him." Lily held her niece away from her. She had an *I'm going to take charge* look in her eye. "I'll get the kettle on – your father certainly looks as though he could do with a cuppa – and then you'd better get me up to speed with the arrangements."

Helen finally explained that she'd booked The Cross House for the wake afterwards.

"Your mother wasn't fond of the place," her father said, as if he'd only just thought about it.

"But it's near the church."

He nodded fretfully. "Will there be an open bar?"

"If that's what you want."

"That's what Joan would have wanted," Lily said with a wide smile.

"You're right," Helen giggled. It sounded strange, embarrassing, really. In less than a week she felt as if she'd forgotten how to laugh.

"Have you thought about sorting out her clothes?" Lily said, looking at both of them.

"A bit soon, isn't it?" Helen said, unnerved by the prospect.

"Just thought while I was here, it would be a good idea. It's got to be done some time."

"What do you think, Dad?" Helen reached over and rested her hand on his arm. He was tracing an imaginary pattern on the table. He gave a worn-down shrug.

"That's settled then," Lily said, pushing back her chair. "Come on, Helen. You can give me a hand."

Helen wasn't at all sure about the good sense of what they were doing, but there was no stopping her aunt. It felt an intrusion to be going through her mother's things. Helen imagined her walking in on them, ticking them off for invading her privacy. Her father wandered in once and suggested to Helen that she might like to take some of her mother's clothes to wear for herself. She didn't like to explain that, in fashion terms, they were poles apart, but more importantly there was a world of difference between what a thirty-something wore and a fifty-something. She came out with a noncommittal remark. Shrouded with disappointment, he turned away and shuffled back out of the room.

Aunt Lily was giving a running commentary. "Oh, I remember this," she said, holding up a polka-dot dress with cinched waist. "She bought it for their holiday in Tuscany. And this," she said, putting a cerise-coloured evening dress against her stout frame,

160

"was when they went to the Hunt Ball. Oh dear," her aunt said, recovering a half empty bottle of Gordon's gin from a wardrobe.

"Here, I'll take it," Helen said. She could add it to the bottle she'd found in her mother's bedside cabinet.

"Funny thing about your mum," Aunt Lily said, "is that she was quite the lady."

"Is that incompatible with being a drunk?" Helen felt her stomach pinch at the shrillness of her voice. Her cheeks flamed pink. She apologised immediately for her brusque response.

"It's not what I meant," Aunt Lily smiled kindly, slipping an arm around Helen's tight-set shoulders. "Just that she seemed to spring from nowhere. For years we'd no clear idea about her family. She never talked about them. At least not before her father died. Didn't talk about them afterwards either. She was like a woman without a past."

Helen never thought of her mother that way but, now that her aunt said it, it made perfect sense. She must have been eleven years old when her mother took her to meet Gran for the first time. She remembered being intrigued by her gran's humble dwelling. It was midway along a row of terraced houses. At the end, there was a newsagent and, just beyond, a boarded-up pub called The Ship. Gran's home had a front room, as she called it, a little hidey-hole under the stairs where she kept a fridge, a back room with open tiled fireplace and a small dining table with three chairs, then the kitchen, which smelt of gas, and a freezing cold downstairs bathroom with a linoleum-covered floor. There were just two bedrooms upstairs and, if you went into the front bedroom, you could feel the rumble of traffic below. Outside, there was a yard and shared

161

alley-way. She'd never been anywhere like it in her life before. Still less, could she imagine her mother living in such claustrophobic conditions.

It had been quite a strained occasion. Fastidiously polite, there wasn't much warmth between the two women. She recognised later that, even though a reconciliation of sorts took place, deep down her mum never forgave her grandmother. It made Helen feel uncomfortable. History had a strange habit of repeating itself, she thought, not in the detail but the broad brushstrokes.

Helen put anything that looked financial or legal into a pile for her father to sort out. It felt odd to read her mother's name but not be able to see her face.

In one of her mother's bedside drawers, among some old photographs, she found a battered black leather-bound address book. Helen flicked idly through it. It must have gone back decades, she thought, judging by the amount of crossings-out. It included some of her dad's old business colleagues. She read the names: Bianci, Deals, Warnes. They'd been like mythical figures in her mind. Now they sounded like gangsters. As well as changed addresses, she noticed, there were a number of changed names, a reflection of modern life, she guessed.

"Thought you might want to keep this," Aunt Lily said, showing Helen a box of her mother's jewellery.

"I think that's for Dad to decide," Helen said. The address book was far more intriguing, she thought, slipping it into her pocket.

The funeral took place on the kind of day her mother would have liked: cold and bright. Helen sat on one side of her father, Aunt Lily on the other. The church was packed with friends and acquaintances. Helen felt glad for her father's sake and hoped they wouldn't desert him afterwards.

Most of the service passed her by. She felt as if she were floating above it, looking down on them all, watching as if from afar, much as her mother had lived her life, she supposed. The most harrowing bit was watching her mother's coffin being lowered into the ground. Her father almost buckled. Bracing themselves, she and Aunt Lily propped him up. As the priest gave a dirge-like incantation, Helen experienced an inexplicable wave of anger. For what, she wasn't sure. Trying to shake it off, she looked up and, in the sea of faces, saw a fair-haired man wearing a pair of large wraparound sunglasses. His skin was the colour of raw pork fat, his mouth set as if his teeth were clenched together. He was standing slightly apart, hands folded in front of him. Who was he, she thought curiously? There was something about his stance that spoke of authority. He looked like he was a cop or a spook. She lowered her gaze.

Afterwards, she talked to as many people as she could. The condolences ran along predictable lines: her mother was a fine woman, greatly missed, a sad and sudden loss. All were too polite to say that she was an alcoholic with few real friends.

Rather bizarrely, Aunt Lily insisted on taking photographs.

"It's not a wedding reception," Helen hissed humorously in her aunt's ear.

"But no less momentous," Aunt Lily insisted. "You'll be glad of it afterwards."

Will I, Helen thought? Do I really want to see myself looking so miserable, my father so traumatised?

While Aunt Lily went back to Keepers with Helen's father, Helen stayed until the last of the mourners left, and the staff cleared away the buffet and dead glasses. She felt generally pleased, if that was the right expression, with how things had gone. There had been a good turnout, including one or two unexpected faces. She briefly wondered again about the man at the graveside. Whoever he was, she thought, he left without introducing himself.

CHAPTER TEN

HELEN WENT BACK TO work. She managed to persuade
Aunt Lily to stay on at Keepers for a few more days.
Aunt Lily and her dad had always been quite close.
More selfishly, she also wanted space for herself.

"You sure you don't mind?"

"Not in the least," Aunt Lily beamed. "I'm going to
teach your dad to cook."

Good luck to you, Helen thought. She'd never seen
her dad do anything more culinary than make a cup of
tea.

"Aunt Lily," Helen began. "Did you notice a guy
wearing sunglasses at the funeral, a stocky chap, of
medium height and build?"

"Uh-huh, I think I know the one."

"Who is he?"

Aunt Lily shrugged. "No idea. I presumed you
knew who he was."

"No. It's odd, don't you think?"

"Strangely enough, anyone can attend funerals."

"Really," Helen said in amazement.

"Some people make a hobby of it."

They must be nuts, Helen thought.

Helen pulled into a local primary school where she
was booked to take some photographs. The headaches
had returned. She wasn't sleeping. When she did, she
dreamt of water, dark and deep, thick like clotted
blood, and most mornings she awoke with a sinking
feeling, sensing that something terrible had happened
but not quite sure what. As she passed through the

twilight zone between sleep and consciousness, the feeling became more pronounced, thoughts took shape until with growing clarity she remembered that her mother was dead. There was regret in her grief, anger in her despair. She guessed some clever-dick shrink would tell her that it was normal in the circumstances, a form of repressed guilt for not having the kind of relationship she'd longed for, for not feeling loved, or for not loving her mother enough.

The school was in a smart part of Solihull. It smelt of cabbage and hamsters but the kids were well behaved. She was halfway through the session when something strange happened. Two brothers were having their photograph taken together. They sat nice and still, happy smiles in place, the camera lined up, everything ready. She bent down to focus and instead of the boys' faces she saw the puffed, bloated putrefying faces of the dead. She leapt back as if someone had thrown scalding water over her.

"You all right?" a teacher asked. "You've gone quite pale."

"Sorry," she gasped, knuckling her forehead with both hands to stop the chatter in her brain. "Felt a bit faint," she mumbled. "Could I have some water, please?"

While the teacher disappeared, the boys, fidgeting with boredom, cupped their hands together, staring at her, whispering in each other's ears. Something in their eyes reminded her of before.

She drank the water in one draught, swallowed down two painkillers to nobble the headache, pulled herself together, finished the session. Stratton called her as she was packing up.

"Not a good moment." She didn't want to talk to him feeling this shaky, this delusional.

"Where are you?"

"A primary school."

"My idea of hell."

"Can I call you back?"

"Promise?"

"Give me an hour or so, about lunch-time."

She drove back, trying to work out in her mind what had happened. It was a bit late in the day to be suffering from post-traumatic stress syndrome, she thought, even if she believed in all that psychological hocus-pocus. Best to blank it out, then and put it down to a one-off aberration, a stress-overload.

By the time she got back to the studio, she felt more clear-headed. Jewel was scoffing a packet of crisps and reading a magazine. On Helen's approach, she hastily bundled both away.

"Any messages?" Helen asked.

"Bloke called Stratton rang."

"Anyone else?"

"Nah."

"I'm just popping over the road to pick up a pint of milk. Do you want anything, another packet of crisps, perhaps?" Helen gave a cheeky grin.

"I'm all right, thanks," Jewel mumbled, looking guilty.

She darted over the road to a nearby row of grotty-looking shops consisting of fast-food outlets, a cut-price booze emporium, newsagents, and an anything for a quid shop. The air smelt of petrol and curry. There was litter blowing about the street and graffiti scrawled across a boarded-up doorway. The place was noisy with traffic, and the sounds of a city working at full-throttle. About to walk inside the newsagent, she froze. A crowd of schoolchildren was surging towards her. Behind them a family of Sikhs. Sandwiched in the middle, was a hat partially obscuring a face. She peered again. Could be wrong, she thought, heart hammering in her chest. Was this another vision, or was this real? She looked again. The hair colour was different, the clothes scruffy, as if she'd been sleeping rough but…

The woman abruptly crossed over the main road, dodging a stream of cars. Helen measured the distance with her eyes, opened her mouth to call out her name, yet what name should she give, she thought, all mixed up? The milk forgotten, and with no regard for her safety, she made to cross the busy main road but was driven back by a surge of heavy traffic as the lights changed. All she could do was stand and watch helplessly as the woman she knew as Freya Stephens vanished from view.

"It's me," she said, agitated, her hand trembling as she held the phone.

"Hello me," Stratton said, a smile in his voice.

"I've seen her."

"Who?"

"The woman."

"Which woman?"

"Stephens, or whoever she is."

"What?"

"I walked over the road to pick up some milk and she was there, walking down the road towards me."

"You're sure?"

"Her hair was different. She wasn't wearing make-up and looked pretty dishevelled, but yes."

"Be right over."

Stratton strode into the building, flint-eyed, flashing his warrant card. Unaware of the nature of the relationship, Jewel gave Helen a go-getting thumbs-up as she led him through to the coach-house. They stood in the kitchen. Helen wasn't quite sure how to react: lover or victim?

"How've you been?" he asked solicitously.

"All right," she said, fingering the collar of her shirt.

"I've been thinking of you." His dark eyes flitted from her to the wall. He looked out of his depth, she thought and briefly wondered whether he regretted sleeping with her. "About Freya," he said, moving on. "You say she looked different."

"Totally."

"Then how come you're sure it's her?"

She smiled, narrowed her eyes in surprise. "Joe, my livelihood revolves around observation. It's what I do."

"Yes, but…"

"I *know* it was her. I saw her this afternoon, the real deal. Freya Stephens wasn't simply an impostor by name. She's created a whole new personality for herself. It was done quite deliberately. She was the hook, don't you see?"

Stratton pulled up a chair and sat down. "Look, Helen, you've had a tough time lately. It's bound to obscure your judgement."

"My mother's death hasn't turned me into a moron." Her voice sounded icy but she couldn't help herself.

"Of course it hasn't."

"And I'm not seeing things." Yes, I am, she thought, suddenly fearful, but this was different, this was…

"I'm just saying you're under a lot of pressure."

"No." She slammed her hand so hard down on the table it hurt. They both looked at each other in shock.

Stratton was the first to break the silence. "Don't push me away, Helen."

"Then believe me," she pleaded, deeply regretting her outburst.

"All right," he said slowly. "If she's the hook, as you say, why would she risk blowing her cover by turning up in enemy territory?"

She sat down opposite him, took a deep, calming breath. "Because she has no choice. This must be where she lives."

Another extended silence.

"Maybe we're looking at this all wrong," he said, scratching his head. "We need to think more laterally. We're assuming you're the target."

"If being half-drowned and mown down by an unknown van-driver doesn't make me a target, what does?"

"But you survived."

"I got lucky."

"Could be more complex than that."

She stared at him, her wits sharpening. "Because I was meant to survive?"

"Yeah."

"All right, then who *is* the target?"

He scratched his head again. "I don't know."

A blind alley, she thought, drumming her fingers on the table.

Stratton looked thoughtful. She could tell from the look in his eye that he was going to press her to report everything and make a full statement. She felt like a witness who, for fear of reprisals, refuses to give evidence. "You managed to turn anything up?" she asked him.

"I wondered whether any associates of Jacks might have got it in for you," Stratton said, "or maybe someone he pallied up with inside. You know what it's like, they all swap tales of derring-do."

"And?"

"I've only skimmed the surface."

It was the old story. He needed more manpower, more resources, more time.

His eyes met hers. She felt herself melt and smiled at him. He was doing everything he could but he was just one guy on his own and she wasn't making it any easier for him. She never seemed to make it easy. "Sorry," she said, reaching over and linking her hand through his. He leant over and kissed her.

"You're bloody hard work, Helen Powers," he said, an amused smile on his face. "Now, I'd better be going before they send someone out to track *me* down. I'll call you later," he said firmly, kissing her once more.

Employing a little lateral thinking of her own, Helen discovered that finding Robyn Roscoe's address was easier than she'd imagined. She simply tapped into the electoral roll website, typed in Roscoe's name, tried several areas of the more salubrious parts of Birmingham and, after the third attempt, struck gold.

It was already dusk by the time she negotiated her way down the narrow private drive that led to *Reynards*. Brick-built, with the kind of square proportions seen in Georgian properties, it looked both expensive and stylish. It also looked empty, Helen thought, noticing too late the dead-end ahead. Abandoning the car, she grabbed her camera and got out to walk the short distance back to the house and take a better look.

Spiked gold-tipped railings and massive wrought-iron gates sealed *Reynards* off from the rest of the world. There were no gardens laid out in the front. A silver-coloured Z8 and a black Range Rover stood like sentries on the brick-paved herringbone-styled drive. Everything about the place seemed to shriek *Keep Out*.

On her approach, Helen heard the familiar click of sensors. Immediately, security-lights flooded the drive, revealing a security alarm high up on one wall. As far as she could tell, there were no cameras. Just in case, she rolled the neck of her sweater up to obscure her face.

Taking out a telephoto lens, she attached it to the camera and fixed one eye to the viewfinder. The house was a showcase for the gallery. Numerous works of art, including several large bronze busts and display cases, as well as the more traditional paintings and sketches filled the living room. At the far end, she glimpsed an alcove lined with walls of books, hinting at a library. Art tomes, she guessed.

The other side of the house appeared to be more lived in. Apart from the large antique rocking horse in the window, there was the usual stuff: television, comfy sofa and chairs, coffee table, plants and magazines. She counted six large windows on the top storey, two chimney stacks either end.

But it didn't tell her anything, she thought, climbing half way up the neighbouring bank to see if she could catch a glimpse of anything more compelling. By straining to her left, she could just make out a room that seemed totally incongruous with the design and style of the rest of the house. With its stainless steel cupboards and work-surfaces, it appeared to have more in common with a morgue than a kitchen. At any moment, she half-expected a body to pop out from one of the steel drawers.

That's when she heard the throaty sound of a fast car.

Jumping onto solid ground and stepping back into the shadows, she hunkered down and watched the slow approach of a dark Porsche Boxster, saw the gates electronically swing back, observed the car drive through and come to a halt. A slight-looking man in his mid to late thirties climbed out, walked up to the front door and slipped a key in the lock, letting himself in as if he owned the place. It wasn't Adam, of that she was certain. Neither was it anyone she recognised, she thought, making a mental note of the car's registration.

Unimaginably cold, she watched and waited, anxiously working out if she could reverse her car up the drive in the dark without drawing attention to herself. And what if she met Robyn Roscoe coming from the other direction?

At last the curtains closed and she made her move. In spite of creeping like a cat, every twig and dried leaf seemed to snap and crackle in the silence, echoing her escape.

Back in the car, she started the engine, opened the driver window and, without switching on the lights, reversed at a painfully slow pace up the drive, and eventually backed out onto the open road.

*   *   *

When Stratton called shortly after her return, she told him where she'd been. He wasn't impressed. "You're a bloody loose cannon. What's it going to take before you realise that the Roscoes are history?"

It was one question she couldn't answer. Then he asked another. "What's Robyn's motive?"

"Well, I…"

"And before you say revenge, from what I've heard, she wasn't too averse at playing Adam at his own game."

Oh God, she thought in dismay, so there was some truth in what Robyn said.

"And I hate to labour the point," Stratton continued, "but it's been four years since you upset the woman."

"Heard the saying about revenge being a dish best served cold?" Helen said, trying to impose an argument she wasn't sure she believed in.

"She's an art dealer, for God's sake, not Lucrezia Borgia."

Helen let out a sigh. "You're probably right – sorry."

"It doesn't matter," Stratton said, clearly relieved to have won her round. "Now, what about dinner tomorrow night. Pick you up at eight?"

"Fine," she said. "See you then."

Later that evening she called her father.

"How are you doing?"

"All right," he said in the way a patient describes their progress after a tricky operation. "And you?"

"Much the same."

"Work OK?"

"Same old stuff."

"Coping without Ray?"

"Yes." But not without my mother, she wanted to say.

"That's good."

"So what have you been up to?" she said.

There was a bit of a pause. "Sorting things out, financial stuff, really."

Her mother's affairs, she thought, quick to pose a diversionary question. "Is Aunt Lily looking after you all right?"

"Yes."

Oh God, she thought, this was awful. They never used to talk in monosyllables. "I'll come out and see you on Sunday."

"That would be nice."

"Maybe we could have some lunch somewhere."

"Yes. Actually…"

"Shall I leave it to you to book a table?"

"All right," he said haltingly. "Erm…Helen?"

"Yes, Dad."

"I was wondering…well, it's a bit tricky, really," he burbled.

"Yes?"

He paused, as if he were winding himself up to say something momentous, then seemed to change his mind. "Do you want to speak to Aunt Lily?" he burst out.

"If she's handy," Helen said, confused.

"He's been rather introspective but he seems a little brighter today, a bit more like his old self," Aunt Lily reported. Really? Helen thought, screwing up her face.

"The Rudges are taking him out to lunch tomorrow. I've made plans to go back on Thursday."

"So soon?"

"It's sink or swim," Aunt Lily said candidly. "In my experience, the longer you leave it, the harder it is to be on your own. At least he's got Vic to keep an eye on him."

"Aunt Lily," Helen said. "You know when Dad was running the business, did he make a lot of enemies?"

"That's a funny question. Why do you ask?"

Christ, Helen thought, how am I going to explain this one? Start with the truth, she thought. "When I was going through Mum's things, I found one of her old address books. There were a lot of names crossed out. Some of them were Dad's old business colleagues."

"Your father didn't build up a massively successful printing business without drowning a few kittens," Aunt Lily laughed. "And there was all that trouble with Ken Bianci."

Bianci had seeped into family folklore, though Helen wasn't entirely certain why. "What sort of trouble?"

"He was one of your father's early business partners. From what I can gather, he wasn't pulling his weight. Your father decided to off-load him."

"Dissolve the partnership?"

"Yes, but Bianci reckoned he was ripped off."

"Was he?"

Her aunt was cagey. "Maybe. Like I said, you have to be ruthless to succeed, especially nowadays."

"So when did this spat with Bianci take place?"

"Over thirty years ago."

Bianci would be an old man, and what had happened to her wasn't an old man's game. Another dead-end, Helen thought.

"Don't think badly of your father for it," Aunt Lily said. "We all have skeletons in our cupboards, dear."

Helen decided to take a peek at her own. She'd been tossing and turning since midnight. It wasn't simply the creaks and sighs of the old building that were keeping her awake, but the clamour in her head. From childhood to present day, she found herself running through a personal list of sins, like the time she'd thumped a girl who was bullying her best friend, the night she lost her cool and mouthed off at a voyeur slowing down at the scene of a fatal road accident. She also had a reputation for getting shirty with cold-callers, and for breaking hearts. More recently, her reserve was sometimes translated as contempt. None were exactly hanging offences. Hard as she might, she couldn't think of anything that she'd done to warrant a grudge – bar her involvement in the Jacks case.

She rolled over again, closed her eyes. Her past was impinging on the present because it was no more than she deserved. Guilt was driving her thinking rather than reason. Stratton was absolutely right: the information about her, including her well-publicised family connection, had been in the public domain for a number of years. Anyone who wanted to track her could, including Jacks, including the Roscoes. So, she thought, opening her eyes again, why did someone want to harm or frighten her now and not then? Didn't add up.

Unless it was unconnected.

And if unconnected, she thought, with a shiver, she really didn't know what she'd done wrong. She really didn't know what to expect next.

CHAPTER ELEVEN

THE CALL FROM HER father came two days later.

"Free for lunch?" There was a positive note in his voice. He sounded much more like the Dad she knew. in control. Back in charge. Thank God, she thought, scanning her diary. A mother and young son were booked for a sitting at midday. She'd been trying to decide how to play it; children were notoriously difficult to photograph unless they were engrossed in something. She kept a box of studio props, stuff like golf clubs, tennis racquets, books, fake flowers, balls, wine glasses and teddy-bears, and hoped she could find something suitably diverting. "I could meet you around a quarter past one, is that all right?"

"Great." He sounded relieved. "Meet me at the main entrance of Rackhams."

Helen smiled. It hadn't been Rackhams for a while. It was now the newly revamped House of Frazer. She thought it an unusual choice, and then remembered it was where he'd taken her mother when she shopped in town.

The sitting went more smoothly than she expected and, after hopping onto a bus that took her into Corporation Street, she arrived a few minutes early. She could see her father waiting near the entrance as she walked along the pavement. Everything about his body language displayed acuity of purpose. He was standing very straight. He had his hands in the pockets of a large grey overcoat. Even at that distance, he looked like a man with a mission. Helen slipped one arm through his and kissed his frozen cheek.

"Waited long?" she said.

He gave a strained smile. She thought she caught a trace of impatience in his expression. "Not really."

"Let's get you inside."

They were greeted by a sudden gush of warm air. At once, she felt transported to a world of luxury and sophistication.

"How hungry are you?" she asked brightly, as they walked through the heavily fragranced cosmetic department to the escalators.

"Not exceptionally."

She gave his arm a sympathetic squeeze. "Why don't we eat in the restaurant here?" The French-inspired menu was consistently good, the service discreet. Because of the careful table layout, it was also the perfect place for confidential conversations, something she felt might be necessary by the look of him.

"Good thinking," he said purposefully.

They were shown to a table and gave their orders to a young dark-skinned girl wearing a Muslim headdress. Helen plumped for Croque Monsieur with a glass of dry white wine. Her father said he'd have the same. The girl disappeared, reappearing minutes later with the drinks. Helen's father briefly talked about the weather, Aunt Lily's vain attempts to teach him to cook, the successful outcome of the holiday he'd been forced to cancel.

"Got the deposit back in full," he declared.

"I should hope so in the circumstances."

He nodded, snatched at his drink. That's not what he wanted to talk about, she thought.

180

"Anyway," he said, forcing a smile. "Now I've got a few extra bob, and no one to spend it on, I thought I'd write you a cheque."

"Dad," she said, embarrassed.

His eyes connected with hers. "We can all do with a little financial help sometimes."

"Yes, but…"

"And I know that money's been tight lately."

Same searching look. Same steel in his voice. What the hell was going on, she thought? "I'm fine, really."

"Are you?" His hawkish eyes were still fixed on hers. He was scrutinising her in the same way a father studies a small child who's done something wrong and won't admit to it; she still remembered that feeling.

"Dad, what's this all about?"

Their food arrived. He lowered his gaze, ran a hand over his chin. She watched him. In the space of weeks, he'd noticeably aged. There were heavy lines around his eyes. His cheeks pouched. The skin on his neck was slack. But he also had a grim determination about him. He took a pull of his drink, put down the glass, refocused on her. "You probably aren't aware, but your mother and I had separate financial arrangements. It was my idea. I didn't want her coming to me every time she wanted her hair done, or make-up or a new pair of stockings," he said, his mouth softening with the fondness of the memory. "I wanted her to feel independent to make her own decisions. She had a number of investments, got clobbered like the rest of us in the stock market crash following 9/11, but she still had a reasonable portfolio. Since she," he coughed.

"Died," she interposed softly.

He flashed a grateful look. "I've made a number of discoveries."

Her gaze sharpened. "What sort of discoveries?"

"In the last five months of her life, she cashed in three of her investments." He looked straight at her and put his hand over hers. "I'm not cross, darling," he said, in a way that conveyed he might be. "I know you've always been proud, liked to make your own way in the world, but there's nothing shameful about needing a bit of help now and then. It's just I can't bear the idea of being excluded. I loathe secrets. I'd hate to think you were in debt, or some sort of trouble, and were frightened to tell me."

She stared at him wide-eyed. "I'm not."

He stared back, raking her face for clues.

"I didn't borrow any money," she repeated stupidly.

"You sure?" The pressure on her hand increased.

"It wasn't me," she said, feeling her nerves jag. Suddenly, what little appetite she had vanished.

Her father pulled his hand away. "That's what I was afraid of."

"When did she make the first withdrawal?"

"August, the 18th."

"How much?"

Her father glanced away, looked back, leaned across. "Twenty-five grand."

Oh God, she thought. What on earth did her mother need that kind of loot for? Her dad paid for everything. "And after that?"

"Two months later for another thirty grand."

She suppressed a gasp. "And the next?"

"A few days after Christmas."

"When exactly?"

"December 29th. This time for forty-five K."

Christ, she thought, the day after she'd been mugged. "Surely, you can trace it?"

"To a point," he said crisply. "She paid the cheques from her investments straight into her building society accounts. At first, I thought there was some mistake."

"Go on," she encouraged him.

"Once the balance cleared, she gave forty-eight hours notice and withdrew the money in cash. You were the obvious beneficiary."

She felt spots dance before her eyes. The room seemed to spin. Her father was speaking again. His voice sounded far away. "What do you think?"

She felt as if her brain were clicking, stimulating the pathways, triggering the zone marked fear. "Apart from the money, did you notice anything different about Mum's behaviour?"

His eyebrows knitted together. "She was drinking a lot."

She was always drinking a lot, Helen thought. Then another idea shot across her mind.

"Did she ever say anything to you about the porcelain in the drawing room?"

Her father looked at her blankly.

"You know, about it being cleaned."

"Cleaned?" he frowned. "She said she fancied a change-around but, now you come to mention it, I'm not sure where she put it."

"Is it worth a lot of money?" she said, her voice low.

He flashed her a knowing look. "It's insured for almost ten grand. There's a lot of hand-crafted details."

So it could have been pawned, she thought, or given in lieu of hard cash. "Have you found any threatening letters or notes?"

"None. It was the first thing I thought to check."

"Did anyone unusual phone or call to see her?"

"No."

"You're sure?"

"Positive."

Wait a minute, she thought, remembering the man who claimed to be a window-cleaner. Was it possible…?

Her father interrupted her thoughts. "We should go to the police," he said decisively.

Talk to Stratton, she thought automatically, talk to Harmon.

"Are you sure she wasn't donating to some charity or something?" Helen asked.

"Not that kind of money," he said staunchly.

"She wasn't seeing a doctor on the quiet?"

"Why? We're fully covered by private health insurance."

"A relative in trouble?"

"Apart from Gran, she didn't have any."

Helen knew that she was clutching at straws but felt she had to consider all the options.

"So what do you think?" her father said, a glint in his eye.

She braced her jaw. "I don't know."

"But you agree the police should be informed?"

She swallowed. It wasn't simply about her any more. It was much bigger than that. "I'll take care of it."

"No, Helen, I…"

I can cut through the red tape, she thought, thinking of Stratton. "I know the right people, remember?" And they'll take my father seriously, if not me.

She was sitting back on the bus, listening to the slow chug of changing gears. Her head throbbed. Her throat felt dry. She could barely stop herself from shaking. People would think it was the cold, she thought, staring blindly out of the window. She ought to be seeing shops, pubs, places where she'd clubbed in earnest as a youngster. Instead, she saw faces: the faces of the dead.

She tried to process the information, to get her thoughts ordered so that she could tell Stratton, and inevitably Harmon, in something approaching a rational manner. Except she wasn't feeling rational. Her father's disclosure made her deeply uneasy. Were they leaping to conclusions, or was it possible that the mugging, the attempt to run her down were neither coincidence nor accident, but carefully orchestrated moves guaranteed to put pressure on her mother in an efficient attempt to extort money? She'd no evidence to prove her hunch. It could all be wild imagination. According to her dad, there were no notes, no unsolicited phone calls, nobody strange turning up at the house, but…

Her only source of relief was the feeling that Jacks and her past no longer seemed a factor. As for the mystery client, if she were an instrumental part of a heist, was she acting alone? Helen wanted to know. With surprise and the night on her side, the woman might have managed to push her into the canal, but had she driven the van? Remembering what Stratton said, was she capable of doing something like that? Helen really didn't know. And because she couldn't think straight, because her thoughts were running away with her, she felt deranged with despair and fury, at both the perpetrator, for what had been set in chain, and yes, her mother, for allowing it to happen. And that faced her with another blizzard of unpalatable questions: why hadn't her mother said something? How had she allowed her fear to take precedence over her own daughter's safety?

Helen remembered the time in the kitchen when her mother came over all apologetic and sentimental. She thought it was the booze talking. Now it seemed as if her mother were making a half-baked attempt to ask for forgiveness. But why was she prepared to sacrifice her in the first place? Helen thought angrily. How could she? Mothers were supposed to protect their children, lie for them, die for them. Was her mother too frightened, too weak, too pathetic to come clean? she raged. Maybe, she thought, grasping at straws, her mother said nothing because she genuinely feared what might be done to her only child. But that didn't make sense either. Her mother knew that she'd come within a whisker of drowning but had, crucially, survived. Another escalation and the outcome could have been quite different. Still she hadn't talked, and, Helen thought darkly, what if her mother were protecting something, or someone else? *Just like you did*, a voice inside her head whispered.

She closed her eyes. She pressed her hands to her temples. She felt fogged with thinking. Maybe they'd simply read it all wrong. There could be a perfectly innocent explanation for her mother's actions. Blackmail happened to other people. Like muggings and threats of violence, the inner voice persisted.

She almost missed her stop and had to fly down the gangway. Getting off opposite the Plough and Harrow, she crossed over and began to walk the short distance back to the studio. It was after three in the afternoon but already it felt as if night were starting to fall. Men with tired-looking faces trudged past. Traffic was bumper-to-bumper. Pedestrians took their chances and weaved through streams of cars to cross the road. Helen glanced idly ahead of her and instantly felt her heart leap into her throat. She rubbed her eyes, felt the chatter in her head, and wondered if she were seeing things again.

Freya was ahead of her. No doubt about it. Wearing the same tatty-looking clothing she'd worn three days before, she had the same purposeful manner, same roll in her hips, same spring in her stride. This time Helen was no longer fooled by the streaked blonde hair. It was nothing more than elaborate subterfuge.

Following her, they passed boarded-up hotels and hostels for the homeless, places that were torched, homes that had been substantial family dwellings, but had fallen on hard times, and were now inhabited by the kind of shadowy figures who only come out at night. The people in this part of town wore shabbier clothing, particularly the shoes. They had the haunted faces of the debt-ridden and dispossessed, Helen thought, rolling up the collar of her coat. It had started to sleet but she barely noticed. For the first time in a while she felt an adrenaline-spike; she felt alive.

After a quarter of a mile or so, they came to a set of traffic lights. The woman stopped and pressed the signal to cross. Helen held back, pretending to look into the window of a newsagent. As soon as she heard the beeping sound, signalling pedestrians could cross, she resumed the chase. It was easier than she imagined. Mothers were out in force collecting infant children from primary school. Shift-workers milled about, lighting cigarettes, cupping their weathered hands against the flame. The health message hadn't fully permeated all parts of the Midlands. Booze and fags and junk food still held sway.

The woman led her past a row of shops. And then it dawned on Helen that, far from being in control of the situation, *Freya* might be luring her into a carefully prepared trap. Helen stopped dead in her tracks. It made sense to turn back, or, at the very least, let someone know where she was going. *Never go anywhere without alerting a colleague,* she'd once been instructed. Reaching for her mobile phone, she decided to call Stratton. Then she remembered his response the last time: disbelief coupled with concern for her mental state. She shifted her weight from one foot to the other. There were plenty of people about. It wasn't as if she were walking down an alley alone. Fuck it, she thought, slipping the phone back into her bag, pressing on.

This suburb of town seemed better off, less run-down, she thought. She actually passed a pub she'd once had a drink in with Ed. It sold Banks's bitter and white wine on tap that tasted vile. She'd searched in vain for somewhere to chuck it. Then, just as the memory faded, the woman tagged onto the end of a bus-queue. Helen moved off a few paces, and waited for some other travellers to line up before falling in behind them.

Two buses arrived, off-loading and redistributing their cargo. The woman moved forward. She talked to nobody but gave a deferential nod to a black man with a scarred face. Stealing a glance, Helen saw the woman's skin had a ghastly grey pallor and, despite the chill night air, she was sweating. Another bus arrived, marked for Smethwick. Some hung back, others got on, Freya included. Helen pushed forward, praying there'd be enough room on the bus for herself as well as the three others ahead of her. She just made it but was forced to stand. Feeling horribly exposed, she tried to disguise her height by bending her knees slightly and shrinking behind a fleshy woman wearing a bright purple sari.

By looking in the window's reflection, she could see that Freya was sitting roughly halfway down the bus. She had her head down as if she, too, were avoiding detection.

At the first opportunity, Helen sat down. They'd been travelling for roughly ten minutes. It felt warm and she felt sleepy. She looked out of the window and viewed the urban hinterland. High-rise flats stood like sentinels. Minarets spiked the skyline. The road was plagued with road works and drivers intent on cutting each other up at every opportunity. Rolled coils of razor wire sat on the tops of walls protecting factories. In among the decay, there were also neat rows of houses with satellite dishes. Handsworth, a suburb of Birmingham, lay further on, midway between the industrial sprawl of West Bromwich and Perry Barr. In sunshine, it looked like a thriving, bustling neighbourhood. In truth, it was the seat of Yardie power where murder and gun-crime were rife.

The bus stopped. Helen wasn't sure where. There was a brief, silent exchange of glances among the passengers. *Freya* got up, walked straight past Helen and got off. Helen did the same. Fortunately, there were others.

The urban landscape changed again. They passed a sex-shop with metal bars at the window and a yellow neon sign promising *Adult Entertainment*. Next to it was a kebab shop that was closed, a dodgy-looking dental surgery with dung-coloured Venetian blinds, and a second-hand clothing shop. Although the woman seemed intent on getting to her destination, Helen couldn't be sure that she was unaware of being followed, couldn't be certain that it wasn't part of a plan. Still she pressed on. She hadn't come this far to turn back.

The shops faded into obscurity and Helen found herself walking through a maze of deprived-looking yet familiar streets and eventually out into a wasteland that seemed to be the result of a battle. The landscape was littered with burnt-out cars and redundant sofas. The mothers were thin, the children thinner. But the young men, black and white, looked strong. Strong with hate. In that underworld of a place, the only things that seemed to move were people's eyes. She realised that she'd been there once before, not on foot, alone, but in a locked police vehicle with many others. SOCO had been called out to a squalid house where six black men had been hacked to death with machetes. Helen gave an involuntary shiver at the memory. She remembered the blood. Litres of the stuff, fresh, not rust-coloured or black, but brilliant, oxygenated red. The floor was slippery with it.

Then Freya turned round and looked straight at her.

Helen froze, stood quite still. They stood there, eyeing each other, for no more than seconds though it felt like for ever. When Freya took up the lead again, she moved more swiftly, dodging in and out of alleyways, displaying a razor-sharp knowledge of the territory. Seriously unnerved, Helen again resumed the chase. It was risky. It was foolhardy. She was engaging in a dangerous game and, worse still, her concentration felt impaired. Fear was taking its toll but she had no choice. She had to stay with it, to know, to find out. Desperate to locate her bearings, she found herself casting her eyes over her surroundings. Boarded-up houses sat alongside their run-down neighbours. Of those that were intact, some had steel doors and waste pipes that only came half way down the walls, the hallmark of the crackhouse. At once, she thought back to the marks on the woman's arms. *Track-marks,* she thought, joining the pieces together. Perhaps this was where she got her fix, she thought, slowing, glancing around, taking her eye off her quarry. Maybe that explained her sweating pallor, her need for money. Stop it, Helen told herself, don't run ahead of the evidence.

Then she lost her.

In an alien part of the city, with no idea where Freya was, Helen reasoned this was no time for panic. It was, nevertheless, time to get out. Retracing her steps back to what seemed more like a main road, keeping her head down, breathing slowly, walking quickly rather than running and drawing attention to herself, she emerged into what passed for a community with the sense of bobbing to the water's surface for a much-needed gulp of air. In spite of her inner grip on her feelings, her head pounded. Her brow and upper lip were beaded with sweat. She felt nauseous as she had a flashback of the time her parents picked her up from hospital and recalled her mum's expression of surprise.

"He?"

"Most muggers are blokes, Mum."

"Silly me, of course."

Was her mother confused because she knew that it wasn't a man? Did she laugh because she'd already crossed paths with the woman who called herself Freya Stephens?

Helen pulled out her mobile phone to call Stratton but just as suddenly Freya reappeared, walked up the road and boarded a bus for Oldbury. Casting caution to the wind, Helen buried the phone in her bag and jumped on behind her. Soon she found herself swaying and bracing in time with the vehicle's stuttering motion. Although it was now dark, Helen easily pictured the brutal landscape. She could already sense the change in density in the air, and the distinctive smell of soot and metal even though most of the surrounding steel and chain factories and engineering businesses had long since shut down. Early on in her career, she'd gone to a disused factory there. She remembered driving into a yard pitted by potholes and dark slicks of oil. It was surrounded by tall walls of iron mesh, through which a street of impoverished houses could be seen, their walls caked in graffiti. Ascending a narrow flight of iron steps, her white protective suit rustling, the heels of her boots, and those of her colleagues, chimed with each tread. Inside one of the offices was the victim of a gangland killing. Thinking about it now made her want to close down inside. The unfortunate male had been flayed before death. She photographed the scene and felt as if she'd personally witnessed his agony. Even after her heart-rate settled back to a normal rhythm, the surge of adrenaline dissipated, leaving her feeling faintly sick, the images had stayed with her for months afterwards.

They'd stopped again. Freya got off the bus. Helen stalked her. A keen wind had picked up, knifing her in the face. For a heartbeat, she wondered again about the intelligence of coming alone, but her need to know, her desire for justice, was stronger.

Freya seemed to be walking with more ease, less urgency, indicating that she thought she'd shaken off her pursuer. She turned off into a concrete maze of decrepit-looking dwellings with sporadic street lighting. They were all the same, broken-down, ravaged, uniformly depressing. Groups of young black men with lustreless eyes watched from shadowy doorways. Helen had only a vague idea of where she was, and it occurred to her, as she walked through ravenous-looking streets, that whether it was day or night there would be no difference here. Suppressed violence permeated the atmosphere. Children with cheap clothes, suspicious eyes and shaved heads stared at her approach. Rap music blasted out of upstairs windows. So this was where the woman who called herself Freya Stephens lived, Helen thought, as she watched her enter a shabby-looking dwelling between two boarded-up units.

The house bore the innocuous-sounding name, Albion Place. Crossing over the road to get a closer view, her foot connected with something. She crouched down, eyes taking in a selection of spent shell cases. Years before, it was an unusual occurrence. Now, it was normal. A symptom of drug culture, the gun had also become the ultimate status symbol, the carrier younger, more reckless, more indiscriminate and cruel. With a shudder, she wondered whose turf she was encroaching on and, hurriedly looking round her, straightened back up as if she'd seen nothing more innocent than a tennis ball lying in the gutter.

In the fading glow of an overhead streetlight, she saw that the garden in front of Albion Place was a weed-infested jungle littered with broken milk bottles and empty cans of lager, crumpled in the middle. A battered pushchair lay dumped on the path to the door. It was difficult to tell whether it was a recent addition or had been there for some time. The front door of the house, which was brick-built and blackened by the elements, had a frosted glass panel that had been smashed once with something heavy, offering little protection from the violence outside on the street. The curtains at the downstairs window were open, revealing grubby nets set at half-mast on the window-frame. A television sat winking in one corner. A long sofa with a swirly pattern was positioned against a wall. An ugly-looking main light, hanging down from the centre of the ceiling, bathed the three scantily clad female occupants in an eerie orange glow. They all held cigarettes. One of them was laughing. Helen heard the click of fast-approaching footsteps behind her and shrank into the shadows. The footsteps receded. There was a sharp rap at the door. She watched as a small, squat man wearing a heavy overcoat was welcomed into Albion Place like an old, much-missed friend.

Making a mental note of the name of the street, she headed back to the nearest piece of civilisation, intent on hailing a cab. There were certain places where it was inadvisable to walk alone. This was one of them.

CHAPTER TWELVE

STRATTON MORPHED FROM LOVER to policeman before her eyes. He was standing in her kitchen, holding her. With each new piece of information, his grasp loosened.

"She *looked* at you?" he said, aghast.

"As clear as day."

"Christ, you were taking a risk."

He was absolutely right. She felt awkward and mumbled an apology.

He didn't speak for a moment, just looked at her pensively. "You figure you were being used by this woman to put pressure on your mum?"

"Seems logical." She waited for Stratton to respond but he didn't. He had that murky look in his eye that told her he was not entirely convinced.

"You say your mother cashed in a series of investments totalling a hundred K, and that was unusual?"

"Very," she averred.

"No sign of any blackmail notes?"

"None, according to Dad."

"No one's asked you or your family for more money since your mother's death?"

"No."

"So there's no real evidence of a crime being committed?"

"Not yet," she conceded. She didn't think her dad would see it that way.

"Or that the woman who calls herself Stephens is a prostitute."

"I know," she said, feeling the shakiness of her argument.

"All right," Stratton said, clearly glad that he'd got that straight with her. "Why not go after the golden goose?"

"You mean my father?"

"Well, he's the real source of finance."

"Because my mum's a soft target...was," she said, reddening. "It explains why I was hurt but not killed. Like we said, I wasn't the target, my mother was. I don't know," she said, struggling to think coherently, "perhaps women go after other women."

Stratton was thoughtful. "Women don't go in for blackmail in the same way as men. If they do, the threat is usually some form of exposure."

"You mean a secret?"

"Uh-huh. Plus, the stakes aren't usually that high. Blackmail for money is a man's game."

"Like driving vans at people," she retorted. "What are you saying exactly?"

"I'm not, simply making observations."

"You're going to give me that sexist stuff again," she said, with a nervous smile. "Maybe she had an accomplice."

"Possibly, but then the money would be split."

She realised he had to be cautious but what she really wanted to hear was some full-blooded conviction. "OK, forget the accomplice. Maybe she gets a genuine kick out of doing it. It's part of the thrill, part of the game."

"That what you think?"

No, she didn't. She waited a beat before she spoke. "She's desperate. She looked dirty and dishevelled, down on her luck. If she's feeding a habit, she's

196

prepared to chuck caution to the wind. All that matters is getting her hands on enough loot for the next fix." As soon as the words left her mouth, she registered the flaw in the theory. If the woman had already extorted a hundred grand from her mother over the past five months, it was worth thousands of tricks and bought an awful lot of smack. Why stay in a shit-hole like Albion Place, presumably selling her body, she thought, when the woman could be hundreds of miles away and feel the wind in her dyed hair. Stratton cut across her thoughts.

"Did she strike you as a drug addict when you first met her?"

She gave a shrug. "I noticed some dodgy-looking marks on her arm but I didn't tumble to it straight away. Not every addict fits the stereotypical down-and-out image, as you well know. There are plenty of well-heeled businessmen who think nothing of using cocaine and heroin. It's as commonplace as a trip to Spearmint Rhino."

Stratton cracked a smile that swiftly faded. His eyes locked with hers. "We need to talk to your father."

"Frankly, he'll welcome the opportunity. No one crosses him or his family."

Stratton frowned as if he didn't like the emotiveness of her language. "Whatever this woman's connection," Stratton continued, "we need to investigate every possibility."

"Possibility?"

"Taken in isolation, the withdrawals from your mother's account are not necessarily sinister…"

"But…"

"Added to the other events," Stratton said, "there may well be more to it, and that means we can't keep this between ourselves any more, Helen. I know there are risks, but you don't have a choice."

And neither have you, she thought. It's what she believed he'd say. Actually, she felt glad. This was too big for someone not to take seriously, and it wasn't simply about her any more. There was her father to consider.

"I'm going to phone in," Stratton said, "initially speak to Harmon, explain what's happened, then we'll take it further. We'll need to speak to your dad. You'll be asked to make a full statement." He looked grave.

"It's all right, Joe," she said, touching his arm. "I'm not going to implicate you. As far as Harmon or anyone else is concerned, you've just come on the scene."

She saw the open relief in his face, but she knew that it wouldn't be easy.

It felt as if the coach-house was erupting with police activity. She'd talked until her voice was hoarse. She'd drunk more tea than she was accustomed to. She felt as if she'd been invaded – mentally and physically.

"I don't understand why you didn't report the incident with the van?" Detective Constable Wylie was speaking. The way he was watching her, with sharp eyes, conveyed that he was a man who'd rather not be there.

"I was afraid," she said. "I wasn't thinking straight. I…"

"You must be aware that the longer it takes to get an investigation underway, the smaller the chance of success."

"Yes, but…"

"And you say you checked Freya Stephens's address and number and found them to be false," Wylie butted in. "That was remarkably clear-sighted of you."

"Habit," Helen smiled hopefully, thinking it wasn't a very convincing argument.

"And was it habit that made you take these photographs?" Wylie said, spreading them out on the coffee table.

"Yes," Helen said, feeling numb.

"But you still didn't think to inform us?"

Look, who's the victim here, she wanted to say? "I told you my mother died," she said, feeling tired. Christ, she could have knocked his head off his shoulders.

"We're both very sorry for your loss," Harmon said, looking suitably sombre.

Wylie grudgingly mumbled a condolence. Helen thanked them and thought hers was a ludicrous response. You thanked people for gifts, for small acts of kindness, for letting you go first, not for expressing sympathy for sorrows they couldn't possibly share.

"So you only found out about the cashed investments this morning?" Harmon's voice was soothing.

Helen turned to her with relief. "That's right,"

"Then you saw the woman and followed her late this afternoon?"

"Yes."

"Have you any idea what you could have been walking into?" Wylie said, back on the offensive, rolling his eyes at what he clearly considered to be her blatant stupidity.

Before she had a chance to answer, to say, yes, she was a complete fool who should and did know better, the doorbell rang. Helen stood up but Harmon signalled for Wylie to answer it. He didn't look pleased, like he was asked to leave the theatre before the final act. Helen slumped back down. There was the sound of the front door to the coach-house being opened and closed. She heard the sound of muffled voices, one belonging to Stratton, then the thump thump sound of two pairs of feet coming up the stairs. Both she and Harmon swivelled their eyes and stood up.

It was Stratton followed by Wylie. Both lower-rank officers leapt into action. An extra chair was brought. Helen became acutely aware of pecking orders. She felt her heart lift, glad that Stratton was in charge. "Right," he said authoritatively, addressing Harmon. "I've spoken to Dukes."

Helen's stomach lurched with shock. The last time she'd come across Detective Chief Inspector Dukes she was being carpeted.

"He's given the go-ahead for Miss Powers to have a WPC stay with her."

Helen stared at him with incredulity.

"We'll also make sure a mobile unit regularly stops by to make sure there's no unwelcome company."

"Is this really necessary?' Helen said, feeling a stab of alarm. She hadn't expected this kind of attention.

"You've been attacked twice. Until we've interviewed the woman and followed all lines of enquiry, we're not taking any chances. Are we all up to speed?" Stratton said, looking in Harmon and Wylie's direction.

"I've got one or two things I'd like to ask," Wylie said.

Stratton nodded a *go ahead*.

"This woman who calls herself Stephens," Wylie said, the question aimed at Helen. "You ever had any dealings with her before?"

"No."

"What about your family?"

"Not that I know of."

"The first time you met Stephens, was that when she booked a photographic session with you?"

"Yes."

"How many photographers work here?"

Helen paused, wondering whether Wylie's dissertation was supposed to impress Stratton. She glanced across at him but failed to read his expression. "Ray, who owns the studio, and myself. Ray's on holiday. Still is," she said, thinking she ought to call him and explain what was happening.

"Where?" Harmon interjected.

"Somewhere in the West Indies."

Harmon looked at Stratton who nodded. Helen read the exchange. They were going to check Ray out.

"So she could only pick you?" Wylie continued.

"Yes."

Wylie stroked his chin and fired another question. "Does she have a local accent?"

"No. She's not from round here."

"Did she say that?"

"Yes."

"Did she say where she was from?" Harmon's voice cut authoritatively through the air.

"She was vague, mentioned the London area."

"Nowhere specific?"

201

Helen shrugged. "Might have been Essex."

"You didn't say that before," Stratton blurted out, making her jolt.

"I didn't think of it before," she said, eyeballing him.

There was a brief embarrassed silence broken by Harmon. "And now you think she's working as a prostitute here?" She was looking at Helen.

"I wouldn't like to be that specific but I think it's a fair assumption." And, aside from being some of the most vulnerable and broken members of society, nine out of ten prostitutes were class A drug users, she thought. It probably explained the marks on her arms. If Freya was a working girl, Helen wondered who her pimp was. Could he have some involvement? she thought with a flash of inspiration.

"With regard to your father," Stratton said, "we're liaising with Staffordshire."

"You're treating it as a separate enquiry?" Helen said, bewildered.

"As a *line* of enquiry."

There was a resounding silence, one Wylie, it seemed, felt compelled to fill. "It's important we know what the motive is."

"It's important we know what the crime is," Stratton countered, a steely look in his eye.

"Thought we were working on the premise that Mrs Powers was being blackmailed," Wylie said, none too pleased, by the tight set of his jaw, to be picked up on a technicality.

"That's a possibility, not a premise," Stratton said, a penetrating expression in his eyes.

Forget the point scoring, the semantics, Helen thought, flickering with irritation. "It's about money," she burst out, a bit too loudly judging by the way the others were looking at her. There were only two other motives she could think of: love and hate.

"All right," Stratton said slowly. "*If* that's the case, she's not asking for much, bearing in mind the risk."

"Maybe it's to pay a specific debt," Harmon cut in. "Or she considers it the right amount to pay her back for some unspecified injustice."

Helen flushed and fixed her gaze tenaciously on Stratton. Should she openly question the current assumption that it was a woman acting alone? Perhaps it was best to let them decide that for themselves. Maybe they thought, like Stratton, that it was too small an amount for more than one person to be involved. She let it drop. In any investigation there was bound to be contradictory evidence and, whatever assumption they appeared to agree on now, it could easily be debated and changed in the privacy of the police station.

"Any other angles?" Stratton pressed. The room, once more, fell silent. Helen could feel her heart clamouring in her chest.

"Good," Stratton said, rising to his feet. "Wylie, I'd like you to drive over and talk to Mr Powers. Christine, you're with me."

WPC Lauren Blazeby arrived. She seemed a nice enough woman, Helen thought. Around thirty years of age, she was of medium height and build, red-haired and freckle-faced. She smiled a lot, which eventually, Helen thought, might grate a bit.

She didn't know the protocol, didn't understand what was expected of her. Should she treat the woman as her protector, a guest or baby-sitter? Embarrassed to eat alone, she offered to cook something for both of them even though she didn't feel hungry. Blazeby said she'd already eaten. Relieved, Helen settled for coffee and a packet of Bourbons in front of the television. She found herself worrying about the state of her surroundings. Although she was meticulous when it came to work, she fell far short on the domestic front. She came from the sweep the room with a glance school of housework. You could scrawl messages in the dust on the television. The carpet needed a good vacuum and the grate was full of ash. As for downstairs, it looked as if half the West Midlands police force had tramped through.

Later on, she phoned her dad and got a policeman named Dyer. After first clarifying her identity with Wylie, Dyer allowed her father on the line. He sounded more upbeat, more determined. A man used to action, he clearly felt better to have his worst fears taken seriously rather than just being plagued by uncertainties.

Lauren made more coffee and told her all about her life: how she'd come from a big family, mum and dad going strong, brothers and sisters climbing up the ladders of their respective careers, how she'd married young to another police officer, how they'd rowed and divorced four years later – no kids, a godsend. While nodding and grunting, and doing her best to show interest, Helen chafed to be on her own. She wanted to think, to try and make sense of what was happening. She felt vulnerable at the invasion of her privacy, unsettled by being treated as a victim, and hated the fact that it felt as if her relationship, if she could call it that, with Stratton was altered. And there was something else.

She was undeniably at the centre of the drama, yet she felt peculiarly excluded. All these people were buzzing about because of her, and yet, in truth, she was the least important part of the investigation. The focus was on the perpetrator. She suddenly realised that this was how the relatives of victims must feel. It made her feel a bit ashamed that, after years of working for the police, she'd only just cottoned on.

She wondered what the police expected of her and what she expected of them. The best outcome was apprehending Freya, proving her involvement, and her subsequent arrest and detention.

That's what made her feel uneasy.

Albion Place, and what it represented, didn't conform to the considered and polished pattern of what went before.

Lauren's cell phone rang. She got up, took the call, and left the room. When she came back, she seemed different but Helen couldn't say how. If pressed, she thought Blazeby seemed held back, not so chatty, less smiley, more like a copper.

Helen waded her way through every soap and home improvement programme on offer. If anyone had asked her about the content, she wouldn't have had a clue. All she could think about was the strangeness of the situation she found herself in. Blackmail, extortion with menaces, violence, however you dressed it up, stuff like this didn't happen to people like her. She was only a humble photographer, doing her best to be ordinary, eschewing the kind of life her parents had wanted for her. Not true, her conscience cut in. You wanted to be a high-flyer, prove yourself, cut a dash, and you didn't care how you did it.

Helen switched to Sky and began to watch the film *Gladiator*. She'd seen it before on the big screen and loved it. A sucker for big moral themes, she found the triumph of the underdog particularly satisfying. One scene in particular stuck in her head. It was the bit where Maximus was taken to the place of execution after the death of Marcus Aurelius. His smart thinking, his insistence on a Roman death – to take his would-be executioners off-guard – and his subsequent escape generally made her spirits soar. Not tonight, she thought morosely.

About ten-thirty, the doorbell rang. Lauren got up and it struck Helen that she'd been expecting it. She listened as Lauren went downstairs, felt the draught as a blast of cold air rushed into the hall and circulated upwards. There was a brief, muffled exchange of voices. Sensing a development, Helen stood with her back to the fireplace. She saw Stratton first, then Blazeby bringing up the rear. Both had serious expressions.

"We found her," Stratton announced.

"At Albion Place?" Helen said.

Stratton nodded. "Called herself Karen Lake."

Helen folded her arms in derision. "That her real name or another alias?"

"Not sure yet." There was a cagey expression in his eyes.

"So what did Miss Lake have to say for herself?"

"Not a lot," Stratton said. "She's dead."

CHAPTER THIRTEEN

"DEAD?" HELEN'S EYES WIDENED.

"Suspected drug overdose. We got there as the ambulance was arriving. Not that it was much use."

"Right," she said, sinking into the nearest chair. Yesterday's suspect becomes today's victim. "You're sure it's her?"

Stratton gave a dry laugh. "We're waiting for a positive I.D. but the girls identified her as the same woman in the photographs."

"You've talked to them?" Adam always maintained that prostitutes were not generally forthcoming with information, stemming from a grave distrust of the police.

"Obviously they were upset, but they were pretty co-operative."

"And the cause of death was definitely an OD?"

Stratton frowned. His brown eyes hardened. "A syringe was found at the scene."

"Heroin," she stated dismally.

"We'll have a clearer idea after the post-mortem. Until then we're treating it as suspicious."

She supposed she should have felt some satisfaction. She didn't. She felt cheated. She wanted answers and, with the woman dead, they'd be even harder to come by.

"According to the girls she worked with, she was a heavy user," Stratton said, as if to bolster his argument.

We die as we live, something she'd been taught a long time ago. "Any previous drugs offences?"

"Incredibly, no."

"And she was a prostitute?"

Stratton nodded. "Moved from Essex seven months ago. Usual story, running away from a pimp."

"And is Albion Place being used as a brothel?"

Stratton shook his head. "No offence has been committed."

"So they just live together?"

"That's about the size of it."

"The other girls say anything about her coming into money?"

"They mentioned *some* money. We're following that line of enquiry."

She gave him a sharp look. *Hello*, she wanted to say, *this is Helen, you don't have to use the jargon with me.*

Stratton sat down next to her. "You mentioned tailing Lake before you followed her back to her address."

"Yes."

"Where exactly?"

"To a rough bit of Smethwick."

"Could you take us there, identify it?"

"Probably, but I don't know where Freya, sorry Karen, went. I lost her, or she lost me, and it wasn't the sort of location you hang around in."

"Was she picking up drugs, do you reckon?"

"Well, it wasn't the kind of place you pick up a loaf of bread," she said, eyes smiling.

"No," Stratton agreed with a short laugh.

"What happens now?" she asked.

"Naturally, we'll be talking to her associates, tracing the family."

And piecing together her history, she thought. "Finding out why her path crossed with mine."

"If," Stratton said.

She expressed surprise.

"What we need is hard evidence, Helen, not imaginative ideas."

It was the nearest he'd come to criticism, she thought. His strict adherence to sticking purely with the facts was so very different to Adam. She ought to be glad. "Any chance you'll recover the money?" she asked speculatively.

He threw her an exasperated look. "Hold up, you're jumping to conclusions again."

"You don't think it was her, do you?" It was impossible to keep the dejected tone from her voice.

"We don't even know for sure whether your mother was being blackmailed."

"Why else would she part with over a hundred grand in cash?" She said, dismayed.

"That's what your dad said."

"Surely, he should know?"

"It's never good to get ahead of the evidence, Helen. People do the strangest things for a host of reasons. Let's say we're keeping an open mind."

Sleep was fractured. Shivering in the drab winter light, she pulled on a robe, and got out of bed. Her life had suddenly taken on a strange, surreal quality. There were some strong similarities with what happened before, she thought. With crowds of journalists and photographers camped outside her flat, then on the other side of the city, she'd felt that same helpless and frustrating sense of being under siege, if for very different reasons. She'd felt so alone, she remembered.

No Adam to cuddle. No job to speak of. No future, it seemed at the time. In haste, she'd fled to Keepers. And there she felt more on her own than ever.

She crept downstairs and made herself a cup of green tea flavoured with raspberry and ginseng. She'd bought it in the throes of a health kick. It tasted of perfumed weeds, but at least she enjoyed the morbid satisfaction that it was doing her good.

She'd once tried to confess some of her feelings to Martin, thought it would make her feel better. Instead it made her feel worse. She felt dirty in the telling. By recounting the story again, rather than absolving her, she'd breathed new life into it, giving it oxygen, feeding it with fresh power. Martin was sympathetic, compassionate and eloquent in her defence. He came up with all sorts of excuses.

"From what you've told me, Adam was a controlling person. The guy seemed to be completely lacking in principles. By contrast, you were naive, infatuated by the man, which allowed him to take advantage of you."

"I wasn't a teenager, Martin."

"But you didn't know or understand the importance or significance of what he was telling you," Martin argued.

A hard lump formed in her throat. "I withheld information."

"What information?"

She hesitated. "Can't say."

He looked shocked. "Come on, Helen. You can trust me. I'm not going to think badly of you. I love you."

"Sorry," she said, writhing with shame. "I just can't."

"Look," he said softly. "At the end of the day, you weren't doing the investigating. It wasn't your job and it wasn't your fault. It couldn't be. You were just a worker-bee."

Soon afterwards, she remembered with piercing clarity, she told Martin that it was over between them. She'd had little choice; her guilt would always divide them. While part of her felt she'd disclosed too much, the other felt that she'd not explained enough. And that's how it would always be. Devastating though it was, it was kinder to let him go.

Her mind roamed back to Karen Lake, and the sheer randomness with which life changes or, she thought, the arbitrary fashion in which death comes calling. We're all an angel's breath away from it, she thought. We think we're immune, protected by luck, God, our friends, lovers, or family. Some of us believe that we're smart enough, tough enough to take care of ourselves. But when death comes it doesn't creep up sweet-talking in your ear. It grabs you from behind. She bet the woman had no idea that today would be her last. Most of us are utterly unprepared for it, she thought. In increasingly violent times, with the threat of terrorism, the chance of being caught in someone's else's crossfire, or the risk of running into a psychopath, who knew whether walking up that specific street, waiting at that precise place, getting into a car with that particular man, would signal the end of life? But Karen Lake had died by her own hand, she reminded herself. Only a violence of sorts then.

Excluding the other end of the market, the high-class escorts, with their fragrant-smelling, well-heeled clients, who did it to pay for the children's school fees, prostitution was rarely the type of occupation selected from choice, or as part of a good career move. The vast majority were driven to it because they were running away from demons. Maybe Karen Lake had experienced a life in care. Maybe she'd come from an abusive background. Maybe she'd got into drugs, found someone to supply then found there was a fatal catch in the transaction. The stories varied but the sub-text was the same: loneliness, unhappiness, vulnerability, oppression. And that, she realised, is what she'd recognised in the woman on the one occasion they'd met, the two occasions they'd spoken. That's why she was drawn to her. The vulnerability in the woman's eyes was mirrored in her own.

Which indicated that Karen Lake was not a ruthless blackmailer but simply a pawn in someone else's game.

CHAPTER FOURTEEN

IT WAS A COUPLE of days later. Helen spent the intervening time going through the motions, pretending things were normal, resisting her grappling thoughts. She blitzed the flat, cleaned out cupboards, and junked rubbish. She sorted through her wardrobe and, with the aid of several bin-liners, divided up clothes and belongings for the charity shop down the road. She ironed miscellaneous clothing that had festered in the bottom of the clean laundry basket for several months. She tried not to reflect on her mixed feelings about Stratton. She told herself that she was busy, under pressure, that's why she didn't respond to his calls. In any case, his life was complicated enough. He had children to spend time with. He had a demanding job. He had excess baggage. So did she. She didn't admit that he didn't see things her way, that he was far too nice a guy for her, that she didn't feel worthy.

Every so often Harmon, or both of them together, would pop up with a fresh morsel of information for her to chew over, swallow, and sometimes spit out.

"Has she been formally identified yet?"

Harmon answered. "By the mother, last night."

Helen suppressed a sigh. "Poor woman."

"She seemed resigned," Harmon said. "Always thought Karen would come to a sticky end."

"Did she say that?" Helen said, appalled.

"Her words exactly."

Helen pushed the pace wherever possible. If she ever had the misfortune to suffer from an illness that was terminal, she'd be the type who'd want to know what to expect, and how long she had to live. It was in her nature to know. Mostly. It was in her psyche to find out as much as she could about her assailant. She quizzed Stratton mercilessly.

"The girl grew up in Chingford, Essex," Stratton said in answer to one of her many questions. "Usual pattern: warring spouses, unruly teenager, rows, you know the kind of thing," Stratton sighed with a dreadful world-weariness. "It appears there was quite a lot of family friction, and she grew up with a history of antisocial behaviour. Karen got chucked out onto the street when her mother found her sleeping with her boyfriend."

"Her mother's boyfriend?" Helen said, pulling a face.

Stratton nodded grimly.

"When did she get chucked out?"

He glanced at his notes. "Five years ago. She was seventeen. Understandably, there's not been too much in the way of contact since."

"Was her mother aware of the company she kept?"

"Suspected, but she said she switched off from it."

Were they also the mother's exact words, she wondered bleakly?

On another occasion, when Stratton and Harmon were about to leave, he asked Harmon to go on ahead and wait for him in the car.

"Does it have to be like this?" Stratton said.

"Like what?" She pretended she didn't know what he was on about.

"As though we don't know each other."

"I don't want anyone getting the wrong idea," she said, eyes glancing sideways towards the door.

"What about me?" he said testily. "Have I got the wrong idea?"

She let out a sigh, and slipped her arms around him. He felt resistant. "I'm not good company," she said gently. "It's the way it has to be for now, sorry." There was a kind of ghastly echo in the back of her mind. She'd heard the words before, *said* the words before.

"Fine," he said with a thin smile. "Goodnight then."

After he left, she went upstairs with a heavy heart. She really didn't understand herself any more.

It was three days before they told her what they'd found. She felt stunned, not simply because of what it meant but because they must have known from the start, she thought. It would have been found by the SOCOs.

"You sure it's the right ticket?"

"We traced it to a pawn shop in Kidderminster," Harmon said.

Oh God, Helen thought. It was where her mother had spent her formative years.

"And the porcelain was there?"

"Yeah," Stratton said.

Helen covered her face with her hands. It made perfect sense. She should have given it more consideration before. Only a woman would appreciate its worth. She thought of her poor mother spending a lifetime trying to escape her past and this bitch, Karen Lake, comes along, forcing her to revisit it. She could only imagine her mother's turmoil.

"Let me get this straight," Helen said wearily, dropping her hands, "you found the ticket under the mattress?" She knew that once everyone involved gave

215

the all-clear to move the body, and the undertakers had performed their task, SOCOs would have examined the headboard for signs of pressure marks – a give-away in sexual killings – and every piece of bedding for DNA.

Stratton nodded. Helen let out a high-pitched laugh. "You mean she was thinking of going back some day to reclaim it?"

Stratton gave an embarrassed shrug. "Who knows what she was thinking?"

Helen rubbed her temples. "You said the girls mentioned some money."

"Karen boasted that she'd come into funds and that there was plenty more where it came from."

"Right," Helen said, recognising that Stratton was right and she was wrong; the woman really had worked alone. "Does my dad know all this?"

"D.C. Wylie and Detective Chief Inspector Dukes are with him now," Stratton said.

Helen gave a knowing smile. With the police, it always came down to pecking orders.

They asked her to go back to the mean streets. They were trying to track down whether Karen Lake had picked up her fatal fix there. Harmon was driving, Stratton watching. It was a bright day though it did little to soften the edge of incipient menace. Helen didn't feel as if she were much use. Every face, every corner, every steel door looked the same. Funnily enough, she felt more under threat in the police car than when she'd walked alone.

"The heroin she was sold was a of a very high purity. It would have felled even the most seasoned addict," Stratton said.

Which means there'll be more deaths, Helen thought grimly. "You going to alert the media?"

"Depends on whether it's a one-off."

"You're saying she was unlucky?"

"Pardon the pun, but you know the score. Heroin's like playing with fire," Stratton said. "Sometimes the gear's dodgy and people get scorched."

Helen gave a depressed sigh and looked out of the window. The sky was livid with stripes of red and blue, like the ribs of a beaten child, she thought.

"I'm sorry, this really is no good," she said.

"All right," Stratton said, signalling for Harmon to take her home.

When she worked for the police, she hated weekends on call. People inflicted the most terrible butchery on each other during the hours between Friday night and Monday morning. It was as if, without the constraints of work, the lid came off all civilised behaviour. She was thinking this as she drove to pick up her dad for lunch. She was thinking a lot about the past.

Afterwards she intended to see Gran. It had been several weeks since she'd last been and, although she knew she wouldn't be missed, she hated to think of her grandmother all alone without any visitors. Like the routine of going to the swimming-pool, she also found some solace in the weekly visit. When the business with Jacks blew up in her face, Helen had gone on an almost daily basis. Gran had just moved into Roselea. Her memory wasn't as bad as it was now, though she was clearly disorientated and upset by the move. Helen didn't begrudge the time spent with her. She was glad to have something and someone else to focus on.

She could have moved right away and started life somewhere else, but, as an only child, she felt a certain responsibility to be within easy reach of her parents. She also believed that it was easier to disappear in the city than in the country. In the country, people let you settle in, then popped round with the village newsletter, asked you to join some committee, Neighbourhood Watch, God forbid, or take part in the local village fete and, before you knew you it, you were being pumped for information with questions you didn't want to answer.

With the pressure off, she'd fully expected to be able to mourn her mother's death, but she felt stalled, stuck, it seemed, in that early first stage of shock and disbelief. In fact, she felt nothing at all, as if closed down inside, a knack she'd developed for blocking out and dealing with distressing crime scenes. Others, outside the police, she recalled, thought she was callous. Her mother certainly alluded to it on more than one occasion. The truth was that, without finding a device to filter it out, you couldn't stay sane.

She was taking her dad to The Crown, a pub with a decent restaurant, a couple of miles down the road from Keepers. In truth, she didn't like going to the house much even though it was full of shared memories. Although the police had been unable to find any further evidence of Lake's involvement with her mother, the family home felt peculiarly tainted.

Her father was making a real effort to be cheerful. Throughout a lunch of roast beef and Yorkshire pudding, accompanied by a bottle of claret, he was almost chatty.

"I've been thinking," he said.

Such a mild-mannered remark, she thought, and yet so ominous. She smiled and inclined her head.

"Ever thought of starting up your own studio?"

"I've often thought about it," she said, "but not seriously."

"Perhaps you should."

"I couldn't afford it." She also didn't think Ray would be very pleased.

"I don't mean in Birmingham. I was thinking Stafford would be an ideal location."

She gave him a shrewd look. She knew what was coming next.

"Until you get on your feet, you could always stay at Keepers."

"Mmm," she said. She loved her father dearly but she didn't want to fill the space her mother had so recently vacated. It wouldn't be good for either of them.

"I could help with the finance."

"It's not that, Dad."

He put his old and crinkly hand over hers. "Will you, at least, think about it?"

What could she say? It was lovely to see him this hopeful, this focused. It would give him the kind of interest he craved. She didn't want to hurt him. Not yet.

They were onto the sweet course before she dared to raise the question that niggled most. "Why do you think that woman picked on Mum, and not you?"

"I've really no idea. I've often thought about it but nothing makes much sense."

"And why did Mum keep it to herself?" It was hard to keep the critical note at bay.

He expelled a sigh. "I've asked myself the same question."

Helen gave him a straight look. "You shared everything."

Her father flinched, indicating that her belief was not entirely true. "Your mother had her problems," he said delicately. "She was a very private woman. She used to have what I called a busy interior life. I daresay she had her reasons, and I tried not to let it bother me. Didn't always succeed," he said, looking guilty.

"But she was being threatened, Dad. Why didn't she confide in you?"

"Because she was afraid. It's the only explanation I can come up with." He flashed a sudden smile. "The threat wasn't to her – the money didn't matter a damn – it was to you. That's why she couldn't say anything. She was too afraid of losing you."

"Oh," Helen said, her eyes misting with tears.

Well-lit, cheery, with no unpleasant smells and a decor heavy on primary colours, Roselea resembled a well-run children's nursery. Helen looked at her gran who, at eighty years of age, was holding a doll to her shrunken chest. In the end they all became like little boys and girls, she thought.

When Gran initially showed symptoms of not being well, Helen's mother was the first to play it down. She maintained that all old people were forgetful. But not all old people put their clothes in the fridge, hoard bottles of bitter lemon and go walkabout at three in the morning, Helen had pointed out at the time. When it got to the stage where her gran could get lost inside her own modest home, Helen's mother eventually, and reluctantly, gave in. Gran was moved into residential care. For the first couple of times, Helen and her mother went together, her mother spending the entire time standing up, eager to keep the visits as short as possible. Then the excuses piled up. Her mother was too busy, too tired, too upset. Helen was told by a nurse that it was more common than you'd think for families to fade from the scene. By all accounts her gran had been a lousy mother so it wasn't such a surprise that, in the final analysis, her mum severed all ties. How could she nurture someone who'd failed to nurture her, Helen told herself, but she couldn't help thinking that, because of her mother's attitude to Gran, there would never be any kind of resolution, that it would haunt her mum forever. As things turned out, she never needed to worry.

Careful not to creep up on her and startle her, Helen tapped on the open door and walked into the room. Her gran struggled to her feet. She was wearing a faded skirt and sweater, and a purple cardigan with all the buttons done up wrong. She wore thick navy socks, and trainers on her feet. Her iron-grey hair was swept back off her wrinkled face by a sparkly slide.

"The place is in such a mess," her gran fretted, looking around her neat and tidy room, "my daughter's a lazy girl."

"That's all right, Gran," Helen said calmly, trying to enter into the spirit of it.

Gran gave her a puzzled look. "No dear, I'm not your grandmother. My little girl isn't old enough to have babies."

Helen gave her an embarrassed smile and sat down. Gran viewed her with some suspicion. "Who are you?"

"I'm Helen. Look, I've brought you some picture books," she said, patting the seat next to her. She always came well equipped. It was the key to distracting her grandmother from some potentially awkward questions.

"Your skirt's too short, dear," Gran said, sitting down, tapping Helen's leg with a bony hand. "You should meet Joan. You'd get on well together. Right little tramp."

Helen choked back a reaction, and rummaged in her bag. She couldn't think of anyone less slatternly than her mother, and wondered, God rest her soul, what she'd have made of the insult. Helen took out a big library book, opened it up and set it on her gran's lap. The old woman looked at it, her face instantly melting into an adoring smile.

"Lovely fur," she said, stroking the picture of a dog with an aged finger. "Lovely fur," she repeated rhythmically.

Helen turned the page. Gran's eyes dimmed with ancient recollection. "Lovely. Special brown," she said, in the peculiarly coded way of the dementia sufferer.

"Did you have a dog like that?" Helen asked.

The old woman turned to her, almost whispered. "Joan killed him. Joan killed baby, too." She stared at Helen with open eyes, waiting for a suitably shocked reaction.

Helen swallowed. She knew that it was common for people like Gran to lose words and memories, and to sometimes recreate their own, but she couldn't help thinking that the old woman, in her delusion, was also voicing some deeper truth, reflecting the hidden enmity between mother and daughter. More than ever, she believed it was the right choice to keep her daughter's death from her. "That must be very sad for you," she managed to say. "You must miss them."

Gran nodded. Her rheumy eyes filled with tears. "And my mummy never comes to visit me. Why hasn't she been?" she said plaintively.

"I don't know," Helen said sympathetically, taking hold of her grandmother's hand, feeling the looseness of her gran's wedding ring in her fingers, " but I'm here, and I've got a bar of chocolate in my special bag for you."

Gran gave a toothless grin and clapped her hands together. "I love sweeties," she beamed, the plea for her mother forgotten.

Helen smiled back, leaned over and took out the bar, unwrapped it and broke it off in small pieces, feeding them to her gran, who popped them into her mouth like a greedy starling, bit by bit. When she took the last piece, she offered it first to her doll before snatching it back. "Babies shouldn't have sweeties. Bad for them," she pronounced, wagging her finger.

"What's your baby called?" Helen said, looking at the doll, a cheap plastic thing with staring open eyes.

"He's a boy," Gran said proudly, clutching him tighter. "My son. I had two husbands, you know."

Gran was only married once, but Helen nodded in agreement.

"Lovely man," Gran said, dreamy-eyed. Then a look of agitation crossed her face. "He'll expect me home soon," she said, gathering up the doll, standing up as if ready to sprint.

Helen didn't know how to respond. She knew from experience that there was no point in argument. It only made matters worse. "Would you like to have a look at my photos before you go," she said, trying to divert her.

"Well, I…" Gran looked around distractedly.

"Come on," Helen said brightly.

Gran sat down again and turned to Helen with wary eyes. "Who are you?"

"I'm Helen."

"Ah yes," Gran said, though Helen couldn't be sure that she really remembered. "I forget, you see," Gran said with sudden and painful lucidity.

"I know," Helen stroked her hand. "You have this illness that makes you forget things. It's not your fault. It just happens to some people."

Gran's face grew serious. There was a pleading expression in her eyes. "Have you come to look after me?"

"To talk to you," Helen said, showing her a photograph of the only time they'd all been together: her father, her mother, herself and Gran. They'd gone out for a Mothering Sunday lunch. It was Helen's idea. Her mother hated every minute of it. Helen was cross with her at the time, she remembered, thought her mean-spirited.

Gran stared at the print and caught her breath. She put a trembly hand to her wet mouth. Her eyes were glassy with fear. "I don't like him," she gasped, pointing at Helen's father.

Helen put her hand gently on her gran's shoulder.

"He's a bad man," Gran said, clearly distressed.

"Is he? Who do you think it is?"

"Don't be stupid," Gran snapped, sending spittle flying onto Helen's cheek. "That's Wyndham."

Helen didn't know what to say. Wyndham had been her gran's husband. Helen had never heard her utter a word against him. In fact she hardly ever spoke of him at all. Neither did her mother, for that matter. Death seemed to have obliterated every trace of his existence. Obviously, something somewhere had got snarled up in her gran's memory bank, Helen thought.

"You won't take me back to him, will you?" Gran said, clutching Helen's hand, a wretched look in her eyes.

"No," Helen promised, taken aback.

"Can I stay here with you?"

"Yes."

"And Lee?" Gran said, looking down at the doll.

"Is that his name?"

"I *think* so," Gran said tentatively. She was often wary of questions. They required knowledge and memory, something she no longer had.

"He can stay, too," Helen smiled.

Her gran sighed with relief. "We'll hide him from Joan," she grinned mischievously, nudging Helen's arm. "We'll keep him a secret."

Helen smiled sadly, patting her grandmother's hand.

She arrived back at the coach-house shortly before six. It felt chilly inside in spite of the heating. She changed back into a pair of jeans, poured herself a glass of red wine and slid a CD into the player, flicking through the tracks, homing in on Bono singing how he'd hurt himself, hurt his lover and discovered that what he thought was freedom was just greed. Feeling a certain, morbid empathy, she decided to give Stratton a call when the phone beat her to it. Expecting it to be him, she snatched it up.

"Hi," she said breathlessly.

"Helen, it's Jen." She sounded different, Helen thought. Not her usual bubbly self.

"You all right?"

"Yes," Jen replied simply. "I wondered…erm…heard any news today?"

Oh great, Helen thought, another of Jen's doom and gloom stories. She snatched a mouthful of her drink. "No, thank God. I've been over at Dad's then I went to visit Gran. Look, Jen, I'm not really in the mood for anything grim at the moment. I've had a bellyful, lately."

"I know, sweetheart."

Sweetheart, Helen thought, pulling a face. Whatever was the matter with her?

"Would it be all right if I pop round? You're not going out or anything?"

"Jen, what's this all about?" Helen said, unable to conceal the sudden note of worry in her voice.

"I'll explain when I get there."

Ten minutes later, Jen was sitting on her sofa, armed with a drink. Although she managed a smile, her eyes looked sad. For a horrible moment, Helen wondered if George had died. When Jen took Helen's hand, Helen felt seriously worried.

"It was on BRMB's five o'clock news," Jen began.

"What was?"

Jen glanced away. "About Adam."

"Adam?" Helen stared, mystified.

"That was his name, wasn't it, Adam Roscoe, the policeman chap you had a fling with?"

A fling, Helen wanted to say. It was so much more than that but she'd only ever told her newly acquired friends the edited highlights of her story. All the comprehensible bits. Hadn't wanted to bore them to death with the rest of it. Hadn't wanted to...

"They said he was from Birmingham, that he used to work for the West Midlands Police and had recently set up as a security advisor in Iraq. Do you think it's the same Adam?" Jen was looking at her anxiously. She was waiting for Helen to deny it. Wanting her to.

"What about him?" Helen blurted out.

"He's kind of got an unusual surname, hasn't he?" Jen said as if wishing he hadn't.

Helen's stomach flipped. "Has something happened to him?"

Jen's clear blue eyes settled on hers. "He was shot dead last night. Some guys loyal to one of those Arab militias. I'm so sorry, Helen."

Later, and alone, Helen stared through a window scarred with rain. The moon was a big, gauzy disc in a star-less sky. She wondered crazily if Adam was out there somewhere, her mother, too. Each in their own separate place.

She'd already downed several glasses of wine. Maybe that's why her thoughts kept crashing into each other, she thought, feverishly taking another pull. That's why she felt as if her brain had finally dislocated.

She felt shocked beyond belief. He'd have put up a fight, she thought. He wouldn't have gone easily. Not like he did with the police. He'd have bucked and cursed and fought against his fate. At least a bullet in the head was quick, she tried to console herself, if that's what it was. She couldn't bear to think of him running away, disintegrating bit by bit, his beautiful body riddled with bullets. She couldn't bear to imagine

227

his anguish, his physical suffering, the blood spattering, the foul 'blow back' effect of close contact wounds, or the ragged, gaping holes caused by shots from further away. It made her want to howl.

She took another snatch at her drink. At least he'd no longer be a figure of speculation and loathing, she thought bitterly. And yes, in spite of the complications, the muddied waters, all the things you can't explain, she'd loved him. Once.

Adam's sudden and violent death brought into focus her mother's untimely demise, her *escape*. And that's what it was, wasn't it, Helen thought, an escape from reality, from pressure, from demand? In the same way human beings can will themselves to live, Helen believed that they could also will themselves to die.

Her heart creased with pain. She had this strange thought that her mother had committed suicide. Ridiculous. Unless you count a lifetime of boozing a self-induced death. The truth was neither she nor her father were enough to sustain her mother. It didn't matter how much love she was shown, how much obedience or loyalty, she couldn't be reached. And, between them, they'd tried hard. Yet, over three decades, her mother became more disjointed, unhappy, vulnerable, clinically depressed, Helen guessed. And nobody knew the reason why. Sure, she'd had a raw deal when younger, but plenty of people bounced back from things like that. Especially when you're loved, when you had tons of money, when you had a child and a pampered life, Helen caught herself thinking angrily. And Adam had no life at all. It had been smashed.

Her mind was grasshopping again. If only she'd been a better daughter, she thought, brushing away the tears as they started to fall, if only she'd fallen in with her mother's plans for her, if she'd made more of an effort, been less critical in private, less fond of her father in public. Oh God, she thought, the tears really falling now. With both of them gone, it felt like the end of an era. And all the things she could have said and didn't, she sobbed, while knowing in her heart that, had her mother survived, she would have said nothing at all.

She got up, spilling some wine onto her hand. Soaking it up with the sleeve of her sweater, she stumbled into her bedroom, almost colliding with the doorframe. Her mother's address book was on the floor by the side of the bed. She had meant to look at it before but couldn't face it. While she had no problem with corpses and trace evidence, blood and bits of bone and brain, she found it peculiarly disturbing to look at the handwriting of her recently deceased mother.

She sat down hard on the floor, resting her back against the solid wooden bed and, steeling herself, opened up the black leather-bound book, starting with the first page. Each entry jogged her memory and conjured up a fresh picture. Under C, she remembered Sam Coles, the good-looking chimney sweep. While other tradesmen failed, Sam always managed to charm her mother into a cup of tea and a slice of cake. She got quite girlie in his presence, Helen recalled with a fond smile. It was lovely to see her mother having fun. Strange, she'd never witnessed it with her father.

She carried on through the D's, E's and F's. It read like a novel. Her mother's friends were all there, each name invoking a name and a memory, heating engineers, garages, schools Helen attended, the private telephone number of Mrs Gillespie, the nursing sister at Roselea, all the small but significant details of her mother's life. Some of the entries were badly faded others fresh and bold. And there were doodles: a cork whizzing off a bottle of champagne next to the wine merchants, a dog's face underneath the veterinary surgeon they hadn't needed in years. Some of the entries crossed over with others so that Aunt Lily appeared twice: once under her maiden name, Powers, once under L for Lily. Helen went to turn the page and stopped. There was another name, squeezed into the corner, tucked away, a single name, three letters, no surname, more surprisingly no phone number or address attached to it. She trawled back through the address book, combing it again to see if the name was cross-referenced. It wasn't. She said the name once, out loud, her voice rasping with surprise.

"Lee."

CHAPTER FIFTEEN

RAY WAS BACK AND in irrepressible form. He looked brown and round and happy. His dark hair had grown long and flopped over his face. He pushed it back in a theatrical gesture with a pudgy hand. "Pour us a drink, Powers, and fill me in on what's been happening."

Helen gave him a warm smile. He always called her Powers, just like he called Jewel, Ronnie – an affectionate bastardisation of the girl's surname, Rono.

Over a couple of gin and tonics, it wasn't long before she confided in him.

"Christ Almighty, why didn't you phone and tell me?"

"So that you could get the next plane back?"

"But your mother…"

"Jewel held the fort," she cut in smoothly. "We weren't that busy. It was all right…honestly."

Ray cast her an appraising look. Are you for real? he seemed to say. "And this other business?"

"It's over," she said, trying to sound convincing. "Just a nasty individual who eventually got her comeuppance."

"Divine retribution, more like."

Helen agreed, but, if she were coldly clinical, the woman's motives were easy enough to identify with. They weren't complicated by hatred or revenge or a desire for power, but simple, unadulterated greed. We all lust after things, she thought, chasing rainbows we can't afford or have.

Ray leant towards her. "You should take some time off."

"I'm all right."

"It's not a request, Powers." He was smiling but his soft hazel-coloured eyes were implacable.

"It's January. It's bloody freezing. Where do you suggest I go?"

"Abroad?"

"I'd have to fly half way round the world to find a suitably temperate climate."

Ray's face split into a grin. "Then how does the Wyre Forest sound?"

"Like hell."

With an almost psychic vision of the collapse in stocks and shares, Ray had invested in a number of properties some years before. They were mostly let out on short-term tenancies. The cottage was rented as a holiday home. *A good little earner,* as Ray frequently informed her. She imagined that after the Christmas break it would stand barren until Easter.

"It's quite cosy. Open fire. All mod cons. You're not exactly cut off from civilisation. Plenty of local pubs and shops."

"Plenty of people asking questions," she chimed in.

"Don't be so miserable," he said with a despairing look. "It would do you good to have a change of scenery. You need to get out more."

Get a life, was what he meant, she thought.

"If you must insist on shutting yourself off from the rest of the world, it's ideal," Ray conceded. "Better still," he said, a playful gleam in his eye, "take a close friend with you." Ruthlessly fishing, as usual, she thought, not without amusement.

"Think I'll stick with my own company."

"Always the dark horse."

Was it that obvious, she thought? She gave him a big smile. "So where is it exactly?"

Ray looked shifty. "It's not really the Wyre Forest – that's just how we sell it to the tourists."

Helen let out a laugh. "You mean it's a shack off some dirt track somewhere?"

Ray shook his head. "There's a proper road leading to it. It's nearer to Clows Top, really."

"Clows Top? Sounds like something from the Archers."

"It's lovely," Ray insisted, "close to Bewdley. There's a river and everything. Pity the Safari Park won't be open. They've got elephants, camels, giraffes and there's a splendid rare breed of white lions."

Helen wasn't listening. Ray mentioned Bewdley. It was a bit further on from the carpet-producing town of Kidderminster. That close, she could make a few enquiries of her own about her mother. She could go where she wanted, visit whom she wanted, and ask all the questions that still needed answers.

All she had were the ramblings of a senile old lady and a doodle in an address book. It was nothing to go on and yet she felt that they were deeply symbolic.

Ray, in a haze of post-holiday magnitude, gave her the rest of the afternoon off. She drove out to Roselea again. She wasn't sure what good it would do. It was impossible to hope that she could get Gran into the right time frame to talk and, even if she did, how could she trust what she was saying? On the last visit Gran accused her own daughter of murder.

When she looked in on Gran, she was fast asleep in her chair, face slack, mouth slightly open. Helen looked round for Mrs Gillespie, the matron who ran the home. A slim, attractive-looking woman in her middle fifties with swept-back hair, she was arranging a large display of flowers in the hall.

"I was wondering if I could have a word about Gran," Helen said.

"Of course, Miss Powers. Come into my office."

The office was a small, windowless room tucked between the day room and dining area. Helen noticed a box of biscuits on the desk. The lid was off and she could see that all the foil-covered chocolate ones had been eaten. Mrs Gillespie indicated a chair and offered her the box.

Helen put up her hand. "No, thanks."

"I was very sorry to hear about your mother. It must be a great sadness to you. So?" Mrs Gillespie inclined her head with a smile, her grey-blue eyes settling on Helen. Helen smiled back. Now that she was there, she didn't know how or where to begin. The silence extended. Mrs Gillespie filled the void. "Have you seen your grandmother today?"

"She's asleep at the moment. I came on Sunday. That's what I wanted to talk to you about, you see. We had this…erm…conversation." Helen broke off. This was daft, she thought. A loose arrangement of words and phrases in no particular context hardly constituted a conversation.

"Go on," Mrs Gillespie said.

"Thing is," Helen said, starting again. "How much do you think she remembers? Is it possible that bits from the past break through to the surface?"

"I'd say that's entirely common at this particular stage of the disease."

"It's as if she has flashes of lucidity," Helen said, "but I can never be certain if what she's saying has any truth in it."

"And that's important to you?"

"Frankly, yes."

Mrs Gillespie nodded. The eyes didn't waver. It was as if she were weighing up what it was that Helen was driving at. There was circumspection in her expression. She intuitively seemed to know to tread carefully. "Many Alzheimer's sufferers retain the essence of their characters. In certain individuals, those traits come to the fore. Someone who's been a bit intolerant when they were well can become quite aggressive when they're sick. Likewise, if the sufferer had a tendency towards depression in earlier life, this can also become a problem later. If they enjoyed a good gossip then, they'll enjoy it now."

"So it's not as if they lose everything that makes them unique?"

"Not at all. Their life stories often give a good indication of how they'll react to change in their current circumstances, which is why we like to know as much about the patient as possible; it gives us a context in which we can work. In your grandmother's case, I gather she had a period of illness during her forties, possibly around the time of her menopause."

Something that hadn't occurred to Helen before. "But nothing was ever found to be physically wrong with her."

"Not physically, perhaps, but certainly mentally. You can't take to a wheelchair for over a decade of your life without something being wrong."

"You mean she was making it up?" Helen said, nerves catching.

"Not literally. It was probably her way of dealing with a certain difficulty."

So now there were two secrets to unravel, Helen thought. "Seems extreme."

"Given enough pressure, we're all capable of extremes," Mrs Gillespie smiled.

Helen shuffled uncomfortably in the chair.

"Going back to your specific question," Mrs Gillespie said. "Alzheimer's patients have a tendency to hallucinate."

"Any particular reason?"

"Failing eyesight and hearing, mostly. Sometimes because parts of the brain are particularly sensitive when the light is poor."

"So what they see and say is just delusion. It has no bearing on the truth?" Helen found it difficult to mask the disappointment in her voice.

"I'd hate to be that dogmatic," Mrs Gillespie said. "Alzheimer's really is a shades of grey disease. Sufferers live in the past for a very good reason – they can access the information better."

"A bit like a computer overload but the hard disk is still intact?"

Mrs Gillespie smiled. "I'm not computer literate, I'm afraid."

Helen tried another angle. "What you're saying is that while the disease alters behaviour and mood…"

"Sometimes leading to paranoia and delusion," Mrs Gillespie chipped in. "It can also release and bring resolution to unhappy or frightening experiences. It's why people with Alzheimer's repeat stories of old traumas and disappointments again and again. It's their way of making sense of the really important bits of their lives. Weirdly enough, people with totally

236

fragmented short-term memory can possess an astonishingly accurate grasp on the past."

So what my gran was saying could contain a grain of truth, Helen thought, shocked.

Clows Top turned out to be a loose association of houses built around a crossroads with a traditional butcher's shop on one corner and a post office opposite. Following the main road to Cleobury Mortimer, as instructed, Helen took a sharp turning to the left and followed the road for roughly half a mile. The scenery was glorious in spite of the rain and the ravages of winter. Badgers Cottage was exactly as Ray stated; brick-built, covered in dormant Virginia Creeper, lying in a cleft, standing alone.

She drove up the narrow drive, lifted a solitary bag from the passenger seat and let herself in, her nostrils flexing at the slightly musty smell. Very quickly she acquainted herself with her new surroundings: small hall, square-shaped sitting room, dining-kitchen. Upstairs there was a tiny bathroom, two double bedrooms and a box-room with an old-fashioned hand-carved wooden toy-box inside. After testing out the bed in the front bedroom, she went downstairs and into the kitchen and worked out how to put on the hot water and heating, then she drove into Cleobury where she ambled about and picked up some basic provisions. Later, she opened a bottle of Merlot and cooked and ate a dish of chicken in a mushroom sauce. As an afterthought she'd popped the latest novel by Nicci French into her bag and was attempting to read it. When she found herself going over the same sentence again and again, she put it down.

She felt like a geologist interpreting the layers of rock to read the landscape. Except she couldn't. It was as if she were continually slipping through shale. She wanted to phone Stratton, to talk to him, to explain that she wasn't really being a cow, that she was trying to do him a favour, but then they'd get talking and she'd blurt out her latest hunch and he'd think she was crackers and that would be that.

It was hard to think of her gran in her forties. Come to think of it, she'd never seen any photographs either of her mother as a little girl or her grandmother as a younger woman. Was it significant? She thought about her own family photograph album. It revealed quite a lot about the players. Her mum was always slightly set apart, even if it was in the way she was looking, not quite focused on the camera, or the way she was standing – one shoulder very slightly turned away. Her dad was always beaming, larking about, the master of ceremonies, keeping things together – easy when you're only dipping in and out. As for her, well, she was the photographer, which probably explained why there were more shots of her father, her home, and pets than of her mother.

Letting her mind go into freefall, she thought back to her childhood self. In her experience, kids were big on secrets – secret places, secret dreams, secrets not to tell. Don't tell anyone, it's our little secret, the molester tells the abused child. But there are other secrets, too, the grown-up kind, the ones to save our skins, our sensibilities, protect others, for the greater good, as Adam always told her, for greater glory. The Mafia code of omerta meant honour and silence – at least if you wanted to stay alive. So what was her mother's big secret? Was it cause for blackmail? Was

238

it linked to her grandmother's flight from reality? The next day she intended to find out.

CHAPTER SIXTEEN

HELEN GOT UP, BATHED, dressed, wandered downstairs and downed some fruit juice. It was too early to intrude on other people's lives so she watched the light purging the last shrouds of darkness. Eventually she made some coffee. She drank it, standing up, catching morning television. With its heavy reliance on confessions and exposures, she soon felt as if her nerve-endings had been put into a pencil sharpener. After ten minutes of some miserable woman slagging off some miserable man, she switched it off, picked up her keys and stepped outside.

The cold gnawed at her limbs like a hungry rat. She shivered, and turned up the collar of her jacket, surrounded by rolling hills and trees and a crushing, cold silence. Her attention was briefly caught by a bird of prey sitting on top of a telegraph pole. It was too small for a buzzard, too big for a kestrel. She reckoned it was a sparrow-hawk. It sat quite still, watching and listening, waiting for the right moment to swoop on its quarry and crunch its bones.

Helen took the main road into Kidderminster, windscreen wipers thumping with the sudden onset of gusty rain. She hadn't noticed on the drive down but there were several locations where bouquets of flowers were tied to lamp posts or railings, or just left by the side of a hedge. This is how we honour our dead, she thought, with roadside tributes, with public reminders for private grief. At the secondary school she had attended there were several benches left in memory of pupils. She could remember their histories even though she'd long forgotten what they looked like. A couple of lads were killed on the road walking from school. One girl died from a long illness, another lad from an undiagnosed heart defect that only displayed itself in the middle of a game of football. As usual, the boys outweighed the girls. She'd taken these things in her stride, she remembered. She was younger and more resilient. There was no counselling on offer then. No public outpouring of grief for losses keenly felt.

She drove around the centre of Kidderminster, negotiating the ring road, and turned off as if she were heading for Stourbridge and Wolverhampton. The traffic funnelled into a narrow, dishevelled-looking street with a sex-shop called Taboo on one side, a used-car dealership on the other. She turned left at the lights and followed the road round. It was the kind of place where the pub landlord's idea of refurbishment was to put new metal grilles up at the windows. Eventually, she came to a row of terraced houses. Her gran's house looked very run down, she thought, as she parked the car and got out. The curtains were thick with dust, the windows dirty, the step to the front door blackened. For an instant, she wondered if she'd come to the wrong dwelling. Then she looked at the house next door, recognised the cactus in the window, the bright yellow curtains and realised that she'd come to the right place after all. Mr and Mrs Wellings lived there, both long-standing friends of her gran, though Helen hadn't spoken to them in years.

Taking her courage in her hands, she banged the knocker on the green painted door and waited. They'd both be in their eighties, she thought. It was quite possible that one of them was dead.

The door was opened by an elderly man with a marked stoop. He was wearing baggy fawn-coloured corduroy trousers and a sloppy sweater with leather patches on the elbows. His face was heavily lined and, because of the stoop, the skin hung down like a bloodhound's.

"Mr Wellings," Helen said with a smile.

"Yes," he said cautiously.

"I don't suppose you remember me. I'm Mrs Painter's granddaughter. We met ages ago when I was a girl."

"Mrs Painter," he said slowly as if Helen were speaking a foreign language.

"Doris, your next-door neighbour. She moved, went to live in a home."

"I remember," a woman's voice travelled from inside. "Let her in, Reg, for Heaven's sake. You'll both catch your death standing on the doorstep."

The old man shrugged and let Helen pass. She followed him through an icy cold room to another where a coal fire was burning. Mrs Wellings sat in a corner near the fire. The window behind her looked out onto a walled, brick-paved yard with a dark brown painted door. Helen guessed that the door led out to a shared access.

The voice was a lot stronger than the occupant. Mrs Wellings, Violet, as she insisted Helen called her, was extremely frail in appearance. She wore several layers of clothing from which her thin wrists and hands protruded like pipe-cleaners. Although her hands were gnarled with arthritis, Helen noticed that the old woman's nails were beautifully manicured and painted a soft pale peach. She wondered if the old man did them for her or whether she had a kind friend or neighbour.

"Sit yourself down," Violet said, indicating the settee. "Aren't you going to say hello, Reg?"

"How do," Mr Wellings said in a bluff, typically Midlands fashion.

"I remember you," Violet said, turning to Helen with a spry smile. "You used to come round for a cup of tea and a biscuit. Talking of which," she said, looking pointedly at her husband, "get the kettle on, Reg."

Reg muttered something and sloped into the kitchen to do his wife's bidding.

"That's better," Violet said, looking delighted to have a visitor. Close-up, Helen noticed that the pale, milk-white skin on Violet's face was broken up by what looked like bruises but were in fact burst blood vessels where the veins were simply too fragile to contain the supply. Her eyes were red-rimmed and the blue irises tinged with yellow.

"This is very good of you," Helen said.

"Get away," Violet beamed. "Now we can have a real good chat. How's Doris getting on then?"

"Physically she's quite well. Her memory's not so good, of course."

"Got worse, has she?" Violet narrowed her eyes.

"She was never going to improve," Helen said simply.

"No," Violet sighed. "I always say if that happens to me, shoot me." Her mouth screwed into a frown. "Can't abide the thought of being gaga."

"Who's to say you're not?" Mr Wellings called from the kitchen in a tone that Helen wasn't entirely certain was humorous.

"Thought you were deaf," Violet called back, winking at Helen. "And what about your mother, dear?"

Helen cleared her throat. She'd been prepared for the question but still found herself fluffing the answer. "She's…erm. She died. Heart-attack."

Violet's red-rimmed eyes widened. "Did you hear that, Reg. Our Joanie's passed on."

"Get away," Reg exclaimed, appearing at the doorway, wiping a teacup decorated with flowers the colour of dried blood.

Violet stretched out her hand and took Helen's. "Sorry to hear that, chick. Had a difficult life, your mother. All came right in the end, marrying your dad, and that, but she had a rotten start."

"Yes, I…"

"Here we are," Reg said, balancing a tray and putting it on the dining table. "Custard Creams or Rich Tea?"

"Custard Creams, of course. We've got guests," Violet said proudly. The old man moved with surprising speed and returned seconds later.

Helen smiled shyly. "You were saying about my mum, Violet."

"Sugar?" Reg said

"No thanks," Helen replied.

"Ah yes, your mother," Violet said, drawing her hand away, her eyes rheumy with recollection.

"Custard Cream, anyone?" Reg said, handing round the packet.

Violet looked at him with irritation.

"Thanks," Helen said, deciding it would be diplomatic to take one even though she didn't fancy it.

"One shouldn't speak about the dead," Reg said, a warning note in his voice. "It's not right."

"Only if you've got something bad to say," Violet countered.

A prickly silence seemed to invade the room. Helen didn't mistake it for integrity. The old man was trying to shut his wife up. She decided to give it another go. Everybody talks. Eventually. "I know Mum had a tough time looking after Gran when she was ill."

"Ill?" Violet snorted, "nothing wrong with her."

"Vi," Reg warned, a threatening look on his face. But Vi was not to be silenced.

"It's true. She led that girl a dog's life, fetch me this, do that, and all because she craved the attention. I didn't hold with it then and I'm not going to pretend otherwise just because Doris has gone round the bend. It will end in tears, I said, and I was right." Violet took a strong sip of tea, clearly glad to get the strength of her feelings off her shallow chest. Reg helped himself to another biscuit and nibbled on it nervously.

"How did my grandfather cope?" Helen asked.

Violet sniffed. Helen noticed Reg's eyes drilling into his wife's. Helen leant forward just a fraction to break his line of vision.

"He was hardly ever there," Reg said, his eyes still on Violet. "Anyway, it was all a very long time ago. You don't remember things that well when you're our age." Reg lowered his gaze. Violet sipped her tea. Helen followed suit.

"Think we could do with a top-up," Violet said spryly. "Any more water in the kettle?"

"I'll have to boil some up," Reg said grudgingly.

Violet looked at Helen with a conspiratorial smile. "I *do* enjoy a cup of tea."

Reg got up, picked up the tray, chucked his wife a look as if he were spitting tacks.

"And shut the door after you," Violet said. "I get a draught on my neck when you leave it open."

"Perhaps you'd like me to stick a broom up my bum so I can sweep the floor while I'm at it," he said caustically.

"That won't be necessary," Violet said, giving Helen another watery wink.

As soon as Reg was out of earshot, Violet leant towards Helen. "We don't get many visitors nowadays," she confided. "Just the odd health visitor, the man to read the meter. The last time someone came it was a fella."

"Right," Helen said with a smile, disappointed that Violet was not more forthcoming.

"A fella asking questions." Violet sat back in the chair, looking satisfied.

Helen felt the smile slip from her face. "Asking questions?"

"Just like you." Violet patted Helen's hand. Her expression trembled with girlish excitement. Her eyes were pinpoints of feverish bright light.

"When?"

"Exactly this time of year, funnily enough. One of those cold dark days we keep getting. Your gran had just moved out."

"But that was about four years ago," Helen said, feeling her stomach churn.

"I daresay," Violet said. "Seemed a nice enough lad, bit rough round the edges, if you know what I mean. I felt sorry for him, to tell the truth. So he never got in contact with you?"

"With me?"

"Said he was going to look you up and speak to both of you."

"Both? I'm sorry, I really don't understand."

Violet leant in towards Helen, took her hand again. This time the grip was tight. "There are some things it's best not to know, but I reckon you have the right, especially with your mother gone. It can't hurt anyone any more. I told you it would end in tears and it did. Your mum was a good girl. She did everything for your gran, washed her, got her dressed, went off to school. Lord knows how she did all the shopping and cleaning – we helped out when we could, of course," Violet sniffed, " but it was no life for a young girl. At heart she was just a kid, a child with too much on her shoulders. It was inevitable, really."

Helen stared at her, mystified. "What was?"

Violet's voice dropped to a whisper. "She got in the family way."

Helen felt as if she'd been hit with a sledgehammer. Everything she'd come to believe about her mother turned to dust and blew away. Even though they'd never been close, she felt, at least, that she understood her, knew her nature, appreciated that she was private, aloof, was at odds with life. But this? She couldn't grasp it. Her mind teemed with questions. "How old was she?"

"Fifteen."

Christ. "Do you have any idea who the father was?"

Helen watched the hesitation. Violet glanced at the door. Helen saw her decide to lie. "We don't know, dear."

"So what happened to the child?"

"She tried to keep it, spitting image of her, it was, but eventually it was put up for adoption. Sadly, the boy spent most of his time in care."

The boy, Helen thought, her pulse racing. Then she remembered the guy at the funeral, the one wearing the wraparound sunglasses, the one with the fair hair.

"Where? Which care home?"

"Not sure if I remember. Somewhere in the West Midlands, I think."

"And was this the man who came back four years ago?"

Violet nodded. "Wanted to trace his birth mother. They can now, you know. Not sure if it's a good idea. It can cause a lot of heartache."

"Did you help him?"

"He never got in touch?" There was a wheedling note in Violet's voice. Helen caught a glimpse of mischief in the old woman's eyes. She wasn't above mixing it, she thought. Suddenly she didn't seem like such a sweet old lady any more.

"No."

"Probably decided it was for the best."

"His name," Helen murmured, already suspecting the answer.

"Lee," Violet replied. "Lee Painter."

She drove back to the cottage in a daze. Lee was her half-brother, her mother's son. As far as she was aware, her dad knew nothing about him. She wondered how he'd react to such a revelation. How it would spoil his opinion of his wife. Not that she was planning on telling him. Like Violet said, there were some things best concealed.

She tried to imagine her mother as a frightened, pregnant teenager. No wonder there was so much discord between her and Helen's gran. No wonder she'd put so much distance between them. Her grandmother was the keeper of her daughter's secret. Strange how senility let it out.

She'd always wanted a big brother, Helen thought grimly, working out Lee's age, someone to care for her, look out for her, to have a laugh with, maybe introduce her to his friends, act as a buffer between her and her mum. If her mother were fifteen when she had him, he'd be thirty-nine now and thirty-five when he first showed back up on the scene. She could just imagine his reaction to his parentage. What must he have thought to discover that his mother was living a life of comparative luxury while he'd been chucked on the scrapheap? Worse, that his mother had a child she'd decided to keep. It would seem like a perverse form of natural selection and would surely stir up a tidal wave of resentment, if not a desire to claw back what he felt belonged to him.

Helen spotted a speed camera and, slowing, immediately changed down a gear. She did the same with her mind, trying to apply some brakes to her thinking. Easy to run ahead of the evidence. Simple to add two and two and make five, she thought feverishly. Could the facts, as they stood, be described as purely circumstantial? Was it just coincidence that Lee started digging around four years before when her own life was breaking apart?

She tried to imagine what it was like to be given up and adopted by the state. If it were her, she'd be forever wondering who she was, who she looked like, why she was given away. The sense of rejection would be immense, she thought and, if your life was spent in the care of strangers, how on earth do you form relationships? As a rogue piece, how do you slot into society's great jigsaw? However much it's slagged off, however flawed it might be, family still counted, still mattered. She wondered what kind of a life Lee had led.

For some, she guessed that it was enough to know who they were, where they were born, what name they were given. For others it would be the start of an emotional and complex and, possibly, harrowing journey, culminating in bitter disappointment. It must be devastating to come face to face with your mother and run the risk of having all your dreams shattered, Helen thought. And how would her mother have felt? Disappointed? Guilty? Ashamed? Had she agonised about giving up her first-born child? Was this the reason that her mother was unable to form close attachments, not even with her own husband, not even with her own daughter? Maybe there was a love story behind it all. Perhaps her mother had always loved and missed the man who'd fathered her son, even after all those years. First love was often the deepest. It explained the haunted look in her mother's expression, her inexplicable despair, the depression. It also explained the reason she drank. Maybe it was the only way to blot out her loss. Helen really couldn't say for certain. All she could do was imagine. She was sailing through uncharted waters, questions breaking over in heavy, white-crested waves, pounding her brain to a hopeless mush.

She doubted whether her mother would have been prepared for the changes in the law enabling children to trace their parents. She might have been persuaded to give her son up precisely because she was promised confidentiality, a promise that was ultimately broken. The thought of such exposure must have truly terrified her. Unglued by her past coming back to haunt her, she would have deeply feared the stain it would leave on her neat and tidy life. What would the Rudges have said, the Mainwearings, her own flesh and blood? No wonder she'd come undone. No wonder she'd succumbed to blackmail, anything to protect her existence. And yet…

Although Helen felt shock, she was also left with a sour taste in her mouth. Being a pregnant teenager, albeit at a time when it was practically outlawed, was hardly the end of the world in today's more liberal climate. It wasn't the sort of thing you allowed yourself to be blackmailed for, your daughter threatened. Her mother had made an error of judgement that many others had made before her and would continue to make. That was all, Helen thought uneasily.

Her thoughts flipped back to Lee. As far as she knew, he'd never embarked on his personal journey of discovery. He'd been going to, or so he told the Wellings, but he hadn't.

And he was still out there.

Somewhere.

Rain sprayed over her face like blood from an open wound. Helen struggled with the cottage keys and let herself in. She phoned Jewel immediately.

"Is Ray about?"

"Yeah," Jewel drawled, "do you want to speak to him?"

"No. I wondered if you could do something for me. I need you to be discreet."

"Go on," Jewel said, voice pricking with interest.

"Can you dig out the prints from the Freya Stephens file?"

"Thought the police had them."

"I had another set made. I want you to see if she's wearing earrings."

"You OK?" Jewel said sounding worried.

"I'm fine. Give me a call back when you've done it."

Helen could almost hear Stratton say, so what? Even if the woman wasn't wearing them, it didn't prove that she was or wasn't driving the van. Neither did it mean that the wearer was connected to the crime. In isolation it was meaningless, but that's how it often was when you were gathering evidence, finding that particular fibre, linking it with that particular bloodstain, that foot or fingerprint.

Her cell phone rang.

"No earrings," Jewel said.

"You sure?"

"Certain."

"Thanks, Jewel. And could you be a darling and leave the prints over in the coach-house for me?"

"I suppose that's all right," Jewel said, though she didn't sound as though it was.

"I can't thank you enough. And one more thing," Helen said.

"Yes?"

"Be good."

There was something else she should have done, she thought, punching in another number. It meant calling someone she hadn't spoken to in several years.

*   *   *

"So what are you saying exactly, Winston?" Helen said, imagining Winston's large, smiley face at the other end of the telephone. Winston Maddison was a Drugs Squad officer.

"There've been no reports of dodgy gear in our patch recently."

"None at all?"

"Not here."

"Where else then?"

"Worcester."

She expressed surprise. Worcester was such a pleasant, leafy city. But then every city has a grim underbelly.

"The purity of heroin on sale at the moment is twice as high as cities like Manchester," Winston told her. "It's to do with geography and the way it's imported. To travel to Manchester it's cut through other dealers so that the purity is around 20 to 30%. In Worcester it's between 50 to 60%. Coupled with this, it's become much cheaper. Does that help?"

Not really, she thought. "You've been great, thanks."

"Keeping all right?" There was softness in Winston's voice.

"Fine. And you?"

Winston gave a big loud laugh. "Me? I'm *always* good."

"Busy enough?" Helen grinned.

"Just holding back the tide, holding back the tide. Know how it is."

She did. And she missed it.

That afternoon she went for a walk to clear her mind. She had two strands of a story, the Karen Lake side of it, and now the Lee element. It didn't necessarily mean that there was any connection, she thought.

When she got back she phoned her dad, but he was out. Then she tried the British Association for Fostering and Adoption and was given a number for the Midlands office. She rang it and listened to a recorded message telling her to phone between nine in the morning and one in the afternoon. She wondered whether to take a shot at phoning one of the care homes in the area but instead plumped for a call to social services where she had the unusual experience of talking to a social worker based in Birmingham who was neither suspicious nor strung out.

"It's different now," he said.

"But?"

"Kids in care still suffer the same psychological problems."

"Like?"

"While some come out well-adjusted and relatively unscathed, leading fruitful lives, there's a high proportion who experience significant problems with anger management and violence. It stems from a basic difficulty in trusting others, especially where there's been evidence of abuse. It's estimated that one in three of the prison population are from care homes."

"I never trust statistics," Helen said with a laugh.

"Me neither," he said, "but the truth is youngsters need money when they come out of care. In a perfect world, they should receive counselling and follow-up, but you'd be surprised how many fall through the net. A fair number end up being homeless within a couple of years of leaving. For those lucky enough to get a job, they may have problems with being told what to do – they identify the individual responsible with authority and abuse, either real or imagined. Sometimes it's just easier to turn to crime."

Pretty bleak, then, Helen thought, thanking him for his time. And which path had Lee chosen?

The wind had picked up, buffeting the tiny cottage. She lay in bed listening to it howling through the trees. Her mind was wandering again. She was thinking about Lee Painter. About Karen Lake. She was thinking about possible connections. No, she thought, ridiculous.

Her half-brother was entirely innocent. There was no evidence to suggest any link to Karen Lake. Like the guy at Social Services said, some kids leave care and go on to lead fruitful lives. She could think of a couple of well-known writers who'd done just that. Why shouldn't Lee be one of the lucky few? Why should he conform to some kind of stereotype? He was understandably curious about his past – at least it showed some spirit – but maybe he'd discovered enough and, after consideration, made the simple decision to walk away, take it no further. Or, fearing rejection, he might have bottled out, might have been wary of bringing the walls crashing down.

But if he'd been tempted by crime, she thought warily, could it indicate something more sinister?

Looking at the worst-case scenario, she guessed Lee would be operating in the place where he'd grown up, the place he knew best, where he had contacts, a base, some geographical knowledge: Birmingham, the obvious magnet.

Then again, perhaps he *had* talked to their mother and, because she was decent and kind, she'd given him some money, no threats, or coercion. That would explain why, if it was Lee, he'd shown up at the funeral. He'd come to pay his respects. But why hadn't he introduced himself, she mused? Because other, more base, more questionable motives were at play?

She considered the sunglasses. Violet Wellings said that Lee was the spitting image of his mother. Perhaps that's why he'd worn them: to deliberately conceal his identity and protect their mum's memory. Yes, Helen thought, drifting off to sleep. She liked that story better.

CHAPTER SEVENTEEN

THE NEXT MORNING HELEN received a call from Aunt Lily.

"How are you, dear?"

"I'm fine. Taking a bit of a break, actually."

"Good for you. After all that hoo-ha with that wretched woman, you deserve it. I gather from your dad the police were unable to trace the money. Beats me why your mother let her get away with it."

"Aunt, can we not talk about it any more? I'd rather forget it ever happened."

"Of course, dear, sorry," Aunt Lily said in a businesslike fashion. "Did you get my photographs?"

"I'm not at home. Ray's lent me one of his holiday cottages for a few days."

"Oh well, they'll keep. You can look at them when you get back."

Yes, Helen thought grimly, what a treat. Wait a minute, what if...

"Staying anywhere nice?" Aunt Lily punctured her thoughts.

"Deepest, darkest Worcestershire."

Aunt Lily made some complimentary remarks about the county, and prattled on about Helen's father.

"How is he?" Helen said, feeling guilty for not being in touch.

"Not at all bad. He spent the weekend with the Rudges. I gather he goes out to lunch quite often. He's joined a bridge club on Thursday afternoons and a computing course at the local college. Would you believe, he's also enrolled in a ballroom dancing class."

Helen smiled. So like her dad to chuck himself into activity, she thought. Despite retirement, he was still a workaholic. It might even be the saving of him.

"That's not to say he doesn't have his moments," Aunt Lily said. "It's always the long evenings that are worst. He'll feel better in the summer."

Helen wasn't so sure. The winter was made for sadness. Somehow it was more bearable because of it. The summer was definitely for lovers. At least that's how she felt. "Aunt Lily, you remember what you said about Mum, about her having no past."

"Yes, dear?"

"Was that your own impression, or did you mean it in the literal sense?"

"Both, I suppose."

"So Dad was as much in the dark as you?"

"I *think* so. We never really discussed it. Does it matter?"

"No," Helen said. "Doesn't matter at all."

She tried the Midlands office of the BAFA again and enquired whether she could trace her half-brother.

"Sorry. You can register your name and, if your half-brother contacts us, we can let him know."

"But can't you put me in touch with him? Can't you alert him to my interest?"

"We're not allowed to do that, dear."

"There's no other way?" Helen pleaded. "I can give you addresses and names, the area where he might have been placed."

The woman was adamant. "As the law stands at the moment, it rests with the adopted person to make

258

contact. There's a new law due to be passed whereby birth parents can trace children they gave up for adoption pre 1975, but that's not much help to you, I'm afraid."

Damn, Helen thought. "Could you explain to me how tracing works then?"

"You mean when the adopted child wants to find his birth mother?"

"Yes."

"All adopting parents are legally bound to tell a child that he or she is adopted. They're usually supplied with information about the natural mother, which they can pass on."

"But what if the child grew up in care?"

"He or she should still have access to their file. If, for some reason, this isn't available, a birth certificate can always be applied for. This will include the mother's name."

"What about the father?"

"Often that information's not available."

"Are there any other details?"

"The certificate will also state the hospital in which the child was born."

"So that might be a starting point for a search?"

"It might," the woman said cagily. "However, some natural parents leave letters or register a means by which their children can contact them, if they wish."

"Really?"

"It does happen."

Helen doubted her mother would have done such a thing. Then again, she couldn't believe her being a pregnant, underage teenager. "What type of information is stored in the files?"

"In the case of an adopted child, the original name, birth mother's name and name of the agency that carried out the placing. The records might contain an address where the mother was living at the time of the adoption."

"Who compiles the records?"

"The social workers involved. Obviously, the more time has elapsed, the more likelihood that information might be mislaid or lost."

"Right," Helen said, wondering how Lee managed to track her mother down. "And when a child decides to find his birth mother, does he receive any form of preparation?"

"Absolutely. The law requires that people, who don't know their birth name and were adopted before November 1975, must be counselled before they're able to obtain the relevant information."

"So there are definitely safeguards in place?"

"Yes."

Helen thanked the woman for her time. Like rules, safeguards could always be broken, she thought.

Helen nipped back to the coach-house over the lunch hour. She was fairly certain she wouldn't be spotted. Ray usually went to the Plough and Harrow for a sandwich and a large gin. Jewel never missed the opportunity to go into town.

On the way in, she stopped off at a newsagent and, though she didn't smoke, bought a packet of cigarettes and a box of matches.

Along with the photographs of Karen Lake, there was a large hard-backed envelope on the kitchen table, with Aunt Lily's writing on it, presumably put there for her by Ray or Jewel. Helen picked it up, took it back to the sanctuary of the car and opened it.

She'd never been a fan of digital photography. Partly because digitals could never be used as evidence in court, mostly, though, because pixilated images lacked tone and definition. Although taken from the best of intentions, Aunt Lily's captured moments of family grief felt like an intrusion, a violation, a bit like the crime scene shot, she thought. As she stared at the sombre-looking faces, the black and grey clothing, the helplessness in her father's eyes, she found half of her brain tuning out, the other scanning, searching for the wraparounds, the white skin, the…

What was it about him, she thought? It wasn't a family likeness – she wasn't even sure if this was Lee –. but more a triggering of a distant memory, the same kind of sensation she'd experienced when she saw him on the day of the funeral. She tried, instead, to look at his hands, which were crossed over in front of him, his stance, feet slightly apart, his jaw clenched. None of it looked natural. This was not a man at ease. Then again, few looked relaxed at funerals. And wait, she thought, staring at the left side of his face. Yes, she felt her heart flutter. The guy was wearing a single hoop ear-ring.

Spiriting the photographs away, she checked the road atlas, and looked for the best route to take to Albion Place.

It didn't look so bad by day. Sunshine painted the sky. The houses looked less threatening. There were no signs of disgruntled youth. Judging from the closed curtains at Albion Place, Helen guessed nobody was up yet.

Praying the car would be all right, she parked it outside and fought her way through a path overgrown by scrawny weeds, and tried the bell. It didn't work. She rapped at the door. When this failed to produce a response, she found a stone and chucked it up against the front bedroom window. Still nothing. She tried again. This time, the curtains were wrenched apart, the window flung open. A woman's face, etched with anger, darted above the window-ledge. She had long red hair of such a synthetic hue it had to be dyed.

"Fuck do you think you're doing?"

Helen blended a smile into her voice. "Sorry to disturb you, but I was wondering if I could talk to you about Karen."

"You police?"

"No."

"Then you can piss off." The window shut with a resounding smack.

Helen exhaled heavily and resisted the urge to kick something. Picking up an empty can of lager smirking on the doorstep, she chucked it up against the window. It fell back down with a tremendous clatter.

"I can do this all day, if I have to," she shouted at the top of her voice, eyes fixed on the closed curtains. "I just want to talk. I was Karen's friend. It won't take…"

The front door swung open, startling her. The woman, who was both smaller and younger than she'd appeared at the window, stared at her with a scathing expression. Her arms were folded in front of her. She was wearing a pale lilac housecoat, the sort Helen's gran used to wear.

Helen coughed, tried to recover her equilibrium. "As I was saying, I'm a friend…"

262

"And I'm the Prime Minister's wife." The woman's blue eyes narrowed to suspicious slits. "You're no friend of Karen's. She wouldn't have mixed with your sort," she said, sweeping Helen with a disparaging glance.

Time to produce the fags, Helen thought, offering the pack to the woman. "You're right there," she gave a dry laugh, "but could we talk inside?"

The woman regarded her for a moment then eyed the cigarettes. Helen produced a light. The woman snatched at the pack, opened it, shook out a cigarette, and took the light, exhaling deeply. "What's wrong with here?" she said, flicking a flake of tobacco from her tongue.

"For one, it's freezing," Helen said, making a pantomime of stamping her feet. "And two, what I have to say is private."

The woman gave another bloodless stare.

"Aren't you cold?" Helen persisted.

In answer, the woman took another drag of her cigarette. This was going nowhere fast, Helen thought. She could stand there all day with the woman bumming cigarettes off her. Desperate measures then.

"You know Adam Roscoe?"

"Roscoe?" the woman said, recognition lighting her eyes. "Haven't heard his name in years." Her voice seemed softer. There was almost a fondness in it. Oh God, Helen thought. "Bit of a sharp bugger. Got slung out, didn't he? And you knew him?"

"I was his friend."

The woman let her eyes travel over Helen's face and body. Yes, she seemed to say, I could imagine you were. "Best come in then."

The darkened hall was illuminated by a single low-voltage light bulb. A steep flight of stairs went straight up from an entrance reminiscent of Thirties-style architecture. The floor beneath their feet was covered in lino the colour of dried-up ketchup. Helen could feel the soles of her shoes sticking to its filthy surface. Looking down the length of the corridor, she saw that the walls were painted in an unflattering shade of green. There was no skirting board and, where the walls met the floor, the paint bubbled. Two closed doors, also painted green, led off to the left. The woman walked down the corridor into a small kitchen, the heels of her mules clicking on the floor. Helen followed, surveying the same toilet-green, the same squalor. Glancing out of the window on to a yard, she observed that it was piled high with rubbish and the remnants of what was once a washing-line.

Inside, four high stools were set against something that pretended to be a breakfast bar. So, minus Karen, three occupants, Helen surmised.

There was one wall cupboard and it was clear, both from the shade of paint and the holes in the wall, that two others had been ripped off. The cooker sat inches deep in grease and spilt food. Strangely, the refrigerator looked quite new and clean. There were two photographs taped to it, one of a young girl, maybe two or three years of age. She looked sickly. Wearing a pale blue sweater, she had the name *Kelly* embroidered onto it. The other snap was of an older woman with the young girl, this time with tubes attached to her nose, sitting on her lap. Next to it was an appointment card for the Birmingham Children's Hospital.

"How's Roscoe then?" The woman parked her rear against the edge of the grimy sink.

Helen slid the cigarettes over to her. "Haven't seen him for a while." That much, at least, was true. And now she never would.

"Good bloke, he was. Fair. Didn't believe in pulling you in, making a bloody song and dance, not like some of the bastards you come across nowadays. And you could trust him," the woman said, "wouldn't get you into any trouble or nothin'."

"About Karen," Helen said anxiously. She didn't want to get into talking about Adam. She didn't want to discover something else she didn't want to hear. Not that it mattered now.

"Didn't catch your name," the woman said.

"Helen. And yours?"

"Stacey." She took another drag. "Didn't know her well, to tell the truth. She hadn't been here that long, really."

"But you got on?"

"Well enough," Stacey shrugged.

"She have many friends?"

"Depends what you mean." There was a salacious note in her voice.

"Any particular clients, any blokes she saw more than others?"

Stacey's eyes flickered with distrust. She took a snatch of her cigarette. Helen could feel the conversation slipping through her fingers again. "What's it to you?"

"We had a mutual friend."

Stacey gave a derisive smile. "Been on the game long, have you? Come to think of it, you never said how you and Karen met?"

265

"We met professionally."

Stacey rolled her eyes. "This is a wind-up."

"Karen wanted some photographs done."

"What sort of photographs?"

"Portraits."

"That what they call them?" Stacey leered.

"Straight up, nothing dirty about them."

"You're a photographer?"

"Yes."

"Got the snaps with you?" Again the same distrustful look.

"They're in the car."

"Get them."

Helen wavered unsure whether this was some kind of test, or whether the woman was waiting for an opportunity to get rid of her. "All right," she said.

"Leave the fags," Stacey said, putting her hand over them, a cunning look in her eye.

Helen nodded, decided it was best to call her bluff. She sped down the corridor, left the front door on the latch, pleased to find that her car had all four tyres and no obvious signs of damage. Unlocking it, she reached in and took out the photographs of Karen Lake and the single digital shot of the unnamed man.

By the time she returned, another woman was sitting in the kitchen. She, too, was smoking. Taller than Stacey, she had a fuller build. Her hair was dark, with bright blonde highlights. It stuck out like a bush. Like Stacey, she wore a dressing gown. Like Stacey, she wore an uncompromising expression.

Helen handed the photographs over. The other woman looked at them, too. Helen watched their expressions change from cold lack of interest to wonderment.

"Fuckin' hell," the other woman said, fingering the prints. Her mouth had dropped open and the cigarette was hanging tenaciously to her lower lip.

"You reckon you could make Jade here look this good?" Stacey said, nudging her friend's elbow with a shallow laugh. "Hang on, who's this?" Stacey said, picking out the photograph of the funeral mourner.

"Oh, a friend of mine," Helen bluffed, watching both women intently for signs of recognition.

"Not much to look at, is he?" Jade gave a coarse laugh.

"Don't know how you can tell with those fuckin' silly sunglasses on," Stacey jeered. "Who does he think he is, some tosser in The Matrix?"

Another theory blown, Helen thought. "So you knew nothing about Karen's plans?"

"Nah," Stacey answered. Jade just shrugged.

Helen wondered how far she could push it before they realised who she was. "What was Karen like?"

Another couple of shrugs.

"Was she happy, sad, depressed?" Helen persisted.

"Wouldn't you be?" The woman called Jade cast her eyes around the room.

"Is that why she took drugs?"

"What do we know?"

"You surprised that she died of an overdose?"

Jade exchanged a knowing smile with Stacey. "Nothing surprises us."

"What the fuckin' hell's she doing here?"

Everyone's eyes swivelled towards the doorway. A slim woman was standing there. She was dressed in a long camel coat, buttoned up to the neck, and she wore long black leather boots. She looked entirely out of place except for her worn-down, pitted complexion.

The skin looked as if it were formed from a natural sponge. She could have been twenty-five or fifteen years older. She turned accusingly on the others. "What have you told her? What have you said?"

Jade spoke first. "Nothin' Shirl. Nothin' we didn't already tell the law."

"She's a photographer," Stacey said, thrusting the photographs towards Shirl, trying to appease her. "Took some lovely pictures of Karen." But Shirl wasn't buying it. She snatched up the prints, cast her eyes over them, and threw them on the floor.

"I've seen the fancy car you drive," she spat at Helen, "seen the clothes you wear. You're that woman, the one they said Karen was blackmailing."

Helen paled, felt three pair of eyes fasten on to her. She wondered how quickly she could run down the corridor and get out of the building. Then she had another idea. Glancing at the fridge, observing the familial likeness, she decided to take her chances.

"How's your daughter, Shirl? Her name's Kelly, isn't it?"

"What?" Sudden fear chased across the woman's face.

"Must be comforting having your mum take care of your little girl, especially with her being so ill. Mind, hospitals are brilliant these days."

"Get out of here before I deck you," Shirl snarled, taking a step forwards. The air felt electric. The others bunched up behind her.

Helen put both hands up. "It's OK. It's cool." Then she bent down, collected the photographs, straightened up, and decided to go for the head shot. "Does the name Lee Painter ring a bell?"

All three women looked at her blankly.

Then she left.

On the way back to the cottage, she decided to call on the Wellings for a second time. She wanted to show them the photograph to see whether the man in the picture could be Lee Painter, her half-brother.

Mr Wellings opened the door, saw who it was, and just as quickly closed it. Baffled, Helen knocked once more. This time, and to her amazement, Violet answered. Bent almost double, she stood inexorably, her eyes drilling into Helen.

"Sorry, dear. We're having our tea."

"Won't take a moment," Helen smiled.

Violet's lips screwed into a frown. "It's inconvenient."

"I could come back later, if you prefer."

"I'd prefer if you went away." And the door was closed.

Helen returned slowly to the car. She sat inside for a good five minutes, trying to work it out. Was someone following her, watching her movements, warning people off?

She picked up the photographs again. They were covered in grime and dust. She flicked through them once, then a second time, more slowly, ran a hand over the passenger seat, checked the glove compartment, leant over and looked in both footwells, moving the seats back and forth to make absolutely certain.

But there was no mistake. Some kind of sleight of hand, she thought, baffled, or maybe it had slid under a piece of furniture. Either way, the digital picture had disappeared.

A pall of darkness hung over the cottage. Switching on the interior light of the car, she searched again, in vain, for the lost print. Resigned, she climbed out of the car and let herself in, taking care to bolt the door. After she'd poured herself a large glass of wine, she picked up the phone to Stratton. She needed to hear his voice.

"Hello, stranger."

"Oh, it's you." He didn't sound as pleased to hear from her as she'd hoped. Not his fault, she thought. She couldn't really blame him. "This a social call or business?" he asked.

"Social."

"No questions, no information required, no theories?"

Ouch, she thought. "Where are you?"

"Home. And you?"

She explained, feeling guilty for taking off and not telling him.

"Sounds nice."

"It's a bit lonely, actually. I'm not far away from you. Do you fancy meeting up? I could drive over."

He waited a beat. She felt her stomach creep with disappointment. "To tell the truth," he said, "I'm knackered. I've only just got home. Yesterday I started at six and finished at two in the morning."

"Of course, sorry, I should have thought."

"It's this fatal stabbing at Selly Oak I'm involved with."

"Right. Another time, then."

Neither of them spoke for a moment. Helen felt desperately uncomfortable. "Did you hear about Adam?" she blurted out.

"Yes." This was followed by a dreadful silence. "I'm sorry," Stratton said, at last.

For whom, she thought? For Adam's sticky end or for her? Or because there would always be the spectre of his ghost haunting them? "Look, I'm sorry about everything," she said. "Life's been a bit strange. Just wanted to say, once I've sorted myself out, I'd really like to see you again."

"Fine."

"I'll phone you."

"Do that."

"'Night then."

"Goodnight, Helen."

CHAPTER EIGHTEEN

THERE ARE STILL PUBS in the West Midlands entirely populated by men. One of them is a tiny boozer in Cradley Heath. Frequented by second and third generation unemployed, it has grand views of a former steel factory. Helen knew this because Adam told her. He drank there, not out of choice, but because it was business.

Through painful experience, she'd become sceptical of the concept of trading information. It seemed wide open for abuse on either side: handlers getting too close to their 'grasses', 'grasses' getting too close to their paymasters. But she wasn't a paymaster, she told herself. She wasn't offering promises, or bribes, or good turns. She was simply trying to track down her half-brother. That was her story. It was also the truth.

Helen parked outside. Criminals are like anyone else, she thought. They stay close to their roots, their friends, their stamping ground. Whether or not Lee was a villain remained to be seen but, geographically speaking, she guessed that this was as good a place to begin as any. More to the point, she didn't know where else to start.

She swung open the door and walked inside. A beery fragrance caught at her nostrils as did the powerful scent of men's bodies. Apart from the noise of a fruit machine, the sound of Muzak, there was little conversation. The room fell silent on her approach.

Six men were clustered around the bar, pints of mild and bitter in their hands. There was a pool table in one corner where, cues poised, four guys stood and watched. The rest were seated on chairs and faded velvet banquettes with the stuffing spurting out. Roughly twenty pairs of eyes fastened on her.

A barman gave her a steely glare. The guys at the bar wordlessly parted, letting her in, then closed rank behind her. She could feel the men's breath on the back of her neck. Feel the intimidation. She'd weathered this kind of stuff before, she told herself. She wasn't leaving.

She smiled hesitantly, ordered a drink. The barman ignored her. He carried on drying a glass with great precision, as if wiping a shotgun free of prints. When a man came up to the bar after her and ordered a round, he was served. Immediately.

She didn't know what to do. She was the only woman in the room. Nobody to appeal to, nobody to reason with.

Another man pulled alongside her. He was short, stocky. His brown leather jacket was open revealing a black open-neck shirt. Apart from that, he had no real distinguishing features. Colourless best described him, she thought, watching as the others backed away.

"What are you having?" he said, turning towards her. He had the smile of an assassin, she thought, warm on the surface, cold underneath.

"Vodka and tonic," she replied, "thanks."

"V&T and a straight Scotch, no ice, no water," the man said.

They were served with speed, without hesitation, no payment required. Helen knew immediately that she was in too deep, too quickly. The click of cue on ball confirmed it. It sounded like a gun cocking.

"Don't see too many women here," he said, his cool eyes razoring into hers, "certainly not girls on their own. A word to the wise," he added, leaning in close so that his lips almost brushed her face, "*not* a good idea." Helen resisted the urge to back away. "So what are you doing here?" he said, pulling at his drink.

"Looking for someone."

"Oh yeah, who?"

"A man."

A slow smile crept over his face.

"My half-brother."

The man arched an eyebrow. "You think you'll find him here?"

"Everyone has to start somewhere," she smiled nervously.

"Did you hear that, Richie?" the man said, turning around theatrically, addressing a man standing nearby who had two fingers missing from his left hand.

Richie let out a laugh. "What did he do? Rob a bank, stick a knife in someone?"

Helen swallowed. "I don't know. I'm not sure."

"What's his name?" her host asked.

"Lee," she said, "Lee Painter."

The man sniffed, rubbed his chin with his hand. "Never heard of him. You, Rick?"

"Nah, either small-time, or before my time," he grinned.

"So why did you want to see him, something important, was it?" The guy in the leather asked.

Shit, better stick with the main story, she thought. "Our mother died and I thought he should know."

"*Should?*"

"I thought it was his right," she stammered.

"Close family, are you?"

"Not really."

"Then why the fuss?"

Helen attempted a smile. "I just told you."

The more he studied her, the more scared he made her feel. She couldn't help but sweat. Her stomach felt completely knotted. "Look, you're right," she said, reaching for her bag, "I can see I'm wasting your time."

"There was a guy," another man said, drawing close. He was taller than the others, didn't look so hard. "Don't remember his last name or nothin' but he was called Lee."

"You know him?" she said, not sure whether this was good or bad luck. Not sure she wanted to stick around to find out.

"He didn't say that," the man in the leather jacket snarled, waving the tall guy silent.

This time she flinched. The aggression in the man's voice was palpable. He turned to Helen with a short, restricted smile. "What makes you think this half-brother of yours wants to see you anyway?"

This was a really crap idea, she thought, trembling. Positively dangerous, and how could she know that the Lee they were talking about was her half-brother? She was just boxing in the dark. With all the courage she could muster, she picked up her bag, making to go. "Sorry, I've obviously come to the wrong place."

"You're in a bloody hurry, all of a sudden," he said, clamping a muscled hand around her wrist. "You on the level? You're not one of them undercover cops, are you?"

"No," she gasped, wincing as his grip tightened.

"Good, now don't be so fuckin' miserable. Drink up. I know a man, if you get my drift. Got plenty of money on you?"

Helen felt the knot in her stomach tighten some more. All she wanted to do was get out of there, go home, go anywhere. He snatched at her bag, opened it, turning it upside down. Coins, lipstick, Tampax, wallet flew out over the counter. She froze in dismay as he picked out her wallet, opening it.

"Don't think he takes Barclaycard," he laughed raucously, stubby fingers moving onto and riffling through the notes. "About fifty quid," he said. "Could be your lucky night," he winked at the others.

The guy in the leather jacket drove a BMW 7-Series. He told her to get in the back. She wanted to protest but her tongue felt too big for her mouth. She was sweating all over now. Shaking. Legs like lumps of lead. Sick with fear. Make a wrong move now, and it might be the last. Once in, she thought, there was no way out. But if she resisted, she'd be hurt, maybe even killed.

"Get in the fuckin' back," he said, quiet but menacing.

She nodded, eyes wide with fear, reckoning her best bet was to go along with him. She had no real choice. She only hoped to God nobody found out about her previous line of work. Criminals weren't that discriminating.

Richie got in one side. The tall guy the other. Her horror complete.

She was taken down streets she'd not come across, past pubs she didn't drink in, through swathes of wasteland she'd never seen before. Every so often, they'd pull over, let two or three cars pass, indicate left then turn off right at the last minute. Christ, who did they think she was, she thought, trying to still the terror bubbling deep inside her? These guys were very good. They knew exactly what they were doing.

She tried to think, to keep her mind alert, to stop the fear from overwhelming her. The kind of places villains hung out in were pubs and clubs, gaming joints, pool halls, boxing rings. So where, in God's name, were they taking her?

They eventually stopped at a decrepit-looking row of shops. The driver got out. He walked along to the end and suddenly disappeared from view. She asked the others, in an anxious voice she hardly recognised as her own, where they were, where he was going, but they didn't answer. She could feel the sweat trickling down between her shoulders, pooling under her breasts. She could feel it under her arms. She could taste fear in her mouth. She had a mental image of her slain body being found by some old dosser.

At last she heard a soft footfall. "Everybody out." The driver had his face squashed up against the window like a demonic-looking gargoyle, his breath making a pattern on the glass.

Richie opened the door and let her out. Nobody laid a hand on her. No restraints, verbal or otherwise. In theory it would be easy to run, she thought, but to whom, to where?

The guy in the leather jacket led the way. They followed him back to a doorway leading down to what looked like a basement flat. The door opened onto a flight of stairs heading down to another door where a big, burly black man stood like a bouncer. After looking her up and down once, he waved them in.

A wall of sound greeted them. It took some time for her eyes to adjust to the light and noise. The place was packed with men and women, the air dense with cigarette smoke and cannabis. Some of the tension eased from her body. She didn't feel exactly safe but, among so many people, she felt slightly less under threat.

Two cages were suspended from the ceiling in which two semi-naked girls, their skin slick with oil, gyrated to a pulsating beat. Underneath them, bodies jerked and twitched like hangman's thieves. Hot-wired on coke or E, their sex seemed indistinguishable in the strobe lighting.

Leather Jacket bumped and jostled his way through to a bar. Cupping a hand to his mouth, he spoke to a pretty blonde who was serving. Following her gaze, he nodded and directed Helen and the others to a corner where an impossibly thin middle-aged man was sitting, legs crossed in an effete fashion, smoking a roll-up.

"Mind if we join you, Blackie?" Leather Jacket said, drawing up a chair.

Blackie blew out a plume of smoke and indicated for them to take a seat. He paid scant attention to Helen for which she was grateful.

"Blackie is blessed with a rare gift," Leather Jacket explained, turning his expressionless eyes on Helen. "Just as the gambler remembers the name of the horse who won the Gold Cup in 1983, the name of the jockey, his colours, his trainer, Blackie is a Who's Who of the lads in the game. But nothing's for free. Everything has its price."

Helen wondered what was in it for him, how much fifty pounds would buy?

"What do you want to know?" Blackie mumbled, not looking at her.

She tried to tame the shake in her voice. "I have a half-brother. His name's Lee Painter. He was born in Kidderminster, was put up for adoption but spent his life in care, possibly somewhere in the West Midlands. He came back to visit my mother's childhood home about four years ago. I haven't heard from him since, but I believe the Midlands is his patch."

Blackie nodded, took a drag of his cigarette. The others watched him like he was the Dalai Lama. Helen felt her skin crawl. "It's possible he might have known a prostitute called Karen Lake," she added.

Blackie frowned, clearly irritated by the interruption in his concentration. He flicked some ash off his cigarette. "Don't know any Karen Lake."

"Right. Sorry," she said.

"Twenty quid," he muttered.

Jesus, Helen thought. She took out her bag and slapped the money down on the table.

"*If* it's the same guy," Blackie said, "he's the nearly man."

Helen stared at him, perplexed.

"Nearly pulled it off, nearly made it, nearly got in with the big boys."

"A loser," the guy in leather interposed.

"Tosser, more like," Richie scowled.

She wanted to hit the pair of them. The last thing she wanted was Blackie put off his stride. "Was this guy blonde, stocky, pale-skinned?"

"Yeah."

Progress, she thought. Oh dear. "So what was he involved in?"

"Small-scale stuff, drugs, burglary, bit of this, bit of that. Spent more time in the nick than out on the street. Eventually got sent down."

Helen felt as if someone had pressed razor wire against her skin. So that's why he was unable to follow up the family connection. "Where?"

"Featherstone."

Wolverhampton, she thought. "He still inside?"

"Cost you another twenty," Blackie said, gazing off into the middle-distance.

Helen let out a sigh and put another note on the table.

"Came out eighteen months ago."

"Then what?"

"Dunno," Blackie said, his small eyes meeting hers. You're lying, she thought.

"Typical woman," Richie sneered, "always asking too many fuckin' questions." The others laughed.

Helen ignored them, kept her eyes on Blackie. "Who did Lee mix with? Who were his friends?"

"Anyone he could use," Blackie said, evasive.

"You said he nearly got in with the big boys. Who do you mean?" She pushed her last ten pound note towards him.

"Cost you more than that."

"It's all I've got."

He sniffed and took it.

"The new kids on the block."

"Which new kids?"

Blackie shook his head, took a drag.

The guy in the leather jacket stared at her. "The Park Lane Boys, you stupid cow."

Stunned, she hardly noticed being manhandled out of the club and onto the street. A rush of cold air brought her to her senses. She was alone with the man in the jacket. He had an iron-grip on her elbow, and was propelling her down the street and towards the BMW.

"What are you doing?" she said, badly frightened again.

He didn't answer. Chucked her in the passenger seat. Got in next to her, locked the doors, drove off at speed. She didn't know what to do, how to react, which course of action might save her skin. Should she talk softly to him, argue, scream, or attempt to get out of the moving vehicle, attack him maybe? No, she thought, watching the streets fly by in a blur. Too risky.

"Where are you taking me?"

"Where do you think?"

Some piece of wasteland, a canal towpath, dark alley, derelict factory, anywhere he could do what he wanted and get away with it, she thought wildly. She attempted to talk again, to keep him connected.

"Shut the fuck up."

Shit, this was looking bad, she thought, desperately trying to keep a lid on her terror. Too often women died because they were too frightened to think.

"I'd like to thank you," she blurted out. "You didn't need to go to all this trouble."

He said nothing.

"I got what I wanted."

"Then you can thank me properly."

"But…"

"Nothing for free, I told you." There was a dangerous edge to his voice.

His words jabbed right through her. She felt a cold chill settle on her stomach, crawl up her spine. Was this some kind of divine retribution, she thought? Was it her turn? A sickening image of Rose flashed through her brain.

Crazily, she tried to formulate a plan. He had to get her out of the car. That's when he'd be at his weakest. Maybe she could injure him, slam his hand in the door, scream for help. But what if he had a gun or a knife…

The car pulled up with a screech, throwing her hard against the seatbelt, winding her.

"Get out," he said. She heard the locks pop up. "What are you waiting for, bitch," he snarled, "I said get the fuck out of here and don't come back."

She scrabbled for the door, expecting a sick joke. But it wasn't. Thrusting the door open, she hurled herself out. With a squeal of brakes, the car took off, laying a thick band of rubber on the road.

She looked around her, feeling dizzy, hardly able to believe her eyes. The pub was closed, shutters drawn up.

And her car was exactly where she left it.

CHAPTER NINETEEN

SOMEONE WAS BATTERING DOWN the door. At least that's what it sounded like. She got up, went to the bedroom window and looked outside, catching her breath in pleased surprise. Joe Stratton was standing there. Then she saw his face. It was dark with anger.

Too exhausted to undress the night before, she'd slept fully clothed. It looked like it, she thought, catching her ragged reflection in the wardrobe mirror as she tried to smooth the creases from her face and clothes.

Glancing at her watch, she sped down the narrow cottage stairs. It was two-thirty in the afternoon. She'd slept for over nine hours.

"All right, I'm coming," she shouted, wondering what was wrong. She opened the door and he plunged straight in, almost knocking her off her feet.

"Well, hello, how are you?" she said, squashing herself against the wall. But Stratton was in no mood for humour.

"What the bloody hell do you think you're playing at?" he roared.

"Tea, coffee?" she said, trying to defuse him.

"This isn't a social call," Stratton said coldly.

"I can see that. How did you track me down?"

"Through your employer."

Thanks, Ray, she thought. "So what crime have I committed?"

His eyes levelled with hers. "Think yourself smart, don't you? Think yourself bloody clever?"

"If you've come here to hurl insults, you can leave now," she said, flashing with anger.

"Have you any idea what you were doing last night?"

She felt her mouth drop open.

"What sort of mess you could have got yourself in?" Stratton persisted.

"How did…"

"Is this your idea of sorting yourself out?"

"Look, Joe, I don't know how the hell you got your information."

"From a reliable source."

She closed her eyes for a moment. The guy in the leather jacket. He'd approached her, taken care of her. In spite of the threats, he'd let her go. How dumb could she be?

Stratton hadn't finished. "In spite of your squeamishness, I gather you paid an informer."

She let out a groan and sank into the nearest chair. "I didn't know. Wasn't like that," she began.

"Wasn't it?" He sat down, too. Not much of the anger seemed to have dissipated.

She rubbed at her face with her hands. "I was looking for my half-brother."

"That's why I'm here," he said uncompromisingly.

Helen looked across at him, feeling her senses sharpen. "You know about Lee?"

"I do now."

"Thing is," Helen said, rippling with excitement. "Painter's the link. He knew Karen, I'm sure of it. He also had an involvement with the Park Lane Boys. Maybe he's pissed people off. Maybe that's why I've been threatened. It's quite possible he's…"

"Dead."

284

"What?" she gasped, hands flying to her head. "No," she said, shaking her head. "It's not true. I don't believe it. Not again." And what about the guy in the photograph? Who was he, for God's sake, a professional mourner, or someone with a different agenda?

Stratton was looking at her in the same way as when her mother died. "I'm sorry, Helen. I ran his name through criminal records this morning. He had a history of theft and drug offences, including possession. His involvement with the Park Lane Boys was minor, bottom rung. He did a bit of gophering. Baldly speaking, he was out of his league, wasn't up to the job. Got sent to Featherstone on a burglary charge, served three years. Came out eighteen months ago. Same month he was released, he was found dead by his landlady."

So that's why Blackie looked her straight in the eye, she thought. How much money would it have taken to get to the truth? Another fifty? A hundred for the story behind it? More? The strangled feeling in her stomach returned with a vengeance. "Murdered?" she said.

Stratton shook his head. "Drug overdose."

She felt her head swim. "But that's what happened to Karen Lake."

"So what? Karen was a prostitute with a habit. Painter was a crook with a habit." He was my flesh and blood, too, she thought, unsure whether she felt relief or sadness. She briefly considered whether to mention the blonde guy in the photograph to Stratton but he didn't look terribly amenable.

"More to the point," Stratton said, "Painter was already dead long before Karen suffered a fatal overdose."

He was right. Just as well she'd never entertained ideas of becoming a detective, Helen thought ruefully, she'd have been lousy at it.

She'd wanted Stratton to stay, to have a cup of coffee, but his caseload prevented it, or so he said. So she watched him leave, saw his car disappear from view, and was reminded of the last time she'd seen Adam. Same grim set of his shoulders. Same departing anger. Her fault. It seemed she was pathologically incapable of maintaining a relationship with a man, even a good one.

Walking glumly back inside, she sat down in Ray's kitchen, on one of Ray's chairs, and stared out of Ray's sitting room window at a landscape obscured by driving rain. She felt as if she were stuck at a crossroads. It didn't matter where she looked there was nowhere else to go. She'd exposed herself to danger. She'd wasted energy in pursuit of a dead man. No wonder Stratton thought her a fool. No wonder he was livid.

In spite of the weather, she decided to venture outside, to feel the rain on her hair, the chill against her skin. At least, these things were real, she thought, concrete and comprehensible.

The road was a mire of squashed animals and mud. Wind whistled through the telegraph wires, making them whine. Rain slashed at her face, stinging her eyes, penetrating her jacket, her clothes. Soon she'd have to return to the real world, she thought, to Ray's studio, to smiling brides and happy families, to visiting her dad and her batty old grandmother, to carrying the family secret.

And still the guilt remained.

After a mile or so, she turned back. It was growing dark. She was soaked through. Her jeans chafed at her shins and thighs. Her socks squelched in her shoes. Water ran off the fields and into the road in a torrent. She felt as wet as the time she was fished out of the canal. It's where it all began, she thought, where it all started to get complicated.

When she got back, she stripped off, took a long hot bath, and dressed in warm clothes. She'd just finished eating an omelette when her cell phone rang. Hoping it would be Stratton, she picked up.

"That Helen Powers?" The female voice was one she recognised but couldn't place.

"Yes."

"We met yesterday."

"I'm sorry," Helen said, racking her brains to put a face to the voice.

"At Albion Place."

"Shirley," Helen exclaimed. Then another more insidious thought took shape. "How did you get my number?"

"Jewel gave it to me, your receptionist."

I know who she is, Helen thought indignantly, wondering what tale Shirley had spun.

"How did you find out where I worked?"

"It was on the snaps," Shirley said sketchily. "Thing is, I've got some information for you."

"What sort of information?" Helen asked, suspicious.

"About Karen."

287

Do I honestly need this, Helen thought? It's done, finished, over. And why now? Why not tell me yesterday? "What about her?"

"I'd rather not discuss it on the phone. Could you come over to the house?"

You must be mad, Helen thought. Here I am, sitting by a nice warm fire, with the promise of an early night, and all you have on offer is a drive in the cold and rain to a Godforsaken rat hole for a nugget of knowledge that at best will prove irrelevant. "Look, Shirley, I really think this is probably a waste of both our time. Things have changed since yesterday. I'm no longer interested."

There was a slow intake of breath. "She wasn't working alone."

Helen felt as if she'd been drop-kicked. "What did you say?"

"Meet me at six and I'll explain."

She knew the risk. Even though she was meeting a single woman, Helen couldn't be sure Shirley would be alone. Remembering her training, she tried to phone Stratton to let him know what she was doing, but there wasn't enough battery on her phone to get a decent signal. She thought about stopping off en route and finding a phone box but, apart from the lack of time, she believed he'd either pour scorn on her efforts, or try to stop her. And she wasn't stopping. Not for anyone. If there were the slightest chance of getting to the bottom of it, she wasn't going to walk away. Not this time. Stupid, maybe, but she owed it to herself and, more importantly, to her mum.

The drive was a nightmare. She had to negotiate the rush hour. There was no let-up in the weather. Rain sprayed like shrapnel.

She pulled up in the seedy street, saw that a light was on in the upstairs bedroom, and made her way up the path. Encouraged by the downpour, the weeds had grown in strength and vigour. They stretched out to her legs as she passed, clinging to her, impeding her progress, intent on taking her down.

She noticed that the door was ajar. She stepped inside, called out softly. There was no answer. She called again, more boldly. Still no reply. She walked down the corridor, opening doors, peering inside, contemplating what she might find, just as she'd done when she'd worked as a SOCO. There were no surprises. Just a shabby house with shabby furnishings.

She made her way upstairs, her footsteps sounding impossibly loud, the stairs creaking with each tread. She poked her head around three doorways, cast her eyes over barely-furnished rooms, two double, one single, stared at the detritus of other people's lives, wondering which bedroom had housed Karen Lake's lifeless body, in which one she'd taken her final fix.

The door to another room was closed. Presuming it was the bathroom, she tapped on it, asked if anyone was in there, waited a few beats, then opened the door, a large part of her expecting a body to be hanging from the shower rail, or floating in the bath, drowned or with wrists sliced open. But there was nothing other than a smell of mould and the sound of silence. She glanced at her watch. It was ten minutes past six. Maybe Shirley had been held up by a demanding client. Maybe she was coming back from the hospital. Maybe she wasn't a very good timekeeper. However

Helen viewed it, she felt it would be a mistake to leave. It was too important. She'd sit it out, she told herself, but she wasn't staying inside. That really might be asking for trouble. She'd wait in the car.

She battled her way back down the path, feeling the moisture flatten her hair against her scalp. The wind had picked up and was crashing against her ears. The night felt heavy on her back.

Hoping to deter car thieves or vandals, she'd taken the precaution of parking underneath a street-lamp. Good, no dents, she thought, hurrying through the rain, but, somehow, the MR2 didn't look right. It wasn't sitting level on the road, for a start. There was a definite list. She ran up to the car, running her fingers down its side, then went round the front, crouching, examining the tyres, feeling the trickle of ice-cold rain down her neck. Shit, she cursed. The rear offside tyre wasn't flat. It was non-existent. She looked around her, furious, wondering which antisocial creature was responsible for the vandalism. There was nobody or nothing to see other than driving rain, empty streets, closed curtains and darkness. She was just weighing up her options when a guy pulled up alongside her in a work-van. He wound down the window, called to her, his voice muffled by the raging elements.

"My wheel's been nicked," she said, craning her head to get a better view of her Good Samaritan. It looked as if he, too, had been caught in the rain. He was hunched over the steering wheel, his features obscured by a hoodie plastered to his head.

"Just on me way home," he shouted to her in a thick Brummie accent. "I can give you a lift, if you like."

Her mother's voice rang in her head. *Never accept a lift from a stranger.* "No, I need to stay here. I have to meet someone."

"Tell you what, you keep dry in your car while I see what I can do."

"Right, thanks," she said, walking towards him. She watched him get out, move round to the back of the van, open the doors.

"Really appreciate this," she said, turning to go back to her car.

The blow from behind came without warning. Pain was her immediate response then shock. Her vision blurred. Her arms shot out at angles. The road seemed to leap up to meet her crumpled body. Then it went dark.

Very dark.

CHAPTER TWENTY

PART TWO

PITCH BLACK.

Helen lifted her head. Tremors of pain shot through her neck and skull as she collapsed back down. She was lying on her side in a foetal position. Half of her felt numb. She had no idea how long she'd been there. Could have been minutes. It could have been hours. There was a coppery taste of blood in her mouth.

She was blindfolded and gagged. Her wrists were tied behind her back, her ankles tightly bound. The space felt airless, hot, too hot. It smelt of oil and grease and petrol and made her light-headed. She could hear the muffled sound of music playing from a radio beneath the throaty roar of an engine. Rain hammered on the roof above her head. It sounded like gunfire. Then, with a chill that stole her breath away, the events leading up to her present predicament rushed in rebellion through her brain, and she realised where she was – in the back of the van.

Fear ricocheted through her. She'd witnessed the outcome of things like this. She knew what happened when people were abducted. She knew about young men trapping young women. What if she'd blundered into the world of the serial killer, she thought crazily, someone who'd taken a chance and seized the opportunity? What if this was his mobile killing-machine? Or was this the person who'd stalked her, the someone who'd lain in wait? You read about it all the time. Crazies with nothing better to do than frighten the life out of women. But no, she thought, her brain slowly forming the connections. It was linked to what happened before. She'd been set up. Perfectly straightforward. Absolutely simple. That's what the call from Shirley was about. There *was* someone else involved. The same someone who was driving the van. Maybe the man in the photograph. And how stupid, stupid, stupid of her to fall for such an obvious trick, she wailed. What was she thinking?

The gag stifled a sob. She'd taken one risk too many. No precautions. No excuses.

Courage was one thing, blind recklessness another.

To be so confined tapped into her most primitive fear. As a child she'd considered death with great seriousness and come to the conclusion that she didn't want to be buried when she died. She wanted to have one of those Viking funerals, like she'd seen in films where they sent you out to sea on a burning boat. That way, she calculated, if by some peculiar quirk of fate someone made a mistake, you had, at least, an even chance of escaping. Not so if you're buried six feet underground in a sealed wooden coffin.

She tried to wriggle her fingers and loosen the rope binding her hands. It wouldn't budge. She tried again, willing her hands to be thinner. Still no use. In desperation, she rubbed the restraints against the side of the van until her wrists chafed and her skin blistered and burnt. Nothing but pain. Panicking, she thought her mind might snap.

Got to keep calm, she told herself, got to breathe. Slow and steady. Mustn't think what might happen. Mustn't think of pain and possibilities, death and dying. Cling on to life, to hope. Without it, you're doomed. You're dead already.

She felt too disorientated to listen for anything out of the ordinary. All she could hear was the noise from the radio, the crackle of rain on the roof, the frightened voices in her head. But wait, she thought. There was something. She had a vague awareness of speed and the fact that they appeared to be travelling in a line. Straight road then? Motorway? Which one? North or South?

She tried to shift position, to feel with her body, to find anything that might aid her escape, but with her senses so severely restricted she felt helpless.

Somebody would raise the alarm, she convinced herself, somebody who knew and cared about her. That's how it worked. But nobody knew she was missing, she thought, flickering with fear. Nobody would realise until too late. She'd just be another body found at a roadside or in a shallow grave. Oh God.

Her mind teemed with images of the dead. She couldn't shut them out. They clamoured at the edges of her consciousness, screaming to get in, the road casualties, the murder victims, the mutilated, young and old. She thought her brain might explode in anarchy and confusion, but wait, she thought, sparking with hope, someone must have witnessed the attack if only from the sanctuary of their home. But it was winter, a nasty little voice inside reminded her. The curtains were drawn. A passer-by, somebody on the street then, she argued frantically, trying to remember if she'd registered anyone other than the van driver. She cast her mind back. It was slashing with rain. The streets were empty. Didn't matter, she told herself stoically. Someone would see her car. A busybody or jobsworth was bound to notice, complain, and report it. Then the police would come out…

Her stomach gave a sick lurch. Cars were abandoned every day. They didn't rate as a priority. They were considered a job for the council. Cars only mattered if there was a motorist inside, someone to steal, to extract money, from.

She twisted her head, trying to shake the cynicism from her thoughts. *Eventually*, she promised herself, someone would check with DVLA, identify the owner, try to contact her and realise that something terrible had happened. For the second time in her life, her face would be splashed across newspapers and television screens and…

No, she thought, with rising panic. Albion Place wasn't in some leafy suburb where people cared about their environment, their surroundings. Nobody would phone the council, or phone the police, or wait for the inevitable spat while officialdom dragged its feet. Nobody would give a shit. The chances were her car had already been towed away, stripped down, the plates removed, and the rest discarded and abandoned. She wouldn't be missed from work because she wasn't at work. She doubted if even her father, stoically fighting off his grief, would miss her until it was too late.

Where is this maniac taking me, she wanted to scream?

She strained to see through the slick of black. Hopeless. She tried to rub her face, to loosen the blindfold. Her right cheek lay against something scratchy, a threadbare piece of carpet or old rug. The fibres would transfer to her body, she thought coldly. Her hair, her DNA, and particles of clothing would be found in the flooring. It would help identify that she'd been there, in this van, owned by this nutter. What the fuck did any of it matter, she thought, stabbed by a blade of fear? She'd already be dead by then.

No, mustn't think like that. Too debilitating. Too dangerous. Got to focus. *You're alive*, she thought, repeating it over and over in her mind.

She tried to move, to wriggle, and relieve the numbness in her side. The vertebrae at the base of her neck, and her head hurt so much she thought one of them might be fractured. If that was the case, she didn't give much for her chances. Was her brain already swelling? Was it already starting to expand and push down on the areas controlling breathing, shutting it down?

Stop it!

No time for hysteria, she thought, breathing hard. She had to believe. Her survival depended upon it. What she needed was a plan. He had to stop some time, she reasoned. He'd need fuel for the van. He'd want sleep, food and water, a toilet, all the things vital to the human body. All the things one takes for granted. Ordinary functions. And when would she sleep and eat again? When would she taste water instead of this saliva-sodden piece of filthy sacking? What if she wanted to pee? She felt almost schizophrenic, one side of her flipping into madness, the other pulling back, constricted by trying to keep sane. Mustn't let fear get a grip, she ordered herself. Use up more air if you panic. Waste energy. Definitely mustn't cry. Don't want to block the airways.

Absurd, can't help it…

The aural landscape was changing. The radio was switched off. The van wasn't going quite so fast now. It felt as if it were twisting, travelling along lesser roads. She felt her body slipping and sliding with the motion. Minutely adjusting her position, she put pressure on her knees, tilting her rear, feeling around with her fingers. She tried to take stock. She'd had a mobile phone in the pocket of her jacket, the side she was leaning on. She tried to make out the outline. It would be bulky, uncomfortable, but she couldn't feel anything there at all. She concluded that he must have frisked her and taken it. What else, she thought? Her bag was in the car. Her keys were probably dropped in the gutter. All she had was the watch she was wearing and a tiny slim-line torch her dad had given her, which she carried in an inside pocket of her jacket. That was it.

Gritting her teeth against the gag, she strained to hear the sound of a clock chiming, aircraft flying over, a factory alarm, anything that could give some idea of her whereabouts. Again, all she could hear was the steady noise of the engine. And it was slowing, she thought. Everything was slowing.

Ice-cold air blasted over her face and body. Her ankles were caught in a painful grip, the rope untied. Then, with one wrenching movement, she was grabbed hold of, pulled out feet first, breech-birth style, and dumped into the outside world.

She felt something cold against her temple. She couldn't see it, but she could feel the shape of the muzzle, feel the weight of the gun. A sharp band of fear tightened around her head. He had her complete and unquestioning obedience. She knew what guns could do. Especially at close-range. She'd seen the star-shaped wounds, the way the skin is stretched and ruptured. She'd seen the ragged exit-holes. This man was clearly a highly dangerous individual.

Although they weren't difficult to come by if you moved in the right circles, it takes organisation to get hold of a firearm. It takes skill to know how to use one. While anyone can grab an eight-inch carving knife from a kitchen drawer, or take a hammer from a workshop, a gun required premeditation, and a measure of expertise. It spelt serious player, serious trouble.

This was a dangerous time for him. Anyone could see them: a guy walking his dog, an adulterous couple. Dangerous for her, too. If she made the wrong move, he might cut his losses, kill her and flee. She wanted to talk, to plead with him, appease him, but all she could make were guttural noises.

"Shut the fuck up," he snarled. This time there was no Brummie accent, no pretence. He sounded rough-cut, rural, small town, though she couldn't place where.

She fell silent. Her legs were stiff and unyielding as if they didn't really belong to her. The rain felt heavier against her face, more textured, sleet or snow, perhaps. She could smell earth. The ground beneath her trainered feet felt soft. She heard the wrenching sound of a door opening. He roughly guided her, ordered her to sit down on a kind of ledge, which she did. Then he swung her legs up, crudely bending them, forcing her into a cramped sitting position. As the door was shut behind her, it sounded like a coffin lid being closed.

She found herself resting against something solid, the side of her head against a kind of grille. She could only stretch out her legs a little way before she came to an edge. She guessed she was in some sort of compartment. Again she could smell oil but this time it was coupled with the smell of leather.

She heard the cadence of her assailant's footsteps recede. There was the sound of opening and slamming doors. A scuffling of boots on earth making her consider whether he was wearing the heavy-duty type with ridges that would leave foot impressions. Then there was the sound of liquid being poured, or rather thrown. She could smell it: petrol. A noise, like a huge gust of wind, battered her temporary prison. She could almost feel the surge of heat. For a horrible moment, she wondered whether she was going to be burned alive, but, as she listened to the crackle of flames, she realised he'd torched the van, destroying all evidence.

All perfectly planned, choreographed and orchestrated.

Again she felt an icy draught to the right of her, felt the air disturb, heard the creak of leather, felt the weight of another redistributing her own, then the sound of an engine starting up.

They bumped along at a terrific pace. She felt as if she were on a roller-coaster ride without any harness. Her teeth rattled in her head, and she wanted to cry out, scream, but couldn't. Eventually, the vehicle crossed back onto road, and the ride became smoother.

There was little or no sound, no noise of passing cars, not a lorry rumble. She'd made two important deductions: she was riding in some kind of four-wheel-drive. Having crossed a field or some kind of track, they were travelling on a road that was both quiet and empty.

She began to wonder about her abductor. She thought about his voice, his real voice, what he might look like, who he was. Was he the mastermind? Was he the man in the photograph, the man she'd mistaken for her half-brother? She thought back to the funeral, visualised him, recalled her sense of recognition. In her blinded state, her other senses felt more heightened. She envisaged him close-up: the pasty complexion, the blond hair. He could have blue or green, brown or hazel-coloured eyes, but she imagined them as blue beneath the sunglasses. A picture was forming in her mind in the same way a photograph develops in the dark room. She swallowed hard. The image came into sharper focus. With a terrible sensation of danger, she remembered the guy who'd smiled at her, the man at the bar in The Pitcher and Piano.

So far he hadn't harmed her, she told herself. Not really. Not fatally. That was good. Very good. It's what all the experts said. She had to work with that.

If she could connect with him as one human being to another, build up a rapport, if necessary play on her vulnerability to satisfy his need to dominate, then maybe everything would be all right. Perhaps she could even talk her way out of danger. Every hour that she stopped him from hurting her was another towards building a relationship with him, another hour bought for someone to sound the alarm. In police terms, she knew that the first twenty-four hours of abduction were the most critical. If he were going to kill her, it would be sooner rather than later.

They'd stopped travelling. He seemed more relaxed, she thought with relief, as he let her out this time, more sure of his territory, more in control. The temperature was much, much colder. The wind seemed to blow straight from the Antarctic, nothing to break its strength, to temper its hostility. He was close to her. She could smell him: citrus and tobacco. She could smell her surroundings: vegetation, maybe gorse or bracken. She felt him loosening the gag, untying it. Right-handed, she thought, croaking a thank-you. He'd given her something back, she thought. Her voice. Words. The ability to communicate. Maybe he wanted to talk to her. Maybe, that way, things would be all right. Then she felt something surprisingly soft brush her skin, caress her face, clamp over her nose and mouth. She tried to cry out but she was smothered by and enveloped in it. As much as she struggled, resisted the urge to breathe, she could not evade the poisonous fumes rushing through and invading her airways. Almost at once, she felt her body stiffen then painfully jerk, uncontrollably, as if she were having a fit. Terror shot through her like an electric current. He held her fast with the same determination with which a cowboy rides a bucking bronco. It seemed to go on forever. Limbs convulsing. Pain. Mind detaching. Her last conscious thought was this was it. This was death.

Hers.

CHAPTER TWENTY-ONE

THE SMELL WAS SWEET, fetid, ripe and personal. The damp air choked with it. Already, she could feel it on her hair and skin, on her clothes. She identified it immediately. The odour of death was unmistakable.

She felt groggy, as if she had a rip-roaring hangover. She was lying sprawled on some kind of cushion or mattress. Even with the stench surrounding her, it smelt horrible, as if dozens of bodies had sweated, had sex, farted and pissed on it. And worse. With dismay she noticed there was wetness between her legs. Fear of being dead was swiftly replaced by fear of being alive.

In spite of her thick winter clothing, she was miserably cold. She could hardly feel her arms, and her hands felt as if they'd been cut off at the wrists. Her ankles were no longer bound together but there was little sensation in her feet and toes. Apart from the near-freezing temperature of her prison, she reckoned she was suffering from shock. Her insides were heaving. She felt dizzy with exhaustion, stupefied. She had a powerful thirst. She felt nauseous. She wondered how long it would be before her assailant returned. Dare she ask for a sip of water? Would he laugh, spit in her face, have pity? And who the hell was this individual who had delivered such chaos to her life? She thought of his many faces: the bloke in the bar, the one at the funeral, her abductor. And when he'd smiled at her was it bluff, or gamesmanship? She suspected the latter.

Still blindfolded, with hands tied together, she rolled and struggled to sit up then stand. She took a number of steps forward but something kept tugging on her, holding her back. She slowed her impulses, tried fractional changes of stance and movement, and discovered there was another rope around her waist, tethering her to some kind of wooden pole or strut. She was like a bear waiting to be baited, she thought.

Trying to decipher the extent of her small world, she took several paces forward, and found that she could step off her tiny island onto what felt like another chunk of solid earth. She crouched down, sniffed it. Soil and damp, she thought, mind bracing. A cellar. A dungeon. A tomb. She tried not to think of the implications.

She strained her ears for sound. No hiss of passing traffic, no human noise, no creak of floorboard, no gurgle of pipes. The silence felt thick and crushing. It pressed down on her. She called a tentative *hello* to try and shift its weight, to lighten the load, but it wouldn't budge.

The vulnerability of her position was obvious. Nothing she'd learnt from self-defence was going to help. She could do nothing unless allowed by *him*. She was at his mercy. Completely. No longer gagged, she could scream her lungs out, but there was no point. Nobody, other than her captor, would hear. It might make him angry. It might provoke severe punishment. It wasn't worth even trying. The only way to change her circumstances was to work out what he wanted from her and give it to him. Anything. Staying alive was all that mattered. Must focus on that, she thought. Think about it constantly, she kept repeating to herself in desperation.

Should she be passive and compliant, or difficult and spirited? One might turn him on and that was dangerous. The other might encourage him to bash her brains out. Unless both were part of the game plan, she froze inside. He'd killed before. That was obvious to her. Once that particular taboo is broken, further killings come more easily.

She sniffed the air. Crazy fantasies about the person whose corpse was lying putrefying somewhere nearby crowded her fractured mind. She wondered if it was a woman, what had happened to her, how she'd died, what weapon he'd used. Gun? Quite possibly. A knife, or hammer, ligature, all three? She wondered if the victim had resisted, if there'd been pain. Her kneecaps began to tremble. She didn't like to consider her own pain-threshold. Mental toughness was not the same as caring whether you had scalding water poured over you or a knife slicing through your flesh.

Got to escape, she thought, wondering if, by some form of contortion, she could telescope her body and force her rear through her looped hands, then slide them down behind her legs towards her feet and over her toes so that her hands were in front of her rather than behind. That way, she'd stand both a better chance of freeing and defending herself. She sat back down, made a vain attempt. Although slim, her clothing was too bulky. She couldn't even begin to push her rear through the gap between her arms. It had nothing to do with physical fitness and determination, but everything to do with flexibility, and she wasn't that bendy. Never had been.

Got to keep strong, she told herself. Must not give in to panic. Must not let the mind roam free. Women died when they lost all sense of reason.

She thought she knew what it was to be solitary, the outsider, reclusive, but now that she was really alone, she realised her mistake. Before, she'd been playing a role, a part she'd chosen and one that suited her, a kind of martyrdom. Now she longed to rejoin the human race, to embrace it, to talk to her dad, to be touched by Joe, to hug Aunt Lily, to share the laughter of good friends like Jen and Ed, Ray and Jewel. Her heart wrenched inside just thinking about them. It was too much, she thought, a sob escaping from her throat, too hard to bear. All the missing and what might have been. Can't remember those I love, she gasped inside. If I do, I'll come undone.

Something was moving. She flinched, let out a small cry of surprise. Whatever it was had a light tread, a scampering motion, mice or, more likely, rats. The smell from the corpse would attract them, she reasoned. The air temperature was pretty cold, making decomposition slower, but it wouldn't essentially stop the laws of nature. Flies were often the first on the scene, laying their eggs in any available bodily orifice, followed by insects doing the same. Some were attracted to leaking body fluids, others to forming body-mould. Small, carnivorous creatures, also attracted by the smell, would come to devour. Judging by the rotting odour, she gauged the body as being several days old. Six, tops? She sighed. What did she understand about anything any more? She had no sense of chronology. She didn't even know whether it was still night, or if day had broken. Without light, how was she going to count the hours? How was she going to measure the time, the time she had left?

She heard another movement. The noise was closer. Could be rats again. Instinctively, she stepped back, set her head and shoulders against the post just to feel something solid against her body. Would they attack living beings? she trembled with fear. Were they like carrion crow that pecked out the eyes of ailing lambs? Would these vile, predatory, scurrying creatures also sense her tethered presence, her weakness, and seize the chance? She shook her head from side to side, trying to kill the idea. But she couldn't. A host of horrible anecdotes whizzed through her brain, tales where rodents nibbled the fingers of neglected babies and children. It was the sort of tale Jen would come out with. Dear Jen, she thought, stifling another sob, what would she make of this? Helen imagined her friend reading about it in some tabloid newspaper, distressed but also rapt, glued with fascination. Oh, how she'd give anything to tell Jen all about it. She wouldn't mind. She could have it all in lurid detail, glorious Technicolour, every last bit. Just to be given the opportunity to tell her. Just the chance to live.

She had a creeping sensation; she was not alone. She must have dozed off because she was slumped on the mattress. Her shoulders hurt from being pinned back. Her bones ached with cold.

By rolling on to her knees, she was able to push herself up into a standing position. She wondered if he were watching her, captivated by her struggle, getting off on it. It occurred to her that she was like a small animal caged for the purpose of scientific experiment. She had no strong views on vivisection. She did now. She felt fury.

She wanted to spit in his eye, hit him, claw at his face, inflict pain, *kill* him. She'd enjoy it, she thought, rage bursting through her body like an erupting volcano. Every connection in her brain fizzed and juddered with energy. She felt molten with anger. How dare this creature take away her rights. How dare he subject her to such indignity. Without warning, she snapped, lost it. Springing forwards, she ripped against the rope around her waist, twisting at it, bucking and tearing at her restraints, yanking on the support, making it creak and groan. Then she whipped round and kicked at it, first one foot then the next, screaming and roaring like a cornered, wounded lioness. She felt no pain at all. If she could have seriously injured herself, she would have done. Like the self-harmer, nothing else mattered except that choice, that freedom. She let everything that had gone wrong in her life boil to the surface. Every disappointment, every grief spumed out of her. She was fearless, reckless, without thought or feeling, and it was glorious. It was intoxicating. It was liberation. Release. Then quite suddenly, the madness passed as soon as it had come. It didn't fizzle away. It just abandoned her. Bruised, exhausted and broken, she sank to her knees. Every part of her shook. She felt finished, done, hollowed out.

This was her lowest point.

She had to be whatever he wanted her to be, she thought miserably, to do what he said. If, by studying her, it turned him on, so be it. If he wanted to defile her, there was nothing she could do. She was hopelessly alone. Just him and her. Locked together.

After a while, she sat up again. Her throat ached. Her muscles felt ripped. Her wrists burnt and throbbed with pain. The skin felt sticky. The rope stuck to it.

"Hello." Her voice was a croak. "Is there someone there?"

Again the scuffling sound. "Look, there's not much point going to all this trouble to get me here if we can't talk."

No response.

"All right," she said wearily. "My name's Helen Powers. I'm thirty-three. I'm a photographer. I take portraits. I guess you know all this already," she sighed. "I don't understand why I'm here, or what you want. Perhaps you could enlighten me, let me in on the secret. I think we almost met. You remember The Pitcher and Piano, the funeral? Are you the person who pushed me into the canal, almost ran me down?"

No answer.

"Who are you?" she said, her voice cracking with distress.

Still nothing.

"Why are you doing this?" she sobbed.

Silence.

She sat back, slowed her breathing, desperate to regain her composure.

"Come to think of it," she said, straining her ears, "it's probably not a good idea to answer." Too incriminating, she thought. "Could I have a drink, a sip of water? Please," she said, trying to stop her voice from sounding too needy. "It's been a long time. And I'd really appreciate it if you could free up my hands. I'm not going anywhere," she attempted to joke. "Where am I, by the way? Scotland or Land's End?"

She could definitely hear something. Breathing, she was sure of it. Not that far away. Somewhere in the darkness, to her left. She got to her feet, took a few shaky paces. Listened. Yes, there it was again. Why didn't the sick bastard say something? Maybe it was a clever plan designed to drive her insane. She wondered what button she needed to press to turn the tables.

"Do you want money, is that what this is all about? I can get you money. You don't have to go to all this fuss. Name your price, and I'll sort it, no problem. And, on my life," she said hastily, "I won't tell anyone what's happened. Why would I? You know I can't identify you. Smart move the blindfold. You could be black, white or Chinese. Frankly, I don't give a shit," she let out a tired laugh. "I just want this to stop for both of us."

She stopped, listened. The breathing sound was quicker, more shallow. Either it indicated excitement or distress. Perhaps she was pressing a nerve, after all, she thought.

"You know something? I bet you're as frightened as I am. Maybe more so, and you know what? Frightened people make mistakes. I understand that. Really, I do. So this is your mistake. A big one, I grant you, but it can be fixed. You're damn lucky. Not everyone gets the chance to make good. And believe me, you don't want be stuck with something so big you can't put it right. Not ever. I know, you see. I'm there, pal, and I can assure you it's pure torment. Blights your life. It's a bastard, isn't it? Your parents give you advice on all kinds of stuff, friends, too, but no one teaches you how to live with mistakes..." her voice lost impetus.

"I can hardly breathe, for Chrissakes. There's a real stink. Can't you smell it, too? Must do. God knows what it is, don't even want to know, blocked drains or something."

"No, not drains," a small voice said.

Helen gasped, moved her face towards the voice in astonishment. It sounded as if it belonged to a girl, a teenager, at a guess. "You're not him," she said, bewildered. Christ, what was going on? Was he holding a kid too, she thought? And why? It didn't make any kind of sense. "How long have you been here? Who are you?"

"I don't know," the girl replied, her voice a dull monotone. She had a definite accent, one Helen had identified before, rural, West Country. Yes, that's what it was, she thought, making the link. He had it, too.

"What's your name?"

"I don't remember," the girl whispered.

CHAPTER TWENTY-TWO

"ARE YOU HURT?" HELEN asked anxiously. If the girl couldn't remember who she was, she was probably concussed.

The girl didn't reply.

"Your head, is it bleeding or anything?"

"No."

"Not bruised?"

"No."

"Good," Helen said with open relief, "has he hurt you at all?"

The girl didn't answer. There was something in the quiet, something pitiable. Helen felt her skin go clammy. "Can you remember anything about how you got here?"

Still the girl didn't answer. Knew but couldn't say, Helen thought, or knew but couldn't bear to remember? Oh Christ, what had they both stumbled into? "Listen, we're in this together now. We can help each other. We can get out of here."

"There's no way out," the girl said, frighteningly submissive.

"There's *always* a way out," Helen said, forcing herself to believe it. "You know where we are exactly?"

"In a cellar," the girl replied.

"Just one entrance?"

"Two."

"Two? Brilliant," Helen said. "Where do they lead?"

"One leads into the cottage, the other outside."

"Outside's good."

The girl gave a hollow laugh. "You don't understand."

But Helen wasn't listening. She was planning. "Any tools, gardening equipment in here, ladders?"

"I think there's a hoe or spade or something."

"Then we can break down the door."

"Too solid."

"Not if we keep at it."

"But we're tied up."

True, and Helen had no idea how she was going to break free. Not yet. But she was determined to work on it. "Any idea what we're tied to?"

"Pig slats," the girl replied.

"This used to be a piggery?"

"Years ago."

"They must be pretty ancient."

"But still strong."

Helen tried to contain her disappointment. "Are you cold, honey?"

"Freezing."

"What are you wearing?"

"Top, skirt and leggings." Thank God, if she'd been in her nightie, Helen would be seriously worried. "Try and move about a bit, get your circulation going. Got anything in your pockets, mobile phone?"

"No."

"Never mind," Helen said, "your family will be looking for you. Your face is probably splashed over every newspaper in the land. You'll feature on every television and radio station. The police will be out in force." She would have clapped her hands in delight if she could have done. Adults who went AWOL were puzzling. Missing teenagers sent a chill through the nation.

"No one knows I'm missing," the girl said, her voice dull, empty of emotion.

"But they must do," Helen said, mystified.

"No."

"Shouldn't you be at school?"

"Don't go to school."

"You bunk off?"

"Never been to school. My mum said school was a waste of time, didn't teach you anything. She taught me at home."

"Then she'll be looking for you."

"She can't."

"Why not?"

"She died two months ago."

Helen's heart gave a sickening lurch. "Oh, sweetheart," she said, feeling her breath catch painfully against her ribs. "I'm so sorry," she said, thinking that it was an entirely inadequate response, " but surely someone's looking after you. What about your dad?"

"Don't know which one it is. Mum said it was either Janus or Star."

Jesus, this was getting more peculiar by the second, Helen frowned. "Then won't Janus or Star be looking for you?"

"They moved on."

Moved on, Helen thought, bewildered. Who were they, travellers, commune-dwellers, or bloody layabouts? A pity one of these weirdly named individuals didn't live up to his responsibilities.

The girl was speaking again. Her words came in short, sharp bursts. "She wouldn't go to hospital, see.

313

Didn't believe they could help. Tried everything else. Crystals, acupuncture, Chinese herbs, psychotherapy, visualisation, you know," she gulped. "Made her feel better but none of it worked. They said I couldn't stay where I was."

"They?" Helen said.

"The people we lived with. It's why I'm here."

"And where's here?"

"My gran's."

Oh God, Helen thought, please no. "Your grandmother, is she…"

"She's over there," the girl said with tremendous calm. "That's what you can smell."

She heard the bolts pushed back and the heavy door swing open. There was a click and the sound of a light switch going on. Even though she was blindfolded, she sensed that her surroundings were more transparent, less dark. Then footsteps, slow and deliberate. The girl began to whimper, then to cry, each sob betraying fear.

"I'm here," Helen called to her softly. "Don't worry. You're not alone now." She felt ringed with fear. It was stronger than the darkness or the silence. Over and above the pervading stench of death, she swore she could smell terror, her own and the girl's.

Helen wanted him to speak, to explain, even if he terrified her with what he might say or threaten, or do. He said nothing. And that was worse. She didn't know whether he was going to curse or assault her; far more alarming to imagine the blow than receive it. The agony was in the waiting.

When he was close enough for her to detect his beery breath against her face, feel it cut through the suffocating atmosphere, she spoke. "Why are you holding us here? Why the girl?" She wasn't demanding – that might antagonise him. She was asking. Nicely.

He pushed the neck of a plastic bottle against her mouth, tipping it up. She drank from it thirstily. Cold water dribbled down her chin. Then he pushed a stale biscuit into her mouth. Right-handed again, she noticed. She felt his fingers brush her lips and realised that he was wearing gloves, not warm wool, but thin vinyl disposables. She considered whether it was phobia or whether the guy was forensically aware. She wanted to ask him to remove the blindfold but didn't dare in case he felt the pressing need to kill her.

"Thank you," she mumbled.

She heard him move away and to her left. The girl let out a shrill cry.

"It's all right," Helen said, "don't be frightened. Have a drink. You'll feel better."

But there was a loud scuffling sound, the sound of clothing being disturbed, ripped, a scream of pure pain, followed by the girl shrieking repeatedly. The noise ricocheted around the cellar, bouncing off the walls. He was panting, grunting, mouthing off to the girl but Helen couldn't hear above the screaming. The noise was incredible, like an animal having its throat cut. Helen opened her mouth to cry out, protest, but the words tangled in her throat, her voice deserting her. She felt as if she were undergoing an operation, immobile but not anaesthetised, able to hear, to see, to feel, wanting to scream, too. Torn apart with terror and distress, she found herself shrinking back to the safety of the pole, sliding down, curling up, wanting to clap her hands over her ears, desperate to shut the noise, and the accompanying images, out. In spite of the cold,

315

she was sweating all over. Her mind raced in anguish. The sound mirrored the fear in her heart, the panic in her brain, the dark imaginings of past events. Why not me, she cried inside. Why pick on her? Then there was the sound of a double slap and the screaming stopped.

The door was closed. The bolts were shot. The girl was sobbing. It sounded as if her lungs were wrenching apart. Helen surfaced from her mute state, longing to offer comfort, to put her arms around the girl, to quieten her. But she was trapped, too, a prisoner of her thoughts and fears. All she had was her voice.

"He's gone now. It's all right."

"He took everything," the girl gasped.

"I know."

"I can't," the girl sobbed. "I can't…"

"Shush," Helen said softly. "Don't think about it, sweetheart. Try to…" Words failed her. Try to what? Forget, pretend, conceal? Is this what Adam told Tracey, Jacks's first victim, the kid from the care home, she wondered? As a result, had the poor girl grown up believing that nobody would listen to or believe her ever again?

She wasn't equipped for this, Helen thought. She didn't know how to respond, what would be best. She was petrified of making it worse. Why was this man doing this, she agonised, because he could, because it was pleasurable, or was it simply a means to torture both of them?

Her mind filled with images of Rose Buchanan and Tracey. Both young teenagers. Both innocents. Just like the girl tethered beside her. She racked her brains, trying to think of a way to connect, to relieve the girl's present suffering. But how could she? "If you don't remember your name," Helen said, at last, "we'll think of a new one."

The girl sniffled.

"Can't have Susan or Jane, far too boring," Helen said, trying to lighten the tone. "I think you're more of a Jasmine or a Saffron."

"No."

"All right, how about Kate or Milly?"

"I like Siena," the girl said, surprisingly sure.

"Great. I like that, too. It's glamorous. Ever been to Siena?"

"I've never been abroad." There was wistfulness in the girl's voice.

"It's one of the most enchanting cities in Europe. You'll go one day."

The girl said nothing. Helen knew what she was thinking. She privately thought the same.

"So Siena," Helen said, forcing herself to sound upbeat, "remember where you're from?"

"Mum said we were from nowhere and everywhere."

Gypsies, maybe? "I live in Birmingham," Helen said, taking the lead.

"I'd hate to live in a city."

"It has its advantages." Like there are people close by, busy streets, taxi-drivers, policemen, someone to notice, to sound the alarm, someone to help.

"We used to live outside a place called Totnes," the girl said.

"I've heard of it," Helen said uncertainly.

"It's in South Devon."

"But it's beautiful there. Is that where we are?"

"Sort of," the girl said mournfully.

"Yeah?" Helen said, inviting further conversation.

"We're in the middle of nowhere."

"Be a bit more specific?" Helen said, blending some humour into the question.

"We're on Dartmoor."

Helen paled. Dartmoor in winter, she thought bleakly. Even if they could escape, how would they survive the moors?

"He's going to kill us, isn't he?"

It seemed like hours since they were offered a drink, hours since he'd created chaos. But, actually it might have been less. It was all part of the process of disorientating them, Helen thought, of creating nightmares in their heads, of subjugating them. It was working. With dread, she wondered what he was doing upstairs, what he was plotting, whether he had torture in mind.

"I'd have thought he'd have done it by now, if that was the plan." It was an honest answer.

"He killed Gran."

Helen's mouth felt dry. "What happened?"

The girl didn't respond straight away. Either she was assembling her thoughts or steeling herself, Helen guessed.

"He had a gun. He shot her." It sounded matter-of-fact to Helen's ears, as if it were an everyday occurrence. Perhaps that was the only way the girl could deal with it.

"How did he get in?"

"Knocked at the door, said he'd taken the wrong turning and got lost, that his car had broken down. Asked if he could come inside and use the phone."

"He didn't have a mobile with him?"

"Said it wasn't working. Not unusual out here."

And granny fell for it. Almost as daft as her falling for the Good Samaritan act outside Albion Place, Helen thought grimly. None of it was random. He'd probably watched and staked out the cottage for some weeks before. An old woman and a young girl were not going to offer too much resistance. "Go on."

"He came inside, shut the door behind him, and pulled/the gun straight away. It happened so quickly and yet so slowly. Gran was terrified. I screamed at him but he pushed me out of the way. She tried to struggle with him. He shot her once in the chest. He was quite close. She went down on the floor. I knew it was bad. Blood bubbled from her mouth," she said breathily. "Blood everywhere. I don't think she was dead to start with. I don't know. I couldn't do anything. There was nothing I could do. Then, then," she said, her voice growing panicky with the memory, "he started on me."

A chill crawled and spread through Helen's stomach. "And you've been here ever since. Any idea how long?"

"Two or three days, maybe. I don't know." The girl's voice was colourless again.

Helen rested her back against the solid wood. She wanted to escape. She wanted to live, to see the sun once more, feel the rain on her face, kiss those she loved, but the girl's freedom mattered more. The girl had lost everything: her mother, her home, her grandparent, and her innocence. Although Helen felt helpless, she knew she had to try to find a way to liberate her. In the meantime, she had to inspire confidence, to keep the girl's spirits alive, fan that single flame every human being has deep inside them.

"Siena, listen to me. When he comes back, tune him out."

"Tune him out?" the girl said, confused.

"In your head. Forget about him, wipe him out."

"It's no use."

"Think of something," Helen said urgently. "Something really nice, your mum or a song. Anything. You like music?"

"I went to Glastonbury last year."

"Lucky you, who did you see?"

"The Darkness."

"Ultimate glam. Think of them. Better still, think of Justin Hawkins."

"No," the girl said, clipped. "I can't."

"You can," Helen insisted. "You're going to think of the lovely time you had. Think of the fun. Was it wet or sunny?"

"Sunny, I think. I don't remember."

"Doesn't matter," Helen persisted. "Think of sunshine and music and love. Whatever happens, you hold onto that. Do you understand?"

"I think so," the girl said apprehensively.

"Good. You leave that bastard upstairs to me, let me make the running, let me do the talking."

"You don't know what he's like."

"Yes, Siena, I think I do." He's just like Jacks, she thought.

The noise of metal bolts scraping back sent a chill through her bones. Suddenly she didn't feel so brave. "Remember what I said," Helen hissed. "Do it for your mum, your gran. Do it for all of us."

He was like a malevolent presence. Even with the stench, the fear, the terror of what might come, the

320

focus was on him. And he knew it. So far she'd tried compliance. She'd tried reason. She'd got nowhere. It was risky, but she needed to try something different.

"What do you want this time?" Helen said, steel in her voice.

She thought she heard a low laugh but she couldn't be sure. Was this the game he wanted to play? Did he enjoy confrontation?

"Stinks down here," Helen complained bitterly. "Can't you get rid of the smell?"

"Thought you'd be used to it."

There was a curdling sensation in her stomach. What did he mean? Did he know about her and what she used to do? Was he aware of her weak spot? She wondered if it all went back to Jacks again. Maybe her captor *knew* about Rose Buchanan.

"But the girl isn't."

"Shit happens, *darlin'*."

It sounded as if he were drinking, she thought, ears pricking. There it was again, the sloosh of liquid against glass. It would account for the beery breath. Perhaps it wasn't such a good idea to push it. Alcohol usually fuelled violence. Even mild-mannered individuals could become raving psychos with enough booze inside them. But what choice do I have, she thought? She had to get through to him, to find out what he wanted, discover his own weak spot.

"That the best you can come up with?" Helen said, scathing.

"Fuck you."

"The girl's done nothing wrong. Let her go."

An ugly silence.

"She's no threat to you."

"You thick or somethin'?"

"What do you want from me?"

"All in good time."

"So you do want something?"

"Doesn' everyone?"

Christ, this was pointless, she thought. "Can't you get us something to eat, something proper, something hot? We're both freezing to death down here."

"I don't do room service, slapper."

"Then what do you do?" Helen snapped.

The blow across her face made her teeth and brain rattle. Her blinded eyes filled with tears. She could taste salt where her lip split. Blood trickled warm and soft down her chin.

"*That's* what I do."

Absent light. No point. No focus. No hope. It felt as if she'd spent the last four years of her life in the dark. This was a further, cruel extension.

She wondered what people concentrated on in captivity. The obvious thought was people, but Helen had already discounted them because she couldn't bear to. If anything was going to send her round the bend, it was thinking of those she cared about.

Instead, she thought of simple pleasures: a hot bath with masses of exotic bath-oil, thick, fluffy towels, Egyptian cotton sheets, white and unsullied, the smell of wet leaves and roses after dark. She thought of music, of favourite songs, books she'd read and enjoyed. She didn't think of a kiss in the rain, an arm around her shoulder or a look of love.

She tried very hard not to consider death. The problem was that most people tended to think in terms of narrow boundaries: disease, old age, at a push, accidents. Conditioned to think about the obvious, we don't entertain the strange, the unusual, the terrifying. That's stuff for other people to worry about. We don't consider the substrata, fear and despair, the incomprehension.

And how the hell do you measure death's close cousin, sorrow, she thought? How do you rate the daily terrors we're beset with, the universal violence, the pain of hunger, the incurable disease, homelessness, loneliness, grief? There wasn't a place in the world free of suffering. There was always some home or city where someone's heart was breaking. Theirs was just another small corner.

She tried to rein in her tortured mind, to contain the demons. Maybe she should concentrate on something she wanted to achieve, she thought, or somewhere special she wanted to visit, focus on the kinds of things people put off for a lifetime because the opportunity doesn't present itself, or there's not enough money, or not enough will. We often find excuses, even for things we really want to do, she thought. In her case, it was simpler than that. She didn't want the experience to be a disappointment. She didn't want it to fail. She couldn't visit that again.

She'd read somewhere about a guy taken hostage. He'd created a garden, worked it all out in his mind. It sustained him through all the crushing hours of boredom, the tense minutes of fear and excitement. When released, he'd stuck by his vision, gone ahead, and then planted the whole thing to rapturous acclaim. It was a lovely story, she thought. She wanted to believe in it, to dream of the day they, too, would be released.

But she couldn't.

*   *   *

"I need a lavatory." Her mouth just about worked. Her voice and tongue felt thick, as if she'd had extended and painful treatment with an inept dentist.

"You can piss yourself, shit in your pants, don't give a fuck."

"Please."

She had no idea why he relented. It could be unpredictability. It could be another means to degrade her. Neither boded well.

"You try anythin'" he warned, "I'll give the girl a seeing-to."

Siena whimpered. It echoed eerily through the cellar. Fighting the urge to be sick, Helen called to her softly, told her it would be all right then pledged to him that she'd be good, she'd behave, she'd do as he said. What other choice did she have? She was still blindfolded, still anchored to him, still under his control. She never doubted he'd carry out his threat if he felt like it. The self-defence course she'd attended didn't teach you about stuff like this. Didn't tell you that someone else's life might be on the line as well as your own.

He ordered her to stand. She got up, feeling extremely dizzy. He warned her not to move a muscle then released the rope from the pole, shortened the length and dragged her behind him. It felt strange to have the freedom. Her legs weren't used to it. They felt weak and wobbly like she'd spent a fortnight in bed with flu. Part of her was reluctant to move. She didn't want to trust him, to be under his guidance, to be this subservient. Maybe it would have been easier to wet herself again.

324

"There's six steps," he said gruffly. She bumped into the first one, the stone catching painfully against her shin. She soon worked out that the steps were quite deep and she had to be careful to lift her leg high enough to stop herself from tripping up. Every time she hesitated, he'd tug on the rope. They went up the steps in a peculiar stop-start motion. It was like struggling to move a heavy set of drawers – except she was the furniture.

At last they were at the top. The air was fresher, less tainted. She took a lungful. The floor felt different beneath her feet. A bit sticky. Lino, she guessed, like the flooring at Albion Place. He was pulling her to the right. She heard a door creak open. He pushed her into a small compartment.

"I need my hands free," she said.

He clicked his tongue but undid the rope binding her wrists. She almost let out a manic laugh of hysteria.

"Don't get fuckin' clever," he warned again, giving the rope around her waist an extra pull to make crystal clear she knew who was in charge.

She pushed the door closed as far as she could, giddy with the luxury of being able to use her hands, and have the strain relieved from her shoulders. As she felt her way to the lavatory, she wondered if there was anything close by she could make into a weapon. In her mind, she ran through a few moves. Maybe she could rush him, take him unawares.

"Hurry up," he shouted to her, snatching at the rope.

"All right," she snapped back, desperately feeling around, touching a cold brick-built wall, feeling a piece of wire netting higher up, indicating a window, but she couldn't even locate a toilet roll holder let alone a makeshift weapon. Dejected, she rolled down her trousers, sat down, and touched her stinging wrists, feeling the broken skin, flinching with pain. Then she remembered the tiny torch inside her jacket, felt for it, pulled it out and slipped it into her jeans pocket.

When she was finished, she flushed the lavatory and returned to her captor. "Hands," he said.

She extended them in front of her, gritting her teeth as he lashed them together. A small improvement, she supposed. Better than having them bound behind her.

"Why are you doing this?" she said, as he began to push her back the way she'd come.

He didn't answer.

"Is this connected to Karen Lake?"

He let out a short laugh.

"You knew her," she insisted. "I'm right. You blackmailed my mother. You used Karen. It was your idea. You're behind it all."

She heard him come towards her, heard, too late, the fist ball and clench, the swing of his arm. The ferocity of the blow to her stomach caused her to crumple and fall. Pain shot through her abdomen in sickening waves. "Cunt, I'm the person who saved you," he roared.

She couldn't speak. Her mouth was filled with bile. Her insides felt as if they were on fire.

"You'd have drowned if I let you," he sneered, standing over her sprawled form, poking her head with the toe of his boot. "Couldn't have that, could we? Seeing as you're family."

The smell was a constant, appalling distraction. She pretended to be normal. She didn't mention the nausea, the racking pain, his unpredictability, his brutality, the morbid thoughts colliding in her brain. For once she was glad they were blindfolded. The girl had no idea of the pallor of her skin, the strain in her face, the fear in her heart.

"Tell me about your mum," Helen said quietly. She couldn't think straight. All she had were fragments like shrapnel in her brain. Karen Lake was in there somewhere. Blackmail, too. And that last remark. She didn't know what he meant or if he meant anything. Could be some throwaway line. *You're family*. What did he mean? Only Lee fitted that description. But Lee was dead. That's what she was told. Surely…

The girl was speaking. "Her name was Malak. I've always called her that. It's Arabic for angel. That's what she was, my mum," the girl said proudly. "A really good person, kind and peaceful. She believed in Karma. What goes around comes around. That everything has a purpose."

Helen sat silently. She thought it sounded a bit too folksy for her liking. She'd seen a lot of death and she was damned if she knew what the purpose was.

"She thought I'd stay in the commune. It's where my home is, but the others said it would be difficult."

"I suppose they had a point," though Helen couldn't think what it might be.

"Before she died, the most amazing thing happened," the girl said, her voice suddenly gathering strength. "It was October and quite warm. She was very weak. We had this kind of bed made up for her outside. Sometimes I'd go and read to her or just sit with her and watch the animals and trees or the sun shining. She loved the colours. Anyway, it was early evening and, quite suddenly, a barn owl appeared. Just came out of nowhere. It seemed to watch us, or rather Malak. She said that the owl signified her death. She wasn't frightened or anything. She just knew that her time had come. She was very peaceful about it. That night she died," the girl finished softly.

"Someone once told me," Helen said, thinking it was one of the old gardeners who used to work at Keepers, "that the barn owl signified the fulfilment of a dream or hope."

"I like that better," the girl said simply.

So did she.

He brought them food.

The girl let out a horrified cry. "I can't eat it."

"What do you mean, you little bitch?"

"I don't eat meat," the girl quailed.

"Fuck you," he sneered. "Had it too good, haven't we? Spoilt little cow. You know what you need," he threatened menacingly. The girl let out a terrified squeal.

"Try," Helen yelled. Anything to stop the violence. Besides, this was no time to be precious. They both needed to eat, to keep up their strength, to help them think, to stay alive.

She cringed as the girl gagged and choked. "For Chrissakes, can't you give her some bread and cheese, or something?"

"Fuck it. You can have hers."

"If she's not eating, neither am I."

She heard the plate shatter as it was thrown against the wall. She heard the door slam shut.

The girl was distraught.

"Don't cry," Helen said. "It doesn't matter. I wasn't hungry." She closed her eyes and lay down.

She felt dizzy with hunger and exhaustion and thinking. She was getting colder by the second. If he didn't kill them soon, she thought they'd die of hypothermia. For the life of her, she couldn't think why he was keeping them alive.

"Try and get some sleep," she said to the girl.

Footsteps again. The scraping sound. Door opening and closing. More footsteps. She felt as though she were in a time-loop. Must be dreaming, she thought, or dying, or both.

She woke up to find him shortening the rope so that she was more securely attached to the strut. Then he untied her hands and shook her to grab her attention. She was again aware of a change in the darkness. She couldn't see but some of the light seemed to penetrate the cloth around her head. He handed her something hot to the touch. She flinched at the sudden heat, suspecting a trick then discovered that what she was holding was made of something thick, like pottery, that it had a handle.

"Drink," he said. She heard him move towards the girl and tell her the same.

Helen sipped at it gingerly, wondering whether it was drugged, or worse. It tasted good. Hot, sweet tea. The best she'd ever tasted. He was after something, she thought.

After she drank it, he gave her a small chocolate bar. She ate it greedily, savouring the lavish sweetness on her tongue. Carrot and stick, she thought, licking every crumb. He enjoys power. Control. He likes being nice one minute, nasty the next. The guy's a sadist, she concluded.

He removed her blindfold. At first, she couldn't focus properly. It was like looking at a shot from a film with the camera playing on the main actor, the rest of the set all fuzzy. She blinked and saw the bricks, the spades, the garden forks, the rakes and hoes hanging neatly along the wall. The cellar must have been sixteen feet square. The floor was indeed made of earth and, as her eyes travelled the length of it, she saw a covered mound along the far side. It was wrapped in a length of carpet. There were stains on the ground, most likely blood and body fluids, she thought, thinking that even a body can lie within the stratas of the earth for a very long time and still be detectable. But this body was not in the ground. It was very much on the surface. The half-chewed, bloated and grey-skinned hand sticking out proved it.

She looked across to the girl. She was still blindfolded, thank God, Helen thought. A small-boned creature, she couldn't have been much more than fifteen or sixteen, Helen estimated. She had shoulder-length wheat-coloured hair, which was matted in dreadlocks. Her clothes had a layered look: a brightly coloured jacket with mirrored pieces set into it, a short orange skirt that was stained and badly torn. Underneath this, she wore black leggings, also torn. Her feet were strangely clad in flat blue leather shoes with a single bar across, the type of shoe you might expect a young child to wear.

Gradually, as Helen's sight improved, her attention turned to their captor. He wasn't that tall but he was stocky. Same blond hair. Same milk-white skin, as though he needed to get outside more. There were two deep scratches on his face, one on each cheek, she presumed inflicted by the girl. This time there were no

330

shades to cover his eyes. She peered into them. Muddy river blue. He wore a black three-quarter length leather coat over a black polo-neck sweater and blue jeans. His feet, which she guessed were around a size ten, were shod in expensive-looking walking boots, Rockports, maybe. He was, indeed, wearing disposable gloves.

As she was watching him, he was watching her, staring at her, slowly combing his short hair with a metal comb. There was something deeply threatening about the action, as if he might, at any given moment, assault her with it. And the way he was looking, she wasn't sure whether it was with cruelty, fascination or satisfaction. Maybe all three. She stared right back, noted the ear-ring in his left ear-lobe, thought how easy it would be for him to catch it and knock it out with the teeth from the comb. She also thought that one of those hairs, even without the root, could condemn him so he wasn't quite as smart as he thought he was. Likewise, the boots would surely leave a trace in the earth. Above everything else, she recognised that this was definitely the man at the bar, the man at the funeral. Her assailant. Her rescuer. And for what?

He put the comb away and took out a mobile phone from his pocket. "You're going to make a call."

Was this her passport to freedom? she thought, hopes absurdly raised.

"To your father. I want a million pounds in cash. He's got thirty-six hours to get it."

Oh God, she thought, crushed. Her dad wouldn't be able to cope with another trauma. The shock, on top of her mother's death, might even kill him. "He doesn't have that kind of money," she said brazenly.

"Don't play fuckin' games," he snapped, his mouth curled in contempt. "Family's bloody loaded."

The words cudgelled her brain, hitting a nerve. "Family? You set me up, pushed me in the canal, ran me down to extort…"

"Shut the fuck up."

"You killed my mother." Her yell ricocheted around the cellar.

He gave a dead-eyed stare, pulled a knife from his jeans and unfolded the blade, which was long and thin, and looked viciously sharp. The tip was pointed low at her stomach. Fear, bright and focused, cut through her. He advanced on Helen and jabbed at her with the tip of the blade. "You going to get this money or do I have to cut you first?"

Helen swallowed. Aside from the sheer pain, one inexpert lunge, especially to the abdomen, could prove fatal. The knife edged closer, glinting in the frozen air. "He won't be able to get his hands on that kind of money in less than forty-eight hours," she stammered.

He laughed with calculated ease. The trajectory of the knife moved from Helen's stomach to her face. For a horrible moment, she thought he was going to slice her cheek. "Yes, he can," he growled. "I know it. You know it. Or maybe I'll cut her," he grinned, indicating the girl with a flick of his head.

Siena's body shook in terror. Helen blinked and mumbled compliantly. Her tongue felt like lead in her mouth. She felt as if she were finally losing her mind.

"That's more like it," he said. "Don't want to get nasty, or nothin'. Tell him it has to be him – no fuckin' couriers – and he has to be alone. I've already got stuff in place to guard against any interference so no police, no heroics. He's to drive to New Street Station, go to

332

the main bank of telephones, Tuesday, two in the morning and wait for a call."

"The station won't be open at that time," she bluffed.

"Shut the fuck up, I told you. It's open and staffed twenty-four hours."

Helen gritted her teeth, nodded. The thought of her dad driving to a phone box, picking up a set of complex instructions, driving on again, crossing motorway networks, covering large tracts of land, exhausting any police back-up, left her reeling.

"What if he can't get the money to you in time?"

"Then you and the kid are dead meat."

She closed her eyes. They were probably as good as dead in any case. Her dad would almost certainly go to the police, she believed, but with so little to go on, she wasn't sure of their chance of success. Blackmail with abduction was a unique crime. With two tiers of victims, the one directly involved, and the relative coerced for payment, the police usually trod very carefully. And that meant slow. They'd try to work out the abductor's motive, she remembered, how careful he was, how confident, whether he was motivated by greed, sexual kicks or some emotional need. She hadn't a clue what was driving her captor, so how could the police possibly find out? "I still don't understand why us."

"Pay-back," he said acidly.

She felt as if he'd slipped a knife in between her ribs. "For what?"

He glared at her, retied her hands, held up the phone, and punched in the digits, deliberate in his movements. She trembled, watched. "No clever tricks," he hissed, holding the phone to her ear.

Sick with confusion, she listened to it ringing. Half of her prayed that her father was out, the other half willed him to be in so that she could hear his voice, tell him she loved him, say good-bye.

"Hello," she heard him say sleepily.

"Dad."

"Darling, it's awfully late."

"Is it?" she said, feeling awkward.

"Doesn't matter. Lovely to hear from you. I gather from Aunt Lily you're taking a bit of a break."

She felt as if her throat were full of stones. She told him immediately what was required, heard the wobble in her voice.

"Oh my God," he cried out, "are you all right? Has he hurt you?"

"No, I'm fine, really," she said, twisting inside. "Please, Dad, it's important you do exactly as he says."

"But…"

"No police. No Stratton," she said pointedly, hoping he'd pick up on it.

"Let me talk to him, plead with him. You're all I have," her father said, his voice soaring with emotion.

Her abductor shook his head slowly.

"It's no good. He won't."

"Please."

"I have to go," she said desperately.

"Helen," her father cried.

"I love you," she managed to cry out before the phone was snatched away and the call cut.

"Oscar-winning," her captor grinned. "Fucked-up middle classes do it so well."

"You won't get away with it."

"Oh, I can. I've had four years to think about it."

334

Four years? Why four, she squirmed, why not one, or two or three? She gawped at him in consternation. It couldn't be, she thought, or could it? "You're Lee," she gasped. "My half-brother."

He grinned, winked at her, pulled out his comb again, running it through his hair in long, smooth movements.

So simple, she thought. She was right all along. He must have faked his own death to cover his tracks then blackmailed their mother, and his own flesh and blood, for God's sake. The nearly man had suddenly made it. "How could you?" she said, eyes narrowing.

"Why not?" he said, dismissive.

"She was your mother. I'm your half-sister. What is this? Revenge because life didn't play out the way you wanted?"

He looked at her with animal cunning. "Revenge, yeah."

"And Karen?"

He shrugged. "She was expendable."

"You mean…"

"I gave her enough high quality smack to kill an elephant."

Helen felt her face drain of any little colour she feared she had.

"Wasn't my fault," he whined. "I didn't make her take it. I didn't inject her. Her own choice to be a fuckin' loser. Just like your mother."

Your mother, *our* mother, she thought. "You bastard," she spat at him. "Mum was a lot of things but she wasn't a loser."

"Mother fuckin' Theresa, was she?" he jeered, taking a step towards her. "She was a lush."

"Shut up."

335

"And a slag."

"I'm not listening," she yelled.

"Got in the club."

"It's not a mortal sin, Lee."

"But shaggin' the old man is."

Her jaw slackened. Her mouth dropped open. She felt as if he'd driven a rapier through her.

"Want me to spell it out, do you? Your mother," he announced with derision, "was fucking her father, your dirty old grandpa, that's how she got up the duff. Filthy little bitch."

"No," she said, trembling. "It's not true. You're lying. You're lying," she let out a dry sob.

"You thought she wanted to protect you?" he mocked. "Should have seen her face when I turned up. She was fuckin' petrified. Shitting herself, she was. Didn't even have to drag it out of her. *Please, I beg of you, don't tell them*," he said, high-pitched in mimicry. "I knows all about you," I says, slapping her around a bit. And the *stoopid* bitch comes out with the lot, whinging on how it wasn't her fault, that her old man was a pervert.

"Believe me," he said, fixing his cold eyes on Helen, "she cared fuck-all about you, darlin'. But she worried about her precious reputation, what people would think, what your precious daddy might say. Come to think of it, we could give him a bell and tell him."

"No," she cried, tears spurting down her face. "Please. It would kill him."

He curled his lip, started to walk away then turned and looked over his shoulder. "Best leave it then. Don't want the old man snuffing it before he gets hold of the cash."

336

*   *   *

"Helen," the girl said.

"Yeah," she said dully.

"He's horrible. He's sick. He was making it up."

Helen shivered and rolled over.

Words are as lethal as knives. They cut with the same clarity. They leave wounds that never entirely heal. They leave scars. Lee was speaking the truth, Helen thought. She recognised it at some deep, unconscious level. It added up. Fitted in with everything else. Explained the animosity between her mother and grandmother. And the result? A psychopathic retard with revenge on his mind.

Lee surely knew that her father would go to the police. He must have factored it in. Most extortionists and blackmailers give heavy instructions not to approach the law but they knew the reality was quite different. He'd probably already thought about roadblocks and bugging devices, funny money and transmitters. Like he said, he'd had four years to consider it.

Her only hope was Stratton. He, alone, knew the risks she'd taken to uncover the truth. He was the only one who could slot the pieces together, who could make the right connections, who knew about Lee. Oh God, she thought, shrivelling inside. Lee was dead. That's what Stratton found out and believed. Lee was the last person he'd be looking for.

She tried to stay sane, go through the moves. Logically. As soon as her father sounded the alert, the police would be faced with a blizzard of decisions.

First, they'd consider whether it was serious or a prank. Picking up on the family's previous history, the local police were bound to realise the urgency. They'd contact the Major Investigation Unit and the case would be passed on to senior officers specialising in kidnap and extortion incidents. And they were bloody good, Helen thought, with a small swell of hope. Lee wouldn't stand a chance.

Briefly buoyed up, she made a stab at what would happen, how they'd play it. News blackout or full media coverage would be a consideration. Going the media route was a mixed blessing. Reports would pour in from all over the country with imagined sightings. Smothered by a mountain of information, the police would be unable to prioritise, let alone process it. Didn't bear thinking about it, she thought, hoping they'd choose the blackout route.

All calls to Keepers would be monitored. Detectives would visit Shirley and her mates, and apply pressure. But would they get anywhere, she worried, skimming over the possibility and focusing, instead, on the options. There were only three she could think of: pay-up, play along, or refuse to negotiate. With a life in the balance, the latter was out of the question. Without more contact, there was nothing to play along with. It all depended on the successful monitoring of the drop. They had to pick him up. Take him alive. Make him talk. Her life depended upon it. More importantly, so did the girl's.

In the meantime, the police would start looking. The obvious choice would be lock-ups, garages, boarded up hostels, ravaged dwellings, but in the Birmingham area. It would never cross their mind to start looking in the West Country, and there was no likelihood that they could come up with a more accurate location without a disclosure of more information. To nail their man, the police needed another call. She wondered if she could trick Lee into making it, but feared he was too cunning. Besides, the consequences of winding him up and him turning nasty made her shudder.

If only he'd written a blackmail note, she chafed inside. So much could be detected from the written word, the level of intelligence, the type of individual, his psychological make-up, his weak spot, a pressure point, *him*. And what did she know about her crazy half-brother? That he was cruel and manipulative. That he had no qualms about administering violence, sexual or otherwise. That he lacked empathy with his victims. That he was utterly ruthless. The Park Lane Boys had taught him well. Wait, she thought, frowning. Either Blackie was wrong, or he was lying. He'd painted a picture of a man not up to it, a loser. Stratton said the same. *He was out of his league, wasn't up to the job*. So both Blackie and Stratton were in agreement. Yet the picture they presented didn't square with the sadist holding them.

She smiled, felt the laughter bubble up inside her. Is this what happens to you when you tip over the edge and lose it, she thought crazily? Do you literally become a gibbering idiot? Here she was in this hellhole of a prison and she was giggling her head off. It was ridiculous, embarrassing, but it seemed so funny, hilarious: Lee, her half-brother, *the loser,* had pulled the wool over all their eyes. He'd run rings around the lot of them, she gasped. He'd…

She peered through the darkness at the girl, her mirth dissipating. She could feel the girl's suffering.

She could touch it. If they ever got out of here alive, she thought gauntly, there would still be horrors ahead.

Helen put her bound hands to her face and ground her thumbs into her forehead. She felt a special responsibility for the girl. She wanted to make the difference. To keep her safe. To give her a future. It was important to her. No, it was vital. Beyond reason. The girl was the light. In saving the girl, she might also save a part of herself. She might not. But that didn't matter.

CHAPTER TWENTY-THREE

SHE THOUGHT IT COULDN'T get any worse. She'd stopped feeling hungry, stopped being cold, stopped smelling death, stopped everything. Her clothes hung like shrouds on her. Every movement took effort. Even rolling over. She hadn't thought of dying like this, life fading away.

They'd been fed with stale biscuits though she couldn't remember when. They were both spending a lot of time asleep. Her dreams were laced with nightmares in which she uttered silent screams. When awake, either her mind was seized by febrile confusion or slow delirium. Each time she stirred from painful slumbers, she believed it would be her last. She wanted it.

The darkness was more inert. She felt steeped in it. In a more lucid moment, she tried to play on the sibling connection. Stupid.

"I could help you," she said.

The light was on. It hurt her eyes. He was sitting on the top step, swigging from a bottle of beer. She couldn't remember the last time he'd offered her a drink. Her throat was tight so she guessed it was quite a long time ago.

His eyes were like slits. The knot of muscles in his jaw pulsed. His expression radiated hate.

"I mean it," she said fervently. "I'm all you have. We're family."

He didn't respond. She thought she saw a smile chase across his shiny lips, but she couldn't be certain.

"You let us go, turn yourself in, and I'll speak up for you, explain why you're doing this."

"What's to explain?"

"About your past, the way you were treated, the disappointments." Her mind was racing again. She didn't think she was making much sense.

"You know nothing, bitch."

"I know enough," she said, hating the pleading sound of her voice. "It would be viewed as a mitigating factor by the courts."

"Bollocks," he snorted. "All they'd do is bang me up in a loony-bin for the rest of me life. No thanks." He took another swig.

"All right, all right," she said, as if he'd worn her down on a deal. "Then what?"

He came down the steps, walked straight up to her, crouched down so his pale face was level with hers, so she could see the wetness of his lips, the chill in his eyes. "We're going to have some fun," he said, rubbing the inside of her thigh with his gloved palm. "All of us," he said, looking over towards the girl. "Then I'm going to kill you."

The girl's crying had long subsided.

"Helen."

"Yes, honey."

"You said you'd done something wrong."

"Did I?" Must have done, she thought vaguely.

"You remember, when you first got here. You talked about something so big you couldn't put it right."

Helen stirred, sat up. Yes, she remembered. How could she forget?

"What did you do?" the girl asked.

Helen exhaled a deep breath. "It's difficult, complicated. It's not easily explained." She knew she was fudging but how could she tell this girl, of all people?

"Doesn't matter."

Helen registered the huge sound of disappointment. The girl was offering to hear her confession, maybe her last confession, and she'd refused her.

"I used to work for the police," Helen began. "I was a Scenes of Crime officer, a person who goes along to crime scenes and records what happened, gathers evidence, that kind of stuff," she said, skating over the surface.

"What sort of crimes?"

"All sorts. You name it, I covered it."

"So you saw dead people."

"Sometimes."

"Strange kind of job."

"Yes." She hadn't thought so at the time. Perhaps it wasn't such a noble calling, after all. Perhaps she'd been a bit touched in the head.

"And?" the girl pressed.

"I fell in love with a married man, a police officer. He was very ambitious and I admired that. I thought he was good for me, that we were good for each other."

"What was his name?"

"Adam, Adam Roscoe."

"Did he leave his wife?"

"No," Helen said, feeling the strain in her voice. "I hoped he would, but it didn't happen." Even if Rose Buchanan had never crossed her path, she suspected Adam had been as wedded to his wife as to his job.

"So what happened?"

Helen experienced a dreadful pain in her chest, a crushing sensation as if her heart were seizing up. "One of the cases I covered involved a serious sexual assault of a young girl. Adam put pressure on the girl to drop the charges."

"That's terrible," Siena gasped.

"Yes."

"But why?"

"He believed that the girl wouldn't stand a chance in court. She'd spent most of her life in care and had a previous sexual history."

"Then he was trying to save her," Siena said reasonably, her voice lightening.

"No," Helen said, uncompromisingly. "The truth was that the guy who'd assaulted the girl was Adam's informant, a nasty piece of work. Adam believed this man could infiltrate and help bring down a gang of vicious criminals. He didn't want his man arrested for what he considered to be a lesser crime. It would have wrecked everything."

The silence was as long and crushing as the pain in her chest. Helen wasn't even sure the girl had heard.

"And you knew about it?" the girl said, at last.

"Yes."

"And you said nothing?" There was an accusing note in her voice.

"No."

And it wasn't because I bought into Adam's argument, or believed in the big picture, Helen thought, everything coming into sharp focus. It was simply because I was a fool for the man. I glimpsed his dream, recognised his ambition, understood his motives, which seemed of the noblest kind, and I believed he was like me. While he didn't engage in any of those things that truly corrupt officers do, she told herself stolidly, he *was* driven and he *was* ruthless, and he got it very wrong. If that made him a bad man, then she was, at least, as bad.

She looked back at the girl. "This man, the informer, later went on to assault another girl, only this time the bastard killed her."

The girl called Siena offered no platitudes, no comforting words. How could she?

He was fired up.

Helen watched him, wondering if he was on speed or E, or something. He was striding around the cellar, bottle of beer in hand, throwing pills down his throat at an alarming rate. The girl looked absolutely terrified.

He seemed to want an audience, someone to play off, to appeal to, to grab a response from. This was probably the last time she'd have a chance to get through to him, Helen thought.

"People are going to start looking for us," she said.

"So?"

"So we'll be found."

"You'll be dead," he grinned.

She stared right back at him. "It's not that easy to get rid of a body." She let her eyes briefly travel in the direction of the flyblown pile in the corner. He eyeballed her back. There was something covert in his expression. Was this simply a family affair or was there more to it, she wondered? "Every contact leaves a trace," she carried on remorselessly. "There's bits of you all over this house, the victim, this room, us. You don't even know it."

"Spare me," he grimaced.

"Where you going to bury us?" This was surreal. But she had to keep up the pressure, had to keep needling him, had to find a way to break through.

"Gonna give me lessons?" he grinned. "Now that would be a laugh."

"I'm trying to help you see the pointlessness. Know the moors well, do you? Even graves yield clues: tyre tracks, foot impressions, DNA." She was bluffing. In spite of massive leaps forward in technology, murderers still got away with it, still managed to escape without trace.

"Who's going to notice a couple of shallow graves?"

"You'd be surprised," she said, cool.

"I can get rid of anything. I've learned, see."

"If you've *learned*," she said, goading him, "you'd know you're talking crap. Even if we're not found for months, the bones won't disappear. What did you have in mind, an acid bath?"

"Fire," he shot back.

Difficult to investigate but not impossible, she thought. "Terrific, a fire on Dartmoor, what a spectacle. Police helicopters will be flying over before you've escaped the county." This was pushing it. She didn't have a clue.

He gave her an alarmingly cold stare. "Why did you do it?"

"Do what?"

"Chase down people like me?"

"I didn't."

"Didn't you?"

"No," she said, feeling nervous.

"So how would you explain what you did?"

"Explain?"

"Your job."

"I'm a photographer."

"Not that one," he snarled.

Oh God, so he did know, she thought. "I was a Mary Bloggs. I gathered evidence," she stammered, her brain racing. Had she helped put her own half-brother away? No, that would be too much of a coincidence.

"Fuckin' weird job for a woman. Messin' around with dead bodies, other people's blood and cum and shit. Get off on it, did you?"

What was the point, she thought? He wasn't going to listen to argument. She remembered that either Blackie or Stratton told her that Lee was involved in burglaries. He probably got careless, she thought, got nailed by some piece of evidence, further fuelling his grudge against the world. She hung her head, closed her eyes, and tried very hard to block him out. She sensed what it was like to be old, limbs creaking, body aching, skin shrivelling. But he kept on going.

"See, if it wasn't for people like you, I'd be carrying on normal, like."

She didn't speak.

"Not so fuckin' clever, huh?"

She didn't say anything. She was too tired, too…

"I SAID NOT SO FUCKIN' CLEVER!" he screamed, smashing the bottle against the strut sending pieces of glass flying over her head.

"No," she cried out in terror. "Not clever." Her teeth were chattering. The girl wailed uncontrollably.

He smiled. "More like it. Got your attention." He threw the rest of the broken bottle down on the floor. "Ever think how many times you've got someone banged up in some prison cell because you got off on

347

potting shit and spunk. Ever think about it?" he said, rounding on her, grabbing hold of her collar, squeezing her throat.

"No," she said, terrified.

"You even grassed up one of your own," he said, spittle flying over her face. "I heard all about it. And you expect me to trust you," he said, shaking her in disgust.

"Wasn't like that," she said feebly. So the past had come back to haunt her, she thought.

"Never is," he said coldly, letting her go. He went over to the steps, sat on the bottom. His eyes levelled with hers. "I'll tell you what it's like, you bitch. I was on a job, see, your neck of the woods, Bournville."

My neck of the woods, she thought. Why not his? Then she tumbled to it. That's why he didn't have a Midlands accent.

"It's a long way from home, isn't it?" she said tentatively, trying to keep some sort of dialogue going.

He gave her an icy stare. "Never shit on your own doorstep has always been my motto. Besides, I know Birmingham pretty well."

"Right," she said, not quite understanding. It was reputed that a lot of villains fled to the West Country, was Lee one of them? He was talking again.

"Fuckin' big house, it was. Mirrors and marble everyfuckinwhere. Fancy safe in the office. Paintings on the wall. Lot of money. Disgusting how some people live," he said, spitting on the floor.

"Got it all staked out, see. No dogs. Occupiers out of the country. Alarm was easy enough to dismantle. Did the homework, know what I mean?"

Helen nodded dutifully, glanced down and closed her eyes.

"Except someone fucked up," he glowered. "I gets in, nice and easy, does what I'm paid to do, and I'm walking down the stairs when I hears a sound. It's coming from the other side of this door," he said, cupping a hand to an ear, his eyes narrowing with excitement, "so I goes up to it, listens and I hears somethin'. Not sure what it is, see, breathin' or snorin' I thinks, which is a bit fuckin' worrying seeing as there's not supposed to be anyone there. Normally I'd have legged it, but it got me curious. Anyway, I goes in, and there's this girl sleepin'. Soundo, she was. Pretty little thing. Not much older than her," he said, gesturing at the girl with his thumb. "So I thinks to meself, Ryan, must be your birthday."

Helen's eyes popped open. Had she misheard?

"Ryan, my *boy*," it sounded like *buy*. "Why waste a perfect opportunity? Besides, I'd got a hell of a hard-on," he leered. "I was clever, see, sharp as a knife," he said, wagging his finger. "Wasn't going to get copped, not for anyone. Nearly choked, she did, but it felt fuckin' brilliant. Dunnit in her mouth, see. Made her swallow. No mess, no evidence. Besides, I had insurance."

"Insurance?" Helen said, mystified.

"Friends in high places. People prepared to cover me tracks."

"You mean police?" she said, jagging with alarm.

He gave her a penetrating look. "The man you grassed up."

The ground felt as if it had shifted beneath her feet. "Adam Roscoe," she said querulously.

"I was on to a good little earner, but then some clever forensic fucker decided to check the door."

349

The door to the girl's room, Helen thought. An alert SOCO would gamble on the offender listening for sounds of someone in the house. "You put your ear against the door."

"Fuckers," he cursed. "Got eight years, eight years of my life rotting away in a shit-hole because of people like you. And even Roscoe couldn't help me."

People like me, she thought. She didn't feel much like a person any more. "But there's no database for ear-prints." The last she heard it was being worked on and developed by a British woman in the field, a fingerprint specialist in her own right. "It wouldn't have been enough on its own," she pointed out reasonably. "You must have left some other evidence." Like bits of your DNA underneath the girl's fingernails, she thought grimly.

He wasn't listening. He was standing up, looking at her with venom. He was holding her responsible, it seemed. *All that time.* "I never grassed on 'em."

Them, she thought?

"We were in it together. The 'A' team. It's what I do, see. My speciality. I wouldn't touch a Rembrandt or a Van Gogh. Nothing that's gonna send alarm-bells ringing, only good shiftable stuff that people pay decent loot for. No point in stealing the Mona Lisa and trying to flog it on the open market," he smiled caustically. "The Art and Antiques mob would be down on me faster than shit off a shovel."

"You mean," Helen said, her voice very small. "The Roscoes were in it with you?"

"Had a good thing going with Robyn," he said with a louche grin. "Not that I ever tried anything on. Wouldn't, would I? But she was classy, cut above. Flogged most of the stuff to the States, not so easy to trace." The grin faded. His pale eyebrows drew together in outrage, his face contorting with anger. "Roscoe saw me all right, see, promised I could pick up where I left off when I got out, but then you goes and shops him, destroys his career, his marriage and balls up everythin'."

She thought she was going to pass out. She'd been such a fool. How she'd clung even now to the conviction that Adam was a good person, misguided, perhaps, but straight and with a heart. She hadn't betrayed him. He'd betrayed her. "I'm sorry," she whispered.

"*Sorry*?" he advanced on her.

She backed away, huddled for safety, waiting for the inevitable blow, racking her brains for a way to divert him. "Which prison were you sent to?"

"Featherstone," he thundered.

That was it, she thought, mildly rallying. That was the connection.

"Been there just over four years, eatin' shit, watchin' me back twenty-four seven, wankin' off," he raged. "Then," he paused, suddenly casting her a clever, disarming smile. "I got me big break."

Suddenly, it all became crystal-clear. "You met Lee," she said.

"Shared a cell. All he did was fuckin' talk. Talk, talk, talk. Drove me fuckin' crackers. He could bloody whine for England. I had to hear all about his miserable life, and his fuckin' *stoopid* ideas, and how he'd fucked up. Thing is, see," he said, his eyes shining with spite, "he had a plan. It was fuckin' brilliant." He let out a laugh, a rattle that came from deep in his throat, "and the sad fuck didn't even realise it."

351

"He told you about us," she said wearily. Old pattern. New twist in the design.

"Before he got banged up, he discovered he had a family. Droned on about it all the fuckin' time, about how much it meant to him, that he'd got a home to go to at last. 'Course, what he really liked, was that mummy was one rich bitch. Had ideas above his station, see. As soon as he got out, he planned to visit and slot back in where he belonged, he said, get his feet under the table. Like a dog with two tails, he was. Stoopid tosser didn't realise he was the last person on earth she wanted to see. Didn't know he was spawned by his grandpa. Mind some of the varnish wore off when he found out about you. Couldn't believe he had a half-sister who'd stoop so low, batting for the other side, and being a grass. Couldn't get his head round it. Went dead quiet then."

"You mean the Jacks case?"

"Lost count of the villains who fancied getting their hands on you."

It had come full circle, she thought, but not in the way she'd imagined. "So you impersonated Lee."

He fixed her with a chill expression. "Had to get rid of him first."

They were plunged into darkness again. She didn't know how long they had. She didn't know whether Ryan was planning to drive all the way to Birmingham, or would orchestrate the drop from the cottage. Either way, she knew that at some stage he'd have to go and collect the money, and that meant he'd be gone for at least a couple of hours. She already knew that he had a good geographical knowledge of the Midlands. That was his stamping-ground. It was where he did business. So there was a chance he'd go closer than might be expected, which would take longer. Not too close, though. That would be dangerous.

She wasn't much of a gambler but, if he played further away, she estimated that they had three, no more than four, hours alone. Up until that moment, escape seemed a remote possibility. Now they were in with a chance. Ryan had unwittingly provided them with it.

"Siena," she hissed.

"Mmmm."

"You have to wake up."

"Why?" the girl said sleepily.

"Because I can get us out of here."

She heard the rustle of clothing, listened to the girl surface from slumber to consciousness. "How?"

"I want you to wiggle the rope on your wrists as much as you can, until it hurts, try and loosen it up a bit. Then we listen."

"For what?"

"For signs of Ryan leaving, a car door slamming, an engine starting up."

"Then what?"

"There's a broken piece of bottle over by your foot. I need you to roll it gently towards me.

"Can't see anything," the girl said crossly.

"But I can. I have a torch in my pocket."

By jack-knifing her body, and running her elbows from the top of her right knee towards her groin, Helen gradually eased the torch from her jeans pocket where it dropped satisfyingly onto the mattress. She sat on it until she heard the four-by-four start up, then she slipped it between her fingers and, after a couple of attempts that set her teeth on edge, flicked it on with the tip of her nose.

A thin light spooled eerily over the cellar floor. Her watch told her it was twenty minutes to one in the morning.

"Stand up," Helen instructed, "and walk as far as you can straight ahead until you can't move any further." She watched the girl stagger to her feet, saw her take a few nervous paces. "That's good," she said encouragingly. "Hold it right there." Helen lined up the light with the tip of the girl's foot and the edge of the bottle.

"All right," Helen said. "Remember, no sudden movements. Easy does it."

"Wouldn't it be simpler if I try and pick it up and free myself first?"

"Too risky, you might cut yourself." A small wound in the right place could lead to serious blood loss. Considering the girl's already weakened state, it wasn't a chance Helen was prepared to take.

"I want you to raise your foot and rest it gently on the glass."

The girl lifted her leg and began to wobble frantically. "I can't," she let out, slamming her foot heavily back down, centimetres away from the edge of the bottle. "Feel woozy."

Helen bit her lip. "It's all right," she said calmly. "Just squat down for a few moments. Breathe in and out, nice and slowly, big breaths."

"But it stinks," the girl wailed.

"Pretend it doesn't. Think of green fields and flowers. Your mum was into all that kind of stuff, wasn't she?" She tried not to sound cynical.

"Visualisation."

"That's right, give it a go." She watched the girl's shallow chest move in and out. "Great," Helen said. "This time stand up very slowly. Think of a plant growing," she said, remembering some faraway kindergarten lesson, "then when you feel secure, raise your foot but don't move it so high. It's just a slight movement, a few inches. That's it," she said, seeing the girl's tongue poke out in concentration. "Can you feel the glass under your foot?"

"Uh-huh."

"Now very gently roll it towards me. Think of sending a ball straight down a bowling alley, but make it slow. We're not going for a full strike."

Helen held her breath, hardly daring to watch, her anxiety turning to joy as the glass rolled towards her and stopped just within reach of her grasp.

"Did I do it?" the girl said excitedly.

"You did great," Helen said, stretching out her foot and moving it closer. By wriggling her fingers, she was able to upturn it so that the bottom of the bottle rested flat on the floor. The hard part was resting enough of the rope against the jagged glass without taking a slice out of her hands. Taking a deep breath, she sawed tentatively back and forth against the glass. Not a lot seemed to be happening. She tried again with a little more vigour, wincing as her right hand almost skimmed a piece sticking up.

"How you doing?" the girl said.

"Not bad. Nearly there."

It seemed to take for ever then it all happened at once. One minute she was bound. The next, her hands were free. With a deep thrill in her heart, she took off her boot and sock, wrapped it around her hand and, picking up the bottle, set about the rope tethering her to the strut. It was much harder. The rope was thick and durable. It took a good ten minutes to cut through it but, when she did, she felt exultant. She ran over to the girl at once.

"Take off my blindfold," the girl said, elated.

"In a minute," Helen said, not wishing her to see the distressing sight of the mess on the far side of the room. "Let's get you free first." Carefully slitting through the binds pinning the girl's wrists together, Helen handed her the torch. "Scarf next," the girl said, raising her slender fingers to the back of her head. Helen rested her hands on the girl's bony shoulders. "Keep your eyes on the outer door, Siena."

"I've seen dead people before," the girl huffed crossly. "I saw Malak. I saw Gran."

"Not like this."

The girl let out a petulant sigh.

Beneath the dirt, the grime, the pallor of her skin, she was very pretty, Helen thought, tenderly stroking a lock of hair away from the girl's face. She had green eyes, almond-shaped, like a cat's. She studied Helen with curiosity, ran her dirty fingers over her face then suddenly clasped hold of her, almost knocking Helen off her feet. Unlikely friends, she thought, hugging the girl back.

"Now cut the other rope," the girl cried, frantic to be free.

Helen handed her the torch, and set to it. She'd almost cut through when the bottle slipped, tearing through the sock and badly gashing the palm of her hand. "Christ," she let out, alarmed at the fast flow of blood dripping onto the floor.

"What happened?"

Helen turned away, shrinking from the light. "Cut myself. It's nothing. Just a bit sharp." She bound the remains of the sock tighter round her hand, helping to staunch the flow.

"But you're hurt," the girl said, shining the light on the cellar floor then staring at Helen's hand and the blood already seeping through the sock.

"It's not serious," Helen said, not knowing whether it was or wasn't. "One more hack at this should do it." She braced herself, picked up the bottle gingerly in her left hand, and drove it through the remaining rope. The girl bolted free like a foal on the first warm day of spring. But they still had another obstacle: the door.

"How long will it take?" They were both out of breath.

Although the door was solid enough, the frame surrounding the lock was rotten and the brickwork was crumbling. While the girl attacked it with a garden fork, Helen picked at it with a hoe. It wasn't easy with her injured hand. Blood had soaked right through. She'd taken off her other sock to rebind the wound. She didn't dare examine it, not because she was squeamish, but because she was frightened of seeing how serious it was.

"Don't know," Helen replied.

"How much time do you think we've got?"

I don't know that either, Helen thought. "Enough. Just keep on going."

She supposed adrenaline must have kicked in. She felt no pain or discomfort. Her brain buzzed. Her body fizzed. She felt warmer for moving about. She felt strangely powerful, too, in spite of the weakening light from the torch.

"If we can escape," the girl said breathlessly, "we can get into the cottage. I know where Gran kept the spare key. We can use the phone."

And lock him out, Helen thought. She didn't know why she expected him back. One man against an entire police force stood no chance at all. The police would spring him, no doubt about it. Another voice deep inside told her not to hope too much.

"Did your gran have a car?"

"Didn't drive."

"But there's a road?"

"More of a track."

"How the hell did she survive out here?"

"Once a month a friend from Okehampton drove out with her groceries."

"And how far's that away?"

"A couple of hours walk, maybe more."

"There's no one nearer?" Helen said, creeping with fear.

"No one."

They got a rhythm going. Helen striking first, the girl second, then repeating the sequence, one after the other. Bits of wood and plaster fell into a heap on the floor. Bricks crumbled. Dust flew up their noses and into their dry mouths. It was tortuously slow. Each time they thought they were nearly there, they discovered that there was another brick, another portion of wood to disable.

"If Ryan comes back," Siena said, sudden fear in her voice. "What should we do?"

"Hide."

"What if we're out in the open?"

"Run."

"If he shoots at us?"

"Hit the ground."

Without warning the lock sprang free, the door creaked and groaned. Together they pushed it open and were met by a rush of freezing night air. Euphoric, they breathed in great lungfuls, laughing, sucking in the icy chill, glad to be rid of the stench, overwhelmed to be free. Helen tilted her face up to a moon masked by cloud, and a sky barnacled with stars. She felt as if she were seeing them for the very first time. They seemed brighter, more abundant, and lustrous. The air smelt of winter, earthy and wet and bleak.

"Come on," the girl said, tugging at her arm.

Helen smiled, handed her the torch, let her shine the way.

The frost-tinged grass crunched as they walked. They went round to what Helen presumed was the front of the building. The girl creaked open a wooden gate and disappeared from view for a moment, then reappeared clutching a key. She shone the light on the cottage, which was long and low. It looked as if it were made of stone or cob.

"I ought to go first," Helen said. In effect, they were entering a crime scene. Out of habit, she realised that it was important not to contaminate the point of entry, the approach path, and inevitable bloodstains on the walls. There was another reason for going ahead. She wanted to shield the girl.

"There's a light switch on the wall just inside," the girl said.

Helen unlocked the door and felt for the switch. The light was so brilliant it hurt her eyes, making them water and squint. As the room gained more definition, she saw that she was standing in a narrow, poorly equipped kitchen with a sort of lobby tacked on housing a boiler and downstairs lavatory.

The scene in the kitchen was one of concentrated chaos. Onions and vegetables that had once hung in large nets were ripped from the walls. Preserved fruits and meats, and jars of jam and honey lay smashed upon the floor. The single drainer overflowed with dirty china. Greasy washing-up water, that looked as if it had been there for weeks, lay stagnating in the bowl. Cheap cupboards lay disembowelled, their contents spilled out onto the blood-spattered lino. On the facing wall was an old cream-coloured Rayburn. Except it wasn't cream any more. It was stained the colour of ox-liver. A slick of blood, dark and clotted, pooled on the floor in front of it. Drag-marks were clearly visible.

The girl was standing next to her. She was deathly white. Helen put an arm around the girl's shoulder, and gently guided her through to the adjoining room, a sort of parlour with a door at the end, which was open, revealing a set of stairs. The room must have been cluttered and cosy once, Helen thought, the place where the old woman spent most of her quiet life. Before Ryan crashed in and snuffed it out.

The carpet was covered in cigarette burns. Discarded beer bottles and bits of rotting food littered the hearth. Some effort had been made to light a fire. Blankets strewn near a chair suggested that Ryan had slept downstairs.

The phone rested on a small dining table pushed back against the wall. Helen seized on it, the words nine, nine, nine playing a soundtrack in the back of her brain. Picking up the receiver, she punched in the emergency number and waited. Nothing. No reassuring dialling tone. She stood there blankly.

Punched in the number again, cursing, until the painful truth slowly dawned on her: there was no line.

The obvious thing to do would be to stay where they were. They had shelter. There was food and water, sanitation. But what if no rescue came? What if, instead, Ryan returned?

She looked back across the room, wondered how to break the news, but the girl was gone. Helen crossed to the bottom of the stairs, called up. She could hear the sound of running water. She took the stairs two at a time. A door ahead of her was closed. She tapped on it.

"Go away."

"Siena, what are you doing?"

"I'm taking a bath."

"No, you mustn't do that." She tried to open the door but it wouldn't budge.

"I *must*," the girl cried, shrill.

"It's not a good idea. Besides, there's no time. The phone's dead. We need to get out of here." She glanced at her watch. It was twenty to two.

"I'm not listening."

"Look, Siena, I understand the reason, truly I do, but…"

"You don't understand anything," the girl screamed back, "how could you?"

Helen retreated. Shaken, she drank glass after glass of water. The girl was right. She had no right to preach. No right at all. There's an ancient saying that warns that those who avert their eyes from evil commit the worst of sins. While Adam wasn't evil, Jacks certainly was. She was no philosopher, no believer, but she understood the message.

She gingerly examined her hand. The gash was across the fleshy part of her thumb. It was deep and open and needed stitches. Racing back upstairs, she found a clean pillowcase in one of the bedrooms and, ripping it into strips, bandaged it as tightly as she could. She also found several sweaters, two of which she put on underneath her jacket, and a pair of bedsocks that smelt of mothballs to replace the ones she'd been forced to use as a temporary dressing. In a worse case scenario, hypothermia, coupled with blood-loss, could prove life threatening. She tried not to think about it. A frantic search for a torch and compass yielded nothing. She needed the girl's co-operation. It didn't appear as if she was going to get it. She didn't blame her.

She went back downstairs and crossed over into the downstairs lavatory. She felt acutely aware of her physical state, her body odour, the smell of pee on her clothes. The dirt. The fear. Mentally, she was in conflict: the pressing need to flee against an overpowering exhaustion. Even the short time in their temporary refuge had the effect of switching off her flight or fight response. She felt drained, sedated with unhappiness, as if she could sleep for a week. With her good hand, she splashed water over her face, hoping it would sharpen her wits.

After a cursory exploration, she found two packets of dried soup and, taking the kettle into the living room, boiled it in there, away from the carnage. She filled two mugs and put the rest in an old thermos flask that, in spite of rinsing, retained a sour, tainted smell. There was no bread, no butter, no milk or cheese but there were dry crackers and cereal, and one tin of baked beans and one tin of salmon. She opened both, stuffed the crackers and cereal into a plastic supermarket bag with the flask, and listened to the girl thumping around upstairs. Minutes later, she appeared. She looked scrubbed but brittle. She'd changed into thick corduroy trousers. Her cleanliness appeared in direct disproportion to her manner.

"Bon appetit," Helen said, handing her a spoon.

"Not hungry."

"You must be."

The girl shook her head, twitched away from her. There was a manic look in her green eyes. She moved as if she had Tourette's syndrome. This was bad, Helen thought, very bad.

"The soup's hot. It will warm you up. Be quick," she said lightly. "We need to get moving."

"I'm not going."

"You can't stay here," Helen said, open-jawed.

"Why not?"

"He might come back."

"This is my home."

"It's not safe."

"And you think out there is?" the girl suddenly yelled, her voice hitting a high note of panic. "I thought I was safe with my mother. I thought I was safe with my friends. I thought I was safe here. And look what happened," she screeched. Her shoulders pumped up and down. The heels of her palms pressed into her eyes. Helen stretched out her arms to touch her. Sensing it, the girl flinched away. Her mouth opened and closed as though she were having an asthma attack. The noises pouring from her mouth were unintelligible. Helen rushed to her side and put her arms around her, feeling the weight of the girl's terror and sorrow. The girl struggled and fought, but Helen held her firm, receiving the blows.

"You're safe with me," Helen told her over and over again, willing her to believe it. "I won't leave you. I'll look after you. I'll get you out of here. I promise."

But the girl was inconsolable. She howled and scratched and sobbed and shook.

After a time the fight seemed to go out of her, the crying grew less intense. Helen stroked the girl's hair, wiped her reddened eyes, her nose, coaxed her to eat and drink. It was after two in the morning. The time her father collected the call from Ryan.

Time to get out.

CHAPTER TWENTY-FOUR

BLUNDERING OFF IN THE wrong direction could kill them, so could the night. To minimise the risk, Helen found hats and thick woollen scarves and gloves. The girl sat sullen.

They carried a limited amount of water as well as raw supplies. Before they left, Helen scribbled their names on a piece of paper and left it by the telephone so that the police would know they'd been there. She also secreted a thin-bladed kitchen knife in the pocket of her coat.

The question was, which way to go? After some attempt to humour her, Helen discovered that the girl seemed to think that, should Ryan escape, he'd return along the most direct route from the main road. For this reason, the girl suggested another way.

"Is it longer?" Helen said, worried.

"Yes."

"Is there a road?"

"We can follow the river."

Follow the river? Helen thought in alarm. "You know it well?" she asked urgently.

"Well enough," was the clipped reply.

It felt as if the moor had its own unique intemperate weather system. The cold was more bitter, the wind more cruel. It bayed at them. The starlit sky, that only minutes before looked beautiful, seemed hostile and glittering with malice.

To start with, they followed the narrow track from the cottage. It was rough and stony and led steeply downhill, swiftly reducing their gait to a slow shuffle. Helen told herself that it didn't matter. Better to make slow, steady progress than go at it like a bullet from a gun and further exhaust themselves.

She tried hard not to think of the wilderness surrounding them. In sunshine, it might seem like a rare jewel. It might look benign and beautiful, but moors, by their very nature, were lonely, desolate wastelands, steeped in dark secrets. They were burial grounds for the dead. Synonymous with Brady and Hindley, and, nearer to her own experience, the Cannock Chase murderer, they echoed with a colossal unnameable fear.

They moved forward, stopped, listened, and keening their ears for sound of another, increased the pace where they could. After a while the land seemed to flatten out though the ground itself was rough and partially sheathed in a thin layer of ice.

Helen felt the wind battering against her face and sensed the bleak openness of their surroundings. She couldn't see the landscape, but she could visualise the desolation, the unforgiving terrain, the utter loneliness. She imagined deep gulleys and fast flowing rivers, rocky peaks and dark wooded gorges. She thought of treacherous tracts of land where the water-logged earth became bog. The girl spoke of a river, but Helen could hear and smell nothing other than peat.

"It's this way," the girl said.

"You sure?"

"Think so, yes."

Helen followed. Her eyes were slowly growing more accustomed to the lack of light. She discovered that, although the night is never completely dark or quiet, it is misleading. What appeared solid could prove insubstantial. A faint outline could be a jagged rock or wild pony. A sound could be no more threatening than the wind chasing through the ferns or ice-strewn wastes. It was easy to feel lost and disorientated. And dangerous.

They must have been walking for forty minutes. Her night vision was better now, more distilled, but the going was agonisingly slow. The ground felt barren and uncultivated. The grass, too, was stubby and unforgiving. She kept bumping into bracken and gorse and tiny hillocks. Neither of them had proper footwear and it was easy to stumble, easy to slip or wrench an ankle. Helen's only consolation was that, if Ryan returned, he would stick to the formal tracks. He'd definitely avoid the marshier terrain enclosing the river.

She tried to keep talking, to bolster their spirits, inspire with confidence. "Try swinging your arms."

"Why?"

"Helps maintain an even pace. And, if you take a tumble, you've got a better chance of saving yourself."

"If you say so," the girl replied sulkily.

"You feeling all right?"

"What do you think?"

Helen curbed a less tolerant response. "Want some water?"

"No thanks."

"No light-headedness?"

"Too cold for that."

"Feet holding out?"

"Stop bloody fussing."

There was a large shape before them. Thinking it was some form of habitation, Helen briefly switched on her

367

tiny torch. The light was poor, signalling that the batteries were running out.

"An old tinner's hut," the girl informed her.

"They used to mine here?"

"It was the richest source of tin in Europe, so Gran said. Back a long time ago. Best tread carefully."

"Why?"

"Open shafts."

"You're not inspiring me with confidence," Helen laughed, trying not to sound worried.

"It's a good sign," the girl assured her.

"How do you work that out?"

"It means the river's close by."

They'd travelled no more than a quarter of a mile before they blundered into it.

"See those lights," Helen said. They were standing side-by-side. The weather had changed. The wind had dropped to light icy gusts. Patchy freezing fog drifted temperamentally across their path. She stood mute, puzzled by the red glow. They weren't tiny fires – too high up – they looked friendly, like leading lights guiding a boat into harbour.

"Look, there's something below them," the girl said, "a flag or…"

"Christ," Helen screamed. There was the most enormous bang, like the sound of a volcano erupting, or massive nuclear explosion. The sky lit up and seemed to shake. "Get down, get down," she yelled, throwing herself at the frozen earth, pulling the girl underneath her.

Flares of light shot into the sky, turning it white. The ground, which had been black and unseen, suddenly flashed and writhed with deadly energy.

Gunfire turned night into day. They lay, paralysed with fear, not daring to move, trying not to breathe while a vast armoured firework display crashed around their heads.

Helen shut her eyes tight, tried to still her trembling limbs, wondering what they had stumbled into. Military manoeuvres, by the sound of it. But, surely, it wasn't possible?

The air burnt with the smell of cordite. The night crackled with the sound of machine-gun and tracer fire. It was like being caught in the biggest thunderstorm imaginable. Right over them. Every so often, the ground lit up, and she was certain they were going to be blown to pieces.

There was no let-up. No time to recover or calm the nerves. She made the mistake of glancing up once. The sky looked like a great illuminated spider's web.

Her heart clamoured. Sweat gathered on her brow. Her hand throbbed and burnt with the pain of injury. She felt quite dizzy with fear. Added to this, she thought of ponies bolting, of being crushed. She tried not to think of the damage one stray bullet could do.

She wondered if they should try and wriggle forwards, using their elbows to crawl, keeping their stomachs and rears firmly down, their movements small, but she didn't know which way to go, which would be safe. Surely to God, she screamed inside, the area couldn't be mined. Wouldn't be allowed. Would it?

Flares arced over their heads, bursting all around them, parachuting through the sky. They must have chanced upon some kind of firing line, she judged, maybe a place where the SAS practised. The moor was probably crawling with soldiers, she thought, but, scarily, she couldn't glimpse any. They all seemed to have melted into the background. She had a mad idea of giving themselves up, surrendering, but they'd be cut down before their hands had left their sides. And this wasn't war, she reminded herself. Just felt like it.

Waiting was purgatory. Hoping was worse. They seemed to be pinned down in a kind of hollow. The chill night air settled in it, forcing the heat to evaporate from their bodies. In spite of being welded together, Helen felt unutterably cold. She wondered if, at first light, the noise would stop. She glanced at her watch. It was almost five in the morning. They must have lain there for the best part of two hours.

The noise was dying. It was less repetitive, more sporadic. Still they didn't move. In the waiting, Helen allowed her mind to leap. She remembered those she cared about and, most oddly, those she didn't. She recalled forgotten faces, strangers whom she'd only ever met in death. But more than these, she thought of the girl concealed beneath her.

Thought of redemption.

The silence was more profound. Slowly and with great care, they stiffly picked themselves up, looking at each other in bewilderment, amazed to be alive. Then they started off again, slowly, moving forward like good and faithful friends. After a short time, Helen heard the river, smelt the water and vegetation. The earth was softer underfoot, less arduous. This was their route to safety, she thought, their pass to freedom, but the mist, which had been patchy, was growing in density and descending with alarming speed.

After a while, she called a halt. Squatting on the ground, they had a small picnic of crackers and soup and water.

"You reckon we're heading in the right direction?" Helen asked.

"Hard to tell. There should be a tor up ahead and then a narrow road."

"A tor?"

"A rocky peak."

"How far?"

"Not sure," the girl said, chewing her chapped lip.

Completely lost, Helen thought, with dread. She glanced at her watch again. It had stopped at five in the morning. She ditched the bag and flask, hung onto the water. "We'd better start moving again."

"Helen."

"Yes?"

"I've remembered."

"What?"

"My name is Ayshea Stone."

"Ayshea," Helen said, trying it out.

"It means life," the girl said.

The climb was steeper now, more rugged. It was difficult to hear the river. Fog muffled the sound. Visibility was down to a few yards. Everything was indistinguishable. Helen hoped the mist would lift with the same fickleness it had arrived. With the light changing, she wanted to be able to see the clefts and gorges, the steep-sided quarries, to know her adversary.

They trudged on, skirting what appeared to be a copse. The ground crackled and Helen could tell, from the sound of Ayshea's tread, that she was limping.

"What's wrong?"

"Blister."

"Better have a look at it." Given the conditions, Helen feared it could turn into a festering sore.

She took the girl's foot gently, eased off the shoe, the thin socks. She had a small foot, Helen noticed, no more than a size four. The skin had almost completely rubbed off the back of the heel, revealing a red and swollen area. It must have hurt for some time.

"Here, I've got a tissue," Helen said, cushioning it, putting the sock and shoe back on.

They both stood up, both heard the sound, both turned. Ayshea's face broke into a radiant smile. Helen shook her head. "Wait," she said.

"But if we flag them down, they can help us."

"Just wait," Helen said meaningfully.

"They'll drive past," Ayshea flared with anger.

She gripped the girl's thin shoulder, squeezed it. "What sort of a fruit-case is out driving at this time?"

"You think it's him," Ayshea gasped, eyes wide.

I don't know, she thought, but she was taking no chances. She pulled the girl back towards the trees, hoping that the combination of fog and woodland would camouflage them.

"But what if?" Ayshea hissed, squatting down next to Helen.

"Quiet."

They both heard it now. The sound of an engine running, a car door opening and closing, footsteps. She heard someone whistle, high and shrill, as if calling a dog to heel.

"It's all right," Ayshea whispered.

Helen shook her head, pressed a finger to her lips.

"You can come out," Ryan's voice pierced the stillness. "I've got what I want. You're free to go. No hard feelin's."

Ayshea's eyes lit up. Terrified she was going to call out, or struggle free Helen clapped a hand over the girl's mouth. As she listened to the crackle of heel on wood, questions pummelled her mind. What had gone wrong? How had he evaded the police? How could they have missed him? Crucially, how did Ryan know to come looking for them here?

He called again. Loud in the stillness. He was closer. She felt distilled with terror. Now she knew what it was to be hunted. Her heart was beating so loud she feared he'd hear.

"I know one of you's hurt, blood on the ground, see."

Shit, Helen thought, staring at Ayshea.

Again the whistle. More footsteps. They stayed absolutely quiet, absolutely still. He was speaking again but the words were swallowed by the wind. He was further away, Helen thought, hoping for it, praying even though she didn't believe. Eventually, the swish of a car door opening and slamming signalled his departure. Relief trickled out of her at the sound of the engine revving, and the vehicle bouncing away over the roughened ground.

Helen released her grip. She felt spent, giddy. Blood had squirted through the makeshift bandage. Some of it was on the girl's mouth.

Ayshea's face crumpled with disappointment. "He said we could go."

You have a lot to learn about trust, Helen thought. "He hasn't gone. He uses smoke and mirrors. He's playing games. And he knows the moors a lot better than we think."

"Will he be back?" the girl's lip quivered. A tear slipped down her face.

What could she say? If you want to understand the photographer, look at the photo. If you want to understand the director, look at his films. If you want to understand the killer, look at the crime. Of course, he'd be back.

CHAPTER TWENTY-FIVE

THE LIGHT WAS CHANGING. The fog had lifted. Winter lent the landscape an exhausted expression. Shapeless shadows gave way to jagged contours, purple-tipped peaks and snow-covered castellated tors. Everywhere revealed evidence of human activity: in the prehistoric remains, the lines of parallel terraces, the relics of open cast tin workings. Yet there was nobody and nothing to see or feel other than a brooding, primeval presence. She wondered how far it was to the prison at Princetown, whether this explained her feeling of foreboding. Somewhere, further off, the barrenness was broken by dark, sinister-looking masses, bogs or forest, she thought, but couldn't tell.

They were by the river. It was wide and in full spate. Brown and swollen with winter rain, it flowed at a relentless pace, gobbling up everything in its path, including boulders and bits of wood, and the bloated bodies of unfortunate sheep. Up ahead, it seethed and swirled, dropping away into a foamy spume of white water. The sound of it was like cymbals clashing in their ears.

Marshy ground, studded with bright green sphagnum moss, made walking difficult and hazardous. To slip would be disaster. Helen imagined the bracing cold, the rush into darkness, the slime. She remembered the canal.

Exhaustion was taking its toll. She'd never felt so cold or so lifeless. Every movement took effort. The throb and burn of injury had diminished, the pain in her hand strangely cooled. Either it indicated something serious, she thought, or her body's natural defences had fully engaged. It didn't matter; her concern was for the girl, only the girl. The girl was her light, her focus, the reason.

However far they walked, whatever ground they covered, yet more stretched out ahead of them in endless purgatory. Helen found herself glancing ever more anxiously behind her, scanning their retreat, watching for Ryan. All she saw were the moors closing in behind them.

She should have noticed, Helen cursed, should have stayed more alert. She had no idea for how long Ayshea had been suffering. The girl's head was lowered. Her gait was stumbling. She shivered uncontrollably. There was no movement in her arms.

Helen caught hold of her. "Look at me," she said in alarm, waving a finger in front of the girl's glassy eyes. Ayshea swayed. Helen tapped the girl's frozen cheeks, pinched them. Ayshea's eyes flickered. She gave a slow wan smile.

"Here," Helen said, gripping hold of the girl with her good hand, supporting her. She looked around for a suitable place to rest, her eyes skimming the wilderness, wondering if, among the tors and craggy heights, she could find temporary sanctuary. Some distance away, she glimpsed a mound of rocks. They looked as if they'd been piled one on top of the other by a Viking god or some other unseen force. Although common sense dictated they stuck to the river's path, their best hope of reaching civilisation, Helen decided a detour was urgent. Ayshea needed to rest, to warm-up, to stave off hypothermia. Out in the open, she stood no chance. And that was unthinkable.

They followed an ancient track through scrubby yellowing grass. Helen half-pushed, half-pulled Ayshea to the rocky outcrop. Once there, they sheltered out of the wind. Helen gave the girl the last of the water. She blended calm and optimism into her expression, into her manner, her voice. She was going to get Ayshea out of here if it killed her.

Helen closed her body over the girl's to try and warm her. As she lay, spread-eagled, she looked through ever-changing shafts of light on to a fossilised landscape of ridges and furrows, of dark chocolate-brown heather, of mounds and crevasses. She played every mental game to mask her fear, her extreme terror of being lost and never found.

"Helen?" Ayshea said, after a time.

"Yes."

"Thank you."

Helen kissed the top of the girl's small head, her eyes shining with tears.

They broke cover under a baleful sky.

The more light there was, the more disturbing the scenery. Ominous-looking standing stones, some single, some in rows or circles, stood, sphinx-like, as if guarding the ancient secrets of the moor. There were few trees. The wind picked up again, snapping through them, forcing the land to seethe in an unforgiving mass of purple and brown. Other than the odd bird of prey wheeling over their heads, there was no sign of bird-life. No sound of birdsong. Just a sustained, eerie silence.

They'd taken to higher ground to cut off the bends, yet the river seemed to meander for miles, thinning and thickening, never losing its power. The river was worthy of respect, Helen thought, not like the canal she nearly drowned in.

Snow covered the peaks, slowing the pace to a weary trudge. It was skin-flayingly cold. Without warning, a loud screeching sound shattered the silence. Ayshea jolted and almost turned her ankle. Helen shot out a hand to steady her. Transfixed, they looked up in the direction of the unearthly cry. The barn owl seemed to fall out of the sky as if from nowhere. A flash of white, dreamlike, swooping down, wings fully extended, screaming low across the land then vanishing from view.

Ayshea was ashen.

"It means hope," Helen insisted, trying not to tremble.

Ayshea said nothing.

Too numb and cold to speak, they trudged in silence. Helen could feel the exhaustion running through her veins, eating into her muscles, settling on her bones. Her hand was throbbing again. It was causing real pain. Fresh blood was seeping through the tattered cloth. She wanted to put her hand in her pocket to soothe it but resisted the temptation in case she should stumble and be unable to break her fall. She needed sugar and sleep and warmth though she wasn't sure which first. She tried to think, to keep herself mentally alert, to stay focused, but her mind was leaping, and that was dangerous. Self-confidence and determination were keys to survival. Self-pity was a killer. It held true for both ordinary and extraordinary circumstances. She glanced back at Ayshea, her face grey in the winter light. The buoyancy had gone from the girl's step, the hope from her eyes. Helen knew that she had to stay positive, keep whatever faith they possessed. She didn't tell Ayshea that she feared the worst was yet to come.

They were higher up now. The snow was thicker, the mist more patchy. From their elevated position, she stared across an expanse of scarred and wounded earth. Ancient tracks ran like a skein of stretchmarks across its skin. It seemed as if the treeless and desolate plateau spread out before her was created from a single solid lump of bone. Ahead, she could see burial mounds, with their histories of legend and secrets, gaping mineshafts and deep gorges, man-made reservoirs and ruined dwellings. It looked like an apocalyptic wasteland and, rather than being comforted by the fast-approaching day, the possibility of escape, she felt terribly afraid.

Still they pressed on.

The sound of rushing water grew loud in her ears. She could smell the river, the dankness of vegetation, the reeds, earth and soil. She could also smell her own sweat, the blood and filth on her clothes.

Pregnant with winter rain, the river led them to an ancient clapper bridge made from slabs of granite. There were lengths of scaffolding pole on the ground as if someone had once intended to carry out repairs and lost interest. Beyond that, a road. And their route to freedom.

The ground was soft and treacherous beneath their feet. The bridge, too, was slimed in moss and lichen. Where the fast, flowing water met the struts, it eddied and boiled and strained. But it was the way ahead that worried her. She couldn't see or hear a thing, yet instinct told her that Ryan was there. Somewhere. Waiting.

"Careful as you go," Helen said to Ayshea, trying to keep the worry from her voice.

Ayshea nodded gravely, took Helen's extended hand. They walked side by side, close together, keeping away from the edges, the sound of their feet drowned out by the tumbling river. As they crossed, Helen had a vision of a family holiday in Scotland. They were driving to Edinburgh and had stopped briefly to stretch their legs in the Lammermuir Hills, a plain bounding East Lothian and the Scottish borders. Sheep grazed in the summer sunshine. Tributaries of the River Tweed sparkled with light and dragonflies. While her parents were admiring the view, she spied some big stepping-stones. As she leapt from one to another, she didn't notice the depth, the speed at which the water flowed, the danger. Her father called out, his voice shrill with fear, but it was her mother who remained calm, coaxing her back, keeping her safe.

A noise. Helen stopped, blinked, and listened, ears keening. It sounded like a twig snapping but, in this strange, sludgy landscape of blacks, greens and greys and whistling wind, it was hard to tell what was real, what was fantasy or delusion.

They were the other side of the bridge. Instinctively, she pushed Ayshea behind her. Scanning the shifting curtains of colour as a watery sun struggled and failed to put in an appearance against a sky the colour of weak tea, she caught sight of a shadow. Coming into focus. Standing ahead of them. Cold eyes impaling her. A gun in his muscled hand.

She stood petrified. Her limbs stiffened. So did her mind.

"Move," Ryan shouted.

The girl was breathing hard behind her. Helen didn't know what to do, what to think or say then she remembered her promise, her private vow. Terror pulsing through her, she pretended she was back on the job: examine the scene, list the order of importance, and view all options. Two against one was good, she thought wildly, but two exhausted females against one armed and physically fit male? They stood no chance.

She stared at the gun. She wasn't an authority but she'd once spent an afternoon with the firearms department and been given a whistlestop tour. By her estimation, Ryan was holding a snub-nosed .38. It had eight bullets, eight opportunities. Worse, he didn't need to be a particularly good shot. Small, compact, extremely powerful, it literally ripped holes in people. Any fool could pull the trigger. It didn't take skill to maim or inflict pain. Even if she could get close enough to stab him with the knife in her pocket, against a gun they stood no chance at all. Her only weapons were mental agility, speed, and the river.

He was walking towards them, slowly, carefully, as if worried about messing up his footwear or leaving an impression in the ground. The gun was pointed low. Helen glanced behind her, past the shaking girl, saw the river, thought of the cold and the current, thought of the danger.

"How did you pull it off?" Helen said, slowly raising her arms, buying time, reeling him in.

"Luck," he laughed without mirth. "Your old man was wired, all right, but the weather screwed them."

"The weather?"

"The fog."

Not only would it have made the drive difficult, she thought in dull realisation, but it would break up any radio link.

"Got what I wanted," he said with a whisper of a smile.

"Good."

"Money makes the world go round. You know that better than anyone."

"What about truth and honesty?" Keep on coming, you bastard, she thought.

His voice hardened. "You've got a fuckin' cheek, bitch."

Helen swallowed. Ayshea began to cry. "Think of the noise of two gunshots," Helen said, standing her ground.

"Who's to hear?"

"You can't just leave us," she said, trying to kill the tremble in her legs. "Someone will find us eventually – even out here."

He glanced at the river. She half-turned as if following his gaze, took a small step back, butting into Ayshea, making eye contact with her.

"You'll have to touch us," Helen challenged him, subtly shifting her stance, slipping her hand into the pocket of her jacket. "Everyone leaves a trace, Ryan. Think of the blood on the ground, the spatter on your clothes. Think of the mess."

He was closing in. His eyes were cruel. He was close enough to blow them away and into the water. He knew it. She knew it.

"Think of your footprints," she said, taunting him, hand grasping the knife. Any second now, she thought. The girl's crying had subsided. Helen could feel

Ayshea's body stiffening, the muscles poised, ready for flight.

"Run," Helen yelled, "Run for your life." She took a step forward, caught the wolfish expression in Ryan's eyes, the tightening of his jaw, saw him turn, swinging the gun wide to his left. She powered into him, slashing at his arm with the knife. She did not see the girl zigzagging, weaving across the moor, sprinting over rock and knoll. All her focus was on him, his outline, his actions, his gun. The pain in her hand was searing and, though she aimed a second blow, he easily twisted the knife out of her weakened grasp and sent it flying. With her good hand she clawed at his face, jabbed two straight fingers into his eyes, making him cry out and stagger. Empowered, she brought up her knee but wasn't quick enough. The next she knew was the muzzle flash, the pistol crack, the smell of cordite, the gun spinning away. In horror, she turned, raking the unforgiving landscape for sight of Ayshea's lithe form. But all she saw was the peat-clad granite, the treeless and uncultivated ground, the rushes, the bright green moss, and patches of standing water. Ayshea was nowhere to be seen.

Because Ayshea was down.

Helen had no time to stare at the body, the bundle of clothes three hundred yards away, to grieve. She had no time to consider the hopelessness of her situation. The blow between her shoulder blades sent her flying. She gave a gasp as her hands automatically stretched out to save her, as her face hit the dirt and re-split her lip, as her hand clenched in agony, but the pain was all for the girl, for letting her down, for failing her, just as she'd failed the others.

He had her by the hair now, his thick fingers gripping the roots, wrenching her to her feet by her scalp. He showed no sign of going for the gun; he was searching for the knife, she thought in misery. He wants to make me suffer, and maybe he's right.

Hot, stinging tears coursed down her cheeks. She was bent over, suppliant. The hair was being ripped from her head. In a flash, she thought of Rose Buchanan, of what had been done to her. Then she thought of Ayshea. And as Helen remembered, rage broke over her like a tidal wave. She wasn't just fighting Ryan any more, but Jacks, and all the other low-lifes. And she wasn't alone. Rose and Tracey and Ayshea were cheering her on. Even Karen Lake. Even her own mother. They represented all the many women she'd come across, who'd been abused.

Raising her left hand, she put it firmly over his, immediately reducing the pressure to her head. Pivoting on one foot, she half-turned so that they were facing in the same direction, his arm fully extended along her left side. Then, with chilling clarity, she smashed her left forearm down hard against his elbow, breaking his hold. Using her height, she straightened up and followed through with a second blow into his body with her elbow. Ryan doubled over, lost his balance and fell dangerously close to the river's edge and the torrent of white water. Helen lifted her leg to kick him but Ryan was one move ahead. With lightning speed, he rolled over, kicked out, tripping her up and sending her flying onto her back. She tried to relax, to roll with it, but the next she knew he was astride her, his solid weight heavy on her abdomen. For one sickening moment, she thought he might rape her. Then his strong hands flew to her throat. She could feel the balls of his thumbs pressing down, choking her, his spatulate fingers squeezing either side of her neck. This time she could do nothing to relieve the pressure. Her knees were pinned and her fists were useless. She knew, from experience, that it didn't take long to render someone unconscious, to strangle them. She clawed at his fingers but he just dug deeper. Her throat was rattling. She was seeing black shapes before her eyes. In desperation, she reached up with her left, uninjured, hand, extending her fingertips, driving as hard as she could into his throat. The effect was immediate. He let go with a guttural cry, his body crumpling as he fell sideways onto his hands and knees. Scrambling away from him, she clambered back onto her feet. The gun was somewhere behind her and she knew that, to grab it, she'd have to turn away, and she'd been taught always to keep facing the attacker, always anticipate the next move.

He was still on his knees, one hand clutched to his throat. He was making strange, animal noises, but his eyes were darting, alert, focused. He dragged himself to his feet. With each sound, he moved closer. Then she saw the knife, its blade glinting in a shaft of brief and unexpected sunshine. She made a grab for it, held the haft in her wounded hand, brandishing it, sweeping in wide arcs in front of him. She should have felt pain but adrenaline-fuelled fury was stronger. As he pitched forward, she lunged with the blade, slicing across his face. He let out an unholy cry and counter-attacked with a knee into her stomach, felling her, the knife spiralling away again. The pain was as intense as a kick to the kidneys. Suddenly it was over, she thought, curled in agony. Somehow, Ryan had got hold of the gun again. There were hundreds of exit-routes, hundreds of different ways to die. This was hers.

One hand gripped the clothing on her shoulder, the other hand flailing wildly with the gun.

"You fuckin' slag," he screamed at her, blood pouring down his face from the open wound which had narrowly missed his right eye. He was dragging her forwards on her knees, bending her to his will, forcing her towards the swirling water's edge. She felt helpless and, in a fleeting moment, she thought of Adam. She wondered crazily if Adam had been this terrified, if a bullet in the head hurt. Would it be better to throw her body full-tilt into the torrent? Might it be a cleaner way to die? Then she thought of the icy cold, the half-submerged boulders and broken branches, the useless, violent, pointless struggle.

Ryan was yelling obscenities. "I'm gonna fuckin' kill you, this time, girl. I'm gonna kill you bit by bit. I'm gonna make you scream." He was completely out of control. The veins on his face were engorged with blood, his bulging eyes possessed by rage.

She let out a scream, trying to resist, failing.

"Shut your big fuckin' mouth."

Was this how it was with the old woman, she thought miserably? Somehow she doubted it. Ryan preferred his victims young and vital. The pleasure was in the pain, of seeing a young life corrupted.

They were right at the edge. It had started to sleet. Both of them were sliding in the marshy earth. The mud was over his boots and coating her clothes. Ryan was trying to gain purchase, to force her head and shoulders down. He still held the gun in his right hand and was attempting to swing it round. But he needed to be steady, she thought, and the ground was as

386

threatening to him as to her. He was cursing now, at the top of his voice, calling her a bitch, a whore, a cunt. He was losing the battle mentally, she thought, and that meant she could still win. Even with the sound of the eddying water clamouring in her ears, she shook off all feeling of a life not lived, of lost hopes, guilt, crushed dreams and despair. She played resistant, twisting against his grasp, then, as he pushed back, she suddenly went with the movement, bowing to his command, taking him off-guard. Ryan stumbled just as she knew he would. At once, she shot out an elbow, smashing it into his nose, hearing the satisfying crack. Blood cascaded over the flint-edged ground. His feet seemed to slide out from underneath him, almost pitching her forward with him, the gun flying out of his hand and into the river where it was consumed by the current and carried away.

Scrambling back from the water's edge, she saw that Ryan had managed to grab onto the platform that was the bridge. Hanging on, he kicked and flailed. For a moment, she thought he might lose his grip and fall. But his hands were strong, she remembered.

He was climbing along, monkey-like, swinging towards her, death in his eyes. That's when she realised what had to be done. And that's when she knew that she had nothing to lose.

Picking up a short piece of discarded scaffolding pole in both hands, she waited until he was near then smashed it once across his shoulders. He let out a scream but still he hung on, his body twisting, racked with pain. Grunting with exertion, she lifted the iron for a second time. There was shock in his eyes as she connected. How could a woman do this? he seemed to say as he plunged into the rolling water, feet first. For a moment he disappeared, bobbing to the surface seconds later, limbs flailing, driven mercilessly by the swirling current.

Helen followed the river's relentless flow with her eyes. She saw the bend, where the undertow was at its strongest, the chevron shape in the water denoting a partially submerged rock, and the way the river twisted and turned in a dizzying eddy further downstream. And she felt nothing.

Ryan was being bumped along, buffeted at formidable speed, head still above the water, just. She wondered if he'd seen the rock, the jagged edge, impending and certain death. She wondered if he remembered those he loved, whether life flashed before his eyes. Probably not, she thought without emotion, as his head snapped against the boulder and his body, finally drained of life, was borne away.

She stood, eyes fixed on the water, watching for bubbles, for movement, for life, checking that he was really gone. Still she felt nothing. Her thoughts, when they came, were cold and practical. If the body went out to sea, it might never be found. If it lodged down river, Scenes of Crime would take over. She thought of the retrieval of the bloated, bloodless corpse, the lacerations, the smashed skull, the river's triumph.

Something cawed over her head. She barely gave it a glance. She was urgently scanning the still and joyless landscape. She was not concerned with the layers of artefacts embedded in the ground. She did not see the heather-covered banks dark as freshly dug graves. She did not see the snowy peaks. All she saw was the lifeless pile of clothes, the girl. For the first time in her life, her professional expertise deserted her. She could not bear to look, let alone approach.

Her throat closed over. She put her wounded hand to her face. With no sense of elation, no joy at her release, she buckled, falling to the frozen ground.

It was over.

She'd failed. Another life lost, she wept bitterly. Everything would be as before. Only a thousand times worse. Nothing to sustain her. Nothing to keep the flicker of hope alive. Nothing to die for. Back into the dark. The future was as desolate as the past, a stark and forbidding place where only a fool would walk. A fool like her.

She vaguely heard the lazy *wop wop* sound of a helicopter circling overhead. She didn't look up. She pressed her face further into the dirt, imagining the girl with the green eyes and wheaten-coloured hair. She didn't think back to the anger in her voice, the fury in her eyes. She only thought of her trusting expression, a trust that was betrayed.

"Helen," she seemed to hear her call.

Delirious, Helen thought. Must have lost a lot of blood. Strange how the mind plays tricks. The voice was so real, so...

"Helen, get up."

She felt death upon her shoulder. Perhaps it was Ryan come back from the dead, she thought feverishly, to finish the job off. What did she care?

"Are you hurt?"

A rescuer, she thought, stirring. "You're too late," she murmured.

"It's never too late."

She staggered onto her knees, looked round, opened her eyes wide. The girl's face was smiling. Helen wondered if it was one of her visions. "Ayshea?"

"You told me to hit the ground if there was gunfire."

"You're all right," Helen said, muddled, raising her hand, touching the girl like some doubting Thomas, unable to take it in.

Ayshea stooped down, putting her arms around her. "And so are you."

The helicopter landed nearby. It should have felt exhilarating, Helen thought, as they lifted her onto a stretcher and carried her to the waiting vehicle, but after so much drama she was just relieved to be rescued from the moors.

They were both taken to Derriford Hospital in Plymouth and given the full treatment by waiting nurses, and doctors with white coats flapping. It felt strange to be whisked inside, and whizzed along sterile-smelling corridors again for the second time in a month. She almost laughed out loud as porters were forced to take circuitous routes to avoid the press. She had to admit she preferred the feeling of heroine to pariah.

She was minutely examined. Her hand was stitched. She was treated for mild hypothermia and dehydration. She bathed until she squeaked with cleanliness. She scrubbed her teeth until her gums bled. She was ordered to rest. People came and went, including Stratton, and she slept and slept and slept.

"How did you know where to find me?" she asked dozily. Stratton was sitting on her bed, his fingers laced through hers.

"We'll talk later," he said, brushing her lips with his.

"You need to check out a car registration."

"Helen, go back to sleep."

"It's important. Dark Porsche Boxster. I saw it at Robyn Roscoe's house." She gave him the number on the licence plate.

"All right," he said, making a note. "Now try and get some rest."

"Someone was firing at us," she said, mind grasshopping, "mortars and stuff."

Stratton's eyes widened. "Jesus, Helen. Didn't you know the military train on Dartmoor?"

"Like to live dangerously," she murmured with a smile, lapsing into sleep again.

Every time, she dozed off and woke up there seemed to be someone else in the room. She was told that there was evidence to suggest she'd been overpowered by chloroform during her ordeal, a nasty, volatile poison that causes a relaxation of the heart muscles, sometimes with fatal consequences. Narrow escape, she thought muzzily. A female psychiatrist called Dr Pellman offered to talk to her about her abduction and subsequent captivity. Helen declined.

"Think about it," Dr Pellman insisted, standing over her. "You may feel quite differently when you're stronger."

No, I won't, Helen thought, wondering if she were displaying an unhealthy family trait. Her mother, for obvious reasons, had wanted to kick over the painful traces of her past. Wasn't she doing the same? "How's the girl, Ayshea?"

"I understand she's making a good recovery." Helen wondered what that meant. The next time she woke, she found her father holding her hand. "Dad," she said, squeezing it, "how long have you been here?"

"About three hours," he beamed, kissing her cheek.

"Did they get the money back?"

"The money's not important, Helen."

"But did they?"

"Yes."

"Good."

They didn't talk much, too much to say, too much to explain. It would all come later, she thought, not as a rush, but in bits and pieces. Like rock formation, it would gradually build up in layers until a solid story eventually emerged. As for her mother's part in it, she wasn't sure how much to say, how much to tell, if anything at all.

CHAPTER TWENTY-SIX

THE NEXT FEW DAYS were a blur. Every time she got out of bed, she was unsteady on her feet. She was interviewed by every policeman on the planet, or so it felt, and made a long and detailed statement. Jen and Ed arrived with flowers and champagne and chocolates. There were hugs and kisses and wide-eyed looks, and a lot of tiptoeing around what had happened to her. It was as if there had been a death in the family instead of her being very much alive. She was the subject of strange fascination, she realised. Not many people have friends who've been abducted, let alone abducted and survived to tell the tale. Jen, for all her gawping, seemed especially fearful of asking too many probing questions. Helen was glad for the reprieve.

Ayshea was never far from Helen's side. They were both fiercely protective of the other. Nobody but they knew what really happened, or how an unlikely friendship had blossomed from degradation and fear. They didn't talk of Ryan or speak of their ordeal. Helen thought it possible they never would. It suited her, but she was worried for the girl, anxious about the possible consequences, the difficulties she would surely encounter, how she'd make her way in a world that was clearly crazy. Helen wondered if she should tip off Dr Pellman, then decided that to do so would betray the fragile bond they shared and discounted it.

As for herself, she felt a vast sense of relief, as if a great slab of stone had been lifted off her back. Every time she looked at the girl, she felt as if something in her world had shifted. She felt hopeful. At peace.

Inspired. It had been a long time since she'd felt such things.

"I still don't understand how you tracked us down?" Helen said to Stratton. He'd virtually camped in her room since her admittance.

"By chucking everything into the mix, looking at the whole situation again. Your car was found at Albion Place. There were signs of a struggle, smashed mobile phone, keys in the road, so we knew that was where you were abducted. Door-to-door enquiries yielded little apart from several sightings of a white van."

"As common as blue jeans and plain T-shirts," she said.

"Exactly. It's why we questioned the girls again."

"You mean Shirley and Co?" Helen said, attentive.

"Shirley Brownlow, Stacey Warren and Jade Jenkins."

"And?"

"Nothing."

She could believe it. Ryan was a terrifying character. One breathed syllable could get Shirley, or a member of her family, killed. And, whatever the police maintained, they were not especially good at protecting witnesses.

"So what then?"

"We looked at all the players, including Lee Painter."

"But Lee's dead. You ruled him out."

"Him, yes. But not his contacts."

"And that included the Park Lane Boys."

"And his prison-chums. From what you told me, Lee had clearly expressed an interest in your family, a very wealthy family, before he got sent down."

"Oh my God," she gulped. "Does my father know about Lee, about Mum?"

"Yes."

"What was his reaction?"

"Shock, as you'd expect, but, to be honest, he was more concerned with getting you back in one piece."

She wondered how her father would feel once the sense of crisis had passed. "I'm still not quite following how you narrowed it down."

"What do guys do in prison?" Stratton asked her.

Ryan's words reverberated through her brain: *eating shit, watching me back twenty-four seven, wanking off.* "I don't know," she said.

"They talk. What else is there to do? And, by all accounts, Painter liked the sound of his own voice. He'd gab on to all and sundry, including his cell-mate who we discovered was Ryan Crees."

"But if Lee talked to everyone, how did you know Ryan was the blackmailer?"

Stratton tapped the side of his nose.

Helen raised an eyebrow. "You mean an informer?"

"Uh-huh."

"Game to you, I think."

Stratton smiled. "Crees was a loner, a skilled thief but he had a weakness – young women. Basically, the guy was a rapist, not in the sense that he went out deliberately selecting victims, but if presented with an opportunity, he felt compelled to act on it, a bit like our friend Warren Jacks. Crees was eventually sent down because a shrewd Scenes of Crime officer gathered the right evidence."

"You mean the ear-print?"

"And DNA found at the scene, but Crees seemed particularly affronted by the print and often banged on about it inside, swearing vengeance."

"It's a bit flaky to deduce he'd come after me, isn't it?"

"There was nothing terribly concrete in our reasoning," Stratton admitted.

"And there's me thinking imaginative ideas wasn't your thing," she said with a jubilant smile.

Stratton smiled back. "Frankly, when you've got thirty-six hours and someone's life in the balance, you're up for anything. The fact you were Painter's half-sister and a former scenes of crime officer gave Crees the perfect opportunity to make a lot of money and satisfy his taste for revenge. Following that possible line of investigation, we did some homework on Crees and discovered that he was born in Plymouth and came from a violent background. As a lad, he escaped his abusive family and spent a lot of time on the moors, specifically the most barren area on the northern edge – an ideal place to hold someone captive."

It was, she thought.

"The problem was the time-factor."

"At least you got there to pick us up. Not sure I could have walked another step," she smiled briefly. "Joe," she said, suddenly reaching out and touching his hand, a serious expression on her face. "I'm sorry."

"For what?" he frowned.

"For being wrong about Adam."

He sighed, shook his head, bent over and kissed her. "Doesn't matter. It's in the past. Except for one tiny factor," he said with a wide grin. "The owner of the Porsche Boxster is none other than Damien Crawley."

"Christ," she said, sitting up, "the guy Adam mentioned in his contact sheets, the bloke he was trying to get Jacks to cosy up with?"

"Yup. Adam was obviously using Jacks to recruit him for his wife's criminal activities. From what we've managed to gather, Mrs Roscoe recently made the professional relationship with Crawley rather more personal."

Another reason for Crees to be enraged, Helen thought. With Crawley on the scene, he stood no chance of picking up where he left off. "What will happen to them?"

"They're both being interviewed by specialist art and antiques officers from the Met. Apparently, they've been after Crawley for some time. They think he's connected to the theft of a number of rare books – apparently there's quite a market for them in the UK. He's also under suspicion for stealing to order for certain crime syndicates who use stolen art as a bargaining chip."

That should knock some of the varnish off Robyn, Helen thought.

"So what happens now?" he asked, squeezing her hand.

"You mean futures?"

"Yes."

"I've got one or two ideas floating around," she smiled elusively. "But, first, I want to get my brain unscrambled."

He laughed.

"I know," she laughed too. "Could take some time."

"What do you want to do?"

It was almost four days later.

Ayshea shrugged. She looked odd dressed in more contemporary clothing, Helen thought. The girl's hair, once matted in dreadlocks, was washed and shiny and styled. It took some getting used to. She guessed Ayshea seemed more grown-up, less innocent. That much was true, she thought, stomach clenching.

"Do you want to come home with me?" Helen wasn't sure about the ethics of it. She didn't know the opinion of Social Services, or whether the fact she was not of traveller stock ruled her out of any caring role, but one thing she was absolutely certain of – Ayshea should not be put in care, not even for a short period of time.

The girl's gaze was steady. "I'd like that." Then her face clouded.

"What is it?" Helen asked.

"I don't think I'm made for city living, do you?"

Helen smiled sadly. The girl was a free spirit used to a simpler way of life, an existence harnessed to the natural rhythms of the world, one that was entirely alien to a hard-edged city-dweller like herself. She could no more imagine life without slick department stores, theatres and cinemas, restaurants and bars, than Ayshea could live without the wind in her hair, the grass under her feet, the sound of birdsong.

"That's all right," Helen suddenly beamed. "I've got a better idea."

*   *   *

Birmingham Children's Hospital was in Steelhouse Lane, not far from the police station. Helen went inside and walked straight up to reception. She was holding a large, fluffy teddy bear. It had brown friendly eyes and wore a jaunty hat and jacket. It was impossible not to fall in love with it.

"I'm looking for Kelly Brownlow," she told a stoutly built female receptionist.

"Patient?"

"Yes."

The receptionist scanned her computer. "You won't be able to visit, I'm afraid."

"Why not?"

"She's in isolation."

"Oh," Helen said, crestfallen.

"Her mother's here," the receptionist smiled helpfully. "Think I saw her taking a breather in the cafe. It's that way," she pointed, craning her neck.

Shirley was unmistakable. Same smart coat, same black boots, same worn-down expression. She was hunched over a cup of coffee. Her fingers trembled. She looked as if she were torn between tears and screaming. Helen knew the feeling. She went straight over to her table and sat down. Shirley looked up. Her sallow, pitted complexion turned grey and her mouth tightened into a short, sharp line. She looked shocked.

"It's all right," Helen said, propping the teddy up on the table. "I'm not a ghost."

Shirley's hands were darting now as if badly in need of a cigarette to steady them.

"About our meeting," Helen began slowly.

"You never showed up," Shirley bluffed, recovering her composure with remarkable speed.

399

"Thought that was my line."

"Don't know what you mean." The cup rattled against the saucer.

"Does the name Ryan Crees jog your memory?"

"I have to go," Shirley said, abruptly pushing the chair back.

"But you haven't finished your coffee."

The woman cursed under her breath and stood up.

"Sit down, Shirley. I didn't tell the police you made the call."

Shirley chewed her bottom lip, swept the coat around her, and gathered up her bag. "Sorry, my daughter needs me."

"That's why you did it, isn't it? Because of Kelly?"

Shirley's mouth quivered. She stepped away.

"Crees is dead," Helen called after her loudly. A number of people stopped talking and stared at her.

Shirley stopped, turned and walked straight up to Helen. "No shitting me?"

"No."

Shirley slumped back down.

"Here," Helen said more softly, pushing the coffee towards her. "Drink it, you look as if you need it."

"Large vodka would be better." There was no accompanying smile.

Helen studied her briefly, wondering how prostitution had chosen her, and if she was as hard as she appeared. "It's why I'm here, Shirley. You're a mum, and you were doing what comes naturally. You were protecting your child. Am I right?"

Shirley cast her a careworn look and ran her fingers through her lank hair. "Crees threatened to take her if I didn't do what he said. He threatened to…" she tailed off. "Anyway," she said, giving Helen a straight look. "He's not the sort of man to fuck with."

"And you knew about Karen and Crees?"

"Yes."

Helen nodded, thought how much she could have been spared if only Shirley had talked. Maybe there was something in this Karma stuff, after all, she thought. "What's wrong with Kelly?"

"She has leukaemia."

"They can cure it?"

The woman grimaced. There was certain hopelessness in her eyes. "It's possible."

It's a slim chance was what she meant, Helen thought. "Tough on you."

"Tough on her," Shirley snapped, defensive.

Helen nodded, stood up, went to leave.

"You've forgotten something," the woman called after her, holding up the teddy bear.

"Give him to Kelly when she's feeling better," Helen smiled. "Give him to her with my love."

They had coffee in the drawing room, just her and her dad. Spring sunshine shone through the windows, bathing the room in a bright warm glow. He'd baked a coffee and walnut cake from a recipe Aunt Lily sent him. It tasted surprisingly good. He looked well, Helen thought, taking another bite. He seemed more rested in appearance and manner. He'd lost some of the stunned look of the newly bereaved.

"I prefer you with your hair longer," he said.

She smiled. Me, too, she thought.

"About Mum," he said cautiously. "Must have been as much of a shock to you as to me."

Wary of breaking the moment, she said nothing, just agreed with her eyes and thought of Gran. Without her, Helen would never have found out about Lee. Neither senility nor death, it seemed, could extinguish the truth or conceal the perverse bond between mother and daughter.

"I guess it rather explains things," he said, "helps us understand how she felt. Why she liked a drink," he added stiffly. "I don't think badly of her for what happened. It was a big thing then, of course, not like nowadays, and I wish she could have shared it with us."

Helen nodded. Didn't say a word.

"Makes me sad to think of her carrying it alone because I think it really blighted her life. But now it's all out in the open, everything seems to have found its place, do you understand?"

"Yes, I do."

"Suppose we'll never know who was the father of her child."

In the fringes of her consciousness, she saw her mother sitting in her favourite armchair, smiling. It's all right, Mum, she wanted to say, your secret's safe. "No. It's not really important."

"You're right," he said in a businesslike fashion. "Probably some lad who's now an old man like me."

She smiled and sipped her tea.

"Had any fresh ideas?" he asked hopefully.

He still harboured thoughts of her giving up her job and returning to live with him at Keepers. This was going to be tricky, she thought.

"I could help get you started, provide you with capital."

"That won't be necessary," she said, taking a last bite of cake, staving off the inevitable.

"Then let me help with your business plan. If you won't accept a loan, I could negotiate one from the bank, act as guarantor."

She hated to crush his newfound enthusiasm but she had little choice. "The truth is Dad, I'm not that interested."

"But I thought you wanted to have your own studio?"

No, that's what you thought.

"So you're staying on at Ray's?" He sounded short. He looked put out, as though she'd chosen Ray in preference to him.

"No."

"Oh," he said, clearly perplexed.

She put her mug down on the table. "I want to go back to the police."

"To work?"

"Yes."

He was open-mouthed. "But, surely, after all that's happened…"

"Don't you see, it's because of what's happened, I want to go back?"

"Will they have you?"

"I hope so," she smiled. Actually, it had crossed her mind that it might not be so simple, but Birmingham wasn't the only place to find work. She had experience. All kinds. Lots of it.

"What about Ayshea?" her father said. "A young girl doesn't want to be stuck with an old man like me."

"I'm not threatening to leave the country," Helen laughed. "Ayshea's perfectly happy, isn't she?"

"Seems so."

"There you are then. Besides, nothing's forever."

She found Ayshea walking through the messy wooded area behind the tennis courts. Everything seemed to be green shoots and fluffy white and pink blossom. Clumps of daffodils and crocuses, like unruly jack-in-the-boxes, popped up among sedate-looking snowdrops and winter aconites. The evergreens seemed greener, blades of sun brighter, air cleaner. Ayshea, with her brilliantly coloured clothes and darting gait, looked like a beautiful plumed bird.

"Hiya," Helen called to her.

Ayshea turned, broke into a shy smile.

"Brought my camera," Helen said, holding it up.

"Oh dear. I'm not sure about this."

"Cold feet?"

"I take a terrible photograph," Ayshea said.

"That's because you've had a terrible photographer."

"If you say so," Ayshea laughed.

Helen beamed. It was a small but significant improvement. Most people took laughter for granted. With Ayshea, Helen wasn't sure if she'd ever hear her laugh again. In an offbeat moment, it occurred to her that laughter was the same as slaughter only with an s in front of it.

"You want me to pose?" Ayshea said uneasily.

"Nope. Just act naturally. Walk over to that tree and turn round. That's it," Helen said, snapping the shot. "This time, tilt your head to the right, as if you're listening…Great. And again…Lovely. Go over to that tree with the pink blossom."

"It's an edible quince," Ayshea informed her with a giggle.

"That's the one," Helen laughed.

In all, she used up two rolls of film. She caught Ayshea smiling, laughing, looking pensive, looking hopeful. She also glimpsed her hurt and sadness, and wondered if, like her, Ayshea would always remember the dark, the cold, the terror, the madness, whether it would make her strong.

As she gazed at the green-eyed girl, Helen knew that, no matter what happened, whenever she thought of her, with all her different moods and expressions, with all her hopes and fears, she'd never forget the girl who saved her. Helen's family and friends believed that, with great courage, Ayshea guided her across the moor to safety. They never knew that Ayshea had led her out into the light and set her free.

THE END

EVE ISHERWOOD

Eve was born in the West Midlands and spent the formative years of her life in an all-male household. Sent away to a girls' boarding school in Malvern, where her Midlands accent was annihilated and some attempt made to curb her natural boyish enthusiasms, she eventually, and happily, became part of an early intake of just twenty-five girls at Dean Close School for Boys in Cheltenham.

Making a swift getaway from institutional life, she headed for the bright lights of the Edinburgh Festival and decided to stay. To pay the rent, she worked as a stationery rep and learnt to repair Parker pens for the boys who attended Fettes College – home to one budding Prime Minister, Tony Blair.

After dropping out of an arts degree, she was recruited to a London public relations consultancy, where for two years she ran the Woman's Own Children of Courage Awards and was once memorably phoned and ticked off by Michael Parkinson.

Previous writing credits include articles in Devon Today and a number of short stories broadcast on BBC Radio Devon. To further her crime-writing career, Eve has worked with officers from both the West Mercia and West Midlands Police.

When not chasing down fictional criminals, she spends a lot of time at home in rural Worcestershire acting as agony aunt and mum to her five children, and one scruffy dog called Muffin.

Also by Accent Press...

The Trevor Joseph Detective Series
by Katherine John

So intriguing . . . cleverly woven together and tensely written – **Sunday Times**

An interesting mixture . . . John is definitely a promise - **Financial Times**

Without Trace	9781905170265	£6.99
Midnight Murders	9781905170272	£6.99
Murder of A Dead Man	9781905170289	£6.99
Black Daffodil	9781906125004	£6.99